'Vintage Malone. Pitch black Glasgow  you like an express train.' MASON CROS‹

'Twisted, sharp and just a little bit he Malone's characterisation is fantastic.' ‹

'Malone gives us his customary mix of to produce a slick thriller with a killer punch.' DOUGLAS SKELTON

BAD
SAMARITAN

Michael J Malone

CONTRABAND 🔒

M

Contraband is an imprint of Saraband

Published by Saraband,
Suite 202, 98 Woodlands Road
Glasgow, G3 6HB
www.saraband.net

298

Copyright © Michael J Malone 2016

ISBN: 9781910192313
ebook: 9781910192320

Printed in the EU on sustainably sourced paper.

2 4 6 8 10 9 7 5 3 1

1

Every time he saw them it was like an assault, a ripping in the bowels, a tightening of the chest so sharp it was a wonder no ribs were cracked. Regardless, he made an effort to observe them whenever he could. It was a reminder of everything he lost all those years ago in Bethlehem House.

A man with a squint could see they were twins, even though one wore a trim white beard to assert his individuality. It was in the walk, the way they held their heads, the way they anticipated each other's movements, as they just did when the leading brother paused at the entrance to the pew, stepping slightly to the side as, seamlessly, his twin moved past him and took a seat. They sat as if synchronised and hitched their trousers up at the knee with the same practised motion.

Ken and Robert Ford, he learned, were prominent members of the congregation and lived on the same street only a couple of doors away from each other, ten minutes walk from the church.

It was sheer good fortune that brought Jim to this church. A job was advertised. Handyman needed for St Aloysius, RC Church, Perth. Father Stephen was absorbed by his well-acted sob story and felt a Christian need to add accommodation to the minimum wage offered for the forty-hour week.

As a former convent child, he knew how to signal that he really did sing from the same hymn book. The lie that he was a former seminarian on his uppers – he told the priest he only lasted a fortnight in the seminary before his parents died and he had to go home and look after his sick brother – sealed his application. From the possibilities of a life devoted to God, he had devoted his life to his brother, he added with a pained smile. Which was a twist closer to the truth than he was prepared to divulge.

What he hadn't counted on were men like Ken and Robert being part of the deal. Surely he had observed twins in action before now? Hadn't he? He trawled his mind for a suitable memory. Nothing rose to the surface. If he had, none had affected him in such a way.

The men – he couldn't bring himself to use the words "The Twins" as that was what people used to call him and John – were not only regulars at the church, they were also active members in the local Catholic community.

Over the months he worked at St Aloysius, Jim came to know both men were widowers, and both were childless. The fact that they both picked women unable to carry a pregnancy to full term was an irony that was only now apparent to them, Ken informed him with a smile at the end of a coffee morning. Being stalwarts, they always stayed back at the end of the event to help tidy.

By this time he was becoming a familiar face around the church and, as such, an easy confidante. He didn't know if it was the near-ness of the confessionals or simply his quiet manner, apparent lack of judgement and ability to appear to be listening, but he found that many people were trusting of him and happy to detail their mean-ingless existence.

A surprising observation he made about Kenneth and Robert was their need to have separateness in their lives. Ken shortened his name and left school early to work in the local bank. Robert kept both syllables and studied English at university. They sometimes went shopping for clothes together just to make sure they didn't buy the same shirt.

One afternoon, while Jim changed a bulb in the sacristy, Robert held the ladder and chuntered away like words were a coin he couldn't wait to spend. The fact he and his brother lived on the same street was an unhappy coincidence, Robert told him. Ken, the older twin by twenty minutes, inherited the family home and he, Robert, fell in love with a neighbour who has since passed on. Neither is willing to sell, Robert added with a grin that was as much Ken's as it was his.

Fury hit Leonard in a hot surge. He almost lost his grip on the ladder.

'Steady, Dave,' said Robert. Dave Smith was the name Jim adopted for this new life. It had a ring of vagueness to it.

'That was close,' Jim mumbled, and forced a breath into his lungs.

'You alright?' asked Robert. Jim managed an answering nod, keeping his eyes away from Robert's face.

Separateness, he thought. They have this amazing bond, and they want to be apart. They want to show the world they are not the same man. I'll give them separateness.

He hadn't felt the need to kill since slicing Mother Superior's wrists open to the bone. That act had lightened something in his mind. But getting to know Ken and Robert had allowed that light to leak until he felt weak with need.

Someone needed to die. He needed to watch as life bled out of a body. He needed to be the one to cause this to happen. The only thing he wasn't sure of yet, would it be Ken, or would it be Robert?

2

The weather is Glasgow-grey with added smirr. The tall buildings on either side of the narrow lane crowd down on me. There's enough space for one vehicle to drive along here, with a pavement that could take one weak-shouldered man either side. A single yellow line tells any driver there's no stopping.

This lane and many others like it lining the city centre are a continual subject of debate. Poorly lit and just feet away from busy thoroughfares, they offer a combination of good hiding places and easy pickings for the ill-intentioned.

A tall figure, full-bellied in a white body-suit, walks towards me. Martin Pierce. Normally nothing alters the stretched, laconic features of his face. He can talk about the weather and a corpse with the same low-level enthusiasm. With twenty years in the job, he's seen it all, but this girl has clearly affected him. His eyes dart from place to place. Muscles bunch in his jaw.

'Just a wee lassie.' He shook his head slowly when he saw me. 'Whole life in front of her and some nasty little prick...' I remember that Martin has two teenage daughters.

'Can you tell if anything's been stolen? Any sign of sexual contact?' I needed to know what I was dealing with here. An extreme mugger, murderer or a killer with a kink? And Martin needed to regain his focus.

'Can't say for sure at the moment,' answers Martin. 'She is fully clothed, but there are some stains of what could be semen on the front of her shirt and jeans.'

'So,' I think out loud. 'He kills her and then masturbates over the body?' I look over Martin's shoulder. All I can see of her are her feet and legs up to the knee as they jut out from her final place of rest.

'Or something that starts as consensual and then turns horribly wrong,' Martin replies.

4

Small feet, in red high heels. Something about them gives me the notion of a young girl playing at dress-up. One foot is pointing skywards. The other leg is at an angle with the toe of the shoe pointing straight at me like an accusation.

I wonder if they were her favourite pair. She's in her best gear and out for a night with her pals when everything is brought to a juddering end. All for a cheap thrill. What a waste. I'll never get used to this. I swallow down any emotion that's threatening to surface. I've a job to do.

'Any other obvious wounds on her?' I ask.

'Only the trauma at the side of her head. The post mortem will let us know whether that happened before or after death. A couple of false nails have broken off. Hopefully she gave him a bit of a clawing.'

Good girl, I thought. *Didn't go down without a fight.* Hopefully there'll be some tissue from the killer under her nails and he'll have a torn face.

Martin looks over his shoulder and then back at me. 'Her handbag is by her side. One of these giant leather jobs. Size of an elephant scrotum.' He aims for humour, and it falls flat. 'Got my lassies one each at Christmas. Enough room for a kitchen sink, but all they carry is make-up and their iPhones.'

'They've both got iPhones?'

'Aye.' Rueful grin.

'You make too much money, mate.' Pause. Enough with the chat. 'Has anyone managed to log the contents of her bag yet?'

'Not yet, Ray,' he shrugs. 'We'll dust everything for prints and get it to you asap.'

* * *

DC Harkness is sitting in front at that morning's muster. He's eying me as if he's about to get his smart-arse on.

'Sir, you're putting on the beef. Does that mean you've been dumped again?'

'Aye, his Thai bride's gone back to her parents,' Daryl Drain jumps in before I can respond. 'She cannae stand the miserable sod a minute longer.'

'Shut up, the pair of you.' I'm tired and feeling a little sick after my alarm call. But, I remind myself, the humour in the room is there to remind me that we're not all monsters. Besides, we're working on a strong solve rate. As a team we are in a relatively good place.

'This is not the kind of behaviour we want to show the new members of our team.' I look at the two new recruits sitting either side of DC Rossi. One male, one female. Both clean out of uniform, both fresh to my murder squad and both so earnest they almost gleam. Makes me feel old. Was I ever that keen?

'Sir, perhaps our new team members can tell us a little bit about themselves?' Harkness suggests. Less from a sense of curiosity than a need to take the piss.

'All you need to know for now, Harkie,' says Alessandra Rossi, 'is that new boy detective's name is Nick, and new girl detective is Way Out of Your League.' Laughter bounces round the room, including, to her credit, new girl detective. Late twenties, blond scraped-back hair and sporting a sturdy build we do so well in Glasgow. It's all those deep-fried Mars bars and Buckfast, don't you know.

'My name's Kate. Kate Harper,' she adds when the noise abates. I offer her a smile of welcome.

'Welcome, Kate Kate Harper,' I say. She'll do fine. I'm not so sure about Nick. Looks like he shaves once a month, and he's so lean that from the side all you'd see is a drain-pipe with a nose and a sharp Adam's apple. An Adam's apple that is bobbing up and down his throat with nerves.

Nick opens his mouth as if desperate to make his mark on the meeting. Then he closes it again. A deep breath, a forced grin, and his testosterone levels take over.

'My name is Nick James, and I'm an alcoholic.' He rubs his hands together, places them on the table in front of him, then changes his mind and crosses his arms, all the while wearing that awkward please-like-me grin.

Harkness and Drain hoot.

'You'll do fine, buddy,' Drain adds.

Alcohol. The Scottish social adhesive. Show you're up for a few jars and acceptance comes that much more quickly.

'Right, people.' I clap my hands, a sharp noise that gets everyone's attention. 'Enough with the nicey-nicey. We have a bad man to catch.'

'There's been a murder?' Harkness rolls his "r" at the end of both syllables like he's a cliché on Taggart. His smile freezes on his face when he reads my expression. This kind of humour is fine after a few whiskies at the end of a case, when the killer is waiting for the Queen's justice. In fact, it's not just fine, it's a requirement. Helps to put the boogieman to the furthest recesses of your mind if you can laugh at him.

However, when a body is cooling in the morgue and a photo of her lifeless face is in the file in front of me, it's bang out of order.

'Time and place, D.C. Harkness, and this is neither.' I raise an eyebrow telling him he should know better. Rossi is staring at him as if she wants to knee him in the groin. He sits back in his chair, crosses his arms and mumbles, 'Only having a wee joke.'

He's a good cop, works hard and has strong instincts. But he's the class clown and often doesn't know when to rein it in.

'Tell it to Aileen Banks's grieving parents.' I pull her photo from the file and hold it up for everyone to have a look at. 'See how funny they find it.'

'What do we know, Ray?' asks Daryl Drain, who then mouths "fanny" at Harkness.

'Cause of death has not yet been established. Time of death, the early hours of this morning. Body found in West Regent Lane propped up between two red dumpsters. Like she was sleeping...'

I realise that everyone is staring at me. I cough and point to the table in front of me where an evidence bag lies, containing the dead girl's handbag.

She had been carrying an iPhone, a couple of tampons, a small make-up bag – with a mirror, lippie and mascara – a leather purse with one of those wee dog tags containing £23.15, a pair of black socks, an e-reader, a set of house keys on a Mickey Mouse key-ring and a matriculation card for Glasgow University.

'The uniforms were out first thing, giving the news to her nearest and dearest.' Everyone squirms with relief. No one likes that job. 'Alessandra, you come with me and we'll speak to her parents. Daryl, you and Nick go and study the CCTV cameras for that area and see what you can come up with. Harkie, you take Kate to the university. Speak to lecturers, friends, canteen staff. Find anybody who knows her.' I hold the photograph up one more time. Hold it there for a good, long minute. I check that everyone is looking at it. They need to remember this isn't just a case.

'Let's get to it, people.'

The team files out of the room, heads down, minds full of the girl's death mask. I study the paraphernalia of her life, now strewn across the desk in front of me. This is what her twenty-one years amounted to. The Mickey Mouse key-ring a small, fun-shaped reminder that for Aileen Banks, childhood had been just a few short years ago.

3

Mr & Mrs Kevin Banks live at Number 5 Anystreet, Anycity, UK, if you have an available three hundred grand. It is a new-build, red-brick, four-bedroom, homogenised version of what society labels ambition. It is bordered with a neatly mown lawn, perfectly sliced in the middle with a monoblock driveway. A black BMW four-wheel and a red Alfa Romeo Coupe, both with personalised number plates, are parked before a white-door double garage.

'Nice,' says Alessandra Rossi.

'If you like that sort of thing,' I respond.

'You wouldn't…'

'…thank you for it.' I do the mental equivalent of girding my loins. Exhale. Say, 'Let's go and rub salt into a tragedy.'

We walk down the drive, and the front door opens as we arrive.

'You'll be the polis,' says the small, tidy man who opens the door. He's white-haired, wearing grey trousers, blue shirt, brown cardigan. Judging by the sad expression but apparent lack of real grief I'm guessing he's…

'I'm the neighbour from number 3,' he provides helpfully and points. 'The bungalow there. Tom Sharp.' He shakes his head slowly. 'Such a terrible thing to happen to such a lovely wee family. Terrible. Just terrible.'

'DI Ray McBain,' I say. 'And this is DC Alessandra Rossi. Can we come in?'

'Sure, sure.' He steps to the side, allowing us entry. 'Kevin is in the front room,' he says in a whisper and points along a cream-coloured hallway. 'Jennie's upstairs. The doctor sedated her.'

The hallway is painted in a neutral cream, and here and there the wall is dotted with family photographs. All of them show a smiling girl through her various growth spurts. Baby to teen. From this I read Kevin and Jennie Banks only have one child.

Tom walks ahead of us, and after a few quick steps he turns left through a doorway. We follow into a large kitchen-diner. A trim thirty-something male is sitting at a long pine dinner table. He's holding a soft toy in one hand. In front of him a white mug full of black coffee. Judging by the way he's staring into space, my guess is that the drink has been ignored so long it's gone cold.

'Kevin, son,' says Tom, 'these police officers need a wee word with you.' He walks over to the hunched figure and places a hand on his shoulder. There is a delay before Kevin takes his eyes from the table top and looks at Tom as if he is a stranger.

'Aye. Aye,' he rumbles.

Tom walks past us, back the way he came in as if desperate to get out of the house. As if grief was catching. 'I'll, eh … I'll head off.' He makes an apologetic face. 'Kinda feeling in the way.'

'Thanks, Tom,' I say and turn to Kevin Banks. He's now standing. Looks about six feet tall. Short black hair, greying at the temples. Navy pin-stripe trousers and white shirt with a patterned tie slung round his shoulders as if he was in the act of dressing for his day when the worst news possible arrived.

'Can I offer you guys a tea, or a…?' His voice is deep, the accent wears the smooth song of the Highlands. The offer of a drink is prompted purely by conditioning, because judging by the way his arms are hanging by his side, the effort to coordinate the required actions would be too great. I realise it's also a delaying tactic. Judging by the way he's biting at the inside of his cheek, he's been fighting to keep a hold on his emotions. The redness around his eyes tells me he's losing.

'No thanks, Mr Banks.' I say. 'Just had one.' I point at a chair. 'Do you mind if we…?'

He nods.

The air fills with the scream of chair legs being scraped across wooden flooring. Out of the corner of my eye I can see Ale cringing against the noise. We sit.

'Did she suffer?' Kevin asks. His eyes move back and forward between Ale and I.

'We haven't had the result of the post mortem yet...'

'I need to know. Did she suffer?' He's holding the toy bear in one hand and twisting a leg round and round with the other. His bottom lip is quivering, and a single tear is sliding down his cheek. 'I turned the news off.' He indicates with a nod of his head where the TV is pinned to the wall. 'They just mentioned over and over again that a girl was...' the word escapes on a breath '...dead.'

'We can't say for sure, Mr Banks,' I say. He opens his mouth as if to ask the same question again. I keep on speaking. 'What we can say is that she didn't give up without a fight. Evidence suggests she had a good go at scratching his face off.'

Ale looks at me as if to ask if this is something I should be divulging. I ignore her. The man needs something to cling on to help him deal with the nightmare of the next few weeks and months.

Kevin closes his eyes. 'Her talons, I call them.' His mouth trembles into the facsimile of a smile. 'She spends hours on those bloody nails. Trimming and polish...' His voice trails off as he realises he spoke about her in the present tense.

'What can you tell us about where she was heading off to last night?' Ale asks.

'She's a young woman.' He shrugs. 'You almost give up asking when all you get is vague answers. "Out", was all she said.'

'Do you know who she was meeting?'

'Friends?' A guilt-laboured shrug. 'You try to keep a balance between knowing what they're up to and giving them space to learn about life on their own.'

'Do you have contact details for her friends?' I ask.

He coughs. 'My wife has some of their numbers on her mobile.' He moves as if to stand up.

'Don't trouble your wife, Mr Banks,' I say. 'We have Aileen's mobile. I'm sure all the details we need will be on there.' If he'd been more aware of what was happening I'm sure he would have then asked me what was the point of the question? I wanted a feel for the family dynamics. They had an attractive living space, but did they communicate? How many answers would the parents be able to provide?

'Her nails and her laptop and her phone. That's Aileen's world right there.' Kevin Banks's eyes go vacant, and I see what I think he sees. A young girl on her bed, connected to her phone by an earpiece and dabbing paint on her toenails as she talks.

'Did she use Facebook and Twitter … all that stuff?' I ask.

'I tease her.' He pushes out his bottom lip. 'Can't you just talk to people?' His eyes return from his thoughts and reach mine. 'What happened to just talking?' He exhales. It is a long and tremulous breath.

'Can you describe her state of mind when she left the house yesterday evening? Does anything strike you as being out of the ordinary?'

Kevin purses his lips. 'She … she was fine. Seemed like she was getting back to her usual self. Gave us the "don't wait up" line.'

'Back to her usual self?' asks Ale.

'Aye. She split up with her boyfriend, Simon, about six months ago. Simon Davis. They'd been sweethearts all the way through secondary school. Then he dumped her and started going out with her best friend.'

'Ouch,' says Ale.

'Aye. Ouch right enough. Wee bastard. We treated him like family. Felt like a betrayal, you know. Even took him on holiday with us latterly.' Pause. 'She kind of went off the rails for a wee while after that. Coming home drunk, or high. We had a few rows I can tell you. And a few attempts to ground her. Which she totally ignored. Strong-willed, just like her mother.' He outlines a scenario that will surely be playing through a million homes across the country.

'Routine question, Mr Banks,' I say. 'Where were you and your wife last night?'

'Here. We're always here,' he answers. 'Don't have much of a

12

life outside of work. And Aileen.' He swallows, picks up the bear and grips its waist. 'After dinner we watched some telly. Can't even remember what we watched. Then we went to bed. Neither of us sleep well until we hear Aileen's key in the door...' He pauses. A sob. His face twists with the pain. 'We must have dozed off eventually because the next thing,' he screws his eyes shut, 'the police were at the door.'

'I got ready for work.' He releases the bear from the torture he is inflicting on it and moves both hands down the air in front of his body as if to demonstrate his work clothes. 'Kept on going with my usual morning routine because it can't be true. It's someone else's Aileen. Not my wee girl.' He holds a hand over his mouth. His eyes screw shut. His shoulders shake in silent pain.

We give him a moment.

'It would be helpful if we could have a look at her bedroom,' Ale says.

'Top of the stairs. Second door on the right,' Kevin manages to answer. He crosses his arms in a movement that comes across like he's trying to hug himself.

'Would you like to come up with us, please?' I ask. My tone suggests I would rather he did. Thankfully, he's in compliant mode. Too numb to be anything else. He gets to his feet slowly, as if age was his problem rather than the early stages of grief.

We make a slow procession upstairs. He reaches a door. It has a small plaster plaque at eye level, pink flowers with the name Aileen embossed in white. He pushes it open and stands aside to let us past.

A double bed rests under the window. Pink fairy lights are wrapped around the metal frame of the headboard. A thick quilt bears the outline of a body that had been pressed against the down. It emphasises how the room has recently been made vacant. Kevin steps forward and places the bear on the pillows. He then smooths out the shape of the body that had recently rested there. From the size of it I guessed it had been made by him.

I look away to study the room. The walls are painted the same neutral colour the rest of the house wears. The wall to the right has a mirrored floor-to-ceiling wardrobe, and a dressing table rests against the wall on the left. It has a pile of books at one end and at the other an array of cosmetics. In the middle sits the glossy black rectangle of a closed laptop. In the corner there's a bookcase. I can see *Harry Potter*, Jacqueline Wilson and more than a few vampire books.

'Aileen loved that *Twilight* series. Kinda grown out of it now, but refused to get rid of the books.' Kevin catches my line of sight. 'When did vampires become the good guys?'

'What was she studying?' Ale asks.

'History,' Kevin answers. 'Such a nothing degree in my opinion. I want her to do something more practical. Something that would lead to an actual job, you know. But girls nowadays,' he shrugs, 'there's no telling them.'

He looks out of the door and across the landing. I follow his line of vision and can see into another bedroom. It's in darkness, heavy curtains closed, but I can make out a shape lying in the foetal position on the bed.

'I'll just go and...' Kevin points towards the other bedroom. As he shuffles out his body language suggests he isn't expecting to be of much use. In a few moments I hear his quiet rumble. A female voice. More soothing male sounds then a sharp, loud, 'Just fucking leave me alone, Kevin,' followed by gut-wrenching sobs.

Ale catches my eye and makes a grim face. 'Horrible,' she whispers.

'Do girls keep diaries nowadays?' I ask her.

'May well do. Online networking is more the thing now I expect. You don't get a reaction from a diary.'

'So it's all about the reaction?'

'Oh yes. We girls like a bit of drama, dontcha know.' Ale pushes her face into a smile.

I look around the room. Assessing. Filtering.

'The laptop is a given. We'll take that. Let's have a look for anything else that might be of help.'

Carefully and as quietly as we can, we look through Aileen Banks's things. At one point I open a drawer to find it stuffed with underwear. I close it as quick as I can.

'You do that one,' I say to Ale. 'I feel like a perv rifling through that.'

'Daftie.' She gets up from her crouch at the floor before the wardrobe and walks towards me. 'No need to feel like that. You're one of the good guys.'

'Whatever.' A predatory male kills a young girl, and it diminishes my standing as a man. Ale may tell me I'm one of the good guys, but I need to do something to remind myself. Like find the bastard who did this.

Sometime later and we've been through everything. There's nothing to suggest that Aileen was anything other than a pretty, normal girl in her early twenties.

'I suspect the phone and laptop are going to be of more use to us,' I say to Ale. 'Let's get back to the office.'

We walk back down the stairs and can see from the hallway that Kevin is back in his seat at the dining table. He's staring at the patterns in the wood, his expression slack, hands flat on the surface as if he's forgotten how to work them.

I cough. 'Before we go, do you have a recent head and shoulder photo of Aileen?'

* * *

Back at the car, I throw the laptop and cables on to the backseat and then climb into the driver's seat. Ale has her seatbelt on and is staring into the far distance.

'God, I hate my job at times,' she says. 'That poor man.'

'Close family members have to be removed from the list of suspects first,' I remind her.

'If that man harmed his daughter, I've a giant set of testicles and

I'm an unemployed drag queen called Cindy.'

There's a knock at the car window and I turn to see the face of the neighbour peering in at me.

I slide the window down.

'Mr Sharp?'

'Aye, son. Kevin...' He nods his head in the direction of number five. 'Do you think I should go back in?'

'Do you know if they have any other family?'

'Don't really know them that well, to be fair. You know how it is. We talk over the fence on the odd nice day during the summer and nod at each other when clearing snow from the drive in the winter. That's about the extent of neighbourliness these days.' He stops talking, makes a face and leans back pressing his hands into his lower back. 'Old age, son.' He barks a laugh, then sobers as if laughter is temporarily banned. 'Creeps up on you and brings a load of unwanted relatives.'

'So – any idea where any relatives might be, then?' I ask. I'm getting the feeling that Tom Sharp is a lonely old man and would like nothing more than to talk to us until it's time to go to bed.

Tom scratches his head. 'Nairn? Up around that part of the country, I believe. His mother has been down to see them a few times. Nice old biddy. Can talk for Scotland, mind. Think she had a wee fancy for me.' He leans forward and aims a wink at Ale.

'Anyone else?'

'I've only been here a few years myself, son. Bought this big hoose, ma wife dies and the weans move down to England. I call them weans. My son's in his forties, and my daughter has just turned fifty. Now I'm rattling about in it. Don't know what to do with myself. I should sell, I suppose...'

'Did you happen to see Aileen leave the house yesterday?'

'There's no much that escapes me, son,' he says proudly. 'She was a lovely wee lassie. Always quick to smile. Mind you she wasn't smiling much after that wee numpty chucked her.'

'The boyfriend?'

16

'Aye. Suppose that's part of growing up, eh? Needin' to try something new.'

'When did she leave the house yesterday?' I try and get him back on track.

'I have my supper every night at nine o'clock. Toasted bagel and banana with a wee sprinkle of cinnamon. Bread doesn't agree with me anymore. I can cope with a bagel, but. And I wash that down with a cup of tea. I was just taking a first bite when I heard the door slam shut and Aileen's feet clipping up the drive.'

'The door slammed shut?' asks Ale.

'Aye. She was a tempestuous wee thing at times. Didnae like her parents telling her what to do.'

'Was she always like that or has that just been since she split up with her boyfriend?'

'Naw, I'd say it was … what … eighteen months ago. When the mum and dad split up. He came back but, tail between his legs. Got the impression he was playing away, if you know what I mean. For a while after, the door would be slammed shut and Aileen would be storming up the drive shouting "hypocrites" as she went.' He looks back up at the house. 'Families, eh?'

'Did you see who Aileen went off with? Was it a taxi or…'

'Not a taxi. It was that new pal of hers. The one with the big mouth and the wee red Ford.'

'Male or female?'

'Oh, she was a female and flashed her boobs at me to prove it.' Tom's face reddens at the memory. 'Young women nowadays. No shame.'

'What made her flash at you?' asks Ale

'She clearly thinks I'm nosy. Just because I have my seat at the window. A red car catches my eye when I'm watching telly. It's difficult not to turn round and look, you know. Anyway, one day she draws up, sees me looking, rolls her window down, shouts "Hey nosy, get a load of this," and opens her shirt.' He grins. 'Fine set, right enough.'

'Apart from the fine set,' I ask, 'and the red Ford, how else would you describe her?'

'I only ever saw her sitting in the car, so I've no idea of height, but she had long dark hair and a plump-ish face. All that junk food the young ones eat nowadays I imagine. And a fine set.' He shakes his head. 'At my age that's likely to set off a heart attack, but. She never parks at the front door when she comes to pick up Aileen.' He pauses when he realises what tense he has just used. 'I suspect mum and dad didn't approve of the lassie in the Ford, and she waited out of their line of sight so they wouldn't know.'

'What about mum and dad? Did they leave the house at all last night?'

Tom looks puzzled at my question. 'Eh. Let me think.' He stands up, stretches his back and then leans forward again. 'Naw. A pair of home birds they two. Never out.' Tom thinks some more. 'I can see where you're going with that, officer. I love a crime drama on the telly, me. First thing you do is rule out the nearest and dearest, eh?'

'Right, Mr Sharp. Thank you.' Save us from CSI devotees.

I fire the ignition to signal my intent to leave. Tom opens his mouth again as if to say something else.

'Got to go, Mr Sharp. You've been very helpful. If we have any more questions we know where to find you.' I drive off.

* * *

Ale and I return to the office. There's a report on my desk to say that time of death was between midnight and 4am. There is no sign of sexual assault vaginally or anally. There are, however, semen stains on her clothing. Tissue was also found under the girl's fingernails, and this would be analysed to check for a match with the semen.

I pick up Aileen's iPhone, switch it on, and I'm asked to enter a password.

'You any good with these things?' I ask Alessandra.

She takes it from me and peers at the screen. 'People are usually quite lazy when it comes to passwords. We can get this down to the techie guys, but I'll have a wee go and see what happens.'

While she's footering about with passwords, I enter our system and do a search. I key in the words 'head injury' and 'masturbation'. I want to see if there are any ongoing investigations in the UK with similarities. The computer thinks for a minute or two and comes up with a request to redefine the search.

An email pops up on my screen to distract me. It's from Chief Superintendent Harrison telling me he is calling a news conference at 5pm. He wants all the information we have.

This I'm happy to provide, and happy he's not asking me to front it. I'd rather pierce my scrotum with a fish hook than appear in front of a TV camera. Especially when I look like I've been bingeing on Mars bars.

Daryl and Nick are still viewing the CCTV footage. I text Daryl to tell him approximate time of death. That'll save some time. I then phone Harkie.

'How you gettin' on?'

'There's lots of snot 'n' tears. People who probably didn't even know Aileen are queuing up to tell us how much she meant to them. Fuckin' rubberneckers. But they've given us a wee office in the main university building, and we're working our way through all of her classmates. There's half a dozen who haven't turned up for lectures today so we'll get on to them once we've spoke to everyone here. Nothing interesting so far though.'

'Keep an eye out for a plump-faced lassie with long, dark hair, big tits and a wee red Ford.'

'Sounds like my kind of woman. She lookin' for an older man to teach her a few lessons?'

'Time 'n place, Harkie. There was a sexual element to this murder, and I find your attitude highly inappropriate.' The words are out before I can stop them. Lighten up, McBain. He's only working the same script we've always used.

'Eh … eh'm…' I can tell he's not sure whether I'm serious or not. I decide to let him off the hook and inject a smile in my voice. 'The

19

girl with the car is important, Harkie. See what you can do to track her down.' I hang up.

I try another search on the system with 'head injury' and 'sex'. There are a number of hits throughout England. The nearest one is Newcastle. Wouldn't be outside the realms of possibility for a predator to jump on a train or a car. I check Newcastle.

Ale's looking over my shoulder. 'Nah, that included rape. Our guy's not going back to having a wank after he's gone the full way.'

'Fair comment, DC Rossi.' I close the screen down. 'This is getting us nowhere. Time for some police work the old-fashioned way. You ready for a pub crawl?'

She makes a face. 'There's a lot of bars in that part of the city centre.'

'Aye, so the sooner we start, the sooner we finish.'

4

It's 10pm, and I just got home after nearly six hours of canvassing through the city-centre pubs. It's one of those jobs I should delegate, but on this occasion I wanted to get stuck in myself. Lets the team see I don't mind rolling my sleeves up. Harrison said at my last staff appraisal that I should be sitting at the centre of the flow of information where I can best collate, weed out and decide on the next part of the investigation's strategy. I say that's how you get fat and lazy.

The canvassing was ineffective. No sign of the girl with the red Ford, and no one recognised the photo of Aileen.

I park, climb out of my car and lock it. Spot the laptop which is still in the backseat. Curse. Unlock the car and pluck it out.

As I walk towards my front door, I look up at the window of my third-floor flat. The light's on. I'm sure I didn't leave it on this morning. There are only two people with a key. Maggie and Kenny. This time of night and it's got to be Kenny. My criminal friend.

Upstairs and inside the flat I'm greeted with the sight of Kenny's size-eleven feet hanging off the end of my brown leather sofa.

'Where the fuck have you been?' he asks as he sits up.

'What? Did we arrange...'

'Na,' he gives me a giant Kenny grin, 'just messin' with you.' He nods towards the kitchen. 'I could murder a coffee.'

'Well, you know where the kettle is, O'Neill. And while you're at it, I take mine black with no sugar now.'

He jumps to his feet. 'Riiiight. Getting fed up with folk talking about how much beef you're putting on?'

I shoot him a finger. He spots the laptop under my arm.

'Finally getting into the digital age, Mr McBain?'

'Black, no sugar,' I repeat.

'Not answering the question suggests this is police work.'

I ignore him and place the laptop on the coffee table.

'Miserable bastard,' he mumbles. 'You people not heard of work–life balance?' He goes into the kitchen. As I power on the machine I hear him organise the drinks. By the time the computer has wakened up he's returning with a pair of mugs.

'So,' he sets them down in front of us and takes a seat beside me. 'You shagging Maggie yet?'

'None of your business.'

'You sound a bit frustrated, mate. I'm guessing that's a no.'

I ignore him and study the prompt in the middle of the screen that's asking for a password. Alessandra got nowhere with the iPhone. It's a safe bet this isn't going to be straightforward either. A small button below the space for the password reads "Hint". I click on it. The word "vampire" appears.

'For chrissakes, Ray. At least respond to my good-natured attempts at banter,' says Kenny as he holds his mug to his mouth.

'Oh, snookums, is nobody talking to you?'

He decides to be direct. 'Fud.' He picks up the remote and, switching on the telly, leans back into the leather. 'Anything decent on tonight?'

Vampire. What the hell could that be? I picture myself in Aileen's bedroom again. I'm looking at the bookcase. Didn't her dad say she was still into those *Twilight* books?

'You got your phone on you, Kenny?' I ask.

'Ooh, I get to help you with police work. What's the story?'

I get him up to speed.

'Shit. I saw that wee lassie's picture on the news tonight. That's what you're working on?' He fishes his phone out of his pocket. 'You're looking for password ideas linked to vampires? Try typing in Twilight.'

I do.

The computer suggests I speak to the administrator.

'Do you guys not have IT specialists who can do this for you?' Kenny asks.

'Aye, but I wanted to have a go. If I get nothing I'll take it to them first thing in the morning.'

'Is that not a wee bit unorthodox, DI McBain? You've been in bother before.'

'Shut it. Do a search on *Twilight* for me. What's that actor's name? English. Big hair.'

'Robert Pattinson.'

'Get you.'

'I am SO down with the kids,' he grins.

'Latent homosexual are the words you're groping for,' I say as I try Pattinson and Robert and then both together.

'Vampire is the clue,' says Kenny as he keys something into his phone. 'Ah, the wonders of Google. Try Edward Cullen.' Kenny spells out the surname.

'Who he?' I ask.

'The main vampire character in the books, apparently.'

I type. The password screen vanishes, and I'm in Aileen's laptop.

'Excellent,' I say, rubbing my hands together. 'You're the man who's down with the kids. What am I looking for now?'

'Social networking sites. Go to her internet home page.'

I do, and the Google legend appears in the middle of the screen with a search box. Below it are quick links to Facebook, Twitter and Glasgow University among others.

Kenny is reading over my shoulder. 'She'll also be using her phone to get on Facebook.'

'You can do that?' I ask.

'Christ, you're pathetic.'

'Naw, I'm too busy locking up arseholes to be bothered with this shite.'

Kenny leans in, takes over the trackpad and clicks on Facebook.

'Hopefully the computer has saved her password,' he says. We go straight in.

'So this is what it's all about,' I say as I scan the page, not knowing where to look first. 'It's a bit busy.'

Kenny moves the mouse, clicks on something. The page reloads and all the entries are from Aileen.

'Right. That filters out everyone else and lets us see what your girl has been up to.'

I read a column on the left. 'She has 285 friends? How can you possibly keep in touch with that many people? Why has she got that wee picture there?'

'That's her profile picture. Some people use a photo of themselves, but you can use any image – a symbol or an avatar. She's using a photo of the actress from *Twilight*.'

'A fucking avatar? Avatar? Isn't that from some godawful movie?' I suddenly feel a huge resentment at the world. People waste their lives on this shit while I'm out there dealing with all kinds of degenerates. I sit back in the chair, crossing my arms and shaking my head.

'OK, granddad. Take a chill pill,' says Kenny. His grin is about splitting his face in two. He turns back to the screen. 'Right. This column down the middle shows your girl – looks like she calls herself LovesEdward on Instagram – and what she's been up to.'

I sit forward, elbows on my thighs. 'This is more like it.'

Under recent activity it says:

'LMAO on Jenny Craig's status.'

'You did WHAT? LOL You go girl!'

'Fucking exam. Fucking hate studying.'

I look at Kenny in frustration. He is still wearing that big-toothed smile. 'Not even going to ask,' I say.

'Our girl has a potty mouth,' he says.

I scroll down the list. Each comment is as inane as the last.

'I'm sure it has some entertainment value,' I say, 'but for fuck sakes, this is what the future of our country is relying on?'

'What age are you?' asks Kenny

I start shaking my head again.

'Get over yourself, ya eejit. You're looking for clues here. Not an excuse to give up on modern society.'

I mentally thank Kenny for the reminder – it wouldn't do to actually say it out loud – and I go back to reading the entries.

After several minutes of this Kenny stands up.

'I can see you're going to be riveting company tonight, so I'll make myself scarce.' He catches my eye and then adds. 'L.M.A.O.'

'Don't let the door hit your arse on the way out,' I say going back to the screen, determined I'm not going to ask him what those four letters stand for.

Ten minutes later and my eyes are rolling in my head with tiredness. I close the lid of the laptop and then go round the flat turning off all the lights and switches. In my bedroom I throw my shirt in the wash basket along with my socks and boxers. My trousers I throw over an exercise bike I bought recently in a moment of full-on insanity. I've used it once. For five minutes. And now it has become a very expensive clothes stand.

Lights out, alarm on my ancient mobile set for 7am, and I'm under the quilt and asleep in moments.

* * *

I wake with a start, heart thumping. I was dreaming. Can't remember what it was about, but I feel that my cheeks are wet as if I'd been crying, and the feeling of menace lingers as I walk through to the bathroom for a piss.

I tuck it away in that place where all my unwelcome thoughts hide.

Back in bed and I'm lying staring at the black space in front of my eyes. I'm wide awake now. I get back out of bed and go through to the living room. Naked, I stand at the window and look up and down the street. Every window is in darkness. Other people next to their loved ones, safe in the hum-drum. Completely unmindful of the dangers around them and the men and women like me who keep them safe.

Taking a deep breath, I dampen down the feeling of loneliness that is my nightly companion. As usual, Theresa's face pops into my

25

head. That fat prick of a husband will be spooning into her back, still with no clue that she and I had an affair and that I could well be the father of his twins.

Shut it, McBain. That way lies madness.

I hear the scuff and echo of footsteps outside. I look along, and to the left I see a man staggering along the street. He's half-singing, half-mumbling, doing the drunk's dance. Two steps forward, one step back and then one to the side. At this speed he'll be sober by the time he gets home.

He finds a note and bellows it. Then tells himself to shhh. 'People are sleeping,' he shouts and then giggles. I shake my head. Glasgow has all different categories of drunk. This man obviously gets his happy on when he's full of booze.

I've had enough of the pantomime, so I turn and move over to the sofa. The skin on my back flinches from the chill of the leather when I sit down. I lift the lid of the laptop and decide to have another look through Aileen Banks's life. There must be a clue in here somewhere.

My mobile chimes. It's through in the bedroom. Who the hell is contacting me at this time of night? The need to know gets the better of me, and I walk through to fetch it. I have a new text. From Maggie.

'Having trouble sleeping again?'

I've given up asking her how she knows this stuff. She's intuitive she tells me. She feels things. She also has a thing for me. We've acted on it a couple of times. The first time was a drunken disaster on my part, and the second time was an emotional disaster for us both, so she decided she only wants to be my mate while I'm still "besotted" – her word – with someone else.

I text back. 'Yeah, thinking of you. It's keeping me awake.'

Her reply is immediate. 'Just have a wank then.'

'Nah. I'm saving my man juice for womankind.'

'How generous. Just a shame none of us appreciate your sacrifice.'

26

I type 'G.T.F.' Add a kiss and then send.

'hehehe. You need to talk, big guy, you know where I am.'

I shut my phone down and walk back through to the living room. If I had any sense I would convince Maggie I didn't care for Theresa and do my very best to make her happy.

Back at the laptop and I look through Aileen's files. Her word documents are all degree essays, judging by the titles. There's nothing in her picture files, but iTunes is busy. The websites she's been looking at are all related to celebs, the *Twilight* movies and social networking sites. Don't know what I expected from a young person at university these days. Evidence of a brain?

Oh, get a hold of yourself, McBain. There's your inferiority complex showing. Just because you didn't get a university degree.

Scrolling through her Facebook entries and I get another side to Aileen. Clips of political demonstrations, wildlife films and links to blog posts from green activists.

Her most recent comments are more reactions to other people's comments, but I work through a time period and I find some of her own status updates.

'Working at the weekend should be against the law. I'm on early at M's Supermarket. Bugger, pee and poop. I'm knackered just thinking about it.'

'I hate the mob mentality on here. Let's be nice people.'

'Laughing at yourself should be a legal requirement. Broke a heel on gorgeous new shoes. Did I laugh? Mwahahahahaha.'

This run of comments makes me smile. I think I would have liked this girl.

There's a few updates about her parents, which are frightening in their honesty and directness.

'The olds are horrible. My dad's a total wanker and mum's a frigid bitch. No wonder he hates her.'

'They think they rule my life. WRONG!!!!!'

'Can't wait till I get a proper job and place of my own. Then NOBODY can tell me what to do.'

Something in me cringes. I wouldn't want a daughter of mine to be this honest on the internet.

I check out the people who are responding to these. They all seem to be mostly girls of the same age. The most regular commenter is someone who posts all the time about some bloke called Jacob. Her 'avatar' is a picture of a book cover. I click on her profile and see that she is much more active than Aileen.

Her whole life is on display. She works in M's Supermarket as well, and I wonder if she is the girl with the red Ford. She has gone out with this boy and that boy. Been in that pub and another pub. Given what has happened to Aileen, it worries me that these kids have no idea of the predators who could be following their every move. There's no need to attempt to groom these kids. They know exactly where they will be and when.

There's a row of photographs at the top of her profile. I click on the first and scroll along. I spot Aileen in the third one along. She's facing the camera, hair shining like an advert and offering a huge smile and a cocktail glass to the world. Beside her is a large-breasted girl with a round face. This must be the one who loves Jacob.

A message appears on the bottom of the screen. A direct message from the Jacob fan. I click on the blue line.

A box appears. It reads:

'Where the fuck r u? I can see u r online. Why r u not answering yur phone. I'm worried sick. The news said you was killed. OMG. What the fuck? Call me PLEEZ.'

My heart jumps. How to deal with this?

I reply.

'This is Strathclyde Police. If you are a friend of Aileen Banks you may have valuable information. Please reply with your address.' I click send before I realise this might not be the best approach.

Nothing.

Minutes pass and still nothing. Then…

'Yeah, fuckn right. It's the middle of the night. Police my arse. Who r u? If this is Aileen u r sick. Totally sick. I haven't stopped crying all night.'

I type as fast as I can.

'This is Detective Inspector Ray McBain. Please call me on 07988 521235. Or come to the police station in Stewart Street, Glasgow, tomorrow and ask for me. It is VITAL we speak with you.'

Again, nothing. I stare at the screen willing a response. Long minutes pass. I'm begging the screen to do something. Then two small letters appear.

'ok'

5

I have no recollection of going back to bed, but I wake with a start, stretched across the mattress, quilt wrapped round my legs. My mind filters out unnecessary information. There was a noise. The letter box clunked. That's what woke me.

I sit up as if spring-loaded. Shit. If I'm still here when the post-man delivers that means I've overslept. I stretch for my phone. It's 8:15.

Fuck.

I jump out of bed and go past the front door on the way to the shower. A small pile of mail waits for me. I bend and pick them up. Two white envelopes. They'll be bills then. And a postcard. I place the bills on a small table at the side of the door and study the post-card. Who sends postcards nowadays?

The picture on the front gives me a chill. I flip it over. Read my address on one side and my brain struggles to take in the words on the other. I flip back to the image on the front. What the hell is going on here?

The picture is a religious scene. A photograph of a giant wooden carving that portrays Christ on his cross with two women kneeling at his feet. I flip to the back.

It reads. "Come and visit. Urgent. Joe."

* * *

Joseph McCall has changed since the last time I came to visit him in Barlinnie Prison just over a year ago. For one thing, he's looking me in the eye and he's sitting back in his chair like he's the one who is enjoying his freedom.

I try to work out what age he is. Twenty-four? He looks younger now that he's clean-shaven. Life without parole was his sentence, and it looks as if he has warmed to the idea.

Still, life on the outside was no jolly for our Joe. His mother was the victim of a childhood rape, Joe being the result of this detestable union. Then he was handed over to a series of faceless men. His soft parts offered as payment for his mother's drug habit. Eventually he ended up as accomplice of the serial killer known to the media as Stigmata. Except Stigmata got free and Joe took on his identity, accepting blame for the crimes. A fact known only to the three of us. I was unable to convince the court they had the wrong man.

'So, how's life in the Bar–L?' I say, looking around the visits hall. High ceilings, long room dotted with tables and chairs. If I was visiting a loved one here it would depress the hell out of me.

'You came,' Joe says with a lift of his left eyebrow. 'Wasn't sure you would.' His right hand is on the table hovering over a piece of card. His index finger is tapping on the table's surface with the speed of a woodpecker. So, he's not as relaxed as he wants me to think he is.

'Do you need anything?' I ask. 'You should have sent a letter with a few requests. I would have been happy…'

'I don't want anything from you, DI McBain. You don't get to satisfy your guilty conscience on my behalf,' he says with a sneer.

I lean back in my chair and cross my arms. 'I don't feel guilty, Joe. You chose to take on the crimes. Your confession was more powerful than my arguments that they had the wrong man.'

'I'm doing a course,' he says. 'Doing lots of reading. Psychology. You're showing classic signs, McBain. Displacement. Your real guilt has nothing to do with me. The old man you and your mates killed in Bethlehem House. That's the guilt you will always live with…'

'Shut up, Joe.' Despite myself I am back in that bedroom. Age ten. Blood splattered, breathing in feathers and terrified beyond movement.

'…and you think being nice to me during your, what, bi-annual visit will assuage … good word that, innit? You think it will help you feel better.'

'Spare me from the I've Read One Book genius. You sent me a card. I came. What do you want?'

'That card said a lot, didn't it?'

'Joe, spare me the cryptic act. Why do you want to see me?'

'I got a card of my own,' he says and slides it towards me. I search his eyes for a clue and then pick it up. The cover is a photograph of a line of trees at the edge of a river. In the distance is the curve of a heather-decked mountain and beyond that a blue sky. A card that would be in any number of tourist traps across Scotland.

My mobile rings. I look at the screen. It's Alessandra Rossi, and I realise why she's calling.

Shit. This thing with Joe threw everything else out of my head.

'Hi, Ale,' I say.

'There's a young girl just left the building. Said you wanted to see her.'

'It's Aileen Banks's pal. Can you keep her till I get back?'

'She was here about half an hour ago. The message has just been sent up by reception. Where are you? It's not like you to be late.'

'Something came up.' I look at Joe. He's staring at the tabletop. 'She didn't happen to leave contact details, did she?'

'No. Said something like, "she knew it was a wind-up."'

'Right. Get over to Morrison's. You know the one on Titwood Road? I'm guessing that's where she works. Ask the manager if they employed Aileen Banks and take it from there. I'll be with you as soon as I can.' I close the connection.

'A copper's work is never done,' says Joe with a half-smile. He looks back at the card. I pick it up. Two words. *Gone hunting.*

There's no signature, but whoever wrote it has signed off with a small symbol. At first glance it looks like a T. But the cross bar is too low down the vertical line. It's a cross.

'It's Leonard,' says Joe, somewhat unnecessarily. I knew as soon as he indicated he wanted to see me that it was going to be about Leonard, aka Stigmata. He stares at me. Chews at a hangnail. His eyes are a mess of conflicting emotion. I think I can name two. Fear, and for a moment there, resignation.

'If you ask me,' says Joe. 'He's about to start a new killing spree.'

6

He watched the two men walk across the road. An image soared in his mind like a gift. He was running after them. A knife in his hand. One of them turned on hearing his footsteps. The blade entered his throat. Disappeared into the flesh like the skin and muscle was hungry for it. A hand grasped at his arm before the old man fell to the ground. Blood sprayed in a jubilant arc. His brother turned, mouth open in a scream as if it was him who had been fatally wounded.

The picture was so strong his knees give way. His thighs tensed at the last moment, and he managed to keep upright. Heart pounding to the sharp rhythm of his blood-lust, he stepped off the kerb. There was a loud scream of protest as a car braked. The fender touched his leg. A man leaned out of his car window. Face bright with fury. Jaw, lips moving. Sounds. Words. He can't hear anything.

Then.

'... fuckin' death wish, mate?'

He nodded. Mumbled. Stepped back on to the pavement.

The brothers crossed the road, faces twisted with concern. One had a hand on his shoulder. He shrugged it off. Can't bear to be touched.

'You OK, son?'

He looked into the man's eyes. The image was so strong, he was amazed this man was not lying at his feet, soaking in a puddle of blood. Shook his head. He couldn't be seen like this. Must focus.

'Aye,' he managed to say. 'Took a wee turn.'

'That priest is working you too hard, mate,' one brother said. Ken? His face a mirror reflecting his sibling's alarm.

'We're just going home to watch the match,' said Robert. 'Pie, oven pizza and a few beers. Not very traditional, like, but we enjoy it.'

'You're welcome to join us,' said Ken. 'We always end up throwing some food out.'

Match?

'Sky sports is too expensive,' says Robert, 'so we go halfers and watch it together.'

'Today's game is Manchester United and Liverpool. Bound to be a cracker.'

'Aye, c'mon. Have the rest of the day off and join us.' Ken's face was up close, kindness a glimmer in his eyes.

'OK.' Muscles tug a smile into place, and he allowed the men to guide him.

* * *

The front door was unlocked. Ken pushed the door open and the other men entered. They turned right into the living room. Above the fireplace the black stretch of a plasma TV came to life when Ken pointed a remote at it. Energetic voices. Bright colours.

Two large cushioned chairs faced the television. The twins in leather. To the side, along the window, rested a matching sofa.

'Have a seat, son,' said Ken, 'and I'll go get us a beer.'

'You do like a wee beer?' asks Robert.

Leonard nodded. Found his vocal chords were working again. 'I'm not much of a drinker, but I don't mind the odd can of lager.'

'Just you take a load off, mate. I'll be two seconds.' He sat. Robert bustled from the room. Ken fell into his chair, pointed the remote at the screen and the noise increased. An out-of-tune, throaty, male chorus hungry for battle.

'Just in good time,' he said. 'The match is about to kick off.'

Robert joined them. Thrust a can into his hand and sat to the left of his brother, eyes locked on to the screen.

A whistle. The noise from the crowd intensified.

'And we're off,' said Ken. 'Hope Liverpool gub them.'

'Not a chance, brother,' said Robert. 'Man U are a well-oiled machine. They're not going to slip up today.'

'Be honest, mate. You'll be happy with a draw.'

Robert flicked his eyes to the side, catching Leonard's attention. 'My brother is deluded. He's going to be a tenner short by the end of this game.'

'Whatever, loser,' said Ken with a smile.

Leonard slid a thumb along the edge of the ring-pull. Crack. Hiss. Placed the can before his lips and sucked at the cool liquid. Eyes never leaving the brothers, he leaned back into the cushioned leather, lifted his right leg and rested the foot on his left knee. He felt his body relax as his mind raced through the possibilities.

This had worked out better than he could ever have imagined.

7

We're in the supermarket manager's office. The girl in front of me has long, straight, dark hair, generous breasts and is staring like she thinks the Grim Reaper is my best friend. Her mascara is a black and grey smudge, and her eyes are puffy and red.

Karen Gardner is her name, and she was Aileen Banks's best friend. She's sitting with her fist clenched, white knuckles pressed against her mouth as if trying to force the grief back down her throat.

'Can't believe it,' she says over and over while shaking her head.

The manager is beside her with her arm across her shoulder, and she is in a similar state but hiding it better and doing her best to offer support to the younger woman.

'Karen,' says Ale, 'Can you tell me some more about what happened that night when you and Aileen went out?' From her tone there is no way you could deduce that this is not the first time Ale has asked her this question. I mentally send her a "well done".

Because I arrived later and Ale already broke the news, I allowed her to carry on with the interview. The girl did look at me sharply when Alessandra mentioned my name. She opened her mouth as if to say something, and then grief stole the words. A sob clutched at her throat. Her bottom lip trembled.

'You picked Aileen up at what time?' asks Ale.

Karen's head falls onto her boss's shoulder, whose name badge reads "Jane Cameron". She has a nose sharp enough to cut a steak with, and her hair is red, straightened to within an inch of its life and thick enough to fill a pillowcase. I feel a childish urge to spray it with water to see if it frizzes up to an afro.

Jane looks at Ale, 'Can this not wait?' she pleads. 'The poor girl's distraught.'

'I understand that,' says Ale. 'However, the first few hours of a murder investigation are crucial. And the time it has taken to locate Karen has already cost us too much.' She turns her attention to Karen. 'Do you understand that, Karen? We need your help to stop this man doing the same to some other poor girl.'

Karen straightens in her chair, swallows and nods. She wipes a tear from her cheek using her sleeve and whispers, 'Yes.' Then, louder, 'But I don't know what happened.'

'Trust me,' I say, 'you don't realise it, but somewhere in the information you give us will be a wee gold nugget that will help us catch this guy.'

'OK,' she says. 'I picked her up at her house after I finished my work. We went into town. A couple of pubs...' Her eyes focus on the near distance as the events of that evening play in her mind. She bites her bottom lip. Gathers her strength and continues. 'We went to a couple of pubs. I wanted to come home early.' Shrug. 'I was driving cos I was skint ... and bored cos I was sober. Aileen got angry with me cos she wanted to stay out.' She stops speaking. Clenches her eyes shut. Her shoulders start shaking. She says something in a high squeal.

'Sorry, sweetheart,' says Ale. 'I don't know what...'

'It's all my fault. We fell out, I went home in a huff, and she ends up deid and it's all my fault.' Her chest is heaving.

'Karen, it is not your fault,' says Jane Cameron. 'You are not responsible for the actions of some sicko.'

'But, but, but, if I hadn't...' She starts to cry again. Sobs like she has an attack of hiccups.

'Look, you people will need to give the lassie a break,' says Cameron. 'Can you not come back tomorrow?'

'Miss Cameron,' I say.

'Mrs.'

'Right,' I reply, thinking, *you've got a husband, bully for you.* 'We really have lost too much time on this case...'

'This "case,"' she actually does the air speech commas, 'being the death of my young colleague, Aileen Banks?'

'Don't think for a minute, *Mrs* Cameron, that we are anything but committed to this *case...*'

Ale interrupts by leaning forward and patting Karen on the knee. 'You have a wee break, Karen. DI McBain and I will just go and have a wee coffee and let you gather your thoughts. OK?'

Jane Cameron sags in her chair. 'I'm sorry, detective. This is such a...'

'No worries,' I say. 'We all need a break for a moment.' I stand up and walk to the door. 'Give you guys half an hour or so for a breather, OK?'

With the door closing behind us, Ale and I walk along a grey corridor towards a glass door at the end and a set of stairs that lead down to the shop floor.

We make our way to the cafeteria, and minutes later, a mug of coffee in hand, we are facing each other across a table.

'I wasn't losing it,' I say.

'Didn't say you were,' Ale raises an eyebrow.

'OK?'

'But I recognised that tone. If she had come back to you with an answer you would've ripped right into her.'

'No I wouldn't, and anyway, who is she to judge me, ginger witch.'

'She seems genuinely upset about Aileen and trying hard to comfort Karen.'

'Only because she's now two members of staff short. I know what these management types are like.'

'She reminded me of someone. The manager,' she adds by way of clarification.

'Aye?' I say, wondering where Ale is going with this.

'That nun. Mother I'm So Superior.'

'Piss off.'

Ale takes a sip of her coffee. Makes a face. 'Just saying.'

'Just talking shite.' I chew on my irritation. Sigh. Ale's right. There is something about that woman. She has the same air of, well, superiority.

'Piss off,' I say again, but with less conviction. We sit in silence, sipping at our drinks. Minutes later, Ale is the first to speak.

'So anyway. Maybe everyone has calmed down, and we can go back and finish our conversation?' Ale stands up.

'How did you get so good, Rossi?'

She raises an eyebrow and smiles. 'I had a good teacher.'

'Well, whoever the fuck he is, tell him to teach you how to be less smug.'

She punches my arm as I walk past. 'See you.'

* * *

Back in the manager's room Jane Cameron acknowledges me with the barest of nods and gives Alessandra a full smile. Karen is sitting by the table, arms crossed, legs crossed, face clenched.

'So, where were we, Karen?' asks Ale. 'Aileen wanted to stay out...'

'And she's been getting right stroppy the last wee while. We always had the code, you know? Never ever split up. Always go home together.' Her eyes fill up. 'And the one time we...'

Ale leans forward and holds Karen's hand. 'Was Aileen on her own when you left?'

'No,' Karen sniffs. 'We met a bunch of people from uni. Barely knew them, but they were kinda familiar, you know. So, Aileen latches on to them. We have another row, so I think, "fuck you hen" and leave her...' More gut wrenching sobs. 'If only...'

'Don't torture yourself, Karen,' I say. 'Sounds like Aileen was a bit of a character?'

Karen nods in agreement. A smile ghosts through the tears.

'The people you recognised from uni ... girls or boys?'

'Girls.'

'Did you know any of their names?'

A shake of the head.

'Sure?'

Then with reluctance. 'The girl with bleached hair. Her name is Emma.' Karen pauses and looks to the side. 'She was a bit of a bitch. It was like, who are these two crowding in, you know? Her and her pal, Claire.'

'Could you describe this girl Claire?'

'Skinny. Black, straight hair. Tall.' Pause. 'Like, model tall.'

'How come you recognised them from uni? In the same building? Same course?'

'Dunno. Just seen them about.'

'We had girls like that when I was at uni,' says Ale. 'The cool ones. The ones that every girl wanted as a friend and every boy wanted to shag.'

Karen snorted an "as if". Quite unconvincingly.

'What can you tell me about Aileen's boyfriend?'

Karen looks up at me. 'Didn't have one.'

'What about Simon?'

'That was long finished.'

'He wasn't sniffing around?'

'I used to warn Aileen that she was leading him on too much. Mind you, he was the one that did the dirty. But then he regretted it. Asked her to get back together. She said she was over him. But then she'd snog him in a corner somewhere, get him all hot and bothered and then walk away laughing.' Pause. 'You don't think...'

'At this stage we are just following every possible line of enquiry,' I answer.

8

Dave Smith, aka Jim Leonard, was getting a guided tour of Ken's house. Like it was some kind of stately home rather than an ex-council house. "This is the kitchen," the old duffer had said, when the room couldn't possibly have been anything else. A master of the obvious.

The units were fairly new, apparently. So were the appliances, but the central heating was a bit ancient. In need of replacement, but a service would do for now, thanks. Jim nodded as if he actually gave a shit.

'Where's your brother today?' he asked.

'How should I know, I'm no his keeper.'

Interesting, thought Jim. *A crack appears in the twin unity.*

'He likes to go for a swim in the afternoon,' the older man said in an apologetic tone. 'He's the fit one. I cannae be arsed with all that exercise. How bored must you be to go up and down the same space in a pool for forty minutes? Better going for a walk or something. Get some fresh air in your lungs, eh? Rather than some chlorinated water that some wee brat has pissed in.' He laughed. 'Anyway, just put your tool bag on the floor there.' He pointed to a space in front of the sink. 'And I'll make you a wee cup of tea before you get started.'

'Thanks,' said Jim, putting his bag down and having a seat at the table.

'The boiler is a good twenty years old,' said Ken. 'I'd get the gas company in to do a service, but they charge you silly money. You sure Father won't mind you doing work for members of the congregation?'

'No need to tell him,' said Jim. 'What I do in my own time is nobody's business but mine.'

'Good man,' said Ken. 'Last time I had the gas man in he kept telling me I needed the radiators drained and a completely new boiler. He kept going on that I should really get a new heating system. But that would cost me a bloody fortune. So, a wee service from your good self will be sufficient as far as I'm concerned.'

'Aye,' said Jim, using as even a tone as he could manage while imagining his hands round the old man's throat. Thankfully there was silence while Ken filled the kettle and waited for it to boil, allowing Jim to drift away into thoughts of his real purpose here.

Death.

It had been a year since the nun. A year of working that memory. A memory of diminishing returns.

At first, reliving it had been enough. The rip in the fabric of life and the continual ache it left in him was assuaged for a time, but the urge to harm was creeping up on him. Fast.

From the moment he met the twins he knew one of them would be his next victim. Twins. Why didn't it occur to him before? And the request to service the boiler had given him the perfect excuse.

A report in the newspaper had given him the method.

A couple were found dead in their bed. Carbon monoxide poisoning. A faulty boiler was to blame. The paper went on to say that carbon monoxide, nicknamed the silent killer, killed on average one person per week in the UK. Mainly down to a fault in the central heating boiler. This is a gas that is odourless and tasteless. A gas that the human blood cells pick up on all too easily and which within a very short space of time can lead to coma and death.

Jim stood up. 'Actually, Ken, I'm not too bothered about a cuppa. Why don't you just see to yourself and I'll crack on with the boiler.'

'Aye, sure,' said Ken while pouring boiling water into a mug. He added a spoonful of dried coffee and then some milk. He then picked up the mug, sipped at it and turned and rested his back against the worktop.

'Do you mind?' Jim said wearing his best apologetic expression. 'I hate when folk stand over me while I'm working. Daft, I know.'

'Och, no worries, mate,' said Ken. 'I'll just go an' watch some crap TV. That Kyle fella makes my blood boil. Love watching him.'

* * *

Jim took the cover off the appliance. Cleaned a few pipes with a rag and looked to where he could cause the most damage. Then he wasted some more time, banged on a few pipes with his screwdriver and then eventually replaced the cover.

He needed to be sure the levels of carbon monoxide generated after his "service" were enough to kill. At lower levels they would only be enough to cause damage to Ken's health. Which wouldn't be enough for his purposes. Migraine, nausea and dizziness ain't fatal. Kidney failure or tachycardia could lead to complications, but again, would be to slow to push the man into his coffin.

The levels needed to be high enough to kill. And by his reckoning, once they were at that level it would only be a matter of minutes.

'That's me, Ken,' Jim shouted above the people shouting on the TV. 'Are you cold? Want me to leave the heating on?'

'Aye, please,' said Ken. 'There is a wee chill in the air.'

9

We're at muster and reviewing the case information so far. Harkie and the new girl are detailing the results of the samples taken from the victim. Semen was identified on her clothing and skin was lodged under her fingernails.

'They're going to run the DNA through the database, see if we can get a match.' The new girl sounds hugely optimistic. Cases rarely run quite that smoothly, but I don't want to ruin her feel-good mood, so settle for a nod by way of thanks. The best lessons are the ones you learn for yourself. Better that than me sounding like a miserable shit.

'Emma and Claire, the two "it" girls from university are proving difficult to find, Ray.'

'What? You were with Daryl Drain, the notorious womaniser, and you couldn't find two attractive young ladies?' I ask.

Daryl leans back in his seat, crosses his arms. 'Changed man, mate. Since I met Cath my days of scouting for talent are over.'

Ale blows through her pursed lip. Then, 'Aye. Right.'

'Honest.' Daryl looks wounded. 'Cross my heart. From now on, I'm a one-woman man.'

Looks of scepticism through the room.

'Naw, don't, DD,' says Harkie. 'My sex life is entirely vicarious. Through your shenanigans.'

Drain shudders. 'Man, that is a horrible thought and jeezuz, what did I do to deserve such a bad rep?'

'Anyway,' I interrupt before someone sounds off a list. 'Anybody got anything else?'

'Aye,' says Drain. 'Spoke to a few more of the neighbours, and they all confirmed that neither Mr or Mrs Banks left the house that night.'

Which means we can score Dad off the potential list of suspects.

'What about the ex-boyfriend? Who was chasing him up?'

The phone rings. Ale answers. Listens. Whatever she hears has her mouth form an "o" of surprise. She hangs up.

'That's Dumbarton Road police station. They've just locked up Mr Banks. Seems he went looking for the ex-boyfriend and tried to tear his head off.'

My stomach lurches. 'Is the boy badly hurt?' The Banks have enough to contend with. No need to add GBH or worse to their lot.

'Didn't say. He's been taken to hospital to assess his wounds.'

'Right. Ale, you're with me. We're going to see Mr Banks. Daryl, you get back on the hunt for Emma and Claire. Take Nick with you. He might improve your chances.'

* * *

Over at the Dumbarton Road office, the desk sergeant is Ron McKie. He's one of the good guys. A don't-take-any-crap attitude married with a generous dollop of common sense goes a long way in his position. Ron and I go back some. He was always a man that was willing to listen to the new boys. Kept them right but tore a strip off them if need be. He rests his capacious belly on the front desk and assesses Alessandra. Not in a lecherous, "who's the totty" kind of way. But, he would have taken in her level gaze and confident stance and immediately thought: *aye, we've got a good wan here.*

'Awright, Ed?' he says when he sees me. He is a keen reader of US crime fiction, and I'd almost forgotten the nickname he had granted me all those years ago. 'Soon as we put your man's name in the system we realised what was going on. Poor guy, eh? His daughter murdered.'

'Aye. Still. You cannae go around beating people up.'

'Cos that's oor job, eh?' His large acne-scarred cheeks bunch in a grin. 'Well, it is down south. Did you hear about those English numpties?' Ron was always fiercely proud of the police service in Scotland, and any chance to laugh at his southern colleagues was quickly jumped on. 'Tasered a blind man when they thought his walking stick was a samurai sword. A fucking samurai sword. How stupid would you have to be?' He slams a meaty hand on the desk top. 'Anyways, the young man Mr Banks attacked has suffered nothing worse than a few cuts and bruises. Possible concussion. The docs wanted to take him in to the hospital just to make sure there wasn't anything more serious.'

'Right. Good to know. Awright if we come in and speak to him?'

'Sure.' He opens the security door and beckons us through. 'He's in Cell 4 the now. Go into the interview room, Ed, and I'll bring him through.'

* * *

Ale and I take a seat, and moments later Ron enters the room with Kevin Banks. He looks about ten years older than when we saw him yesterday. He sits in a chair as if his bones are aching.

'Mr Banks, my name is…'

'Aye. We met yesterday. Forgive me if I don't shake your hand.'

Looks like Mr Banks is firmly in the "anger" stage of grief.

'You attacked a young man today, Mr Banks. Care to tell us why?'

He sags in his chair.

'I just thought … I wanted to…' He leans forward, places both elbows on the table and rubs at his scalp with the palm of his right hand. 'I don't know what the hell I was doing.' He then puts a hand over his mouth as he fights to control himself. A tear slides down his cheek. He sniffs. 'Is Simon OK?'

'He's currently being assessed by a medical team at the Western,' I answer. I don't want to let him off the hook too quickly. He needs to learn the consequences of this particular action. Grieving parent or not.

He mumbles into the desk top, 'Stupid. Stupid. Stupid.' He shakes his head. 'Simon was only guilty of betrayal. He wouldn't…' He stumbles over the word "kill". 'The boy doesn't have a vicious bone in his body.'

'So why go after him?'

'You're awake all night. You go through all the possibilities, and you remember all these cop programmes where the boyfriend did it. I couldn't shake that thought from my head. I just wanted to speak to the boy. Speak to him, you know. He loved her too. At one point. But when I saw him walking along the road ... He was on his phone, smiling. Actually smiling. How dare he fucking smile when my daughter had been murdered.' He exhales. A long, juddering breath. 'I lost it.' He turns sharply to the side as if he doesn't want us to see the pain he's in.

'Aye.' I'm wearing my disapproving face. Catch Ale's face. She doesn't speak, but her face says exactly what she is thinking. How can you ever get used to this level of grief?

Kevin turns back to face us. Closes his eyes and fights with his emotions. He coughs. Opens his eyes and looks from me to Ale and then back again. 'So what happens now? Is Simon going to press charges?'

'That's not how it happens in Scotland, Mr Banks. The evidence goes to the procurator fiscal, and he decides whether or not there is a case to be brought against you.'

'Christ. The missus is going to go nuts.'

Exhale.

'Jeezuz. You hear about this happening to other families and you wonder, don't you? If something happened to your daughter, what would you do?' His face blanches. 'I always thought I was a reasonable man. I thought, if something ever happened ... to ... I would rely on the police and the courts to see that justice was done. But now...' His eyes search mine for something. Judgement? Accord? We're men together. Surely I know how it must feel. 'But now, I know. I could wrap my hands round his neck, squeeze with everything I had and feel his last fucking breath.'

His unasked question. Do you have kids? A daughter maybe? What would you do? I think of my erstwhile lover, Theresa. The last time I saw her she was heavily pregnant and refused to confirm

47

whether the baby was mine or her husband's. I never dared to check the gender. If I knew, I knew I'd never keep away. I'd bang down Theresa's door till she proved either I was or wasn't the father. And I realise I'm a coward. Not knowing the gender has helped me keep my distance. Helped me avoid taking any responsibility. Sure, Theresa doesn't want me around, but if I'm the father, she doesn't get to decide that.

'Mr Banks, you are in a police station, and you have just stated how you could kill someone to two police officers.' Ale stares at him, her expression a warning. He just stares back, blank.

Ale softens her attitude. 'We'll have no more talk about killing anyone, eh? How do you think your wife is going to react when she hears you're locked up in here? Does she not have enough to contend with? And if you had killed Simon, what then? Your wife has no daughter and a husband who is locked up for murder?' Her tone is just the right one in this situation. That of an angry mother.

Time for a change of tactic. 'When you were lying in bed last night thinking that the ex-boyfriend did it, did anything else occur to you?' I ask.

'What do you mean?'

'I know daughters can be secretive, especially where there father is concerned. But there just might be some clue she let escape? The people she met, the places she went to?'

'Ha! I tried to friend her on shitbook, and she ignored my request. Told me nothing.'

'What about her mum? Did she confide in her?'

'A little, I guess. More, when she was younger. Lately they always seem to be at loggerheads. My wife was a bit of a tearaway when she was young, saw Aileen making the same mistakes and wanted to keep her safe.' At that last word, he buckles again. Buries his face in his hands and allows the grief to flow.

Ale's eyes are filling up. I have a huge lump in my throat. I've been in so many situations like this over the years, but something about this man's love for his dead daughter really gets to me. Is it because I may well be a father myself?

I take a deep breath, lower my shoulders, force calm into my voice. 'Ale, would you see if Sergeant McKie can show you where the tea and coffee is? Maybe Mr Banks would like something?'

She gives me a look of thanks and darts out of the room without asking what the man wants, as if she's about to be overcome herself.

* * *

Driving back to the station and I get a text from the guys at the hospital. The boy is fine. Nothing more than cuts and bruises. He has given a few names as alibis. The team will check them out.

Daryl phones in to say he has a lead on the two girls.

'Excellent,' I say. 'So The Drain hasn't lost his touch after all?'

'Stupid question,' says Daryl.

'Let me know when you get them in. I want to be there for the questioning.'

Ale is driving. The traffic is heavy. We've barely gone above ten miles an hour in the last twenty minutes. My thoughts are with Kevin Banks. His grief was palpable, like another person in the room.

'How can a parent ever come to terms with the loss of a child?' asks Ale, like she was reading my thoughts.

I shake my head. Say nothing.

'Sorry I nearly lost it in there, boss,' says Ale. 'If you hadn't sent me away for the coffee...'

'S'alright. You're only human.'

'Aye, but as a woman in the force, I don't want the guys thinking...'

'You know what, Alessandra? I was close to losing it as well, and as far as I'm concerned you're a human first and a woman second. Next comes the job. And keeping all that in mind helps you become more effective in the job. But that's just me. We all want to be the cool, calm professional, but there will always be times that the people you meet will get to you. Something in them speaks to the human in you. It's inevitable.'

Ale focuses on the road for a moment. Nods her head. Says, 'Aye.'

The phone rings again. It's the boss. There's a press conference on the Aileen Banks murder, and he wants me to front it. Hate doing that. Some of the guys, soon as they hear they're going to be in front of the camera they rush off and get their best Ralph Slater suit on. Me, I hate being a public face.

'Make sure you are back here in time, McBain.'

'Sir.' I hang up with a curse. My mind goes straight back to Kevin Banks. 'Fathers and daughters, eh?'

'Aye.'

'You never talk much about your dad.'

Ale looks at me. 'You know he was in the polis, right?'

'Think I knew that.'

'He died when I was a teenager. Hit and run. They never caught the guy. Or woman.'

'Do you have good memories of him?'

Ale smiles. 'Yeah. Worked long hours. But when he was present he was *present*, you know? We used to see him sitting in the car before he came in the house. As if he was leaving the shit of the day out there. As if he wanted to protect his girls from all the horrible stuff he had to process in his working life.'

'Sounds like a clever man.'

'What about your dad?'

'He was an arse.' Smile. I search my memory. Don't come up with much. 'He was drunk a lot.'

The grief we experienced from Banks earlier on is making us both melancholic, and in the confessional of the car we are just two people who happen to be police. Listening to Alessandra talking about her dad, I wonder what kind of parent I might be. Would I have the sense to leave the job behind me when I walk in to the family home after a hard day dealing with the worst that people can do? I wonder about parents and their children. At the pain they feel at their loss. From what I can see, parents view children as their better selves. What they themselves might have become had life and its vagaries not intruded. They emotionally invest in that potential, and the grief becomes more acute because the potential will never be realised.

I wonder if I should shut up about the parental thing. Theresa made it quite clear she wanted nothing more to do with me. I haven't told anyone in the job about my suspicions of potential parenthood and I regret the words as soon as they come out of my mouth.

'Did I tell you I might be a dad?'

10

The day of the funeral was warm for autumn. The sky was a peerless blue, the breeze no more than a huff from the mouth of a bored god. The trees that bordered the cemetery were a burnt auburn and the pathways through the headstones provided a crisp litter bed for those leaves that had given up the fight.

The surviving twin said he wanted the funeral to be a celebration of Ken's life. The colour black was banned, and in keeping with this request the attendees fought to outdo each other, wearing the gaudiest colours in their wardrobe.

Robert Ford himself was wearing cream trousers, a post-box red jacket and a paisley patterned tie with God knows how many colours on it. Jim was by Robert's side for most of the day, wearing the only jacket he had, which was a dark green. Robert insisted he borrow a tie, so against his better judgement he went for one with luminous pink and blue stripes.

The service was mercifully brief, Jim thought. Being in such a prominent position, so near the family of the bereaved, he was aware that he would be in the vision of most of the people there. How to keep the bored expression from his face and wear something that approximated grief was almost beyond him.

Robert almost inevitably was the one to find the dead body. And almost succumbed to the gas himself had his first action not been to turn the heating off when he walked into the house. The house was like a sauna, he told Jim. As he described events of that afternoon, he said that he felt the heat as soon as he walked in the door. Shouted for Ken, got no answer. He walked through the living room and through into the kitchen. No Ken. He turned off the heating before he then went upstairs. To find Ken, fully clothed, face down on the bed. As if he'd been making his way there for a lie down and fatigue had overtaken him before he could get into a proper sleeping position.

Jim was a wonderful listener. He gripped the older man's forearm in a show of support and silently willed him to continue, hoping that his mounting excitement would not be recognised for what it was.

Robert detailed his puzzlement at his brother's position on the bed. Then his chest began to tighten, he felt that he couldn't breathe. His head was pounding and he felt alarmingly dizzy. And confused. What was Ken doing lying like that?

And how he had the presence of mind to open the bedroom window, he'd never know, he told Jim. Which, on learning what had killed his brother, was something of a minor miracle. And the action that had saved his life. The doctors told him his higher fitness level might have been why he had been able to stave off the effects of the gas longer than his brother.

Tea and sandwiches were being served back at the church hall after the burial, and while Jim listened to the great and the good of the parish eulogise the deceased, he dreamed of the moment he would have Robert to himself.

It was back at Robert's house later in the day, when all the mourners had gone home to their own living, breathing families, when Robert crumbled. He had been at attention all day, his bearing rigid with his refusal to publicly show his grief. Only when he and Jim were on their own did he give in.

They'd been sitting side by side on the sofa in silence for many minutes when Robert gripped Jim's knee.

'You were the last person who saw Ken alive,' said Robert. His face long, eyes anguished. 'Tell me again what he said?'

'He made me a cup of tea,' said Jim. 'Said he wasn't your keeper when I asked where you were.'

'The old git,' Robert half-laughed half-sobbed.

'Said he couldn't understand why someone would spend all that time swimming up and down the same stretch of water...'

'Ha.' Robert shook his head slowly. 'Anything else?'

'Nope,' said Jim. 'Apart from saying he wanted to watch some guy on the TV called Kyle. The man he loved to hate, apparently.'

'Yeah,' said Robert. 'He loved to watch that crap. Joked that we should make up some rubbish so we could get on the telly.' He jumped up from his chair and ran into the kitchen as if he was going to vomit. Curiosity drove Jim to follow. Robert was hunched over the kitchen sink. His legs gave way and he fell to the floor. He managed to get himself into a seated position and drew his knees up to his chest. Holding everything tight.

He was stuck there. Anchored to the spot with anguish. A line of spit shone from his lower lip, down past his chin. He rolled his head slowly from side to side, moaning his brother's name.

Tea, thought Jim. That's what people do in this situation. They deflect their thoughts by making tea. But he couldn't move. He was transfixed by the beauty of the other man's sorrow, by the drama of his hurt. He wanted to be up close. Forehead to forehead. Breath to breath. Pain to pain.

He took a step closer and soaked up the other man's energy. His eyes smarted, his chest puffed, adrenalin sparked in his fingertips. He stumbled to his knees, rapt, his arms out, wanting to touch the older man.

Robert misread his intention and held a hand out to take one of Jim's.

'You really cared for him, didn't you?' he asked in a whisper through his clenched throat.

Jim nodded the lie. The ability to speak momentarily lost, his mind reeling. Until now, the black hole in his life had only been filled by the death of another. But this was an incredible charge. He felt replete. Sated.

Grief would be his feast from now on.

11

The clock never stops. It is inexorable. One moment moves to the next with an inevitable but inaudible tick. People go about their daily lives: what gadget to buy next, what processed crap to shovel down their neck for dinner, what wine goes with what meat, who said what to whom? And the pettiness of it drives me fucking nuts.

That's probably why I'm still single. I can't switch off. I can't leave the horrors of the day in the car before I enter my front door with a genuine smile on my face. I unlock my front door and think of Kevin Banks. How will that man ever find normality again?

But the clock keeps on moving. One tick before another tock. Unceasing and soon the unbelievable becomes the normal. Mankind's greatest trick. The ability to adjust. We have to or the species would never have survived the millennia.

One of the first cops I worked with, Harry Fyfe, was always going on about how mankind was doomed. *A pathetic pile of shit*, was how he succinctly put it. *We do some God-awful things to each other*, he would say. *We're ruined. Hopeless cases.* I used to laugh at him. After a day like today, I'm on his side.

Jeez, I'm full of it tonight. Need to switch off. But I slump before the telly and switch it on. Some magazine show on the Beeb blares into the gloom of my living room, and they're talking about the nation's greatest fucking casserole.

'Oh for f ... Turn that shite off,' I shout and aim the remote at the telly. 'Dinner,' I say out loud. 'What will I have for dinner?'

You do that, don't you, when you live on your own? Talk to yourself.

There's feck all in the fridge. And nothing apart from a tin of tuna in the cupboard. That'll do. Hardly filling for a growing man. I pat my expanding belly. It'll do.

Aileen Banks's laptop is still on my sofa. Oops. How did that happen? I need to get it into the office and recorded into evidence. Tomorrow.

I push open the lid. Bring up Facebook and before I even articulate the thought I'm looking for the two girls as described by Karen. They were the "it" girls, so surely Aileen would want to follow them? I find her friend list. I'm looking for a Claire and an Emma.

As I scroll through Aileen's list of friends I have to fight down the old curmudgeon in me. How can people be arsed? There's nearly three hundred "friends", and an alert is telling me she's had over fifty friend requests … since she died.

As the online peeps say: WTF? Even I have heard of internet trolls. Are these internet ghouls? Befriending a dead person?

There's a Claire. Skinny with black, straight hair was how Karen described her, and that's how the picture looks. Claire Baird, it says. Tells me she works at Starbucks. Goes to Glasgow University. Lives in Glasgow.

Feeling ridiculously pleased with myself, I click on 'About'.

Her birthday, email address and mobile number are noted. Her favourite quote is "I am the one who knocks." She's lost me there. Some horror movie quote maybe?

Is nothing sacred in this online world? All kinds of creepsters could get their hands on this information and do all kinds of weird with it.

Her timeline – that's what they call it, right? – is banal taken to the edge of boring and beyond. With an added pinch of dull and a twist of trivial. She shops, like, a lot. Goes to clubs, like, a lot. And uses 'like' a lot. And LOL comes up fairly often. Lots of love? Lots of lollies? Look out lippy?

A picture of red shoes with the words, come to momma. And then a few rants about a TV show with too many initials to work out what it actually is.

I look for posts on the day of Aileen's murder.

'SO want that top out of Cruise.'

'Never thought I'd say it but yuks to more coffee.'

And the last one for the day, at 7:17pm: 'It's a school night, but fuckit, who's up for a pub crawl?'

This has eleven comments. One from Aileen. To my unpractised eye it looks out of place with the other comments. Like she's desperate to join in. Claire replies to Aileen's comment with 'yeah, whatever, don't wait up sweetie.'

I recoil, and it's not aimed at me.

One of the comments in this thread is from an Emma. Emma Smith. Her details are much more scant than Claire's, and her profile picture is a photo of a male pretty-boy – not Emma, then. Her date of birth just has a month and a day. No year. And her mobile number is missing.

I scan her photos. Nothing much until I see two girls. One is tagged as Claire Baird, the other, a girl of similar age and height with blond, spiky hair, as Emma.

Emma Smith, hello there.

Her timeline for tonight says, 'A quiet night out at Cafe Gandolfi. Who's coming?'

Don't mind if I do.

* * *

Cafe Gandolfi was pure jumping, as the young ones say, when I arrived. Not been in here for ages. A bit expensive for my tastes. Haggis, neeps and tatties for £13. What's that all about? I could rustle that up on my own for a couple of quid. But then I wouldn't get to experience the L-shaped room, high ceiling, dark wood panelling and the tables and chairs that look like they were made from materials washed up on a beach.

Looking around the people in the room I feel like I've landed in an alternative Glasgow. When I do go out, I'm more used to the cheap and cheerful "whit's your fuckin' poison, mate" kinda pub. This is where you hang out if you're on trend, wear the latest clothes and carry the newest iPad.

'Ray McBain, what the hell are you doing here?' a voice chimes in my ear. I recognise it and feel a huge smile form on my face.

'Maggie.' I turn to face her, lean down and draw her into a hug. 'I could ask you the same question.'

She beams up at me. 'The girls…' she sweeps her right arm dramatically towards a table. Four inquisitive, shiny faces stare back. '…invited me out. Seeing as it's my birthday.'

Shit. 'It's your birthday? Why didn't you tell me?' She's looking great. All clean and primped and pink with a touch too much booze.

'Cos then I get to crow at how rubbish you are as a mate.' Four faces are still staring at me. 'Anyway, what the hell are you doing here?'

'Would you believe it, work?'

'Coming from you, aye, I would. Has there been a murrrdurrr?' A drunken squeal of laughter follows this question.

Taggart, you have a lot to answer for.

'There has, actually.'

'Oh shit,' she makes an apologetic face. 'You know me, I don't watch the news.'

I pat my pocket, check I have my wallet on me. 'Anyway, it looks like the birthday girl isn't nearly drunk enough yet. Can I buy you a drink?'

'No thanks, Ray,' she says with a smile. Flicks her hair away from her face. 'It's getting to the point of no return. Fast. If I have much more they'll be pumping my stomach down at the Western.'

'Would you no rather get something else pumped?' one of her friends shouts. Laughter erupts from everyone else at the table. High pitched enough to pierce an eardrum.

'Did you just turn down a drink?' another friend asks. 'You mental?'

'We're drinking champagne, Ray,' says another one.

'Are you one of the boys in blue, Ray?'

'Why don't you join us?'

'Sorry, ladies. I'm working.'

A chorus of "awwwww" rings round the table.

Then.

'Disnae mean you can't buy us a drink.' It's the one with the brown bob. Mediterranean tan. Cleavage reaching all the way down to the table top. She catches me looking and winks.

'So what it is then? What are you all drinking?' I ask, caught up in the good mood flowing from the table.

'It's alright, Ray,' says Maggie, patting the top of my arm. 'We've more than enough, thanks.'

'A bottle of their finest Taittinger,' says one.

'Naw, that's cheap crap,' says another. 'They've a cheeky wee Dom Perignon on the menu.'

'But you can only buy it if you join us,' says another.

'Seriously, Ray,' says Maggie. 'I apologise that my friends are badgering you...'

'She's thirty-one today,' someone shouts.

'Gawd, that makes me feel ancient,' another responds.

'Shut it, cheeky,' says Maggie. Back to me. 'There's no need, Ray.' She looks embarrassed.

I've got to milk this.

'Now what kind of friend would I be, Maggie...'

'From what we've heard you guys have been way more than friends.' More high squeals. Maggie looks like she wants to run away. I just grin. She throws me a "see you" look.

'I'm going to have you, Littlejohn. And you, Weir.'

This is rewarded by a snort from one and a giggle from the other.

'Excuse me a moment, ladies. I'll just go to the bar,' I say to a chorus of cheers.

Maggie follows me. 'You don't have to get me anything, Ray. My birthday isn't really until tomorrow. But this was the best night to get everyone together.' We reach the bar. 'But if you insist.' Cheeky grin. 'You can get me this one.' She pulls a menu out from a stand, and her finger-nail, painted deep red and crested with a diamante, rests on the description: "The granddad of all prestige cuvee champagnes, truly iconic. Moët ensure pristine quality, regardless of the volume produced. The 2000 vintage is full of life, with vibrant fruit and a piercing intensity of dried fruits, cocoa and vanilla." It is indeed a Dom Perignon and comes in at a wallet-busting £140.

'You can fuck right off,' is my succinct reply.

A waiter approaches. Male. If he's a day over twenty-one, I've got fifteen toes. Shaved head, skin so fresh it looks like he applies it each morning and sporting a beard so thick and bushy it could have come right out of a photo of the troops in the American Civil War.

Surreal.

'Am I drunk already?' I ask Maggie.

'What can I get you, sir?' he asks.

I drag Maggie's finger up the page. Find a price that suits. £47.

'That one.' I fish my credit card out of my wallet.

'What? No moths?' grins Maggie.

'It is a special day.' Caught up in the moment, I lean forward and kiss her. On the lips. Maggie steps back. Flushed. I hear a comment from the table.

'Oh, Maggie could be getting a birthday shag after all.' Cue more giggles.

'Ignore them,' Maggie says.

'They seem a good bunch,' I say.

'Could do a lot worse,' she replies with a fond smile. She touches her lips with the tips of her fingers. Lightly. Then scratches her cheek, deflecting my vision.

'So,' she says.

'So.'

'Haven't heard from you…'

'Been busy. Lots of bad people out there,' I say, thinking, *when did we get this awkward? Is it because her pals are here?* I lean forward with a grin. 'I suppose a birthday shag is out of the question?'

She laughs. Head back. Sounds like the scatter of gold coins on a cobbled street. God, she looks gorgeous.

'Takes more than a fifty quid bottle of champagne,' she replies.

'We could do a lot worse than each other, you know.'

'Yeah. Well. Not going there, Ray. Not tonight.' She opens her mouth as if she's going to say more. Then changes her mind. 'Did you really come in here tonight on a case?'

'Aye.' Shit. I'd momentarily forgot. 'Looking for a couple of young women.'

'Oh, aye?'

'Aye. Friends, sorry, acquaintances, of a girl that was murdered.'

Maggie shivers. 'Right.' She coughs. 'Let's not go there either. It's my birthday.' She turns to the bar. 'And where's that handsome young barman with my champagne?'

Just then Beardy appears. In his hand the foiled neck of a bottle jutting out from a silver bucket full of ice.

'How many glasses, sir?'

'Don't worry about glasses, son,' says Maggie. 'We've got a sufficiency. Unless, of course, you want to join us, Ray?'

'I'll just have a glass of fresh orange.' I say to the barman. I scan the room. No sign of the girls I'm looking for.

'Not here?' asks Maggie.

'No.'

'Come and sit with us then.'

'Ach, I'll just be cramping your style.'

'Ach nothing. Get over yourself, McBain.'

The women at the table cheer when they see us returning with the gold-foil-topped bottle. And give each other knowing looks. I carry a chair over from another table, take a seat and the next half hour flows past in a flurry of laughs and chatter. I almost hold my own, but the women are too quick even for me. Taking the chance when the conversation moves to the far end of the table, the woman beside me, Gillian, moves in close. She puts a hand on my thigh and says, 'You could do a lot worse than our Maggie, you know.'

'I know.'

'You men. I'll never understand you.'

Maggie looks at us, a quizzical expression light on her face. 'What are you cooking up, Littlejohn?'

'Me? Nothing.' She leans back in her chair and takes a sip of her champagne. 'Just telling Ray here that you're not getting any younger.'

'Ha,' Maggie laughs. Then she shakes her head. 'See what I've to put up with?'

The rest of the conversation goes past me as I noticed a group of young people enter. Three boys, two girls. I recognise the girls from their photos – thank you, Facebook. I consider how I'm going to get a chance to talk to the girls on their own, when I see the group split by gender. Good. I wait until the girls are settled at a table with their drinks before I go and talk to them about a murder.

12

There's a line of weak light coming through a small space in the curtains. It divides the room, slices through a pile of hastily shed clothes on the floor, before it reaches the bed and the naked woman lying beside me. She turns to face me, a smile on her face.

'Well, happy birthday to me,' she sings.

I lean forward and kiss her. Long and slow.

'Ooh,' she chuckles when our faces part. 'Tongues and everything.'

'Well, it is your birthday.'

She laughs.

'Don't know how many times you said that last night,' I say.

'How many times did we…'

'Three.'

'Well, there you go.' She cuddles into me, her naked skin lining mine. Makes a small groan of pleasure. 'Can we stay here all day? I don't want to leave this bed ever.'

My belly rumbles in response. We both laugh.

'Can we leave it for some food?' I ask.

She nods. 'And while you're up, making me bacon and eggs, have a shower first, eh?' She sniffs at my armpit. Makes a face. 'You're minging.'

I jump out of bed and feel incredibly energised despite having had little, make that no, sleep. 'Kitchen?'

'That's right.' Maggie sits up on the bed and makes a face. 'You've never been in my flat before. Second door on the left as you go into the hall. The first door is the toilet. Where the shower resides.'

'OK. Towel?' I ask with a distracted tone. I'm too busy enjoying the view of her naked breasts.

'There should be one in the bathroom. And don't stare at a lady. It's rude.' She grins and makes no move to cover up.

The shower is one of those power ones. The water drills onto my scalp and shoulders. I turn my face up to the flow and feel it drum on to my forehead. Then I realise I'm humming. Bugger me. Ray McBain making happy noises. So that's what a night of sex can do for you.

Then I realise it's not the sex. I'm not anxious to run for the hills. I want to stay.

It's Maggie.

Another realisation. I hadn't thought of the case for hours. Welcome to the human race, Ray.

My chat with Aileen's Facebook "friends" was a bust.

They were both sitting with a glass of something, spiked with a straw, their iPhones face up, resting just a fingertip away. They barely looked at me when I introduced myself. Made a slight face of recognition when I mentioned Aileen's name and scarcely raised enough interest to acknowledge that they knew her. I asked a few questions and got a series of 'dunnos' in reply.

Thinking about it while I am standing in the shower, and it occurs to me that they were more concerned that I was putting a dampener on their evening than they were that someone they knew had been murdered.

'So, what can you tell me about that evening?' I asked again.

'Nothing,' the Claire one said, flicking her long, black hair out of the way before she leaned forward to sip at her drink through a red-striped straw.

'Look, mate,' Emma said, finally showing some animation. 'We didn't really know her that well. To tell you the truth, and I don't want to speak ill of the dead, but she kinda, like, stalked us, you know? Made the mistake of making her our Facebook friend and she knows everything about us and always makes sure she's with us and trying to worm her way into our company. Not cool, man.'

When did we all suddenly become American?

'Did you see her that night? Anything you can tell me might help catch the man that killed her.'

Emma blew out of her pursed mouth, sat back in her chair and crossed her arms. 'She came over and joined us, her and that chunky mate of hers.' She looked over at Claire. 'Karen?'

'Aye. Karen,' Claire snorted. 'They're still into *Twilight*. How sad is that? I'm like grow up, ladies.'

'How would you describe the relationship between Aileen and Karen?' I asked. Don't know why I did, but the words come out before I could edit.

'What?' Claire leaned forward. 'Do you think they were lezzies or something?'

'There are all kinds of relationships. Family, friends, colleagues … not just sexual ones. We're relating right now.'

'Ewwww,' both girls grimaced at exactly the same time.

Claire thought for a moment. 'Aileen was the boss. Karen followed her about like a wee puppy. Like she was totally in love with her or something.'

'Hence the lezzy response,' Emma said. The insouciant pose had momentarily gone and I could see from her direct gaze that there was a sharp mind in there. She just didn't want me to see it.

'And she was delighted when Aileen and her boyfriend fell out. Even we understood that.'

'Simon?' I asked.

Claire squinted. 'Don't think that was his name…'

'Ian,' said Emma. 'Or…' Looked at Claire. 'Jack?'

'There was a Ian and a Jack?' I asked.

'Yeah, after Aileen and Simon split she had a couple of one-nighters. Nothing serious you know?'

'How do you know all this, Emma?' asked Claire.

'Hello, Facebook,' she answered. 'And Aileen pure cornered me one night in the loos over at the student union and poured her heart out.' She made a face.

'You poor thing,' said Claire. 'Where was I?'

'You were shagging that English guy you said had a tiny penis and could barely get it up.'

Both girls threw their heads back and laughed. We'd moved from barely wanting to speak to over-sharing in just a few short minutes. It was like some silent signal had passed between them that it was OK to talk.

Someone's phone pinged. Both girls looked at theirs. Exchanged a glance that said it was nothing, really.

'Back to Ian and Jack?'

'Yeah…' Emma looked pointedly at her empty glass. I took the hint, asked what the girls would like to drink and went to the bar.

Drinks replenished, I steered the conversation back to the boys.

'So. Ian and Jack. What can you tell me about them?'

'Not much. Both were one-offs from what I could gather. Aileen dumped Simon. Realised it was a mistake. Tried to get him back, and then when he didn't come running back with his tail between his legs Aileen went out with other guys to try and make him jealous,' answered Emma.

'I got the impression that Simon dumped Aileen to go out with her pal?'

'Nah, Aileen said that was what she told her olds…'

'Olds?'

'Parents.' Claire gave me a look that asked: don't you know anything?

'Yeah, so, she told that to her parents.' Emma made a face. 'You don't want them to really know what's going on, do you? And besides, Ian and Jack are players. Well, Jack is. Ian hangs on his rep. They're all about shagging as many girls as they can, you know? And when Aileen didn't give them everything they wanted, they moved on. But they'd hang out now and again. Like pals.'

'Hey.' Claire pushed at her friend's shoulder. 'How do you know all this?'

Emma tried not to look too pleased with herself and had a sip of her drink. 'I pay attention, Claire. Gossip are us.'

'Simon. What do you know about him?' I asked.

'He didn't do it, did he?' asked Emma as she crossed her arms and furrowed her brow.

'My dad says there's no smoke without fire,' said Claire.

'Yeah, it's all over Facebook that Aileen's dad kicked the shit out of him.'

'How did I miss that?' asked Claire.

'There's no evidence that links Simon to her murder. He's just helping us with our enquiries,' I said, trying to calm the conversation down.

'Yet,' said Emma. 'No evidence *yet.*'

'Yeah, Aileen's dad wouldn't take a flaky like that without something concrete, eh?' said Claire. She shivered. 'Jeez, we could have been speaking to a murderer.'

'You wanted to go out with him at one point. You could have done more than just speak to him,' said Emma.

'Man, you are creeping me out.' Claire crossed her arms and her eyes clouded. Then she reached out and pushed her drink away from her. Looked like a good time was no longer on the menu.

'Look, ladies,' I said. 'We have to speak to Simon given their past relationship, but that doesn't mean he did it. I can't say any more than that. So please don't go making any assumptions.'

Claire looked over at Emma. 'I'd quite like to go home now. Should we phone a taxi?'

'Our flat is just up the road, Claire,' said Emma.

'Yeah, but...' and she looked like a wee girl who is missing her father.

'Listen, guys, I'm sorry. I didn't mean to frighten you. You're in no more danger out on the streets now than you were when you came in an hour ago,' I said. Two pairs of large eyes looked back at me. 'Finish your drinks. Look after each other, eh?'

* * *

Maggie sticks her head in the bathroom door.

'You turned into a prune yet?' she asks. Steps inside and hands me a towel. She looks me up and down with a grin. 'Least I know you're clean.'

'Stop leering at me.' I wrap the towel round my waist. 'Unless you want morning sex?' I grab her and hold her close.

'No thanks, Ray. I need fed, and I need to get to work.' She sheds her dressing gown and steps beyond me into the shower. I stare at her small but pert breasts, the narrow of her waist and the flare of her hips. I make a yum sound.

She laughs and pushes me away. 'Get dry and make me some breakfast, will you?'

'Say pretty please.'

'Piss off. And bacon and eggs will do nicely, thanks.'

* * *

At the breakfast bar in her small kitchen we're sitting on stools facing each other. Both of us grinning. It occurred to me that the last time we were this familiar it didn't end so well, and I'm trying to work out why.

'It was just a birthday shag,' Maggie says.

I feel my stomach twist. 'Right,' is all I can say, and I study my plate.

'I was using you for birthday sex.'

I look up at her, and she's wearing a huge smile.

'It was more than that, and you know it,' I say.

'Do I?'

I get off my stool and walk towards her. Move in between her open legs. Kiss her bacon fat smeared lips. 'Aye. This is the happiest I've felt in a long time.'

'One shag doesn't make a summer.'

I laugh. 'If that's not the expression it should be.'

Her expression shifts to sombre. 'I fell in love with you a long time ago, Ray.'

'Feels like I just caught up with you.' I kiss her again, and I don't want to stop.

She pushes me away. 'Let's just take it one day at a time, eh?'

'I've just had a thought.'

'What?'

'It's really your birthday today, isn't it?'

She smiles.

'So we can do the whole birthday sex thing again tonight.'

13

The only light in the room was a flicker from the television, sound turned down to allow the older man on the sofa to sleep.

From his vantage point on the armchair, Jim Leonard assessed Robert Ford, stretched full length on the sofa, head propped on the cushioned arm, hands on his stomach, and thought it looked as if he was posing for his coffin. The only sign that the man was alive was the slight rise and fall of his chest.

They had been watching one of those Scandinavian crime dramas, so beloved of the great unwashed, when Jim became aware that Robert was no longer engaged in the programme and had fallen into sleep.

Jeez, it was boring, thought Jim looking back at the TV. Who cares if these people get killed? And he could care even less if the murderer got caught. And was it supposed to make it more interesting if they all spoke some indecipherable language? And what's with subtitles?

Father Stephen had been in earlier. Pleased to see that Jim was still keeping Robert company after his brother died. Said Jim was a saint. A Samaritan for helping the old fella cope with his grief. A bad Samaritan maybe, thought Jim.

The initial kick was fantastic. It was close to the feeling he got after a kill. But killing people could get him locked up, and he hoped this might be the next best thing. But as the old man's grief inevitably quietened, and he became a shuffling, mumbling wreck, the charge he received from feeding on it was almost unnoticeable.

He had attempted to stoke it up on a couple of occasions. Asked Robert to remember happy times with his brother, but the response was less than gratifying. He wanted to talk about his brother less and less and would wander in to another room in the house, fall into a chair and stare at the wall. He was Scottish, he told Jim. He didn't talk about his feelings unless it was about football or if he'd just drunk a barrel of whisky.

Jim looked at the TV screen. Someone was running for their life. He stretched out his legs and crossed them at the ankle. The poor sap on the telly, and of course it was a woman, would inevitably trip and fall, allowing her potential killer to catch up with her.

Yup. There she was. Caught. Now she was kicking and squealing. Fighting the inescapable fate the TV writers had dreamt up for her. Jim watched the killer, and it was *his* hands round the woman's neck. His knee pinning her to the ground. His nose that could smell her panic. His heart that was racing to the charge of an impending death.

The programme ended with a blare of music and was replaced with some adverts and then a news bulletin. A familiar face filled the screen. McBain. Wearing an ill-fitting collar and tie. Talking about a recent murder. Jim could lip-read the words "helping us with our enquiries" only because it was such a cliché. And didn't McBain look pleased with himself. Jim considered turning up the volume so he could hear what he was saying, but he couldn't take his eyes off the TV long enough to locate the remote.

McBain.

All these years later and he, apart from Jim, was the only one of the kids involved in that death in Bethlehem House – his first murder – who was still alive. Something needed to be done about that, thought Jim. He gripped the soft arms of his chair. Felt the twist, then the surge and soar of cleansing, purposeful hate. Unfinished business.

There and here.

He looked over at Robert. It wouldn't take much and the old man would be dead. He needed to move on, and it wouldn't do to leave behind too many people who might recognise him in the future.

Pinch his nose, cover his mouth and it would all be over in moments. Or, he could make it look a suicide? Wouldn't take too much effort to get him into the bath. Slash his wrists. The police wouldn't look too far into it all. People would say that his grief was so great he couldn't go on. And the man would surely be grateful for an end to his misery. In fact, many would consider it a mercy.

Now, *that* would be the act of a Samaritan.

14

Alessandra Rossi looked over the man driving the car as if he was a complete stranger, not her boss. As usual, the words were out of her mouth before she could press the edit button.

'Ray, did you get your end away last night or something?'

'What?' He took his eyes from the road for a moment to quiz her with his expression.

'You were actually singing there.'

'Was not.'

'You were. We've been working together for, what, two years now, and I have never ever heard you as much as hum.'

'Crap. I sing all the time. And … get my end away? Did you actually use those words? You've been working with Drain and Harkness for too long, Ale.' He chuckled. 'End away.'

'Well, did you?' In for a penny, she thought.

'Wonder where that comes from,' Ray mused. 'It's a weird expression.' Another chuckle.

'Jeez. You did. You totally got lucky last night.'

'Detective Constable Rossi, I find this line of questioning completely inappropriate, and what's wrong with me singing?' He looked over at her. Then back at the road, making sure he was a car length away from the vehicle in front. 'What was I singing?'

'Dunno,' Alessandra shrugged. 'Couldn't make the words out.' Pause. She let an imaginary tune run through her mind. 'Sounded like *I Kissed a Girl*. You know, that Katy Perry song?' She slapped her thigh and giggled.

'No fucking way. You made that up.'

They both laughed.

* * *

The hospital entrance hove into view. McBain parked the car, they climbed out and Ale followed him through the main entrance. A couple of people were standing just beyond it, wearing dressing gowns and pyjamas, taking in their fresh air along with a mouthful of cigarette smoke.

In the lift, McBain leaned against the wall and asked Ale, 'You ever smoked?'

She shook her head. 'Never saw the appeal. You?'

The lift door opened. McBain walked out and as he did so, looked over his shoulder to answer her question.

'No. But I did get my end away last night.'

'Wait. What?' Ale charged after him. She pulled at his sleeve. 'Details, man. Details.'

'Oops. Too late.' He smiled. 'We're at the ward.'

'Bastard,' Ale said to his back as he walked into the small room and over to one of the beds. She watched him and noticed that there was definitely a bounce to his step. And adding that to the singing, she was sure there was more to this than just some groin action.

First, however, there was the small matter of a young man, a possible murder suspect, who'd been put in that hospital bed by the father of his deceased ex-girlfriend.

Ray was already doing the introductions by the time she caught up with him at the side of the bed.

'We just want to talk to you about the other night, Simon. You feel up to talking?'

The boy on the bed nodded. 'You mean when Aileen's dad gave me a doing?' He had a line of stitching on his left eyebrow and plasters over the bridge of his nose, which was badly swollen.

Ale sized him up. Under the bruising there was enough on show to suggest he was a handsome young man. The width of his shoulders and the line of his legs under the sheet gave a suggestion of height. He brushed his hand over his cropped, dark hair and steeled himself to briefly look both Ale and Ray in the eye.

'That and the night Aileen died,' said Ale.

A large Adam's apple bobbed up and down the boy's throat as he swallowed. His hands were on his lap, fingers twisting. 'I was with my pals that night. Craig and Douglas. And I met my brother, Matt, later on. You can ask them. I didn't touch her. Didn't even see her.'

'That's fine, son,' said Ray. 'We'll get your statement later. We just want to ask you a few questions for now.'

'Statement. You want me to make a statement?' He sat forward on the bed.

Ale pulled out her notepad. 'Just some questions for now. Where were you exactly?'

He told her. She wrote it down.

'From when to when?' she asked. Same again.

'And could you give me the full names of the guys who were with you?'

The full names and addresses of Matt, Craig and Douglas were supplied.

'So you didn't see Aileen at all that night?' Ale asked.

'No,' Simon answered, his eyebrows raised in a "see me, I'm being totally honest" expression. He couldn't meet Ale's eyes for long, and he looked away. Out of the window. Then back to Ray and Ale. 'Didn't speak to her at all that night.'

'We have her phone,' Ale went for the bluff, inwardly cursing the fact that they still hadn't worked out how to unlock the machine. 'We can read her texts.'

'Good.' Simon stuck his chin up as if bracing himself against a lie. 'Then you'll know I'm telling the truth.'

'There was some semen on her top. Mind if we do a wee DNA swab?'

'Of course not,' said Simon, a flush forming on his cheeks.

'Hot in here, innit?' asked Ray. 'We should ask them to turn the heating down. Hospitals, eh? Must waste a fortune.'

'What's the swab thing then?' Simon asked.

'It's like a cotton bud. We swipe the inside of your mouth. It picks up some cells from the inside of your cheek, and we compare the DNA structure of that to the DNA found on Aileen's body,' answered Ale.

'Easy peasy,' said Ray.

'So anything to tell us before we go ahead and get it all organised?' asked Ale.

His Adam's apple bobbed up and down a few times before out squeaked, 'No.'

'Sure?'

A silent nod while Simon studied the sheets covering his legs. *Poor kid*, thought Ale. *Looks like he's about to shit himself.* Then she studied her response to the guy. Had she already written him off as a suspect? She mentally corrected herself. This was way too early in the investigation to be making any assumptions.

'Look, we all know that things can get out of hand,' said Ray in a consoling tone. 'You have a wee knee trembler out the back of the pub, for old time's sake, and before you know it, there's an argument. It gets heated and...'

While he spoke, Simon continued to study his sheets, but he was shaking his head in a rhythm to match Ray's words. His lips were pursed tight and his nostrils flared. When Ray stopped, he said, 'No, no, no, no. No.' The last "no" was almost a shout. Then he looked at them both defiantly with a final, 'No.'

Simon crossed his arms. Sucked in some air like he had just remembered to breathe.

'I loved Aileen. I wouldn't harm a hair on her...' His voice cracked. He held a hand over his face and started to cry.

Ale heard footsteps as someone entered the room. When whoever it was reached hearing distance, they speeded up, and Ale saw a small, heavy woman with straightened blonde hair and full make-up on barrelling to the bedside. She was in a dark trouser suit, wearing a cream raincoat and carrying a voluminous tan handbag. Ale guessed she was in her early forties.

'Who are you people?' she asked. 'And why are you upsetting my son?'

'It's OK, mum,' said Simon. 'They're the police.'

'Oh they are, are they,' Simon's mum said, pulling her coat tight around her. 'Well, I hope they are going to be charging the man that put my son in this hospital. I know his daughter is dead, and God knows I share his pain, but you can't just go around battering innocent children.' She quickly looked Ale and Ray up and down and, dismissing them, turned to her son and forced a lighter tone into her voice.

'The doctors are saying you can go home now. That's great, eh?'

Simon nodded, but looked as if he'd rather have all this teeth pulled without anaesthesia.

'You okay, son?' she asked and, leaning forward, pulled him into a hug.

Simon tried to extricate himself from her mothering, but was no match for the power of her solicitation, so he settled for mumbling into her hair. 'I'm OK, mum. I'm OK.'

'Mrs?' asked Ray.

'Davis. Helen Davis,' she answered and pulled herself up to her full five feet nothing.

'Mrs Davis,' said Ray. 'I fully understand that you are concerned for your son's welfare, but this is a police investigation. And if you don't mind, we would like to ask your son some questions.'

'Aye, sure, sure,' she answered and looked over Ale's shoulder.

'Who are you looking for? Matt?' asked Simon.

'Aye,' she answered. 'He brought me up in that wee death-trap of a car of his.' She took a step to the side and tried to look down the passageway beyond the door. 'He was right behind me. Must have carried on down to the drinks machine at the…'

'We'll only be a few minutes more, Mrs Davis,' said Ale. 'If you could…'

'Aye, sure, hen. Sure. I'll … eh …' She was clearly torn between her mothering and her duty as a law-abiding citizen to comply with a request from the police. Ale thought it was delightfully old-fash-ioned, and her heart went out to the woman. She didn't see enough of that kind of respect these days. 'I'll go and find number one son.' She offered a small smile. 'He of the shitty car.'

'Thank you,' said Ray. 'We won't be long, and then you can take your son home.'

Mrs Davis took a couple of steps out of the room. And then turned back.

'Here, do we need a lawyer? Cos I'll get one. I'll find the cash. Anything for my boy.'

'There's no need for any of that right now, Mrs Davis. But if we do, Simon will be fully appraised of his rights.'

'Right. Sure. Aye.' And her face crumpled as she turned and walked away.

Ale waited until the woman was out of hearing.

'Your dad?' she asked.

'Dead,' answered Simon in a flat tone. 'Afghanistan, about eight years ago.'

'Sorry to hear that, son,' said Ray. 'Must have been tough on you guys.'

Simon shaped a what-can-you-do shrug.

'How many of you are there?' Ale asked.

'Just me, Mum and Matt.' He squared his shoulders as if he had made a decision. 'Just us three against the world.' Had the sound of an often used expression. He exhaled. 'So, what else do you need to know?'

'Tell us what happened between you and Aileen. Why you broke up.'

'She said we'd been together for too long for people who were so young. That we needed to see a wee bit more of life before we settled on each other.'

'You didn't agree?' Ale asked.

'Other people make childhood romances work. Why couldn't we?' He looked out of the window. Stared at the monochrome sky. 'University life. There's so much going on. She wanted a taste of all of that. ' He turned to face Ale and Ray, his weak smile painted with every grey in the spectrum. 'When a parent dies when you're young, you mature quickly. Know what really matters. The people you're with. Not the fashion, the bling, and certainly not The Only Way is bloody Essex.'

Ale noticed Ray making a face of enquiry.

'It's a programme, Ray,' she explained. Then, looking at Simon, tried to make an ally of him by nodding at Ray as if to say, what a numpty.

Simon smiled, and Ale felt herself warm to him a little more. And then steeled herself against the feeling. This young man was their main suspect.

'We heard she wanted you back,' said Ray.

'Funny way of showing it.' He looked at Ray, a question in his eyes.

'What do you mean?'

'Snogging those guys down at the student union. They were all over her. Made me sick.'

'Sick enough to have an argument with her?'

'If someone tells me they don't want me, I've enough self-respect to take that on the chin and try to move on.'

'Why didn't you take her back then?' Ale asked.

'One, she didn't actually come out and say anything. Two, I think she needed to get it out of her system. If we'd got back together, something else would have caught her attention, and she would have dumped me again. I'd be the comfy slipper dude she came back to after other guys messed her around.'

His speech sounded to Ale like one that was a rehash of a conversation with some mates late at night in the student union after a few pints of beer. Also sounded like he was a young man with a good deal of self-awareness.

'Weren't you tempted?' Ale asked.

'I might have been, if she'd asked. But she would do that flirty thing with me, expecting me to read her mind and...' He stopped speaking and moved his hand to his mouth as if to stop the words from pouring out of him. 'It's my fault. It's all my fault.' He closed his eyes and a solitary tear slipped out. 'If I'd read the signs, I would have gone back with her and she would have been with me that night, and she wouldn't have died.' His right arm was across his chest, and with his left hand he was pressing into his eyes, as if trying to push the tears back in. Grief took over and his shoulders moved to its lament.

'I should have been the comfy slipper guy for her. She'd still be alive.'

* * *

Helen Davis had a fatalistic view on life. Shit happened and then more shit piled on top of it until you were sitting in the shadow of shit mountain. She was a teenage bride to a soldier, and she knew, just knew, that the army would be the death of him. Then, when her sons were born, she took the view: hope for the best, but expect the worst. Then the worst happened, and it was just her and her boys, and by God she would do everything she could to protect them.

She saw the way that detective looked at her. The female one. Poor bitch, she was thinking. A dead husband and two strapping boys to look after. She felt her jaw muscle twist and her stomach sour at the thought of her sympathy. She didn't need anyone's pity. Her and her boys would get by. They would survive.

But then there's the loneliness. The weight of it surprised her. It was a physical thing. Straining her thighs, her back, pulling at her eyelids until all she could do was close the curtains, crawl under the covers and sleep. People give you a year and then expect you to recover. The first birthday, the first Christmas, the next wedding anniversary, get them over and you'll be OK, they told her.

Ha. Idiots and liars, the lot of them.

The boys acted out, got bullied, bullied back – all spit, fists and fury for a time – then friends, school, routine helped them adjust to the father-shaped hole in their lives.

But she had moments every day when she was elsewhere, listening for his voice in a crowd, looking for his face in a photo, searching for his underwear among the laundry. Just that morning, when she woke up, her first question, even before she was fully awake, was why wasn't there an impression of his head on the pillow beside her. Then the gut-punch of realisation and the soft moan into her quilt before she pulled herself together. Her boys needed her.

She heard footsteps, and the two police officers were walking down the corridor towards her. She pulled her capacious handbag to her midriff as if it was giving her heat and sustenance.

'We have everything we need for now, Mrs Davis, but we may need to get back in touch,' the male detective said.

Mrs Davis nodded slowly as if a weight was being balanced on her head. Several thoughts passed through her mind, each reflected by her expression, before being moved on for something else. And each one of them brought her pain. Except for the last.

Then she stood up and brought her phone out of her coat pocket. Quickly thumbed through some pages and held it up for them to see.

'You people need to do something about this,' she said.

'What are we looking for?' Ale took the phone from her.

'Bloody Facebook. Some wee bastard is mouthing off about my Simon. Saying he's guilty. Saying Aileen's dad gave him a doing and that the police had arrested him.' She looked from Ale to Ray and then back again. 'And it looks like there's a lynch mob going on in Twitter. Somebody has cooked up a hashtag: #Simonisguilty. And everybody is sharing it and...' She sat back down on the chair. To Ale it looked like she sat down before she fell down.

Helen knuckled a tear away from her cheek. 'My boy did not kill that girl. I know my son.'

That girl.

Helen recognised what she was doing as soon as the words left her mouth. She was distancing herself from Aileen Banks in her mental war to help her son. The kids had been together for a few years. Most of their "winching" had been carried in and out of each other's houses. Plenty of time for Helen and Aileen to eat together, play together. Plenty of time to form a strong bond. They'd even gone shopping a couple of times after her and Simon split up.

The power of Helen's desire to protect her son surprised her, and it was all caught up in those two words. "That girl".

Helen closed her eyes, felt a pang of missing for Aileen. Opened them, looked at Ale. 'I was really fond of her. She was like the daughter I never had. She made my son happy, but I can't grieve for her until I know my son is safe.'

'It would also be good to have a word with Matt. Is he still here?' asked Ray.

The switch in topic, from one son to the other, threw Helen momentarily. She looked around herself. 'He … he said he forgot he had a class today. Had to go back to uni. Forget his head that boy.'

* * *

Ray and Ale travelled the lift in silence. Walked past another group of smokers at the hospital entrance, each holding their own counsel. Ale noticed a young man hanging about at the foyer. There was something in the way that he looked at her. And something about his face, across the eyes, but before she could snag the thought Ray held open the door for her and they were out into the late autumn chill.

In the car, Ray was the first to speak.

'Well?'

'That boy is either innocent, or he's an actor in a class of his own.' Pause. 'You?'

'Mmmm. Not sure.' Ray inserted the key and fired the engine. 'The best lies are the ones that stick closest to the truth.'

15

It's breakfast time. I've made Maggie an omelette and, bless her, she's tucking in like it actually tastes nice. While she eats I look round the kitchen at some of the stuff she's chosen to surround herself with. There's a shelf of cookbooks that even from the state of the spine I can see have been well used. In among them there are books on poetry and mysticism. The clock on the wall wears the face of the moon and the aluminium fridge door is wearing pictured magnets of cats and dogs. And the odd feel-good slogan.

'Feel the fear, eh?' I say.

'Mmmm, Mr McBain, you make a good omelette,' Maggie says mid-chew.

'Liar.'

'No. Really. It's very tasty.'

'It's perfect bachelor food, is what it is.' I hear the coffee pot reaching the boil. 'More coffee?'

Smile. 'Yes, please.' Bigger smile. 'I could get used to this.'

'Ah. Therein lies the problem. After the third date and the clock strikes twelve, the pumpkin disappears and I revert to grunts and scratching my balls.' And I wonder when Maggie is going to set the programme for the continuation of our relationship. Last time, she felt that I was still in love with someone else and didn't want to be second choice.

'That's a change? In what way?'

'Cheeky.'

She reaches over and holds my hand. 'It is what it is, Ray.'

'I hate that expression.'

'I'll take what you're prepared to give me.'

'Eh?'

'Loving you is easy in some ways, Ray. In others,' she offers a

83

conciliatory smile, '...not so much. It's less like you come with baggage, more like an airport luggage carousel.'

'Well, thanks for that appraisal.' I move my hand away from hers.

'Don't get defensive, Ray. It's true and you know it.' She takes my hand back. 'What I'm trying to say...' and it's like she's reading my mind '...let's just enjoy the moment and let the future take care of itself.'

I feel my chest heat and throat tighten with affection. I stand up and move closer. Pull her into an embrace. Feel my body respond. She laughs, pushes me away.

'Don't be getting any ideas, buddy.' She grows sombre. 'I was thinking about that young girl who was murdered. Aileen Banks.' She reads my expression of surprise. 'Your name was in the papers. And you were on the telly, Ray.'

'Right.' There's no way I want to bring my work into this relationship and rather we didn't talk about it all.

'Life's too short. I'll take what you can give me, Ray, knowing you are a good and caring man. And if it doesn't last, it doesn't last. But I'll enjoy it while I can.'

'Jeezuz, that's a fatalistic point of view.' I put a hand on both of her shoulders, and the realisation comes as fresh as my words. Along with the realisation that the feeling had been there from the first time we met. 'I'm in love with you, woman. Can't you see that?'

A small tear forms on a lower lash and hangs their like a crystal. 'It's just ... I have a sense...'

'What?'

'Nothing. It's nothing, Ray. It's just a lack of sleep.' She reaches out and strokes my cheek.

'It's something, Maggie. Enough to get you upset.'

She shakes her head.

'C'mon. Spill.'

Maggie goes to say something and from the shift in her expression, thinks better of it. Then she says, 'You not sleeping well?'

'You're changing the subject.'

'You were crying in your sleep.' The expression of empathy on her face was enough to trigger a tightening in my throat. I coughed, hoping that would loosen the emotion. 'Then I heard you get up in the middle of the night. You were in the living room for ages.' There was a question in that comment that I didn't want to acknowledge.

'I'm fine.' I brush it off. 'But there's something else on your mind. Something else you were going to say.'

'It's alright,' she says and reaches over to grip my hand. 'Not urgent.'

'Maggie, please. What's on your mind? I'm not going to stop nagging until you tell me.'

Her expression softens. 'It's … just I have this sense that we don't have long together. So,' she turns up the wattage on her smile, 'I want to enjoy you, us, while I can.'

'Maggie…' I say. My phone rings. 'Hold that … no, change that thought.' The number is withheld. *Probably the office*, I think and press accept.

'DI McBain,' I say.

'Sorry to disturb you, boss.' I recognise the voice of Daryl Drain. 'That's somebody at Barlinnie on the phone. Not sure why they're phoning you, Ray.'

I do.

'Joseph McCall had you down on his notes in place of next of kin, seemingly.'

'Aye?' I don't know why I'm asking, because I know.

'He's topped himself.'

16

There's a song on the radio. Love is all around, apparently. And it's Marti Pellow's voice warbling along to the swell of the violins. I reach across and pick at the car's controls. Change channels. I like cheese as much as the next man, but not today.

I look out of the car window, across the rooftops before me and up to a granite-grey sky. A world of monochrome to suit my mood. Poor bastard. Joseph McCall, deceased. You go through all kinds of unmentionable stuff, take on the crimes of a serial murderer and then commit suicide with a short rope and a long drop. Then you have a funeral where your only mourners are a prison guard, a chaplain and a slightly podgy police detective.

A feeling rolls towards me. Sours my mouth. Sits in my gut like a weight. Mood, thy name is guilt. I could have, should have, done more to help the boy. Insisted for longer and louder that he was not the Stigmata Killer. I should have pressed for an investigation into the crimes. Proved that McCall couldn't have been the guilty one.

Instead I hid. Took an easy life. Ignored the nightmares and the night sweats. Tried to push to the back of my mind that a man called Leonard had tried to kill me after murdering a number of people from my past.

I hold my hands in fists. Look down at my knuckles, turn my hands over and check the scars that pucker the pale flesh of my wrists. Close my eyes to the fear that surges from my bowels to my heart and imagine it as the white heat of rage. I will not be bowed by that man. I will not.

I need to make things right.

McCall's belongings are in a small box in the passenger seat beside me. As I was named as his next of kin – I shit you not – I was given his belongings, and what a pathetic assortment it is.

I need to sort this. While poor Joe's flesh is beginning the long slow act of decomposition, the Stigmata Killer is out there, doing whatever the fuck he is doing. And given his previous activities, I very much doubt he's crocheting blankets for the poor.

That can't be right. And I'm to blame.

One gold signet ring. One gold chain with crucifix. Six novels. A gun-metal cigarette lighter and two postcards.

The sum of a life.

Nope. Not having it. I've got to do something. Take responsibility at least.

At last.

I look out of the window and into the distance, seeing nothing of the Glasgow vista before me, feeling resolve work its way through layers in my mind. Gaining acceptance in all those places that shrank from action in the past.

Or, as our American cousins might put it, growing a pair.

I recognise one postcard. Joseph showed me it the last time I visited. The image on the front was a Highland scene. Could have been taken almost anywhere north of the Scottish central belt. The words on the back read "*Gone hunting*".

The other is a Glasgow scene. And my gut twists when I recognise it as being near the place I stayed when I was on the run from my colleagues as the main suspect in the Stigmata murder enquiry: St Andrews Square. What the hell is going on here?

I turn it over. Three words. The hand-writing on the address side is different from the three words on the message side.

I compare the writing with that on the earlier card. The address and message match the address on the Glasgow card. So whoever wrote on the first one addressed the second one but left the message side blank.

Before I've articulated the thought, I pick up one of the novels. It's Craig Robertson, whoever the fuck he is. A book called *Random*. I open the cover. McCall has signed and dated it. And given it a rating. Five out of five. Looks like we are all critics nowadays.

The writing matches the message on the card.

I examine the postcard. It's dated three days before McCall killed himself. I read his message from the grave and fight to still the chill that slowly rises the length of my spine.

McBain, you're next.

17

One of the benefits of not having killed for a while is that there's less chance of being caught. But then you have to constantly fight down that beautiful hunger. The desire that demands expression in the shedding of another's blood or in the delivery of pain.

Oh, you can imagine the act. Spend seductive hours in speculation. Pick a position, send your limbs to sleep and your mind on a journey of tragic imaginings. Of course, if you have memories to call on, you can insert just the right detail into your mind's weavings.

Remember that last breath. The last agonised sigh. Or the moments at the beginning of the attack, when fear first surges in their gut, before the brain can articulate what is about to happen. A recognition of danger that is linked to the pre-socialised animal. Atavistic. Certain. Bowel-loosening.

Hanging on the edge of the surviving twin's grief worked.

Then it didn't.

So he had to act. End him. End it. All of life before that moment was a sham. Scrubbing in the shallows. Waiting to die. Being nothing but breath and hunger. And that moment of release was all there was.

All there needed to be.

18

'Where are you, Ray?' asks Alessandra.

'Mmmm?'

'Jesus, man. What is up with you today?'

'Sorry. What were you saying?' I mentally give myself a shake. The resolution that formed in my mind has not worked its way into action yet. I know what I need to do, but I don't know how to do it yet.

Well, that's not true. I do. I just have to gird myself to face the consequences.

'I was saying that we should keep an eye on Simon Davis. Guilty or not, there's a social networking lynch mob piling it on him, and we need to keep an eye on it,' Ale says and pushes her laptop into my line of sight.

'Don't you mean, unsocial networking?' I ask while making a face. I look at the screen. Read out loud. Trying to focus. '**Never liked him. Always thought there was something dodgy about him. Got to watch out for the quiet ones.**'

Ale nods. 'People are quick to judge, eh?'

'Aye, who needs a judicial system. Let's hand it all over to Facebook and Twitter.'

Ale scrolls down the page. Reads. Says, 'Look at these twats.'

I read a conversation with three young guys trying to outdo the others with their solidarity with their sisters and their unbridled testosterone. '**What would you do if it was your sister, man?**' '**Yeah, wee prick needs to suffer.**' '**Bring back the death penalty.**' '**I'd swing for him.**' '**Cops are crap, we should do him.**' '**DM me. We need to sort this.**'

'DM?' I ask.

'Direct message.'

'And we can't read it when they go direct?'

'Nope.' Ale's face is grave when she says this.

'Something to worry about, do you think?' I ask.

She looks away from me and out of the office window. Glasgow is wearing a clear blue sky, and judging by Ale's face she would rather be out under it than in this boxy office with me.

She chews on the inside of her lip before answering. 'Could be bravado. Could be playing to the gallery … See how many likes they have here? But if they're taking it off the public viewing, it could mean they are serious.'

I read the names. Ian Cook. Jack Foreman. John Snow. Study their images.

'There was a Ian and a Jack who were seen going out with Aileen.'

Ale nods and clicks on Ian Cook. Two posts down has him at The Horseshoe Bar.

'This says he was there half an hour ago,' says Ale.

'Why do they make it so easy for us?' I ask while grabbing my car keys. 'You coming?'

* * *

The Horseshoe Bar is an institution in Glasgow. Largely unchanged since Victorian times, it's reasonably priced despite being in the city centre. And the first floor is the place to go if you've a hankering to sing your lungs out to the karaoke machine. Apparently. You wouldn't catch me up there without a knife at my throat and a bomb on the doorway of everyone I love.

Thankfully, the lads we're after are on the ground floor, lining up alongside the, wait for it, horseshoe-shaped bar. They're both tall, skinny and tanned, with trim beards and what I'm guessing will be trendy hairstyles. They both look like their photos on Facebook. I'm beginning to love that site.

'Ian Cook? Jack Foreman?' I say as I reach them.

They both turn. Look us up and down, surprise evident in their expressions. 'Aye. Who's asking?' Ian says.

I do the introductions.

'How can we help you guys?' asks Jack, leaning against the bar, completely at home in his surroundings and with who he is. I find myself wishing I was that confident when I was his age. His mate tries to affect the same indifference but lets himself down with a quick chew on the inside of his right cheek and a scratch at his perfect head of hair before he meets both of us with a strained smile.

'We're just looking for some background info on Aileen Banks.' I say.

'Aye, that was a total shame, like,' Jack says with what feels like genuine concern and a twist of pain. 'She was a lovely lassie.'

'Aye,' says Ian. 'You guys any closer to finding out what happened?' He looks at both of us with an eager expression. Eager to help. Makes me wonder what his motivation might be. Real or fake concern? Or does he have something he wants to make sure stays hidden?

'We understand you guys both had a wee thing for her,' says Ale.

'Just a wee snog up the student union,' answers Jack. 'She had too much class to be interested in the likes of me.'

'Must have been a disappointment to you, Jack,' I say. 'A man of your reputation and all you manage to get is a snog.'

'Don't know what you are on about, mate,' says Jack. 'And why are you bothering me when you should be interviewing that ex-boyfriend of hers?'

Touchy. I clearly hit a nerve.

I ignore him and face Ian. 'What about you son? You get any more than a wee kiss from the lassie?' I hear the irritation in my tone and realise that I see their version of cool kids, read into it a sense of entitlement and want to slap them down on behalf of every geeky child on the planet.

I catch a look from Ale. She recognises my tone and wants to talk me down off the ledge of my indignation. I force a wink in reply.

'No,' says Ian. 'As the man says, she was way too nice to be interested in us.'

'I do hear you guys have a bit of a reputation with the ladies,' says

Ale with the suggestion of a smile. 'Towie comes to Glasgow, kinda thing.'

Both lads smile, their egos suitably buffed up from Ale's comments. It doesn't harm that she's very pleasing on the eye.

While I wonder what the hell Towie is, Ale asks, 'What can you tell us about Aileen?'

'Didn't really know her that well, to be honest,' says Jack.

'Yeah, we used to see her about the union and the pubs and stuff,' says Ian. 'She was kinda hot,' he admits and then fights a blush as he realises this might be disrespectful of the dead. 'You know what I mean.' He picks up his drink and tries to hide his social gaffe behind it.

Ale catches my attention. Nods to the side. I follow her movement and see a young couple at a table. As I look over the female looks up, meets my eye and then goes back to studying her phone. Or whatever she was doing.

I look back at Ale with a silent question, then I realise that both lads are watching us, wondering what the hell we are doing. Hiding my irritation at Ale, I get back to the case in hand.

'Do you remember much about the night she died?' I ask, now officially off my high horse and still feeling the heat from Ian's face. They really are just kids, and the ability to blush, to my world weary eyes, suggests honesty and sensitivity. Not qualities I crash into much in my day-to-day.

They both shake their heads.

'Was it a Friday night?' asks Jack. 'We were wasted, bud.'

'What about the boyfriend?' Ale asks. 'Do you know him?'

The smiles slide off both boys faces. 'Not really,' says Ian. 'He's a bit of a college boy, Mr Try Hard. We wondered what Aileen saw in him.'

'Aye,' Jack agrees. 'Do you think he did it?' He looks eager to know, and I read more into his asking the question than curiosity.

'Nothing's been ascertained yet,' I say. 'He, along with a group of people, are helping us with our enquiries.'

'That's polis talk for, "he's guilty as sin, man."' Jack has lost his comfortable slouch against the bar. His shoulders are squared off, and he looks braced for a couple of rounds in an MMA gym.

'Calm down, Jack,' I say. 'It's polis talk for "we don't know enough to be charging anyone with this death yet."'

'Fuckin' waste of space, man. He fuckin' did it.' He pushes past us and walks out of the bar as if his jacket's on fire and he's hoping it's raining outside. As he does so, he all but knocks over a couple who are just ahead of him. Strangely for Glasgow, the male of the couple doesn't challenge him to a stare off at five paces and carries on his way.

'What the…?' I ask, looking at Ale and Ian. The change was so abrupt it took us all by surprise.

'I'm sorry,' says Ian. 'I'll go and talk to him and calm him down.'

'What's the problem?' Ale asks.

'His sister was raped a couple of years ago. He takes this thing kinda serious. Has a zero tolerance you might say.'

As he tries to walk past us, Ale puts her hand up. He stops with her palm on his upper chest. She looks him in the eye and says, 'Tell him to calm down. We've been watching your activity online. If anything happens to Simon Davis, we know where to go.'

Once the boy leaves, Ale looks at me as if she's annoyed.

'What?'

'Nothing.'

'That's not a face with nothing going on behind it.'

She says no more. Her mouth firmly closed. She distracts herself by buttoning up her jacket and then walking over to the table where the couple she looked at were sitting.

I join her. 'Aye, what was that about?'

'The girl sitting here. It was Karen Gardner.' Aileen Banks's friend. 'The guy. I swear I recognised his face.' She examines their discarded drinks as if seeking inspiration. 'That's it. He was at the hospital when we were up seeing Simon Davis. Even looks like him.' She waves a hand across the middle of her face. 'Has the same eyes.

I'll bet you anything that's the brother.'

'And?'

'Ray, you need to wake the fuck up. What's wrong with you today?'

It stings. I know she's right. Don't want to admit I'm not on my game.

'Rein your neck in, Rossi. What are you on about?'

'Karen Gardner was here. At this table with a boy who is very probably Matt Davis.' She pauses and looks into my eyes, waiting for the proverbial penny to drop and catch. 'The best friend of the deceased and the brother of the deceased's boyfriend getting all nice and cosy. Doesn't strike you as odd? Or worthy of comment?'

'What of it?' I say. 'There's any number of reasons why they might want to offer each other support.'

Ale examines the abandoned drinks. Picks one up. Looks like the drinker had about two sips from it before leaving.

'Why did they leg it as soon as they spotted us?'

19

We're in the car, shaking drops of rain from our heads.

'Jeez,' I say. 'It was glorious sunshine when we went in to that place.'

'Aye,' agrees Ale. 'Typical west of Scotland. Give it five minutes and it will be snowing.'

Ale and I rarely indulge in such mundane chatter. It's a clear sign that there's something we need to air, but the thing is, I'm not in the mood to get talking. I fire up the engine, check the traffic in my mirrors, indicate and then enter the flow just before a double-decker bus.

Silence.

And I'm stewing in it. If you were to ask me what I'm annoyed about, I wouldn't be able to tell you. I'm just fucking angry. Aware that my hands are trembling, I hold the steering wheel tighter.

Ale is first to break the quiet.

'Karen Gardner and Matt Davis. Wonder what's going on with them.'

'You sure it was Matt Davis?'

'We don't have a firm ID on him, but there is a strong resemblance to that boy we talked to in the hospital.'

I take a moment to think about which lane I need to be driving in. Realise I need to change, do so and earn a loud note of warning from the horn of the car I narrowly miss. Looking in the car mirror I can see a red face mouthing a few obscenities. I shout a few of my own.

Ale shifts in her seat. Looks out of her window.

'What?' I ask. And flinch at the aggression in my tone. Ignore it. I'm not the one in the wrong here.

'Nothing.'

'Nothing?'

Ale ignores me. Crosses her arms. Looks straight ahead.

'What?'

'Nothing, Ray. Just drive.'

'Jeez, it's like being fucking married.' I have a moment where I recognise I need to take a deep breath. The traffic feels too busy, the buildings are crowding in on either side and Ale is doing that judging thing.

'Christ, who'd want to marry a crabbit git like you.'

'Now we're getting personal. You on the rag or something?' As soon as the words are out of my mouth I regret them.

Ale looks at me. I risk a glance. Her lips are a tight, narrow line. Her jaw clenched. She looks away as if considering her response.

'You know, a certain amount of sexist shit comes with this job. All that banter with the boys crap. Fine. I can take it. I've got broad shoulders. But that ... rag comment, I don't expect from you, Ray. You're better than that.'

I exhale. Screw my eyes shut for a moment. Force my shoulders down.

'Sorry.' It's a mumble.

'Can't hear you. Did you say something?'

She's not for letting me off.

'Sorry.' Louder.

'For what?'

'For being a sexist prick.' I actually manage a half-smile.

Ale grins back. 'Knob.'

I relax a little. Throw her a grin of relief. We're good. I owe Alessandra a lot. She was one of the few people who stood by me when I was on the run, suspected of being the so-called Stigmata Killer. It almost cost her career. She deserves more from me.

'Did you just call me a knob? A gendered insult could be construed as sexism, Detective Constable Rossi.'

'I could have called you a cunt, but that is a powerful, beautiful thing. And from me could be construed as a compliment.'

'Really?'

'Yes.' Ale thrusts her chin out. 'I'm reclaiming the word "cunt" as a thing of beauty and declaiming the insult it has become through a male-dominated Christian religion that is terrified of the power of the female.'

'Good for you,' I say.

Ale smiles, pulls out her mobile. Gets thumb-busy. I feel relieved that there is no bad feeling and recognise that my earlier irritation has receded somewhat. I know I should delve, try and get to the source of my earlier mind-set, but my courage is lacking.

'Excellent,' says Ale, studying her phone.

'What?'

'I sent a friend request on Facebook to the two guys we met in The Horseshoe, and they've both accepted.'

'Really? Won't they recognise you?'

'I set up a fake account a while ago for this kind of thing. My name is Sandra Ross, and I used a photo from a young, American actress. So, I'm all pretty and everything.'

'Ah. Alessandra Rossi becomes Sandra Ross. I see what you did there.'

'And our friends are already busy.' She reads. 'Jack is saying that he better not meet Davis when he's out at the weekend. Can't trust that his actions will be entirely sane.' She looks at me. 'I'm paraphrasing. He says he'll slice his balls off.'

'Do you think he's just blowing off steam? Trying to look tough to his home boys?'

Ale giggles. 'Did you really just say home boys?'

'What, is that not how these guys talk?'

'Yeah. If they're in the 'hood. And I'm not sure that the Merchant City comes into that category.' She laughs again. 'Home boys.'

She reads some more. 'His comment has over a hundred likes and a whole string of comments encouraging him to teach Davis a lesson.' She makes a face. 'I'm worried, Ray.'

'Forgive me if I'm wrong, unsocial networking newbie speaking here, but my reading of this malarkey is that people like to sound off, be seen to be strong and active. It's all about having the image of being a certain way rather than actually doing something about the stuff you say you are concerned about.'

'Yeah, and normally I would agree with you, Ray. But there's a tone here. Just not sure about it. And what if Jack does actually meet Simon Davis when he's on a night out? You saw how he was when we were talking to him in the pub. That was not a normal reaction.'

'True.' I say. Ale does have good instincts. 'Keep an eye on it, will you?'

We've reached the office. I spot a free parking space and manoeuvre into it. I apply the handbrake and pull the keys out of the ignition. Instead of stepping out of the car, Ale remains in her seat.

'I'm going to ask you a question, Ray, and I don't want to hear the words "fine" or "nothing" in the answer.'

I slowly release my seat-belt. 'Right…'

'What is going on with you?'

I open my mouth to speak.

'You're not allowed to say "nothing".'

'Honestly, I'm fine,' I reply. She gives me a look. 'OK. I'm OK. Honest.'

'Pants on fire.'

I feel my face heat and the earlier irritation return.

'DD…' she means Daryl Drain. '…tells me you were at a funeral the other day.'

'Drain has a big gub.'

'And shiny blue contact lenses, but let's leave that for another day. The funeral?'

She stares. My eyes move away first. Cursing the confessional of the car, I tell her everything, and as I speak, her chin drops lower and lower.

Ten minutes later and I'm still talking.

'Fuck,' she says. Giving the syllable good length. 'So, Joe was never Stigmata. You knew, told no one and allowed that poor guy

99

to go take on several life sentences?'

'We think he did murder his carer, Carol,' I say and cringe at my weak attempt at mitigation.

Ale stares ahead as if trying to assimilate all this new information. 'Fuck,' she repeats.

I cross my arms. Hold myself tight, tucking my hands into my underarms until I feel them go numb with the lack of circulation. Ale looks at me and reads my expression.

'Ray,' she says. 'Jesus.' And I can read her compassion and lack of judgement and feel my eyes spark with tears. I exhale in an attempt to quell my emotions. Then cough. Now I'm clenching my teeth.

'And Leonard? He's the bogeyman?'

I can only nod. Her question sums him up perfectly, and I acknowledge this, feeling weak and ridiculous.

'Why does he have such a strong hold over you, Ray?'

As children, Jim Leonard and I shared the same space in a convent orphanage. He and his twin brother lived in each other's shadow. There was something uncanny in their communication with each other which, combined with their joyless demeanour, freaked out all of us other kids. Then his brother died from pneumonia, and Jim became so distant from reality that he was removed to another form of care. One that the other kids were sure consisted of padded cells.

Just before he was taken away, he had taken to following me. I would often wake up in the morning to find him standing over my bed. Each time he would be chanting, "We're going to kill them all."

The other kids just laughed at him, but there was a fixed look to his eye as he said this that I couldn't shake from my dreams.

It doesn't take much digging into any man's psyche to reach the tender child, and it's only now that I can see that the boy I was never recovered.

The last time I encountered Leonard, he drugged me, murdered an aged nun before my eyes and then sliced my wrists to the bone. In his twisted mind, he thought he could stage the murder to show that I killed the nun and then, torn with guilt, turned the knife on myself.

If we were standing face to face, I know I could take him no problem. I have height on him and weight. And yet.

'We? You said we, Ray?' Ale asks when I stopped talking.

'Sorry?'

'Why would Leonard chant "We're going to kill them all"? Was he including you in this somehow, Ray?'

'Ale. Leave it.'

'I'm just trying to make sense of it all, Ray.'

I silence her with a look. We aren't going there. Enough with the sharing. But Ale is no longer easily cowed.

'And what about Joseph McCall?'

I'm holding my right arm by the wrist and rubbing the scar with a thumb. Realise what I'm doing and go back to the cross-armed position, hiding my scars in the damp dark of my armpits.

Looking out of the window, I offer nothing but silence to Alessandra's question. In the distance I see a stretch of blue sky, skirted by another weather front rolling in on Glasgow. A mass of cloud stretches across the horizon. Dark and heavy, like a conscience gravid with guilt.

20

Jim Leonard was in Father Stephen's office in St Aloysius Roman Catholic church using the parish computer for purposes it was never considered for.

Father Stephen was so naïve and trusting it doesn't occur to him that his odd-job man might have purposes other than social networking for using the machine. It was Jim that talked the priest into having a Facebook and Twitter account. And once these were live, the priest quickly ran out of interest and left them to Jim to update.

Which suited him fine. So he began every computer session with a quick scan of the banal and then added to it. Once his boredom threshold was truly tested, which took all of ten minutes, he would then get on with his main occupation online.

Hunting.

First, he had to stoke the fire. He searched for Ray McBain and clicked on a link to a recent news bulletin. A young girl had died. She had a boyfriend who was helping the police with their enquiries. McBain's fat face was spewing police speak and Leonard felt the adrenalin surge of hate. He allowed the sensation to rise and felt his hands shake. The video ended and he replayed it.

McBain was wearing a dark suit. Leonard could see that the top button of his shirt was open behind the knot of his blue tie. Putting on the weight again, Ray? Too much fat on your neck to button up your shirt?

Confidence was apparent in his stance, the way the words flowed, but Leonard could read impatience there. He'd rather be out there investigating the case than speaking to a camera.

A reporter interrupted with a name. Simon Davis. Leonard noted it. Spends the next hour doing some online digging. Before long he knew more about the youth than his mother did. He was a twin. One of the good guys. Or he was before Aileen Banks's death.

He was a counsellor on a website for twinless twins. 'Help yourself by helping other twinless twins' was the strapline. Made total sense, thought Leonard. Why didn't he think of joining something like this before?

He found a twin site. Signed up. But he couldn't find a mention of anyone called Simon Davis. He got into a chat with one woman. She was grief-stricken when at the age of thirty-two her other half, as she called her, took an overdose. Then followed the usual blah about how could she not have seen it, how could her twin do this to her, how could she not have stopped it? Leonard played the part of online listener to perfection. Drew this woman out so that she was telling him stuff that she wouldn't even tell her counsellor.

Once that trust was established, Jim played her like a fiddle. Started to remind her of how bad she felt when her twin died. Suggested that suicidal impulses were genetic. Stayed up all night in the chat room with her telling her how lonely he was and that if only he was braver he would join the suicide club. Planted a seed that they should do it together. Talked about the best methods of joining their twins in heaven.

'See you on the other side' was the last message he received. And six words never had such an impact on Jim. Kept him awake for nearly forty-eight hours while he thrilled at the conclusion of his efforts.

But then the woman came back online with a meek, 'I couldn't do it. Could you?'

He hadn't replied. Let her think he had ended his life. She could add that to the guilt of the death of her twin.

Nope, this online stuff could only achieve so much. The problem with that woman was that she was in the States. He needed someone local. Someone he could meet. Someone whose life he could watch ebb and end.

He went back to watching McBain. The familiar face filled his screen. A reporter interrupted, repeating Simon Davis's name.

And Leonard saw that the media were itching to start their own blame game.

He could have fun with that.

He was on Simon Davis's Facebook page. There wasn't too much activity with status updates, and Leonard almost found himself liking the boy. Then realised that with the recent death of his girl-friend and "helping the police with their enquiries", he was going to be too busy to post what he's having for breakfast.

There was a photograph with a girl. Pretty. Virginal. Could she be the girl who died?

Underneath it there were a number of messages calling Davis a murderer and demanding he removed this picture from his feed. A few young men were threatening to hurt him if he ever showed his face in their part of the city.

Why hadn't he closed this down, Jim wondered? You'd think a possible murder suspect would be asking to get this kind of thing removed. Either he wasn't that savvy, or the Facebook authorities weren't too quick to respond.

He clicked on another photo. Simon with an older woman and another young man. There was a clear family resemblance between them. The caption read 'Mum and twin bruv.' It was followed by a few sycophantic comments on how good everyone was look-ing. He scrolled down past a ream of inane posts so boring they almost lulled him to sleep. Something jarred. Knocked him out of his stupor. He scrolled back up the page, unsure what it was that caused him to stop.

Found 'Just confirmed as counsellor on Time4Twin. V excited' followed by a list of comments where people pretended to be pleased for the poor sap. So that's where he was.

At last, thought Leonard. Gold.

21

Back in the office and Ale is throwing Ray meaningful looks. Was it just a couple of days ago that Ray had that spring in his step? Whatever had given him a lift hadn't lasted long. And now he is back to his overwrought, over-sensitive self.

She wishes he would go and speak to Chief Superintendent Harrison. She feels he won't be able to recover properly from his mental and physical wounds until he gets it all off his chest. Even she can see that it's weighing him down.

Daryl Drain enters the office along with Harkness. They've been speaking to people over at the student union. Daryl looks over to Ray with a disappointed look on his face.

'Nothing interesting, boss,' he says.

'Put it in your report and we'll go over it later,' Ray says.

Alessandra catches Daryl's eye. 'Coffee, DD?'

Daryl picks up that there is more to this request than a need for a hot beverage. 'Aye,' he says. 'Just what I need before I get on with this.'

Rather than head to the cupboard with the kettle and the dried stuff, Ale heads towards the office door, signalling she wants to go to the cafeteria.

'What's up?' Daryl asks when the door closes behind him.

'Not here,' Ale whispers.

They walk round a corner and down a stairwell.

'Right, can you tell me now?' Daryl asks.

'It's Ray. I'm worried about him. Really worried.'

'Aye?'

'I think he came back to work too soon. He's been even more irri-table than normal. He's clearly not been getting much sleep. Then,' she steps closer to Daryl as if proximity will ensure no one else will overhear, 'he told me that Joe McCall was not the real Stigmata, and he knew about it all along and kept quiet.'

Daryl takes a step back.

'Wow.' He turns away, hand to his forehead. Turns back.

'What made him tell you?'

'Dunno. But I wish he hadn't.' Ale chews on the inside of her cheek. A thought stills the movement. 'I'm not going to Harrison with this. I went to the bosses during the Stigmata thing and look what happened.'

'Yeah, well. Ray got charged with the murders, but that wasn't your fault. He put you in an untenable position.'

'Oooh, get you.' Ale manages a grin. 'Untenable.'

Daryl welcomes a break in the tension. 'Yeah, I've got one of those loo rolls with a word of the day on it.'

'Really?'

'No, piss off. I do have an education, DC Rossi. I just prefer to stay down at your level. Don't want you to feel inferior.'

Ale laughs. 'Oh look. You lost this.' She shoots him the finger. Then grows serious. 'It has to come from him this time. I'm not getting involved.'

Daryl nods in agreement.

'And there's this case,' Ale says.

'What about it?'

'If we had the Ray McBain I started working with, we would have the truth of Aileen Banks's death tied up in a neat wee bow.'

'Maybe we need to take up the slack?'

'Aye. There's something about Aileen's pal Karen and Simon Davis's brother, Matt, that bothers me.'

'What about them?'

Ale explained about the sighting at the pub.

'What do you suggest, boss?' Daryl asks with a grin.

Ale feels a small thrill that Drain is taking her seriously, despite the smile.

'I suggest you go and count your toes in front of a moving train.

But not before we speak to Matt Davis,' Ale answers. Then she pauses for a moment in thought. Turns as if going back to the office.

'What?' asks Daryl.

'Och, it's probably nothing.'

'Just spit it out, Ale.'

'I think Ray's got PTSD.'

Daryl nods slowly, as if digesting this latest comment and finding he agrees with it.

'You don't think I'm nuts?' asks Ale.

'Well ... yes ... but I also think you might have a point. Ray has been in hospital twice in the last, what, twelve months after being seriously wounded. He could have died at that convent. And he has been more of a crabbit bastard than normal.'

'And this guy Leonard has some sort of hold over him. It's like he mentions his name and Ray reverts to a ten-year-old being kicked by the school bully.'

'What are you going to do?'

'Why is it down to me, DD? You've known the guy for years. Why don't you do something?'

'You know what the police are like with this kinda thing. One of my mates was at Lockerbie...' He stares off into space as if recalling some of the horror stories. 'Before the guys went back to normal duties they were lined up. Asked, if they were suffering from PTSD, to take a step forward.' Shakes his head. 'Of course, no one did. You don't want to be that guy.'

Ale nods her understanding. The weak link in the chain.

'But that was what, nearly thirty years ago? Things have changed.'

Drain snorts. 'Sure, the processes are in place. The help is available, but guys are still reluctant to ask for it.'

They stand in silence. Each lost in thought.

'You're his confidante, Ale. He told you this stuff. Not me. Besides, he has a soft spot for you. I come at him with this shit and he slaps me down. He'll listen to you.'

Ale leans her back against the wall, crosses her arms.

'Yay, good for me. Woop.' She shakes her head. Makes a decision. She crosses her arms as if protecting herself against what she sees as her own betrayal. 'Why does he always put me in this position?' Wipes a tear from her cheek. 'I went to Harrison the other day about the PTSD thing. The prick didn't want to hear. Said I was over-thinking. And now there's this thing about McCall. Jeez.'

'Right,' says Daryl while he processes this. 'If you already went to the boss, why are you talking to me about this now?'

'Thought if I heard myself saying the words out loud I wouldn't feel so bad, you know? I'd hear the words and I'd hear the sense of it all and I'd feel like I'd done the right thing.'

'And?'

'It still feels like I'm a number one arsehole.'

'You had valid concerns, Alessandra. Ray is not himself, and as you said, this case has lost its focus – Ray doesn't have any. Meanwhile a family is mourning a daughter and wondering what the hell happened and what the hell the police are doing about it.'

22

My suspicions are founded when Daryl and Alessandra walk back in the office without any coffee.

'Was the brew that good you drank it all on the way back?' I ask. They both have the decency to look shame-faced. I give them the stare and go back to doing the same thing at my computer screen. Staring. It's what I've been doing since they left the room to talk about me.

I just can't focus.

My mind is a litany of wrongs.

Bethlehem House.

Joe McCall.

Jim Leonard, aka Stigmata.

The old man, of mistaken identity, whose only sin was to be resident in that convent. An old man that Jim and I murdered with the help of three other children. With a stab of shame I realised that I'd never ever discovered his name. I'd been complicit in his death and I didn't even know his name.

Patrick Connolly. Leonard's first victim. Found out *his* name eventually. And I can barely form the syllables of his name in my mind and I'm in his shed, up the back of the convent garden, while he forces himself into me. My tender parts a sheath for Connolly's need to slake his lust.

It's strange that I can barely recall the actual attacks, but the smell of cut grass and creosote immediately has me choked with emotion.

Why now?

Why is this all coming back to me now? I was over this. Right?

I stand up. Aware of Alessandra's eyes following me, I leave the room.

Knock on the door down the hall.

'Come in,' orders my boss.

I push open the door, and aware of the tremble in my hands stuff them in my pockets.

'Ah, Ray, just the man,' Harrison says with that almost smile of his, and I want to lean over the desk and untidy the perfect knot in his tie. 'Kevin Banks.'

'What of him?' I ask and ignore the faint relief that I may get off telling him. I steel myself. After he's done talking, I start. No excuses.

'Just had a communication from the fiscal. He's decided that Kevin Banks has a case to answer.'

'OK,' is my non-committal response, but I'm thinking, *shit, this is going to be a mess.*

'We can't have people going vigilante. We have to remind them that there is a rule of law. So, be a good boy and have him arrested.'

My mind returns to the reason I walked in this office. I need to do this. Can't hide behind silence any longer.

'Still here?' Harrison asks.

I close my eyes. Take a breath. Focus on the rise and fall of my chest. That's where they say the calm lies, don't they? It doesn't work. My heart is a heavy metronome thumping out a loud rhythm of self-loathing. I look at Harrison, wondering why he can't hear the knock in my chest.

'Ray...' he moves his eyes from his computer screen. 'Is there something else?'

'Joe McCall was never Stigmata. He was so scared of the real murderer, he took on the crimes. Felt he would be safe as a lifer in Barlinnie. The real killer is a man called Jim Leonard.'

'Are you still seeing that shrink of yours?' He looks at me as if seeing me for the first time since I sat down. Then he mentally dismisses me. 'Get out of my office, DI McBain, and carry out this order from the Fiscal.'

'I watched ... I was drugged right enough ... couldn't move ... while Leonard slashed the wrists of ...'

'Ray!' Harrison shouts. 'Get a grip, man. That case is closed. McCall is on record admitting the crimes. Let's leave it at that. And take a couple of days off. Make another appointment to see your counsellor.'

It occurs to me that Harrison is all about ego. His rise in the force came from his ability to play the game. He has a real knack of saying the right thing to the right people at the very best time. All the while wearing his best fucking shirt and tie. A number of his high profile cases were solved by yours truly, which reflected well on him as my commanding officer. Doubtless, if I maintain this assertion, he can see it all collapsing like a tower of Jenga bricks.

Now that the words are out I feel exhausted. Like all of my emotional coin has been spent. I sag in the chair.

Harrison watches me. Calculating. I don't care. He can do what he wants. The truth is out now, and if he doesn't want to hear it, I'll find someone who does.

He reaches into a drawer and pulls out a brown file. He places it on top of the desk between us in the manner of someone moving a piece on a chessboard. When he opens it I can see a small pile of paper. On the front it reads: *Health and Safety Executive. Managing Post Incident Reactions in the Police Service.*

'PTSD is a terrible thing, Ray. We have processes in place in the force to help people like you.'

'What the hell are you on about?'

His gaze is resolute. It says, "I will protect my career at the cost of yours, if that's what it takes".

'You've had two terrible incidents in a very short space of time, DI McBain. When that happens, there is a very real danger that it may lead to the development of chronic psychological distress, the use of poor coping strategies and alienation from family and colleagues.

'I've already had one of your colleagues in here, concerned about your behaviour. You need to take care of yourself psychologically and emotionally, Ray.' His tone manages to be patronising while wearing a note of warning.

'Wait. What do you mean, one of my colleagues has already been in here?'

'The person concerned came to me in confidence, and my officers need to know that my confidence is sacrosanct.' Look up the definition of smug in the dictionary and it will show an image of this man's expression. I want to wipe it from his face with a half-brick. But I'm too numb to act. I fall back into my chair. He takes this as a good sign and continues with his game of chess.

'Take some time off, Ray,' he says. His tone more conciliatory now. 'I'll set up another group of sessions with your counsellor, and we'll get you back on the job in no time. The Ray McBain we all know and love, eh?'

I look at him. Feel a surge of anger. Grab at the arm of the chair and just manage to damp it down. *Fuck's sake, Ray. One moment it's as if you're anaesthetised. The next it's as if you're going to explode.* My mind is a slew of words, emotion and half-articulated thoughts. I stand up and take a step to the right. Put my hands in my pockets. Look around the room seeing nothing.

'Right,' I say. *Well done, mate,* I think. *That told him.* Then realise I actually don't care what this prick thinks, and without another word I leave the room.

* * *

Next I know, I'm in a church. I can remember walking. And walking. A tiny woman shouting at me when I moved to step in front of a bus. The comment, "Nearly got your suit pressed there, son" when I stepped back onto the pavement. Don't think I even flinched.

My response, 'Aye.'

See me with the Glasgow banter.

The church is old. Faces the River Clyde. High, vaulted stone ceiling. Cool and echoing, but the calm inside speaks to me. I move into the far side of a pew at the back, where I will be invisible.

'Bless me Father, for I have sinned.' The words chime in my head.

Once a Catholic.

I push down the knee-rest and fall forward as if in prayer. Placing my forehead on my clasped hands I think of something I might say to whatever God is listening, but there's nothing. I have nothing to say, and the silence I hear back is ringing.

I get off my knees, sit and look around me. I can see some artwork in regular spacing along the walls. Carvings in wood all showing the same male, long-haired figure. That will be the Stations of the Cross then. Reminding us sinners of Christ's suffering. Requiring a blind faith that the nuns did their very best to inculcate in me. Failing for that very same reason.

Footsteps, a polite cough, the sound of a backside sliding along the wooden seat.

'Haven't seen you here before?' A young man wearing a dog-collar. Sounds about fifteen. I focus. He looks about fifteen and is all but shining in his need to help. Makes me think I really must look like shit.

'Nah, I don't tend to frequent these kind of places.'

'And yet, here we are.' His hair is blonde, and he's wearing a trim goatee as if it might add some age and weight to his presence. I revise his age upwards. Old enough to grow a beard. He'll be about seventeen then.

I say nothing. He takes the hint and stands up. 'I'll be over there if you need me.' He points at the confessional box. I watch as he walks over, his footsteps echoing in the cavernous space. He pulls open a small door and disappears inside.

I follow him. Pull open the door and kneel in front of the small grilled window that separates the space between the confessing and the confessor.

'Haven't said those words for years,' I say.

'Bless me Father,' he says, and I can hear the smile in his voice. Despite the I-hate-the-world stance I've been taking on these days, I find myself drawn to this young priest.

'What age are you, mate?'

'Does it matter?'

'Nah, not really. Maybe. Age brings experience that helps when people come for advice.'

'If people wanted to hear my advice that might be the case,' he says ruefully. 'Mainly people just want someone to listen.'

'I used to go every week when I was a kid. To confession. It was a crock of shit. I never did anything wrong. Had to make stuff up.' I put on a childish voice. 'I told three lies this week, said the word "fuck" twice and looked up Mary Smith's skirt.'

The priest laughs.

'Aye, me too.'

'What, you looked up Mary Smith's skirt?'

'I was meaning that I made stuff up. But I was probably looking up someone's skirt. In my case it was a big cousin.'

'Tut, tut, Father,' I say, and it feels absurd to be calling this young man "Father".

'Well, what can I say? I'm only human. And it was long before I took my vows.'

We settle into a moment's silence. My phone buzzes in my pocket. I ignore it.

'Why do you think you came here?'

'Got into something at work and left in what you could call a bit of a huff. Next thing I know, here I am. And here we are.'

'Did the church let you down, Ray?' he asks, and I'm startled by his reading of me.

'Big time.'

'And yet...'

'It's the quiet. I think I was drawn in by the calm. The building I can take, but I'd rather leave the organisation that built it.'

'Why's that?'

'The blind faith thing. We don't really know what's out there. Nobody does, but demanding that we give in to blind faith is so fucking manipulative it does my head in. I'm pretty sure it was devised by some high heid yin, way back when, as a way to keep the peasants quiet and themselves in power. Our ignorance is bliss to the powerful. Our silence, their coin. Don't question, play the role we give you and you'll get in to heaven.'

'What's so wrong with wanting to get into heaven?'

'Nothing. If it even exists. What if all we have is this? The here and now? Our time in these shells of bone and meat? Shouldn't we make the most of that rather than abdicating all responsibility to a greater power in the hope that they will look after us? Make it better in the next life?'

'Is that what you're doing? Making the most of this life?'

'Good question, Father. Good question.' And I consider. If I did answer the question, it would be with a resounding no.

23

Jim Leonard often contemplated death, but it was rarely his own that was on his mind. That day, for some reason, he could think of little else. What would it be like? Would he experience pain? Might it be quick? Or slow? In his sleep or at the hands of one of his intended victims?

The thought of some great nothingness didn't scare him, because he believed in the afterlife. The nuns had performed their duties well. He was looking forward to that future. Breathing nice and slow during an endless day where he would know some form of equilibrium. Islamic Fundamentalists could keep their thousand virgins. He was looking forward to a sense of peace.

Native Americans say there is no death, simply a change of worlds. Fine. But it's the transition from one to the other that interested Leonard.

He knew with the certainty of the devout that he was aiming for heaven, despite everything. God was great. All-knowing and all-forgiving. Didn't he promise to forgive all of his lambs? *Psalms* 103:12 reads, *As far as the east is from the west, so far has he removed our transgressions from us.* Does that sounds like a vengeful God? He would see and understand that his actions were the result of a drive outside of his control, a need that was greater than any one man could harness.

Therefore, forgiveness was a surety.

Leonard looked at the computer screen in front of him. Concentrated on the shapes there instead of the silent notes inside his head. 'Time4Twin' read the banner. Who came up with this nonsense? The homepage explained this was an online support network for twins. They stressed that it didn't matter whether the support required after the loss of a twin was from a bereavement or an argument. They even offered a willing ear for those who were tired of being only seen as one half of a pair and demanded to be recognised on their own merits.

This was the third time he'd been on the site, hoping to get in touch with Simon Davis but landing with a different counsellor each time.

He read in one testimonial from someone called Rhonda that she hated when she and her sister were continuously forced together by their mother, endured any number of identical outfits right up to their late teenage years and how she chafed against the limitations of being a twin. And how, with the help of her new best friends at Time4Twin, she had successfully dealt with the guilt she suffered from daring to strike out on her own.

Rhonda signed off with, 'Go, Time4Twin'.

Holy Mary, Mother of Christ, thought Leonard. Some people don't half have to work hard at earning themselves a problem. Go volunteer in a warzone, Rhonda, he thought. Work on some perspective rather than torturing yourself over nothing.

A dialogue box came up on the screen. He was asked if he wished to talk to someone.

'Yes please', was his response.

'US or UK?'

'UK.'

There was a moment while the dialogue box appeared to freeze and he wondered if his internet connection had been lost. Then, 'We will be with you momentarily.'

How very formal, thought Leonard with a jolt of pleasure. So many of the things he read online were overly friendly and any pretence at grammar was entirely accidental.

'Hi, my name is Simon and I'm here to answer any of your questions and to help you register.'

'Hello, Simon', he typed, thinking, well, that was a slice of luck. How many Simons could be counselling on this site? 'Very nice to meet you', he typed. 'My name is' – he paused and then with a smile added – 'Jude Michaels'. He doubted the young man would recognise the significance of this name. Few people would in this more secular age. St Jude was, of course, the saint of desperate situations. Very fitting, he thought with a smile

'Welcome, Jude.'

As Simon, his new best friend, wittered on about the benefits of Time4Twin, Leonard reflected. Yes, he was looking forward to eternal peace, but there was still so much pleasure to be had on this mortal coil before his last accepting breath.

'What do you hope to gain from your sessions with me, Jude?'

We have sessions, thought Leonard?

'My twin died suddenly when I was a child,' he typed, 'and he's been a dark cloud hanging over me every day since. I have never been brave enough to meet a counsellor face to face, to be honest. But I'm hoping the distance we have physically on this' – he struggled to find the right word and settled for 'forum' – 'I hope this kind of forum will encourage me to open up.'

'I certainly hope so, Jude. We've helped many people here. At least, we like to think so.'

'Before I open up to you, Simon, can I ask what experience you have yourself? I mean, I could be talking to anyone here. Apologies if I offend you.'

'No, no', replied Simon. 'That's a fair question. I may be the youngest counsellor here, but I've built up a wee bit of experience. I volunteered with the Samaritans. Went through all of the training they demand.'

Leonard felt a charge of excitement at that last answer. This guy had a lot of promise. He was young. Driven to help. You don't get many kids doing this kind of thing – and he must be a kid or he wouldn't even have mentioned his age. And the use of the word "wee". Classic Scottish understatement. With a thrill, Leonard realised that this was almost certainly the Simon he was looking for. There was a lot of promise here. Messing with this guy's mind would be a challenge and hugely rewarding.

His fingers hovered over the keyboard. He typed, 'You're obviously a compassionate young man, Simon, or you wouldn't be doing this. But why specialise in helping twins? Surely that demands a particular form of expertise.'

'Of course it does! I'm a twin myself!'

Holy Mary, thought Leonard again. Young people and their propensity for exclamation marks. He responded, 'I'm sure you guys have rules about how much you share online, and I'm sorry if I have been too intrusive with my questions. But one more, if I may.'

'Sure thing. Ask away.'

'Is your twin alive or dead? I mean how can you possibly understand if you've never gone through that kind of trauma?'

'My bro is very much alive, Jude. But I have suffered loss in my life.' Of course you have, thought Leonard, or why else would you be doing this? In his experience, those people who enter this field are also looking for some kind of help themselves. 'In any case, we're doing this to provide an ear. To empathise. To enable our clients and to help them move on. Anybody can listen, but it takes a special skill to listen properly, without judgement, without jumping in with advice.'

All very textbook, thought Leonard.

He typed, 'And you can do all that on here? I'm almost afraid to suggest it, bearing in mind what I already said, but would we get the chance to meet up?'

'That's not a service we offer, Jude. Our funding doesn't cover that.'

'How about a telephone conversation? Can we do that? I'm already finding that there are limitations here.'

'Let's see how we get on here first of all, please?'

'Of course,' wrote Leonard, his pulse racing with anticipation. 'I'm already feeling that this is going to be a great benefit to me.'

24

Outside the church, I stand on the pavement and watch the flow of traffic. People in cars. Each of them locked in their own world. Chasing the next gadget, the next pair of shoes, the next big thing, and it's all so pointless I want to scream at them.

Across the road from the church is the River Clyde, and I feel the pull of the water. Judging the flow of cars, I sprint across the road and over to the white railings at the water's edge.

The great River Clyde. The river that Glasgow built and which, in turn, built Glasgow. Helped it to become the second city of the British Empire. And now, I lean forward and examine the slow slide of water. It's a sleeping giant. The water is calm, fractured reflections sit on the surface. But it is too far away for me to see my own sullen image in the water.

I look up. Just on the other side of the river from me is Carlton Place. The address of my police-authorised counsellor. I look away quickly with the absurd notion that my looking at them will somehow attract their attention.

I pull my phone from my pocket. Three missed calls. Two from Alessandra and one from Daryl. I click on Daryl's details and press call. Can't face Ale right now. She demands too much honesty.

Daryl picks up immediately.

'The Super said you were taking some time off, Ray. What's going on?'

'Ach, don't listen to him. Talks out of his arse. What's happening back at the ranch?'

'We've just brought in Kevin Banks. He's up before the beaks tomorrow morning.'

'That was quick.'

'Yeah, he brought in Peters to take over the case while you were out of action.'

DI Peters. Sees me as his professional nemesis. Which is posh speak for someone who hates my guts.

'That was quick.' I swallow my anger at myself. I've got no one else to blame. 'Well, he'll just have to take him back off the case. I'm going nowhere.' I pause a beat. 'Can you come pick me up?'

'Sure. Where are you?'

I look around me. Place my back against the railings to take in the wide, tall wooden doors of the church and the crucifix hanging above.

'Nowhere,' I say with a rueful laugh. Then I tell him. He snorts in response. I look over to my left and am reminded that the casino is in that direction. Thinking this would be an easy pick up point for him, I tell him to meet me there in five minutes.

* * *

Waiting at the corner for Daryl, my mind goes for a search of the sense in the last hour. I can recognise that everything is clear now. Rational Ray is back in control. But what the hell happened after I walked out, well, minced out of Harrison's office?

I remember little of how I came to be in that church.

And what was I thinking? A church? I haven't been in one since that time during the hunt for the Stigmata Killer. Before that it would have been just before I got chucked out of the seminary.

A gap opens up in the clouds, and I feel a little heat from the sun. I turn my face to it and enjoy the warmth. The little things. I like being able to notice them, for a change. The traffic is a loud hum. A door opens, and I catch the scent of roasting coffee from the bagel shop behind me. A couple walk past. Judging by the looks on their faces, the world doesn't exist outside their bubble, except to supply them with essentials.

All of this was going on around me when I made my way to the church, yet none of it registered. What's wrong with me? Maybe, as Harrison suggests, I do need time out? Speak to the counsellor? I look over my shoulder, across the river.

Nah, fuck that.

Moving forward, that's what is required. Taking that next step is what will keep me focused. And sane. Time off work will just give me too much time to think. Too much time to dwell on the sorry mess my life is in.

Footsteps. A deep voice.

'Looking for some action, mate?'

I turn round. This isn't who I expect to see. I'm grabbed into a bear-hug. Take a moment to feel the security of this man's solidity before pushing him away. Emotion chokes me for a moment. I cough. Smile. Realise I'm pleased to see him.

'Wanker,' I say in greeting to Kenny.

'Good to see you too, mate.' He's wearing that grin.

'What, has it been all of two days since I saw you last?'

'And my, look how you've grown.'

I pat my stomach. 'It's the deep-fried bagels, don't you know.'

'You deep fry bagels here?' he asks, smiling.

'Such a tourist.' I place a hand on his shoulder. Give him a smile of thanks and look around. 'You were just passing…'

'Glasgow really is a small city, eh?' He gives me a look as if assessing whether or not I'm in the right state of mind to hear the truth. 'Your friends are worried about you, Ray.'

'So this is some kind of American-style intervention?' I stiffen and take a step towards him, all grunt and gristle.

He puts a firm hand on my chest to stop my forward momentum, completely unfazed by the switch in my mood. 'Get over yourself, McBain.' He reaches out, pinches my right cheek and gives it wee shake while laughing, and I find myself reacting to his good humour. Only Kenny O'Neill could get away with this.

'I thought Daryl…'

'Alessandra took over. She has me on speed dial. Brains and beauty that one.'

'So…'

'So, she called. Said you needed a distraction.' He holds his arms wide. Again with the grin. 'And I'm it.'

'What do you have in mind?' I relax and decide to go with whatever scheme he and Ale have cooked up.

'Not sure.' He makes a face. 'But I predict that copious amounts of alcohol will be involved.'

* * *

Next morning and I'm rueing that last whisky and ginger ale. Thankfully, Kenny is a bit of a light-weight when it comes to booze, and I'm not much better.

In the car park at work, I breathe into my cupped hand. A sniff as I try to assess how much of last night's drinking has made it into this morning's breath.

Apart from one brief flirtation with alcohol while I tried to deal with the effects of a Catholic convent upbringing, booze has never been my escape route. I want to make sure that no police eyebrows are raised while asking that question this time around.

Satisfied that all they're going to get if they get close enough is a minty-fresh exhalation, I exit the car and come face-to-face with Daryl Drain.

'Awright, boss?' he asks.

'Getting there,' I answer while trying to read the expression on his face. He looks silently back at me.

'What?' I ask.

'In a better place today?'

I set my jaw. He looks like he's been storing something up since yesterday and needs to get it off his chest. I owe him, and he knows it. But my response has a more caustic edge than I was aiming for.

'Brilliant, big man. Just brilliant,' I say.

Daryl shoves his hands deep in his pockets as if trying to keep them away from my throat.

'There's something going on in your head, and you have to sort it. If you need to keep working while you do that, great. Ale and I put our careers on the line for you before. Don't take us for granted now. Everyone else in that office would be happy to hang you out to dry. Get real and get help, for all our sakes, eh?'

I take the scolding. Say nothing. Sometimes when you are presented with a plate of shit, you just have to eat it.

* * *

Hoping that the butterflies in my stomach will all start flying in the same direction, I walk into the boss's office.

'Just back from the counsellor,' I lie.

Harrison looks up from the file on his desk and stares. Assesses.

'I managed to get an emergency meeting with my counsellor,' I say. Substitute counsellor for Catholic priest and I'm being truthful. 'And we've agreed to start a course of therapy. Once a week.' That's a stretch, but I'm sure the young priest won't send me on my way. And with a start I realise my intention to return.

Harrison sits back, clasps his hands on his lap. 'I'm impressed, Ray. I didn't think you would respond so positively.' He oozes a smugness that's so thick I wonder why it doesn't clog his pores.

'Yeah ... and the thing is, the counsellor thinks it would be a mistake for me to take time off. Says it would hinder any progress. I need to keep busy.' I leaven this statement with a smile of apology.

'Right. Ah. Well.' He thinks about his next move. 'We had to move things on quickly.' He leans forward on his desk. 'We brought in Kevin Banks, and DI Peters is now in charge of the investigation.'

I pretend I don't know and give it an awfurfuckssake.

'By all means, keep busy if that's what your mental health professional says you should do, Ray. But I've moved Peters over and can't go chopping and changing. So, you'll just have to join the team, but report to him as chief investigation officer on this one, OK?'

No, it's not ok, but I don't have too many options.

* * *

Peters has gathered the team around him, and they're getting organised.

'Good of you to join us, Ray,' he says, looking up when I approach. Everyone else has a quick look, then with a degree of awkwardness, returns to face Peters. Ignoring the heat of shame that flares in me, I move closer to the group. He does me the courtesy of recapping on what has just been agreed. Less out of politeness and more out of a need to remind me what I crap job I had been doing. Fair enough. I deserve it. But he only gets one cheap shot before I launch myself at him with a cocked fist.

'Listen up, people,' he says, surveying the office. 'This case is getting a lot of airtime, meaning the suits want it over, pronto. There are a number of things still to be sorted...' he looks over at me and I can't stop myself from growling. 'For example, Kevin Banks says he was at home that night with his wife. But we still haven't confirmed that with her...'

I take a step forward, but before I can say anything, Ale has her hand on my arm and has stepped forward.

'And I was just saying that DI McBain and I were about to go and pick up Matt Davis for questioning, sir,' says Ale.

'Right. Aye,' I reply, managing to rein myself in. 'What are we waiting for?'

'And Daryl and Harkie were going to bring in Karen Gardner,' she adds, eyes focused on Peters, and I'm thinking, *Go Ale. You've manipulated the situation nicely to allow you to follow up on your hunch.* I'm happy to let it play out. Besides, Peters is just standing there feeling like he's been had and not sure how or why. Which is very pleasing.

'I'll just grab...' Ale walks over to her desk, collects her bag, shoulders it and walks towards the door. Realising she's taking the initiative before Peters says anything, I follow her. She doesn't want Peters to countermand our actions, and he is awkward enough to try.

Before I turn and walk out of the room with Ale, I catch Daryl's eye and give him a quick nod of thanks. He gives me a nod in return, but his expression is laced with a warning.

Don't fuck this up.

25

'It's *déjà vu* all over again,' says Ale as she buckles up.

Smile. 'Aye.' Seems like weeks since I last parked the car and walked into the office, rather than just a matter of hours ago. So much has happened. At least, in my head it has. 'Where are we headed?'

Alessandra pulls her notebook out of her bag. Flips it open and reads an address on the south side of the city. I scan my mental map and work out the direction I need to be driving in. If police work ever gets too much for me, I can always get a job driving one of the city's taxis.

I fire the engine. Put the gear into reverse but stop as I hear a knock on the car window. I turn and spot an eager face.

'What the...'

I roll the window down.

'Gordon Murphy from the Glasgow Telegraph,' the man says. My vision is filled with his lean face, white teeth and short-cropped hair. He's wearing a waterproof jacket over a blue shirt and tie, with a proper knot and everything. His voice is followed into the car by a strong whiff of garlic.

'Well, Gordie, if you don't move the fuck out of my way, I'm going to do you for possession of a dangerous weapon,' I say.

'What? My Dictaphone?'

'Naw, your breath, mate. Chicken with forty cloves of garlic for your tea last night?'

He has the decency to step back. 'Sorry, DI McBain. My missus gets a wee bit heavy-handed with the garlic.'

'Jeez, what's happening to the journos in this city?' I ask. 'And what's wrong with pie and chips?'

'Mind if we have a quick word?'

'Sprint,' I say.

'Just wanted to ask you about the arrest of grieving father, Kevin Banks?' He's already talking in tomorrow's headlines.

'No comment.'

'Care to comment on the heartlessness of a country where a parent gets arrested after justifiably acting out after hearing about his daughter's murder?'

'No comment,' I say. 'Now kindly move the fuck out of the way while I go and do my job.'

'Social media is alive this afternoon. People are furious with the police about this poor man's arrest. The hashtag #fuckthepolis is actually trending. Care to comment on that?'

'No comment.' I slam the car into reverse, lift my foot off the clutch, none too carefully, narrowly avoid hitting the journalist with my wing mirror as I move out of my spot. Brilliant. Just brilliant. The powers that be make the decisions and we, their servants, are blamed for everything. As usual.

Ale has her phone out and her thumbs are a blur. Sharp intake of breath. 'Right enough. People are going mental on Twitter.'

'Bunch of fannies.'

'The word "fanny" is on the same word embargo as "cunt".' Ale looks at me out of the corner of her eyes.

'Am I allowed to use male genitalia?'

'Whatever floats your boat, Nancy.'

'What's the plural for penis?'

'Pee-nye? Penises?' Ale says. We share a grin. She grows sombre. 'We're good?' she asks.

'As good as it gets, Alessandra Rossi.' I answer one question and ignore the subtext. 'That was a clever wee gambit you played there,' I say.

'What do you mean?'

'Getting me quickly out of the way of Peters.'

'Well, you two have history. He won't waste time in trying to piss you off, so I'm thinking, let's get McBain the hell out of Dodge.' She looks at me. 'It's best for you to fly under the radar for a few days.'

'I always said you'd go places, DC Rossi.'

'Yeah.' Sigh. 'South side of Glasgow here we come.'

* * *

Helen Davis is sitting in a large cushioned chair staring out of her window when she sees a car pull up and two formally dressed people, a man and a woman, get out. *Hope they're not trying to sell me something*, she thinks when they walk towards her path. She discounts that when she notices that neither are carrying anything that might be promotional material. And the studied expression on each of their faces.

Then she recognises them and feels a twist in her stomach. These were the cops who visited Simon in the hospital. She pushes herself up from the chair, and with hand over her heart waits for them to reach the door and knock.

'Will somebody get that?' she aims a shout at the room above her head, not expecting an answer. Simon will be on his laptop, trying to save the world one person at a time, and Matt will have his headset on and be playing some daft game. A pause. Neither boy responds, so with heavy, grudging footsteps and a weary, 'For God's sake,' she walks to the door.

As she reaches out to twist open the lock, she notices a piece of paper on the floor. She bends down to pick it up, opens it and with a souring in her mouth recognises the print and the shape of the word on the page. It's a page of A4 and has one large word in bold black ink in the middle.

Murderer.

'Bastards,' she says, and opens the door.

When she reads the expressions of surprise on the faces of the man and woman in front of her, she offers a weak smile of apology. 'Not you,' she says, and waves the paper at them. 'You're the cops who came to the hospital to speak to Simon, eh?'

'Yes, we are, Mrs Davis,' the heavy guy says, and reintroduces himself and his female colleague.

'So, why…?' she asks. She crosses her arms, and despite a stab of worry, can't help the stray thought that questions why someone as attractive as this girl would want to work in the police force.

'Can we come in for a moment, please?' the man asks. She can't work out if he said McBean or McBain. 'Best not to give the neighbours anything to talk about.' Settles on McBain.

'Sure. Right enough,' she says, and hands him the piece of paper she's holding. 'It's not like they don't already have enough to go on.' She turns and without another word enters her living room. She can hear the paper unfold as the cop opens it and senses them follow her into the living room.

She reaches her chair, turns to face them and bends into her seat, the cushion accepting the shape of her body like an old friend. Crossing her arms and her legs she gives a nod at the paper in the male cop's hand.

'We get that at least once a day.' She rubs her eyes and then pulls her hair back behind her ear. 'Arseholes. What happened to innocent until proven guilty?' She looks from one to the other. 'My boy did not kill Aileen. He couldn't harm a fly.' She feels the emotion swooping in on her. Doesn't have the time to fight it, and her face crumples and her chest heaves. She wipes away a tear while gathering her resolve.

'Simon's up in his room. Him and his brother are on the Xbox,' she says, not sure why it was suddenly important that she presents her boys as a united front. Simon hates the Xbox. Thinks it's juvenile.

'It's actually Matt we want to speak to, Mrs Davis.'

'Oh.' She leans forward on her chair. Hands clasped as if in prayer, elbows resting on her knees. 'What … I mean … why…'

'Just for routine questions, Mrs Davis. We'd like him to come down to the station with us.' McBain says.

She stands up, and it's as if her whole body is quivering. 'But…'

'As we said, Mrs Davis,' says DC Rossi while taking to her feet and holding a hand out as if she's afraid Mrs Davis is going to fall. 'We just want to clarify a few things. If you could…'

Just then the drum of footsteps and two young men appear at the door. Helen notices the look of recognition on Simon's face and reads his apprehension. Her heart gives a lurch. She wants to rush over to him, swoop him up in her arms and hold him tight. The way she did when he fell as a toddler. It's a mother's job, isn't it? To keep her children from harm? She takes a step back. Reminds herself that he's a grown man now. Old enough to vote. Old enough to have sex and get married. Old enough to bear arms for his country. Old enough to kill, then? She sloughs off that thought like it's a shit-stained coat. Not going there. Her Simon is innocent. And why do they want to speak to Matt?

She looks at her other son. Her other twin. Matt is a taller, stockier version of his brother. With darker hair and a less welcoming countenance. If he hadn't popped out of her vagina, she herself would have doubted the fact that these boys were brothers. Let alone twins. He refused her breast and had resolutely been his own person ever since. A difficult boy to love, she admitted, and remembered the boys' seventh birthday party and how Matt had walked up to another boy and slapped him in the face in front of all the other parents. She couldn't even recall the reason, but would never forget the horrified look on the other parents' faces. Or the look of satisfaction on Matt's. Simon couldn't hurt a soul, she asserted inwardly, but she had always worried about quite what Matt was capable of. She quashed the thought with a guilty blush.

Realising that she'd been lost in her own thoughts for the last few moments, she checked the two cops and both her sons to see if anyone noticed. Nope. Everyone was studying Matt.

'Matt, we haven't met,' McBain says, and introduces himself and Ale. 'We'd like you to come down to the station to help us with our enquiries.'

'But...' Simon takes a step forward. 'Why would you...'

'Matt. If you would just come with us?' McBain holds a hand out as if to guide Matt to the door.

'Oh, Jesus,' says Helen Davis. 'As if the neighbours haven't got enough to talk about.'

Matt snorts. 'I'm going fucking nowhere.'

Without realising what she's doing, Helen takes a few steps forward and slaps Matt across the face. Then she hides the offending palm, tucking it under her left oxter. 'You're going,' she says. 'No bloody arguments.'

'Mum!' says Simon. 'What the hell are you doing?' He turns to Matt and puts his hand on his brother's shoulder. Matt shrugs it off, as easily as he had shrugged off the slap. Or was that the way she wanted to see it, thought Helen?

She turns to face the cops who are both trying to hide their surprise.

'Got to keep them under control. Been difficult without a father,' she mumbles and then holds her lips tight, afraid what else might spill out, utterly ashamed of her reaction. Then she stifles that thought with a compensating one that demands to know why Matt is always showing her up.

'If you could try and get some proof as to who is leaving those notes, Mrs Davis, we'll arrest them for harassment,' says DC Rossi, and Helen is grateful that she is trying to erase some of the tension.

'What notes is she talking about, mum?' asks Simon, his face bright with concern.

'It's nothing, sweetheart.' She shakes her head. 'Absolutely nothing.'

* * *

It's only when we pull in at the station that I realise since the moment we first met Matt Davis, and for the forty-five minutes or so it has taken to negotiate Glasgow traffic, he hasn't said a word.

We get the nod that Harkness and Drain have just collected Karen Gardner and, traffic allowing, they should be back in just over an hour. We make ourselves nice and comfortable in room three.

Matt sits where we direct him, hands clasped on his lap and legs stretched out before him. He's a cool customer. Let's see how we can unsettle him a little.

I go through the usual protocols and then say, 'State your full name please?'

'Matthew Stephen Davis.' His voice is a deep bass. I'm thinking that whenever he goes into pubs, he must get asked for proof of age, and then that voice will swing it for him.

'Really?' I ask. 'Was your dad a snooker fan?'

'No idea, mate. He didn't live long enough for me to ask him.' He's stating a fact, not looking for sympathy.

'Date of birth?'

He tells us.

'I didn't realise you and Simon were twins,' says Ale.

'There you go. Every day's a school day.'

'Who's the oldest?' she asks.

'He is. By fifteen minutes.'

I give Matt another look over. The resemblance is not as strong as I've noticed with other identical twins. As Ale had said, it was across the eyes and the forehead. But where Simon's features are fine, Matt's are heavier, more masculine. He crosses his arms and his biceps swell, stretching the fabric of his shirt. He catches me noticing and smirks.

'Rugby?' I ask.

He nods.

'Wrong shaped ball, if you ask me,' I say.

He makes a face as if to say, whatever, your opinion doesn't even register, mate. He clearly wants to project an attitude of someone who isn't that bothered about being here. His languid pose is an attempt to show us that he has nothing to worry about, but that's all it is, a pose. Even the most basic knowledge of body language tells you that crossed arms is a defensive position. His outstretched legs and crossed ankles also tell me he is apprehensive. The mind may have an agenda, but the body will often betray. Despite what he wants to tell us, he's worried. We just have to find out the why and the what.

'Tell me about Aileen Banks,' I say.

'What do you want to know?'

'What was she like? Your memories of her? Stuff like that,' I answer. I want to get him talking about her in a personal sense, not in the abstract. The first thing we do to distance ourselves from guilt and grief or blame even, is to de-personalise. After all, *they* weren't really human. If he had any form of relationship with her, I need to see that being played out on his face.

'She was my brother's burd. Came round the house loads.'

'Did you like her?' asks Ale.

'She was nice enough,' he shrugs. Going for non-committal.

'They split up before she was killed,' I say. 'What do you know about that?'

'Shit happens, mate. Who really knows what goes on in a relationship apart from the couple themselves?'

'Sounds like you have experience of that yourself,' says Ale. 'A handsome boy like you must have girls queuing up for a date.'

He exhales through pursed lips. 'As if. Not interested. More bother than they're worth.' Then he closes his mouth tight, like he has reminded himself to only answer the question and not provide any additional information.

'What do you remember about the break-up?' I ask.

'Tears and snot, mate,' he says. 'Simon was gutted, but he's too proud to go begging and left her to it.'

'Why do you think they broke up?'

'Ran its natural course, didn't it. They were together right through secondary school. Uni life gives a different perspective, eh? The big bad. Much more to experience.' His hands are on his lap now. A little more relaxed. It's like he's confident that we will know all this and is therefore more happy to give details. Suggests he and Simon ran over his conversation with us.

'That day in the hospital. When we came to see Simon. Why did you run off?' asks Ale.

'Dunno what you mean?' he answers and scratches at the side of his forehead.

'Your mother said you were with her. I'm thinking you saw us and legged it. I want to know why.'

'That's not what happened,' he answers. 'I just remembered, like.' A weak smile. 'I dropped mum off at the hospital, and then I remembered I had a class.'

'So why were you hiding at the hospital reception when we came out?'

'What?'

'I saw you at the reception area,' says Ale. 'You were waiting for us to leave before you went back in. Why did you want to avoid us?'

'Don't know what you're talking about.' He sits up, slides his feet under the chair, crosses his arms.

'And we checked your class timetable for that day.' I gamble and go for the lie. 'You had a free afternoon.'

'Yeah, it was an assignment I had to finish. I was late. Had to get it done for the next morning.'

'So why say you had a class?' Ale asks.

'What is this?' he asks. 'Am I being arrested or something?'

'No, Matt. You avoided us that day and when someone does that it suggests they are hiding something. We want to know what you are hiding.'

'I'm hiding nothing, mate.' The skin on his neck is mottled. He gives it a scratch. 'And I wasn't hiding from you. Don't know what you are talking about.' As he continues speaking his voice gets louder.

'Then we saw you in The Horseshoe with Karen Gardner. You legged it as soon as you spotted us,' says Ale.

'It was the guys you were with,' he answers. 'Foreman and Cook.' He sits forward, chin jutting out. 'They've been saying shit on Facebook about Simon.' He slumps back in his seat. Crosses his arms. 'Karen dragged me out of there before I...' realising he was about to suggest a violent act, he paused, '…made an arse of myself.'

'Wise move, son,' I say. 'Wouldn't be the brightest thing to do with two police officers as witness.'

'Aye … well.'

'You and Simon, did you ever double date?'

'Do what?' He's not wondering what the words mean, but why the question is being asked.

'It's when you and a pal each take out a girl,' answers Ale.

'I wasn't … ' Exhales. 'Now and again. Simon and Aileen have been, like, forever. I've not met any that've stuck. Women are nuts.'

Ale smiles. 'None taken.' Her expression a request for more information.

Matt is unrepentant. 'One lassie. I'd been seeing her for three weeks. Three weeks, yeah? Told her I was thinking of getting a tattoo. She was like, nope, not happening. Said she could deal with a couple but that was my lot. ' He purses his lips and blows. 'Three weeks and that makes her my boss? No chance. I was like, take a walk, hen.'

'What about Karen Gardner?' I ask.

'What about her?'

'Double date?'

A shrug. 'We went out in a foursome kinda thing a couple of times. Simon and me don't socialise much really. He always had…' he pauses before he says Aileen's name, ' …and I had my own pals and the guys down at the rugby club. Anyway, Karen's a good laugh like. A mate. Don't see her like that.'

'Does she see you the same way?' asks Ale.

'Aye,' says Matt, his expression as adamant his tone. He's leaning back in his chair, long legs stretched out in front of him, hands soft, resting on his thighs. He's in safe territory, and from his perspective, dealing with everything that we're throwing at him. Time to mix it up a little.

'What about Aileen?' I ask.

'What about her?' He presses his hands on to the sides of his chair, switches his weight and is now fully upright in his chair.

'She was a bit of a babe,' I say. 'Ever rub one out while thinking about her naked in your brother's bed just through the wall?'

He looks from me to Ale and presumably sees nothing but the same frank curiosity on her face.

'Jeezuz. You people are sick,' he says. 'She's not long dead and you're…' He shakes his head, and I'm thinking this is interesting. He's defending her honour. A wee spot of chivalry, and he cares more than he is letting on.

Is it really just on behalf of his twin brother? Or is there something more at play here?

'Ever listen to them going at it and wish it was you?' I ask.

'You're sick.' He shakes his head. And scratches at the skin on his neck.

Realising that at this stage we're not going to get much more out of him, we escort Matt out of the secure area and in to the public part of the station. Explain that we're going to arrange a lift for him back to the house.

'Don't worry about it, mate.' He sticks his hands in his pockets. 'I'll find my own way home.'

Just then Harkness walks in the front door with Karen Gardner.

Matt and Karen lock eyes. Say nothing. Matt walks past her and out of the door.

'Interesting,' mumbles Alessandra. Then. 'Hi Karen. Thanks for popping in.'

'Sure. No worries,' she replies just above a whisper.

* * *

In the interview room, Ale takes the lead. Goes through the legal stuff.

'Before we start,' she says. 'Can we get you a wee cup of tea or something?'

'No,' answers Karen. Then, as if she has remembered her manners, 'Thanks.' And offers a weak smile. In contrast to Matt, she's sitting upright, spine pressing into the back of the chair, knees together, hands clasped on the table top. She looks like she has just discovered she has brittle bone disease and is scared to move.

'I know we've spoken before, Karen,' says Ale. 'But that was an informal chat. This is nothing to worry about, but we just need to get that all on record. OK?'

'OK,' Karen squeaks. And I'm struggling to place this girl with the one in the red car who flashed her boobs to the old man next door to the Banks house.

We ask Karen to outline the events of the night Aileen died. For the record. She complies. Spelling it all out, exactly the same as when we first talked to her. And it's almost too perfect. People get it this exact when they have rehearsed. Ask someone for details of an event, particularly when they appear to be under stress, and something in the story will change. Sure, if they are being truthful the facts will repeat, but something in the telling will change.

I scan my memory. Yup. As far as I can make out it was word-for-word.

'How did you and Aileen meet?' I ask.

'At the supermarket.'

'Hit it off straight away?'

A nod. Her eyes shine a little bit more.

'What drew you together?'

'Dunno,' she answers. 'My parents are divorced. Hers were having problems. I'd just broken up with a boyfriend.' A long pause as she stares at the table top, sifting and sorting through memory. A smile laden with affection. 'We both loved *Twilight*.' A tear escapes and she wipes it away.

'You two were great friends, eh?' asks Ale.

Karen nods. A sob escapes. 'Sorry,' she says. 'Still not quite used to...'

'No need to apologise, Karen. We understand. You've lost someone you care about.' Ale reaches forward and pats her hand. Realising this isn't entirely professional, she withdraws and sits back in her chair. 'I'm sure Aileen would be proud of you. The way you're dealing with this.'

'Yeah?' asks Karen, as if desperate for approval from the grown-ups.

'Yeah,' answers Ale, her tone like a hug.

Karen sniffs. Wipes away another tear. Settles into her chair a little more.

'Tell us a little bit more about that night. Before you two split up. Was there anyone around, anyone who caught your attention apart from the usual people you would expect to bump into when you were out?'

Karen shakes her head. Stares at the tabletop. Thinks some more. 'No.'

'Sure?'

A nod.

'Please think carefully, Karen,' I say. 'There may be something in your head. A clue that could help us catch this person.'

'It was just the usual crowd. With a few randoms. But nobody who sticks out.'

'Did you see Simon that night?'

'No,' she answers. 'Although he did text Aileen. Just to say hi. But she ignored it.'

'Why?'

'She said he was being a dick.'

'I never met the girl, but I don't think she knew what she wanted,' observed Ale.

Karen loosened her hands a little. 'You're right. One minute she was like, let's find some guys to party with. Next she was missing Simon and texting him.'

'How do you think that would have been for Simon?' I ask.

'Must've driven him nuts. I told her she was being a crazy bitch. She had to cut things off with him, like, completely, you know? Or they'd never move on.'

'Makes sense to me,' says Ale. 'What do you think would've

happened eventually with Simon and Aileen?'

'They would've got back together,' she answers with certainty and a slight note of regret.'

'Why do you say that?' I ask.

'Jeez, they were made for each other. Totally. You just had to spend five minutes in their company to see.'

'How did that make you feel?'

'A wee bit jealous, if I'm honest.' She tucks some hair behind her right ear. 'I'd give anything to have someone like that. And she just throws it away.'

'Tell us about Simon.'

A note of suspicion forms on her face. 'Are you asking me if I think he did it?'

'No,' I replied. 'Just looking for the best friend's perspective. Is he a nice guy? Did he treat her badly? Did he ever hit Aileen or verbally abuse her?'

'You don't really know what goes on in someone else's relationship do you?' she says, thinking aloud. 'I always thought Simon was too nice, really. And a bit boring. No one's that nice, eh?' She's a little more animated as she says this. As if she's enjoying the chance to have a bit of a gossip. 'Or that safe.'

'What do you mean by too nice?' Ale asks.

'Well,' she draws the word out as if it was made of two syllables. As if trying to build up her energy to convince herself as well as us. 'I mean, he was a volunteer on the Samaritan phone line. Apparently he did quite a lot of online … what do you call it … counselling. On a couple of other sites an' all. He's only in his early twenties for God's sake. Get a life mate,' she sniffs.

'What about Matt?' Ale asks. 'Ever fancy a wee slice of that? He's a handsome guy. Got those rugby-player thighs.'

'If you like that kind of thing.' Her tone is defensive.

'Oh come on,' laughs Ale. 'He's fit.' They're girls together.

Karen allows herself a smile. 'And he bloody knows it.'

'Did you guys ever…?'

Karen tosses her head. 'He wishes. We had a snog once when we were drunk.' She holds a hand up and slices her long fingernails back and forward across her throat. 'Electricity was zero, mate. Was like kissing a fridge.'

'Whose idea was it?' I ask.

'His. Totally. Said we needed to get it out of the way or we'd be,' she holds both hands up and does the air-quote thing, '"haunted by the possibility of it for the rest of our lives".'

'What a shit chat-up line,' says Ale.

'Yeah, and it worked.' Karen offers a smile. 'He got the kiss.'

'And nothing else?'

'Nothing else.'

'Disappointed?' Ale asks.

'Not bothered really. Would be nice hanging off his arm, but it wasn't to be.'

'Is Simon more your type? The silent, nice and safe one?'

'As if,' she sneers. 'Apart from the boring fart thing, he was my mate's ex. Out of bounds. Totally.'

'Disappointed?' I ask. 'The nice guys are the ones you go back to, no?'

'Not even going there,' she answers. 'A friend's ex?' She shakes her head. 'Too much grief. Besides, they weren't really over. Not really. The only person who couldn't see that was Aileen.' She tails off. Stares into space. Finds a knot of grief and rubs at it. Tears spark in her eyes before shining a trail down the pale of her cheek. She sniffs. Palms her face dry. It is a gesture that is awkward and serves to remind me how young she is.

I push aside any thought of her youth. I can't let that influence how we deal with her.

'Karen,' I say, and pause. Wait for her to look up from the table and meet my gaze. 'What are you not telling us?' I don't realise how harsh my tone is until I catch a warning glance from Alessandra. Fuck it. This girl needs to know how serious we are. 'We need to get to the truth here. Your best friend in the world is dead. No more

140

nights out, nights in, girlie chats over fucking *Twilight*, Facebook or *The Only Way is Essex* … this is as real as it gets. And in your head is a vital clue that will help us…'

'I've told you everything I know,' she interrupts, as if desperate to shut me up. She's hugging herself now.

'I don't believe you.' I allow my frustration to seep in and slam my hand down on the table top. She jumps. 'You're holding something back. I can smell it. What is it?'

'Nothing.'

'Liar.'

'I'm not lying.'

'Pants on fucking fire.'

'Ray,' says Ale quietly. I throw her a warning scowl. Time she got real as well. Yeah, there might be times when I go over the score, but this time I'm on the money. I'm certain of it, and Karen just needs a wee fright to make her tell us what she knows.

Karen is even whiter now. Her eyes dart about the small room as if she's looking for a safe place to land. Somewhere far away from my accusing glare.

'You're hiding something.' I point at her, my finger like a dagger, invading her space. 'And you need to tell us now.'

She shakes her head. Shuts her eyes tight.

'Karen,' I say.

She crosses her arms.

'Karen.'

Crosses her legs.

'What are you holding back?'

She puts a hand over her mouth. A word escapes. 'Matt…'

'What about Matt?'

'He…'

There's a knock on the door. It opens slightly and a head sticks in. It's Daryl Drain.

'Boss.'

'We're in the middle of something here, DC Drain,' I say, and

141

notice the release of tension in the room, like dirty dishwater escaping down a plug-hole.

'Sorry. I wouldn't interrupt but this is...' I can tell from his expression that whatever is eating his gusset, it's extremely important. I stand up.

'Excuse me, Karen. I'll just be a moment.' I leave the room, inwardly cursing. She was on the verge of telling me something, and I doubt we'll ever get back to that moment.

In the corridor I turn to Daryl. 'Right. This better be fucking good.'

'It's Kevin Banks, boss. Just took a dive under a truck.'

26

I thumb a text to Maggie. 'Your place or mine?'

Her reply arrives ten minutes later. Ten minutes while I sit outside her house in my car. It's still early days in our relationship, and I don't want to take anything for granted. Which is a weird thing to say when I'm sat outside her house.

Hers reads, 'yours?' Followed by a double kiss. Then a moment later, 'Eejit. I saw your car as you arrived. Come on in.'

She stands at her door with hand on hip and her head cocked to the side. Smiling. She stretches up for a kiss as I reach her.

'If you saw me arriving, why did you wait ten minutes to answer?' I lean down and push my lips against hers. Savour the press and the warmth. Feel a stirring. Lean in to her to stoke the fire. Her face is against mine and I can feel her cheeks press up as she smiles.

She moves back into the hall and I feel a pang of disappointment. 'Cos, I thought you'd just come in,' she snorts a laugh. 'Instead of sitting out there in the car like Ray nae pals.'

'We hadn't arranged anything, and I didn't want to just arrive unannounced.' I put on my best sad face.

She goes to say something. Pauses. 'A mix of consideration and impatience. How could a girl not love that?'

'Do we shag first, or should I make dinner?' I ask.

Maggie throws her head back and laughs. 'Again with the consideration and impatience.' She moves towards me. Kisses me long and hard, her tongue caressing mine. Stops. Breathes deep. 'Dinner can wait.'

* * *

We make it as far as the sofa and after, we lie there naked and sated. I close my eyes and feel sleep about to take me. Maggie nudges me.

'Hey. What about my dinner?'

'Right enough.' I grin. 'We have worked up an appetite.'

She cuts off my chuckle with a kiss.

'What do you fancy to eat?' I ask.

'There's nothing much in the cupboard. Mrs Hubbard's been a lazy bitch, frankly. Couldn't be arsed going to the shop today.'

'Want me to go for a carry out?' Her hand is stroking my chest. Now I know how a cat might feel when it's on the receiving end of some affection. I resist the urge to purr.

She nods. 'There's any number of take-out places at the end of the road.'

'Well, this is Glasgow.' I sit up, reluctant to do so as that means her hand will stop stroking me. But judging by the growl from my belly, food is becoming essential. 'Preference?' I ask.

She shakes her head. 'As long as it's hot.'

'What, like me?' I stand and shake my hips. My naked groin is level with her face.

She puts a hand over her face and mock screams, 'My eyes! My eyes!'

'Better put some clothes on before I go down to the shops.' I grin. 'Not everyone appreciates what a hunk of man I am.'

Maggie laughs. 'Which reminds me. Nothing with cheese, please.'

* * *

Fed and watered, empty cartons congealing on the table in front of us, and we're back on the sofa staring at something or other on the TV. I feel almost relaxed. The news comes on. Kevin Banks's attempted suicide is the lead story.

'Shit,' I say. My face fills the TV screen and police speak issues from my mouth. The reporter then goes on to say how social networking sites have gone into meltdown. People are furious that a man whose daughter has died under suspicious circumstances has been driven to such a desperate act.

'What happened, baby?' asks Maggie.

I'm rubbing both hands over my head while posting to the back of my mind the fact that Maggie is comfortable enough to use such a term of endearment. But today's events are in a storm at the forefront of my mind, and the nice stuff will have to wait. 'Fuck Twitter. Fuck Facebook and all the sad bastards who use them.'

Maggie changes channels.

'What are you doing?' I turn to her. Hear the note of aggression and instantly regret it. 'Sorry, I'm…'

'Do you really want to hear any more? You need to switch off for the day, Ray.'

I fall back into the cushions. 'For sure,' I agree.

'How is he?' asks Maggie. Her face full of concern for Kevin Banks.

'He'll survive.' My sympathy for him is tempered by the fact that his actions have put us thigh-high in the shit. I close my eyes and allow my head to slump back into a cushion at the thought of the headlines the next morning. Sure, the online sites will be alight with all of this, but I can ignore them, can't I?

Nobody could say how he'd managed it. He was being escorted back into the station after appearing at the court. And just before the uniforms brought him inside, he'd taken advantage of a slip in concentration and wrestled himself out of their grip.

Folk make a run for it all the time, said Daryl Drain afterwards. But they tend to run for safety, not the wheels of the no. 77 bus. The uniform who tried to re-capture him reported that it was as if Banks was aiming for the bus, rather than trying to get away from him.

Was his grief fuelled purely by the loss of his daughter, or was there something more? Guilt perhaps? We did get confirmation from Mrs Banks that her husband was home that night. Even the nosy neighbour confirmed that. Could the neighbour be wrong? Certainly Mrs Banks was doped into a stupor, and it's quite possible she had no idea what she was saying when she answered our questions.

Sadly, I've spoken to many grieving parents in my time, but I can't remember one who was driven to kill himself in such a dramatic fashion. At the least they want to find answers. They want to know what happened to their loved one before fully giving in to the tumult of emotion that such an event rouses. To attempt suicide before they are given that detail? I've never come across it, and it makes me question exactly what is going on in that man's mind. Does he know more about this than he is telling us?

To me, this is an act of guilt. Not grief.

27

Helen Davis waits at her living room window, arms crossed, anxiety hanging like a twisting weight just under her heart. Each breath a challenge. Each second until her son returns from the police station hangs on her as heavy as dredged-up sin.

What could they be asking him?

Why are they even interested in him? Yeah, he's been a difficult boy, but surely they don't think he could have anything to do with that girl's death?

The fact that she still can't say her name, even within the confines of her own mind, gives her a little tug of guilt. She swipes it aside with a silent acknowledgement and the words: once her boy is safe from accusation. Or, make that boys?

No smoke without fire. The words scroll through her mind and memory helpfully adds her mother's scolding tone. That was her favourite saying. The old witch. She expected the worst of everyone and couldn't wait to tell you if she was ever proven correct. Even if that proof was only in her own mind.

Her mother's attitude had gifted her a healthy dose of cynicism, but she didn't ever reach the depths of imagination her mother plumbed on a regular basis. It made looking after her in those final years extremely difficult. The number of home helps they went through before she finally died didn't bear thinking about.

Helen turns on the television. Hopes that the sound distracts her. The news comes on. Is that really the time? She checks her phone. It's after 6pm. Where has Matt gone? Surely he's not still at the police station? And if she finds out that they finished with him hours ago and he didn't bother to get in touch, she'll bloody kill...

A name sounds out from the TV. Worries at her attention. Kevin Banks. She steps in front of the screen, the better to see, and the detective who was in her house earlier fills the screen. Handsome guy, she thinks, but needs to cut out the pies, she hears her mother speaking.

With a shake of her head, as if banishing the spirit of her long deceased mother, she tries to make sense of the words coming out of the man's mouth.

As their meaning becomes clear, an involuntary movement has her hand covering her mouth. *Oh my God. Kevin ran under a bus? Is that what McBain said? What would possess him to do that? Grief must be driving him crazy.*

She recalls the first time she met Kevin Banks. They were waiting to collect their respective children from some event or other. The kids playing it cool. Not wanting the olds to meet. *Of course I was curious*, she thinks. *This girl was taking up a lot of space in my son's head. I wanted to know where she came from.*

Kevin had an easy smile, a trusting cant to his eyes, and who wouldn't love that Highland accent? His wife on the other hand was a torn-faced cow. Barely gave her the time of day. Knew she was single and translated that into a threat to her marriage.

She read all of that in the seconds it took to shake that wet fish of a hand and remembers thinking, *you don't know the half of it, darling.*

An endearment that sparks another memory of her mother. Her voice sounds in her mind. She tuts it away. Brushes it from her thoughts like she might flap at a wasp. Her mother was the worst judge of character she'd ever come across.

Then her mother is louder than ever.

It saves you time, darling. She even managed to imbue that endearment with the tone of doom. *Expect the worst from everyone and sooner than you know, someone is going to prove you right.*

* * *

Jim Leonard has been sitting at the church computer, just an hour distant by car from the Davis family. He's been waiting with the patience and focus of a hunter. Waiting for Simon Davis to go active on the twin counselling website.

He has a strong feeling about this one. A thrill in the gut that he's not felt since he took a knife to that old hag of a nun. *Doing God's work my backside*, he thought. The woman was clearly on the same side of the good/evil divide as he was.

Closing his eyes, he focuses on the excitement of it. The hunger. The charge. Wills it to every cell in his body. Feeling it surround him like a full body halo.

The word "halo" causes a snort of laughter. He revels in the irony. Then dismisses the thought, gathering the sense of excitement to him again. His own dark aura.

Feeling a tremble in his fingertips and a shortness in his breath, he opens his eyes and releases the sensation. It's too much. Demands release. And he's too far away, in every sense of the phrase, from his target. Better not get too caught up at this stage or he'll need to go out and hunt now. That would be sloppy and get him caught.

He acknowledges the debt he has to McBain in finding this target. If it hadn't been for him he'd never have come across Davis. *So, you're good for something, Ray, other than eating.*

An alert sounds on the computer. Just thinking of him and the internet sends notice of his appearance in the world. He enters a screen and sees that McBain has hit the news again. Another few clicks on the man himself appears. He turns the sound up. Some sap … scratch that, it's the dead girl's father, has run under the wheels of a bus and the media are giving the police a hard time. Grieving parent reacts to arrest. Blah. Blah.

McBain is giving it the usual police speak. As if words of more than two syllables are supposed to be a sign of intellect. At the end of his speech, before the camera stops filming, Leonard notices that McBain gives a small look to the woman on his left. As if checking that his performance was acceptable. She moves her head very slightly in response and raises an eyebrow.

She's a good few years younger than McBain. Clearly in the force or she wouldn't be standing there. The look passing between them suggests something more than just colleagues. Could McBain be having an affair with a workmate?

He pauses the screen. Examines the look that passes between them. Congratulates himself on spotting it, as it would have been missed by everyone else. He hunkers down in his chair, legs stretched out before him, crosses his arms and tries to work out what is going on.

McBain looks hale and hearty. And far too happy for his liking. Sure, he's pale, too heavy and there are dark circles under his eyes. But he's breathing, moving about and far too functional for Leonard's liking.

Of all the people affected by that night in the convent, they are the only two left alive. He really must do something about that. But first. He turns his attention to the female cop.

Attractive face. Slim. A brightness about the eyes that he finds appealing. There's a brain there, not withstanding her connection with McBain.

She's good looking, intelligent and is clearly drawn to McBain.

This won't do, he thinks. This won't do at all.

28

Next day and Alessandra Rossi has just listened to my latest theory.

'No way, Ray,' she says with certainty. 'No way did that man kill his daughter.'

'So why, then? Why run under a bus?'

'Who knows?' Ale is driving. Takes her eyes off the road in front of her to look at me. 'Grief does crazy things to people.'

'Couldn't sleep for thinking about this last night.' I repeat my theory. 'Surely, as a parent you want answers? You want to know what happened and that keeps you going.'

'No two people react the same way, Ray.'

I make a non-committal sound in answer and look out of my side of the car. We're in a line of traffic on the M8, crossing the wide, grey ribbon that is the River Clyde. The driver in the blue Vauxhall alongside is moving his mouth rapidly. As if accompanying his favourite song on the radio. I study him some more. Read the furrowed brow and think, nah, he's shouting at some poor sap on the other end of the phone. His top button is open and his tie unloosened. I can see his hair is damp with sweat. That's technology for you. We don't even get respite from the world when we're in a car.

Ale speeds up and we lose him.

'Seems we're all under pressure, eh?'

'What?'

'Is grief the only pressure Kevin Banks is under?'

'I think everything else will be relegated to the Who Gives a Fuck file.' Pause. 'Do you think she'll be in?' asks Ale.

'If she's not at home, she'll be at the hospital, by her husband's side. And we'll get her there.'

'What are they saying? Coma?'

'A medically induced one until the swelling in the brain goes down. He's also got a large selection of broken bones.'

'Jeez.

We both lapse into our own thoughts, and fifteen minutes later we're in suburbia and rolling up outside the Banks's house.

Jennie Banks has a long, lean face that has been hardened by recent events into her judgement of the world. And planet Earth can go nuclear for all she cares. Her arms are crossed tight, as if to hold in her crushing disappointment.

'Yes?' she asks, with one foot placed behind the door as if she can only allow the world entry one tiny piece at a time.

I explain who I am and ask if we can come in. She simply turns round and walks into her living room without speaking. We follow, Ale first, and I close the front door behind me.

'I was just heading out,' Jennie says as she cushions herself into a chair. And not one person in the room is convinced by this statement. Least of all her. She drums the fingers of her right hand on the arm of the chair. Her left hand is wedged firmly into her armpit. She stills the movement of her fingers and stares at the carpet in front of her. Looks from me to Ale. Her sight lighting on each of us so briefly, as if to look at someone else hurts.

'Need to go and visit my husband. He's been in some sort of...' It takes a real effort for her to speak, and I wonder if she has been medicated against the worst of her pain.

'We know, Mrs Banks,' I say. 'Have you been in touch with the hospital to find out the latest news?'

'I'll get...' she searches for the name of her neighbour, '...Tom from next door to phone for me.' She wipes at her eyes as if trying to improve her vision. 'It's all so confusing. All that medical speak.'

Alessandra tells her what we know.

'Oh,' Jennie Banks says. 'Right.' She looks out of the window. 'Funny that, eh? Another head injury. Like father, like daughter.' Her bottom lip trembles for a moment. Then stops. It's like she's gone to the well to find there are no more tears.

'We're really sorry to bother you again, Mrs Banks. We just wanted to run through the events of that night again.'

'I don't...' She shakes her head so slow it's as if she's on a different clock than us. 'Aileen went out with her pal. Just like she'd done a hundred times before.'

'She didn't say where she was going? Who she hoped to meet? There were no new friends in her life that you were aware of?' Ale asks in the most apologetic tone she can muster. And as she speaks, Jennie Banks's head maintains the same slow movement from side to side.

'Aileen was a secretive wee madam. Even kept changing her Facebook name so I couldn't find what she was up to.'

'And you and Mr Banks stayed in that night?'

'Barely have a social life. Been married too long.' A small snort is as close to laughter as she can manage. 'I went to bed at my usual, just after ten. Kevin stays up late when Aileen is out. Says he can't sleep till he knows she's home and...' she stumbles over the word, '...safe.' She crosses her legs. 'One thing you can take to the bank. That man truly cares for his daughter.'

From the way she trails off after saying this, I can't help but read she doubts that the same level of care ever extended to her.

Ale stands up, signalling an end to the questions. She looks at me as if to say, enough, the poor woman can't take any more.

'Mind if I use your...' Ale asks.

'It's at the top of the stairs.'

* * *

Back in the car. Before Ale drives off she turns to me.

'Well?'

'Seems Mr Banks still has his alibi,' I answer.

'Interesting though.' She stares out of the window with an enigmatic smile.

'Go on, spill,' I say.

'I didn't need to go wee-wee,' she says, and the smile is now a full-blown grin. 'I was checking. Mrs Banks has a well-stocked drug cabinet up there.'

'Aye?'

'She's got some heavy-duty stuff. And the thing is, the date on her pills is for a few months ago. She was prescribed this stuff yonks ago. She's on 500mg for Christ's sake. Something was not well in her world before this happened. Kevin Banks could have had a brass band playing in there and she wouldn't have had a clue.'

'So, he could have gone out and she would have been none the wiser.'

We both say at the same time, 'The nosy neighbour.'

* * *

Tom Sharp is all but wringing his hands with excitement at the thought he might be able to help us. He offers to make us a cup of tea. We refuse, saying we don't have time to come in. Last time we saw him, I remember thinking this guy could talk for Scotland.

'You want to run through the events of that night again? Aye?'

'Please,' I say. 'We'll get you down to the office to make a formal statement in due course, but we just wanted to check a couple of things first.'

'Sure, sure.' He nods and runs through his original story. Dwelling on Aileen's pal, Karen with the big boobies, for so long that I feel the urge to slap him out of it.

'So, you're having your toasted bagel with banana,' I'm impressed by my own power of recall. 'Aileen comes down the drive. Gets in the car and off they go.'

'Sure, sure.'

'Anything happen after that?'

'You guys want a nice cuppa tea?' he asks again.

'No thanks, Mr Sharp,' I answer. 'We have a lot to get through today.'

'Any more comings and goings from the Banks' house?' asks Ale.

He shakes his head. 'I closed the curtains and put on the telly. If I remember right it was NCIS I was watching. Good stuff that. Keeps the old grey matter tuned in, you know. Must be right smart people coming up with all those stories. There was one...'

'And what time did you go to bed that night?' I interrupt before we get a blow by blow account of the entire series.

'Same time as every other night. 10:30. A fella needs his routine, you know.'

'And you heard nothing more from the Banks?'

He cocks his head back. Thinks. Shakes his head. 'Nope. Not until the next morning at least. Soon as my head hits the pillow, I'm out. It's all about the routine. You young people could learn something about that from your elders. I expect you are up and out and about till all hours?'

'You don't know the half of it, Mr Sharp,' I say before he can continue, and take a step back from his door. 'Thanks for your time.'

'You're welcome, son.'

I take another step. Stop and turn back.

'One more thing. You said last time that about eighteen months ago you believed that Mr Banks was having an affair?'

'Aye.'

'Any more developments on that front recently?' asked Ale.

'I'm not exactly their confidante, hen. Who knows what's going on in a marriage, eh? What I do know is that the shouting might have stopped, but Jennie Banks still wasn't a happy woman. Always has that drawn look about her, you know? As if she's the camel and she's waiting for that one last straw to fall.'

29

We're back in the office. I'm staring at a dark computer screen and thinking I'll switch it on in a minute. Ale is looking at me as if I've got a ponytail growing out of one of my nostrils.

'What?' I demand.

'What was that all about?' she asks, and with a sharp movement of her head indicates Peters' desk.

'The man's a bawbag, Ale. The sooner we all accept that the better,' I answer, trying to dampen down my irritation at the man. As soon as we were back in the office, he was over checking if we had anything to add to the investigation. A perfectly reasonable thing to do, but coming from him, and in addition being a reminder of how I had fucked things up, I all but told him to go fuck himself.

'You'll get no argument from me on that score, Ray. But if you want to be kept on this case ... kept in the office and not forced to take leave ... you need to accept he's chief investigating officer and give him the details he needs to know.' She leans forward and pins me in my seat with a look.

'I know,' I say and exhale. 'Every time I see his ugly face I just want to take a cheese grater to it.'

'Take another deep breath, Ray,' Ale says. Smiles. 'Out with anger and in with love.'

'Fuck off, Rossi.'

We share a laugh, and I feel a little of the tension lift.

I push a button and my computer flares into life. My email inbox is a tad on the busy side. *You have 187 unread emails,* it tells me. I groan and scroll down the senders and headings. One jumps out at me and with a self-satisfied smile I aim my mouse and click. The satisfaction comes from the fact that the medical guys don't know that Peters has taken over the case and that this should have gone to him.

It's the post-mortem report, and I have to read it several times before I can make any sense of the medical speak. It seems that poor Aileen Banks suffered from an extradural haemorrhage caused by a ruptured middle meningeal artery.

The forensics person has invited me to phone them if I have any questions. I dial their number.

'DI Ray McBain here,' I say when they answer. 'Thanks for your report...' I read the name on the email, 'Doctor Flannery.'

'You have questions?' she asks with a soothing lilt that has strains of the song 'Molly Malone' running through it.

'Yeah. If you could translate for this thick Jock, that would be grand.'

'Happy to, DI McBain.'

'Call me Ray.' And I want to keep this young woman talking. For hours if need be.

'Happy to, Ray...' She infuses my name with a smile that carries down the line. 'This is the file for Aileen Banks, yes? Extradural haemorrhage or EDH is most often due to a fractured temporal or parietal bone damaging the middle meningeal artery or vein, with blood collecting between the dura and the skull.' Before I can interrupt, she adds quickly, 'It is typically caused by trauma to the temple just beside the eye.'

'Right,' I say.

'Remember that young Aussie cricketer who died last year?'

'You're speaking to a Scotsman and you're referencing a cricket incident?' I say, but a TV news report flashes up from my memory. A fast ball to the temple and in a terrible accident a young man dies playing the sport he loves.

'Sorry,' she laughs.

'No worries,' I say. 'I have a faint memory of some poor kid getting hit on the head and dying a couple of days later.'

'Well, this is the same kind of injury. But in this instance death happened a good deal sooner. I would suggest within minutes, rather than days.'

With that pearl of information, my instinct to continue to flirt with Dr Flannery is completely curbed.

'And another thing you need to consider,' she says after a pause for thought, 'is that people who suffer this often have a lucid period straight after the injury. So your girl might not have suffered the injury where she was found.'

'So she could have been struck and moved, of her own volition, somewhere else where she deteriorated and died?'

'Yeah. This happened late in the evening? In the city centre?'

'Aye.'

'Someone could have seen her. Thought she was drunk and without realising that she was dying, left her to sober up.'

I shudder at this.

'Any way of telling if that's what happened here?'

'Sorry, no. I'm just giving you a hypothetical. She could have been struck and died on the spot, but in many of these injuries ... we reckon about a third ... the wounded is able to move and speak and all that before they deteriorate into death.'

I thank her and she rings off.

'And?' Ale is in my face.

I relay the information.

'Bloody hell,' she replies and shakes her head. 'Poor girl. The thought of her staggering about, dying and people thinking she's just pissed...'

We lapse into silence, each of us lost in our imaginings of the Aileen Banks's last moments. Guilt sours my mouth. If I hadn't been so lost in my own troubles we could have found the guy who did this.

'Don't go there, Ray,' says Ale.

'What are you...'

'I can tell what you're thinking. What's past is past. We're in a better place now. Thinking what might have been isn't going to help.'

'Sure, sure,' I reply in imitation of the nosy neighbour. Humour is my line of last defence as I deflect from how accurately Ale read me. But still...

I see her again. Beside the dumpster. Confused. Scared. Dying.

'We need to go and have another look at the CCTV pictures,' I say. Something is nagging at my mind. There's something obvious here that we're missing.

'DNA results in yet?'

'No.'

'You're chasing them, right?'

Ale gives me a look, as if to say, *don't push it, mate.* Then reaches for her mouse. Clicks a couple of times. Reads something from the screen and then punches a number into her desk phone. Speaks. Listens. Hangs up.

'There's a backlog.'

'There's always a fucking backlog.'

'Another couple of days is what they're saying.'

* * *

We've been sitting here for hours, and I'm wondering if your eyes can get repetitive strain injury. We're in CCTV central. Banks of screens and rows of seated viewers. How the hell can they keep their concentration, I wonder?

The staff were incredibly helpful. Probably relieved to get away from the tedium. They provided a desk and a screen and quickly linked in to the date and area of the city we were interested in.

I lean my head back, twist from side to side and hear the bones grind. I stretch my arms out to each side and groan.

'If this was TV they'd have seen something by now,' Ale says.

'Yeah, well, what can I say? Life disappoints.'

'And on that philosophical note...' Ale moves her eyes from mine to the screen in front of us. 'Jesus, the things you see when you've not got a gun.'

The street is empty apart from one man. He's walking strangely. Then he stops. Looks around to see if he has an audience. Then he reaches back between his cheeks and has an energetic scratch.

Clearly this isn't sufficient, because then he slips his hand under the waist band of his trousers and goes at it again. We can see the look of relief on his face and Ale giggles.

Just then a couple walks into view. Hand in hand. They exchange a look as they assess the antics of the young man. They are too far away from the camera for us to make out their features. But something about the woman has me on alert.

'That's Helen Davis,' I say and pause the action on the screen.

Ale leans forward. Peers. 'So it is.'

We both look at the man. And if my expression is a mirror image of Ale's, my mouth is hanging open.

'Oh my God,' we both say at exactly the same time.

30

'Tell me about your twin', Leonard types.

'Happy to. But this is about you', Simon replies.

'I'm still a bit shaky discussing this. I've never talked about it with anyone. It helps me to know that you understand how it feels. To have a twin. Are you identical?'

'Yes. Although, as we've grown older we're looking less and less alike.'

'How come?'

'He's into sports. I'm a desk jockey. Spend most of my time on the computer.'

'What sports is he into?'

'Rugby. Trains hard for it. Has a neck thicker than one of my thighs.'

'So, people won't ever mistake you for one another?'

'They used to. All the time. We had fun with it. But now it never happens, cos I'm so skinny. With a grey complexion. Did you and your twin get mixed up?'

'Constantly.'

'Tell me more.'

'The nuns put a sticking plaster on the back of our necks. With our names written on them. People used to have to turn us round to check who they were talking to.'

'Nuns?'

'It was an orphanage and old folks' home, run by an order of nuns.'

'Were they nice?'

There's a pause while Leonard counts out a minute.

'They were not.'

'I'm sorry.'

'What for? You weren't there.'

'If I hit a nerve.'

'I was trying to work out a way to answer. I went with honest and succinct.'

'Always a good combo I find. Back to you and your twin. Did you have fun with the whole identical thing?'

'No. We were too scared.'

'What do you mean?'

'Of being caught. The nuns were a bit too handy with their fists.'

'I'm sorry.'

'You need to stop apologising. What kind of things did you and your twin do?'

'It was mostly at school. One of us would misbehave and then we would blame each other until the teacher was dizzy with it. And we both got detention.'

'In my day it was The Belt.'

'Mum used to talk about that. Was it sore?'

'Depends on who was giving it to you. Some teachers used to make it their mission to cause suffering. Others hated it and would barely use the thing.'

'What was your twin's name?'

Leonard paused before answering. Counted out two minutes on the computer clock.

'John.'

'Sorry. That was clearly difficult for you.'

'You're going to have to stop saying sorry. Lol.'

Leonard hated the use of "lol", and even using it with a sense of irony made him want to hurt someone. But sometimes you had to use all of the tools at your disposal if you wanted to make a connection.

'Oops. Almost did it there again. Tell me about the orphanage.'

'We used to call it The Home. And it just occurred to me that there is a subtle but powerful distinction between calling it home and calling it The Home.'

'Yeah. I "hear" you. Did it feel like home?'

'Felt like a place where we were parked until the adults worked out what to do with us. The word "home" has connotations of safety, love and comfort. The Home had little of any of those three words. What kind of home did you and your brother have?

Dad died when we were young. Army. Afghanistan. Mum was amazing. And tough on us. Didn't let us away with anything.'

'Good for her. Did you miss having a positive male influence in your life? Boys do need their dads.'

'You don't think about those things as a kid. You just get on with it. As long as there was food on the table, cartoons on TV and a decent internet connection, I was sorted. What helped you get through your time in the home?'

Leonard considers typing the truth for a moment. Helping a group of friends, including an almost famous police detective, murder an old man we thought was terrorising us. He grins at the thought of the impact this might have. Goes for...

'Comics. I loved Superman and Batman and all those guys. Perfect escapism for a lonely wee boy.'

Which is of course a lie. Why would you want to help people? Unless it was for your own brutal ends.

'Do you miss your twin?'

'Every day.'

'What's your abiding memory of him?'

He pauses. Knows the boy is really looking for something pleasant. Considers the truth. And nods to himself.

'He wet the bed pretty much every night. The usual cure was to be woken up at 5am and dumped in a bath of cold water. This morning his "carer" decided that he should learn a lesson and she stripped his pyjamas from him, wrapped him up in his piss-sodden sheets and left him there for hours while the rest of us went to morning mass and had breakfast. He was suffering from bronchitis at the time. It developed into pneumonia and he died.'

'Man, that's awful.'

'Yup.'

'How did you feel?'

Leonard stops. That's enough, he thinks. If the boy wants more, he's going to have to earn it.

'I've said enough. There are some places I can't quite go yet. At least not remotely like this.'

'That's a shame. It feels like we're making some kind of break-through here. Please go on.'

Leonard can almost see the desperation to help. This boy really is a Samaritan.

'Can't. Just can't.'

'What would it take?'

'In person? I could maybe open up in person.'

'Can't do that. Not part of the deal.'

'Please? I really do feel we would get somewhere if we were face to face.'

'Sorry.'

He takes a gamble.

'I live in central Scotland. We could meet up in, say, Glasgow?'

'It's really not allowed.'

Leonard counts out two minutes. It feels like such a long time while online, even to him. Then…

'Please?'

There's a pause for about forty-five seconds while the boy debates. Then two letters appear.

'ok'.

31

'Bless me Father, for I have sinned. It has been a few days since my last confession,' I blurt out, like the words are scalding me.

'Would you rather go into the actual confessional box for this?' the young priest asks. We're sitting side by side on one of the pews.

I shake my head.

'Thanks for opening up for me at this time of the...' I try to assess the weak light coming in through the high windows of the church and settle for '...morning.' I haven't managed to look him in the eye yet, embarrassed that I'm here. But the space around us is having the effect I hoped it might. The air is cool and filled with the scent of old wood and incense, and the air around me echoes with the easing of sin.

'Your need was urgent. Judging by the energy you were putting in to knocking the door.' His tone is chiding, but his expression is soft with a heavy-eyed smile.

'Sorry,' I say and look up at him. His eyes are thick with sleep, his hair dishevelled and his breath wears a hint of smoke, peat and the isles. This note of whisky makes him seem more human, and I offer a weak smile of acknowledgement. 'And thanks.'

'We do suffer the odd piece of vandalism here, so there's a wee CCTV camera above the door. I saw it was you and came down.'

I suddenly feel cold and cross my arms. 'Thanks,' I repeat, and I'm aware of his scrutiny. Empathy is cast in the shape of his eyes and the slump of his shoulders. I want to punch him. I want him to hug me and tell me everything will be alright.

'What's going on, DI McBain?'

'You know me?'

'I recognised you last time. You were on TV talking about a big case.'

'Call me Ray.'

'What's going on, Ray?'

I look up. Meet his eyes, open my mouth and the words are trapped down the swell of my throat along with every anxious moment.

'Take a breath,' he says. 'We've got all...' his turn to look at the windows. '...morning.' I hear the humour in his tone and manage a laugh. To my ears it sounds like a grunt.

'I'm OK when I'm at work. Or, I should say, I'm almost OK at work. But when I'm home ... the TV, a wee cuddle with the girl-friend distracts for a wee while, but when the world's asleep...'

'You're alone with your thoughts and a tuned-up imagination?'

'Something like that,' I answer and think of Maggie curled up on her side, facing away from me and knowing that she's awake and worried as I go through the pantomime of silently dressing and leaving the house. But that's preferable to the roar of my pulse in my ear and the silent scream locked into the muscles of my jaw.

'Do you have any support available from your employers?'

'I had a good day today.' I look at him. 'So why was I so...' I can't find the right words. 'I had to get out of the house. If my girlfriend had said anything to me I think I would have exploded.' I feel the shame of that last sentence burn and hang my head.

'It's a pity that the ones we love often get the worst of us,' the priest acknowledges. 'Tell me why was today such a good day at work?'

'This is under the confessional seal, right?'

'Aye.'

'We saw CCTV footage from the night Aileen Banks died. Her boyfriend's mother was out on the town. Walking along the street just yards from where her body was found.'

'Right.' There's a note of interest from the priest.

'But that's not all. She was with someone. A man.' I know he's not going to say anything to anyone, but I can't bring myself to say his name.

166

He recognises this and asks, 'And that feeling of having achieved something didn't last when you got home?'

I shake my head. 'I have no control. There's no rhyme or reason. Everything feels fine. Until it isn't.'

We sit in silence. The shout of pulse in my ear has receded, and my breathing is slow and measured. I follow the in breath with my mind, acknowledge the rise of my chest. Being mindful is the new treatment they say. But how to be mindful when the black dog charges, full of teeth and wrath.

I manage a smile. 'The irony isn't lost on me,' I say.

He cocks his head to the side by way of a request for an explanation.

'The church has been the cause of most of my problems, and yet I seek refuge in a church.'

'Why do you think that is?'

'Fucked if I know.'

'That's a cop-out, Ray,' he says kindly.

'You know, I watch the odd thing on the TV on a Sunday morning. Listen to people say how Jesus helped them get over their addiction or other problems, and I shout at the telly. Tell them to fuck off. Jesus had nothing to do with it. It was you. You did it. Take responsibility for your problems and acknowledge the resilience you found to overcome them.'

'Why is that important to you?'

'I can understand the temptation to hand it all over to someone else. Some*thing* else. But ultimately we're on our own.'

He pauses for a beat. 'Interesting word that. Resilience.'

I nod and look him in the eye properly for the first time. 'Yeah, and right now it feels like it's completely beyond me.'

32

From the hush of the church to the confessional space of a car. I'm sitting in the passenger seat. Alessandra Rossi has just pulled on the handbrake.

'You awright, Ray?'

'Aye.'

She says nothing.

'I've been better,' I fill in the silence she leaves.

'You look like shit. Did you sleep last night?'

I hold my hand up. Thumb and index finger almost touching. 'Today is another day, DC Rossi.' I muster the energy from somewhere. Consider the word, resilience. Let the sense of it work through my muscles. Pray that something takes hold.

I look at the house we're sitting outside of. 'Let's do this.'

We walk up the path, and the door opens before we can reach to knock.

'The boys aren't in,' says Helen Davis. The way she's holding the door open reminds me of Jennie Banks, though Helen looks less haunted by events. She's wearing a pair of grey trousers and a long, grey cardigan. A cream blouse and a warm pink patterned scarf finishes off the look. Very Marks & Spencer. I'm getting the impression she doesn't do joggers and t-shirts.

'Can we come in?' asks Ale.

Helen pushes the door fully open and walks through the hallway and into her living room without a word. We follow.

'Any more threats being posted?' Ale asks, the concern in her tone real.

'Not through the letter box,' Helen answers as she takes her seat. She crosses her legs. Places both hands on her lap. Keeping everything contained.

'Oh?'

'Simon doesn't go online much these days.' Worry for her son is etched into every line. 'Some of the stuff people leave on there is utterly vile.'

'Have you reported it?' I ask.

She answers with a shrug. 'What's the point? Most of these people are hiding behind fake accounts. Silence one and another two would spring up in its place.' She smiles. 'Even I opened a fake account. Don't worry, I'm not about to go trolling. I just wanted to keep tabs on what Simon was having to put up with.'

She fidgets with a strand of hair at her neck, twisting it between her index and middle fingers. 'At first he refused to let these eejits stop him going into these sites. Why should he allow a bunch of cowards to dictate how he spends his time, is his view. Used to spend half his life doing all that online social stuff. Still does all his online counselling stuff. It's something about twins these days.' She shakes her head, her eyes leaking love and concern.

'Anyway.' She crosses her arms and focuses on Ale. 'What's going on? Why do you want to speak to me?'

'It's about Kevin Banks,' answers Ale.

'Terrible thing that. I heard it on the news. Whatever possessed him? Grief makes us act in strange ways, eh?' She switches position. Left leg over right, as if bracing herself for wherever this conversation is going next.

'When did you last see him?' I ask.

'Why do you want to know that?' she asks, and I recognise the delay tactic. Everything that has come out of her mouth since we walked in the door has been part of that strategy. Interesting. Feels to me that at some level she's worried we know something. She leans forward and looks from me to focus on Ale as if seeking an ally.

'As you say, he's acting in grief,' I reply. 'But we want to get a clearer idea what's going on in his head, and his wife's not in a fit state to answer our questions.'

'I had a boyfriend when I was a teenager,' says Ale, aiming for solidarity. A shared experience. 'My parents and his parents used to meet all the time. Started off as a safety thing, you know? Make sure the boy that their daughter's in love with isn't from a family of nutters. Turned into a good friendship,' says Ale. She shakes her head fondly. 'They still go away for weekends together ... and I dumped him years ago.'

'That's nice,' says Helen with a smile as false as a plaster Madonna's tears. She's worried, and it's not just about her boys. There's a personal factor here. Ale and I then sit still and say nothing. First one to speak loses.

'I'm trying to remember the last time I saw Kevin. Must have been some university thing. An open day or something.' She's slowly moving her head from side to side as if trying to access the memory. 'Can't believe he would do that. The papers are saying he aimed for the bus rather than, you know, to pass it?'

We stay silent. Out of the side of my eyes I can see Ale nod in answer to the question. She's struggling to stifle her instinct to communicate.

'Terrible. Just terrible. The whole thing,' says Helen as she loosens her scarf and places it on the arm of her chair.

'You haven't spoken to him since Aileen died?' I ask.

'No. Don't think my family is at the top of his favourites right now.'

'And you haven't spoken to him since the last university ... thing?' Ale asks. 'Which was when, do you think?'

'Jeez, must've been...' Her expression falters and alters. She allows irritation to take over. Attack being the best form of defence. 'What is this? What the hell are you people doing here, and why are you asking me these questions?' She stands up. 'I want you to leave now.'

'Fine,' I say, and both Ale and I stand.

We follow her out of the room and down the hall. Just before she opens the front door, I do the Columbo thing.

'Just one last question...'

'What?'

As I turn to look at her, I see her features are beginning to relax with relief. They tighten again, like a boxer might hold up his gloves to fend off a blow.

'The night Aileen died...?'

'I was here. Early bed, cos I had work the next day. Working on a Saturday, eh?' She aims for a lightness in tone and fails. 'Should be illegal.'

'Then why are you on CCTV walking up Renfrew Street, hand in hand with Kevin Banks?'

33

Helen stares at me. Her face pales and her neck sparks with deep, pink Rorschach blots. I wonder if she could read them what she might see.

She stands with one hand reaching for the door handle. The other strays to the heat on her neck, and her thumb rubs there as if trying to erase them. The mouth might obey our brain, but the body often betrays.

'I'm not a bad person,' she says. 'And Kevin would be an easy man to fall in love with.' Tears brighten the dull ache of regret in her eyes.

Would be. She's not quite there yet then.

'We're not here to judge you, Helen,' I say. 'We want to find out as much as we can about the night Aileen died.' I think about her situation. Devotes her life to her two boys after her husband dies in service overseas. Can't have been easy.

'How long have you been having an affair with him?'

'We didn't start until Aileen and Simon fell out,' she asserts, as if in her mind this mitigates having an affair with a married man.

'As DI McBain says, we're not here to judge you,' Ale says. 'The why and how don't matter. We just want the facts.'

'We met in a supermarket would you believe...' Helen carries on speaking as if keen to unburden her conscience. 'The one that Aileen works ... worked in. Hadn't seen him for ages. I'd forgotten what a charming man he was. Always made me smile. Made me feel better about myself, you know? And I always wondered what he saw in that stuffy cow.' She looks down at the carpet. 'God. Poor woman. What must she be going through...'

I see again the images from the CCTV feed. The way he held out his hand. The way she accepted. A small skip in her step while she reached up with her other hand to fix her hair. There was a fresh-ness about their body language. Initial attraction evolving towards something deeper.

'I've been thinking about him running in front of that bus. Must be guilt. Can't deal with the fact that while his daughter was dying, he was out with me.' She bites the inside of her cheek. 'The good ones are all taken, eh?' It's like she's finally accepted that whatever she had with Kevin Banks, it can never survive this. She lifts up her chin, crosses her arms.

'Yes, we were having an affair. Yes, we were out that night. Anything else?'

With these words I get a glimpse of something else. A hardness. A shell she has grown to protect herself. To hide herself.

'The CCTV camera we saw you from was sited just round the corner from where Aileen's body was found. Did you see her at all that night?'

'No.'

'One thing I've learned in this job is that there's no such thing as coincidence. Especially when it comes to murder. I'll ask you again, did either of you see Aileen Banks that night.'

'No.'

'What kind of relationship did you have with Aileen?' asks Ale.

'She was my son's girlfriend. What kind of relationship do you think we had? She was in and out of my house. She made my son happy. That was enough for me.'

'Until she didn't make your son happy any longer...'

'Don't want to speak ill of the dead and all that, but she had the best of her father and the worst of her mother. Charm and humour to spare. Then a complete lack of self-awareness, flighty and spoiled. Used to drive me nuts. But it was up to Simon. He had to deal with it all himself. You learn quickly as a parent that often the opposite of what you advise is what happens. Once they get to a certain age, it's best to keep your opinions to yourself. Especially when it comes to girls.'

'Did you ever fight with Aileen?' I ask, and as the words fall from my mouth I'm questioning the instinct that has me pose the question. But a flash of memory has her slapping Matt just feet from where we are standing. Is she only that quick to strike with her sons?

There's something more at play here.

'What kind of...' Helen looks from me to Ale. 'You don't think I've got something to do with her death.' As she speaks she places a hand over her heart. I look up from there to her neck and can see that the blotches are back.

Ale fires me a look as if I've just taken a dump on the carpet.

'I've never heard anything so ridiculous,' she replies, all but spitting at me. 'Time you were leaving.'

Ale reaches for the door and pulls it open.

* * *

In the car she gives me that same look.

'Really, Ray?'

'What? Cos she's a woman she's not going to be violent?'

'You know that's not what I mean. Do you really think she's a suspect?'

'Stranger things have happened. CCTV puts her in the vicinity. She's known to the deceased. She's fiercely protective of her boys. Motive and opportunity, Ale.'

'What about the semen on the girl's top?'

'That was Bill Clinton.'

'Piss off,' she laughs.

'She goes outside with some poor sap. My money's on Simon. Gives him a knee-trembler. Meets Mommie Dearest on the way back into the pub, arm in arm with her old man. They have a fight. Bang.'

Ale looks out of the window, back at the house. Chases my theory through her mind. 'Nah. Not buying it. Kevin Banks isn't going to stand by and let her hurt his daughter. And Simon's denying he was there.'

She fires up the engine and drives off. A few minutes of silence as we each ruminate. Two families. Two mothers. One father. Two brothers. One friend.

One dead girl.

I'm certain that someone among her living connections knows the truth.

Without warning, I feel my breath shorten and my chest grow tight. I wipe my palms dry with a slow movement up and down my trouser leg, hoping that Ale doesn't notice. I lick my lips, the moisture welcome, and looking out of the car window at my side, I study a building in the distance. Realise it's the water tower at Cranhill and focus on it like a seasick traveller might hang on the thought of reaching dry land.

I silently send a prayer to the god of panic attacks. Not now, you bastard. Not while I'm at work. To distract myself I ask Ale a question.

'What about your story about your ex-boyfriend's parents going on holiday with your mum and dad?' I ask.

She shoots me a grin. 'Complete and utter pish.'

We both laugh, and for a few moments at least, the sound of it chases away the rising breath of the black dog.

34

Back at the office, and Ale and I are walking along the corridor on our way to DI Peters' office in order to update him on our activities.

'Do we have to?' I ask.

'Get over yourself, McBain,' answers Ale. 'He's the chief investigating officer now. Deal with it.' She softens her comment with a smile and a weak punch to my shoulder.

'Is that your version of tough love?'

'Aye.'

'If he wasn't such a prick.'

'Ray...'

'Or a dick...'

'Ray...'

'I mean, his version of living dangerously is going in to Tesco with a Sainsbury-branded plastic bag, for fuck's sake.'

'True. But is any part of that you learning to deal with it?'

We're walking along the corridor towards the office. A door opens. Peters walks out of it and almost collides with us.

'Talk of the devil,' I say. 'We're just coming to report in.' *And it's costing me about ten years of my life*, I want to say.

'Right,' he says and looks from me to Ale.

Ale fills him in, and he stands there with his arms crossed as if trying to look more imposing. Might work too if his arms weren't as thin as the flex feeding a laptop.

'Right. Right,' he says. 'Any word back from the hospital yet?'

'Far as we're aware, Banks is still in a coma.'

'And the DNA sample?'

'Still waiting,' Ale answers.

'Bloody hell. How long does it take these people?

'That'll be the cutbacks,' I say.

'Convenient excuse,' he answers. 'Chase them up, Ale.' He looks at me. His eyes meeting mine for little more than a second. 'Ray,' he says by way of acknowledgement. Then his eyes stray down my neck and chest. 'Have you got a nicer tie than that?'

'Whit?'

'Press briefing in twenty minutes. The boss wants you to front it.'

'I hate doing those fucking things.'

'We've all got our cross to bear, Ray,' he says, his eyes saying that I am his. Without another word he turns and walks away.

'Missing you already,' I say.

'Ray,' Ale scolds while choking on a laugh.

'What a fud.'

'Love that word,' says Ale.

'It's not on the same word embargo as…'

'Nope. Brings up warm memories of wet Saturday mornings and Bugs Bunny cartoons.'

'Some consistency would be nice, DC Rossi.'

'Where's the fun in that? Got to keep you old men on your toes.'

'I'll "old man" you.'

Ale picks her phone out of her pocket. Checks the time.

'Didn't realise it was that late.'

'Jeez, do you young people not use watches anymore? And what's for dinner tonight? Pot noodle and EastEnders?'

'Something like that,' she smiles. 'Care to join me?' And I read a note of loneliness. But I decline. I'm not even good company for myself these days.

'Nah. As much as that combination appeals, Maggie will be expecting me.'

'Oh,' Ale nods. Crosses her arms, leans against the wall. She's expecting a story from me then. 'Things still going strong then?'

I see the light dance in her eyes and feel a surge of affection. She's happy for me, and I can't remember the last time I observed that reaction in anyone. Want to give her a hug, but that might not be appropriate. I settle for reaching out and touching her arm.

'Pot noodle,' I say. 'Yum.'

After the press briefing, in which I manage to use many words without saying anything of real value, I make my way to my car. My tie is unknotted and in my pocket before I leave the building.

I'll give you "nicer tie", you prick.

My phone pings. It's Maggie. If I'm coming over, she's asking me to bring some bread, cold ham and salad stuff. Tomatoes and the like. If not, she'll make do.

I drive to hers. Realise when I'm sitting outside her building that not only do I have no recollection of the twenty-minute journey, I haven't stopped at the shop for the food.

Should I go upstairs?

I don't articulate an answer. Instead I reignite the engine. Driving off, I throw a glance over my shoulder. See a pale face at her third floor window and feel a stab of guilt.

* * *

As I reverse park into a space just feet from my front door, I see a man standing there. He's holding a small, white plastic bag.

He holds it up and waves it in my face when I draw near. I smell spices.

'You'll have had your tea?' he grins.

'Kenny.' I give him a look, which judging by his answer, he correctly translates as, *what the fuck are you doing here.*

'Maggie called. Said you'd be needing some food. Said you were fading away to a mountain.' He looks at my gut.

'Fine,' I reply. Don't have the energy to tell him to piss off.

I unlock the door. We walk inside. Kenny makes for the kitchen and starts to plate up. I go to the toilet. Aim a weak string of piss at the bowl. Didn't really need to go. This is more of a delay tactic.

'Hope you washed your hands,' Kenny says as I accept a heaped plate of food from him when I walk back into the kitchen.

'Nah,' I say. 'Didn't even get my fingers wet.'

'Clatty bastard,' says Kenny. He's the kind of guy who washes his hands before and after he goes for a pee.

'Couldn't help but notice, Ray…' Kenny speaks with a mouthful of half-chewed chicken, '…there's barely any food in your cupboards.'

'Yeah, cos if I buy it, I eat it.'

'Is that not the idea?'

'Yeah, but I buy the bad stuff. The "go straight to my artery and clog it" variety.'

'So you starve?'

'Does it look like I'm starving?' I pat my gut.

'Instead of bad choices at the supermarket, you're then making bad choices at the carry-out place?'

'There's a kind of logic in there somewhere,' I grin.

He gives me a look, shakes his head and shovels in another mouthful. 'Fucking eejit.'

We eat in silence. I eat much more than he does, his body being a temple and all that. I use the last piece of naan bread to wipe up the last streak of sauce. Chew until it's gone. Lean back in my seat and belch. One thing about me, doesn't matter what kind of mental state I'm in, hand me a plate of food and I'll hoover up the lot.

Leaning back, I think about Maggie. Her strained face at the window. She knows me better than I know myself. Knows exactly what is going on in my head, but I wonder if knowing makes it easier to accept without being wounded by my actions. It takes a special kind of person to set aside their own needs in that situation.

Maggie is that kind of special. My chest tightens with equal parts love and guilt. I should be better, I know it, but there are times I only have room in my head for the snarl of my own thoughts

'Maggie sent you?'

'Not "sent" so much as suggested I pop over.'

'Right.'

'You're not going to self-harm are you, Ray?'

'Fuck off.'

'Want me to go?' he asks. There's no side to the question, just a request for honesty. If I want him gone, he'll leave. But the evening stretches ahead of me, and it's too quiet, too long, and my heart beats a leaden pulse at the thought.

'You're here now,' I concede less than graciously.

'You're welcome for dinner by the way.'

'And I was all set for a baguette, cheese and ham. With salad.'

'Ooo, salad. Get you.' His expression shifts. Softens. 'Maggie phoned an hour ago. Only takes twenty minutes from hers to yours.'

'She saw me then?'

'Aye.'

I sighed. 'I'm not fit company.' And the words *I don't deserve her* sit heavy on my heart.

'Don't worry about it. Sometimes I think Maggie knows you better than you know yourself.'

'Wouldn't be difficult. Self-knowledge isn't exactly my strong point.'

He says nothing in response. Sits back in his chair, waiting for me to speak.

'I went to church last night.'

'Did you say a prayer for me?'

'You're beyond redemption, mate. And not everything is about you, by the way.'

'It's not?' He grins. 'I'm the centre of my universe. Thought it was the same for everyone else.' He pauses. Adopts his serious face. 'So, what's eating your gusset?' Typically Kenny. No hanging about.

'You should go into counselling. Make a fortune.'

'Nah,' he replies. 'I find shouting "pull yourself together" at people isn't really that effective.' He leans forward, elbows resting on his thighs. 'So. The church?'

I look out of the window behind him, at an unfathomable sky clothed in a palette of dark grey. Fatigue pulls at my eyelids. Not sure if it's the feeling of satiety from the food or a feeling of safety from Kenny's reassuring, non-judgemental presence.

'Not in the mood for talking, Kenny. D'you mind?' I allow my head to fall back onto the cushion and stare at the stipple on the ceiling.

'Fine by me,' says Kenny. 'There's only so much of your shite I can stomach anyway.' I hear the smile in his voice and feel myself respond. Want to offer a *fuck you* in response, but I don't have the energy.

* * *

It's dark when I'm woken by a pressing need to go to the toilet. I'm in there for a good five minutes, and when I come out I hear Kenny ask, 'I take it the loo's a no-go zone for the next hour?'

'Still here?' I go back to my seat and see from the weak light coming in from the street that he's stretched out on the other sofa. Judging by the touch of light in the sky, it's early morning. About five-ish.

'It's a mirage,' he says, his voice thick with sleep. 'The real Kenny is actually spooning into the back of his favourite working girl, hoping she's ready for another session.'

I smile into the gloom of the room. And realise that this has been the longest unbroken sleep I've had for a long time. I want to thank him, but he'd only tell me to piss off.

Instead. 'Coffee?' I ask.

'Have you got any in those barren cupboards?'

'There's no calories in coffee, so I trust myself with that.'

'Milk?'

I snort in reply. 'If there is any it's bound to be halfway to cheese by now.'

'Black coffee it is then,' he says.

I go to my bedroom, take off my shirt and suit-trousers and put on a t-shirt and a pair of joggers that are lying at the side of the bed. Then I walk to the kitchen and set us both up with a coffee.

The light has grown by the time I get back into the living room, and there's enough to see that Kenny doesn't even have the decency to look like he's slept on a couch. Looks like he's just come out of make-up at the film studio.

'Prick,' I say as I offer him the coffee.

'Wanker,' is his reply.

I sit. We sip.

First light is my favourite time of the day. Dreams fostered by the dark no longer have the power to wound, and the damaged and the deranged are still asleep. The day stretches ahead with a hint of possibility unthreatened by reality.

I put my empty cup on the low glass table in front of me and lean forward, my elbows on my knees. The thumb of my left hand finds the inside of my right wrist and caresses the embossed edge of my scar. My permanent reminder of Leonard's hate for me. I survived while his twin brother didn't, and for that sin he wants to rub me out.

After the attack, I used to wipe at it for hours, as if to erase it, but instead it bled. Now I've learned to control that urge.

I can feel Kenny's eyes on me. My scars.

'I could've died.'

'I know,' he replies. 'I love this time of day,' he says, changing the direction of the conversation. We both know I'm grateful, and Kenny has no need to hear it expressed again. 'If I had my gear with me I'd be off for a run.'

'If I could be arsed, I'd join you.'

'I'm curious,' Kenny says, his head cocked to the side. 'You mentioned the church last night. What's that all about?'

'I know. Not sure I understand it myself. It's like that poem about parents fucking you up. 'Cept with me, they were aided and abetted by organised religion.' It wouldn't need an expert to draw causal link from my childhood, the Catholic Church and my present issues. And yet, the draw of the familiar, the cool echo of the building and the young priest's eagerness to help overcame all of that.

'What do you think sparked this latest episode off?' Kenny asks.

'McCall dying.'

'Yeah?'

'It was too easy to go with the official verdict, let him take the blame and allow Leonard to escape.' As I mention his name, that final tableau rears up in my mind. Mother Superior lying at the foot of the altar with her throat cut. I'm fighting to move a muscle, any muscle, not knowing that Leonard has injected me with something. His face entering my vision, all leer and hunger as he draws a knife across my wrists. His plan was to kill the nun, avenge his brother and lay the blame on me. In his narrative, I then cut my own wrists.

All of this was ruined by the timely arrival of Kenny O'Neill. He completely missed Leonard and huckled Joseph McCall to the floor while he waited for the police.

'Would you recognise Leonard if you saw him?' I ask.

He shakes his head. 'I saw you in a daze, lying in a pool of your own blood. McCall was the only living, breathing person in that wee chapel. Leonard was long gone.'

I shiver.

'What are you going to do?' Kenny asks.

'He's the bogeyman. Can't have that. I've dealt with enough disturbed people to know that they're only scary if you invest them with that quality.'

'Any ideas where he might have gone?'

'We find a Catholic organisation that has recently taken on a handyman.'

'Easy as that?' Kenny gives me his sceptical look.

I think of how at my recent moment of crisis, my automatic movement has been back to the familiar and nod.

'It's what he knows.'

'I've got a guy,' Kenny says. 'Does "research" for me. I'll get him on the case.' Pause. 'How can I narrow it down for him, Mr Detective?'

'He vanished that night. The only sight of him has been via a couple of postcards. Nice Scottish scenes. All that was missing was a tin of shortbread.'

'So, he's stayed in the country.'

'Aye, and he thinks I'm public enemy number one, so he won't have gone that far. Not Glasgow, but only an hour or two away.' I think of the postcard. 'Somewhere to the north.'

He was on a handyman's wage. Can't have much cash, surely. He'd need a job quickly, and a job like that at a local church could well come with a bedsit type of arrangement. Leonard would know exactly how to worm himself into that kind of situation.

'Tell your man to check job adverts in local newspapers being published north of Glasgow. Might as well go as far as Inverness. Jack of all trades kind of thing.'

'What will you do when we find him?'

Not if. When. Kenny is confident in his guy, and this confidence causes a vibration deep in my mind. I think of the blade, cold on my skin. The desire in Leonard's face. And despite myself I shiver. This man will not control me any longer. I cross my arms, as if trying to preserve heat, to steel myself against a small boy's fear.

'Have you ever killed anyone, Kenny?'

35

They arranged to meet in a public place. Leonard suggested a bookstore with a cafe. Waterstones – Argyle Street branch. He arrived a good thirty minutes early. Slowly walked through each of the three floors. Pretended to look at the stacks of brightly coloured books.

He'd only ever bought one book: the Bible. White leather cover with gold embossed lettering.

He heard a member of staff in conversation with a punter.

'It has a red cover,' the would-be customer began. 'It's called *The Girl with* something or other. My book club were reading it. They all said it was great. Sorry, I can't remember the full title.'

The bookseller went through a list of titles all beginning with *The Girl*. The customer shook her head at each of them. Shaking his head, Leonard walked away. He thought people using these kind of places would be smarter.

On the first floor, he turned left at the top of the stairs and walked through the coffee shop. Took in the glass-fronted cooler and the selection of cakes.

'Help you?' asked the barista, as if he did actually want to help.

Leonard shook his head and walked past the counter. He scanned the other customers. Not one of them was reading a book. Why come into a bookstore coffee shop and not cop a free read of some of their books?

He walked in a large circle, past cookery, poetry, kids and fantasy, before arriving back at the top of the stairs. There was a chair by the window. From there he could see everyone coming and going. He could study the boy as he arrived.

Seated, he plucked his phone from his pocket and checked the internet connection. It was strong. He connected and opened his emails. Nothing. They'd agreed the boy would email if he was held up.

He looked at the time. Five minutes to go.

He picked a book from the table to his right. Opened it to the first page and pretended to read. Someone walked past. A girl. Then an old couple. Then a couple of booksellers.

Then, right on time, Simon arrived.

He could tell it was him from the way he scanned the people around him. Searching for a look of connection, possible recognition. Leonard kept his expression neutral and allowed the boy's eyes to skim past.

Simon was taller than he expected. Broad across the shoulders with long lean legs. There was a softness in his gut and in the line of his chin, suggesting little exercise and long hours at the keyboard. An untucked red and blue check shirt, jeans and a three-day growth completed the look.

The boy approached the counter, which took him out of Leonard's line of sight, so he moved, took a few steps forward and pretended to study the books piled high by the side of the chiller cabinet.

Simon ordered a can of Irn Bru. Collected his drink and took a seat.

Leonard approached the counter. Ordered a black coffee and sat one over and watched as the boy studied every person that entered the space.

His own drink arrived, and he gave a nod of thanks to the server. He hated coffee, but it was part of his disguise. He lifted the cup and pressed the lid to his lower lip and pretended to sip.

After ten minutes of watching the boy eagerly looking at everyone who comes in, he pulled out his phone and thumbed out an email.

Can't make it. Can't do this. Sorry. And he pressed send.

He heard the boy's phone sound a warning. Watched as he pulled the phone out of his pocket and read. Saw the look of disappointment on his face and allowed a smile to tug at the corners of his mouth.

The boy stood. Pocketed his phone. Took a last, long pull at his can and walked away.

Leonard followed close behind, thinking, *at last, the hunt is on.*

36

Kenny's certainty in his guy is justified, and a couple of hours later we're headed up to Perth in Kenny's Range Rover.

'What happened to the BMW?' I ask.

'All the best crims are in four-wheel drives these days.'

'Crims and yummy mummies. How can we tell you all apart?'

'The tattoos and the cauliflower ears,' Kenny says with a grin.

'I'm guessing a few not-so-yummy mummies could challenge that assertion.'

My phone pings. It's a text from Alessandra.

'Hey bossman. You up for kickin some arse today?' She's checking up on me. Doesn't normally text at this time in the morning. I must have looked particularly shitty yesterday.

'Sorry Ale. Got a lead on Leonard'

'Where you going? Want me to tag along?'

'Best you don't know.' The boss wants me to forget all about Leonard and McCall, and he'll be furious when he finds out I've got my own investigation going on. I need to protect Alessandra from that.

'Just so our stories are straight. What will I say to Peters?'

'Tell him no amount of playing the big man will make up for having a micro penis'

'Ray!!!'

'I'm owed some time off. Tell him I'm using it to get some root canal treatment. The prick will enjoy the thought of me in pain so much he won't ask any more questions'

'True dat' A pause. Then, 'Don't do anything completely stupid'

'Not sure I can promise anything'

I pocket my phone and look out of the window. We're now well out of the city and almost at Stirling. The castle comes into view on my right. And beyond it, the gothic tower in commemoration of William Wallace stands out in bas relief against the Ochil Hills. I have a vague memory of an outing here organised by the nuns. I must have been about nine or ten. After a severe march up the hill, all the boys were gap-mouthed at the size of Wallace's sword housed inside. But now I can't see it without thinking of the shit movie Mel Gibson made about the man himself.

'FreeDOM!' I shout.

'Fuck!' says Kenny. 'Nearly gave me a heart attack there, you prick.'

'Serves you right for driving so fast. There's a speed limit, you know.'

'That's alright. I've got a pig in my car.'

'Won't save you, mate. Traffic cops love doing other cops.'

* * *

Before long, Kenny is pulling up outside the church. The gable end of the grand building backs up right onto the street. A wide stretch of sandstone and a tall stained-glass window. Just to offset the apostolic grandeur, Perth and Kinross council have thought-fully placed a large black bin and a small green electric box just underneath the window.

There's a house to the side that shares a drive. It has a low wall with tall railings in front. A patch of freshly turned earth fills the space up to the front door. This area is home to a bed of severely pruned rose bushes. Dozens of them. Must be quite a sight in the height of the season.

I turn to Kenny. Say, 'Stay.' And exit the car.

I crunch up the gravel pathway, but before I can knock, the door opens.

'Yes?' a small woman asks. She barely hits five feet tall and is as thin as a church candle. Her long, white hair is pulled back to perch on the top of her head in a bun. Adds a couple of inches to her height.

'DI Ray McBain,' I say while pulling my warrant card out of my wallet. 'I wonder if I might speak to Father...' I leave a gap in the hope she might complete the name.

'Father Stephen is at his breakfast.' She pulls herself up to her full height. 'He can't be disturbed.'

I hear footsteps and a man in black appears at her elbow. He's chewing.

'It's alright, Martha,' he says. He wipes his mouth with one hand and puts the other on her shoulder. 'I have time for the officer.'

'But you need to eat properly, Father,' she stretches her neck back to look up at him. Her expression softens, becomes motherly, which strikes me as a little odd when it occurs to me that they are fairly equal in the wrinkle department.

Then I revise my opinion when I remember the reverence with which the nuns treated visiting priests in the convent. Not odd at all.

Father Stephen smiles benignly at Martha and guides me into a sitting room that looks like it was furnished in the eighties. Floral print sofas with wooden arms and feet and a thick shag-pile carpet. I half expect a framed Duran Duran album cover to be on the wall above the mantelpiece. But of course, that prideful place is taken with a crucifix.

Father Stephen motions that I should sit and folds himself into a chair. He picks at his teeth. 'Martha and her bran cereal will be the death of me,' he smiles. 'There's not enough time in the day to chew that stuff.'

'I prefer a bacon roll myself, father.'

'Now you're talking, young man. But Martha is worried my arteries will clog and I'll be kicking up the roses before you can ask if I want red sauce or brown.'

'Has to be brown sauce for me.'

'Me too,' he laughs. A sound that is hearty and without nuance. This is a man who strikes me as having no sides. One face fits all. What you see is all there is and ever will be. Amen.

'It's actually your new handyman that I wanted to speak to,

Father. Is he about?'

'Dave?' He cocks his head to the side. 'Actually, haven't seen hide nor head of him since yesterday morning.

Dave. So that's what he's calling himself.

'Is there something wrong?' he asks, his face shaped in concern. A concern that appears to be wholly about Dave's safety rather than any suspicion he might be involved in any wrongdoing.

'We just need some help with our enquiries, Father. Other than that I can't say too much.'

'Hang on.' He stands up. 'He has a room at the back of the house. I'll just go check...' He turns and walks out of the room. I follow. Don't want *Dave*, if he's there, to do a runner.

We come to a wooden door. Father Stephen knocks.

'Dave? Are you there?'

My heart is beating like a bass drum. At the other side of this door could be the man who has haunted my dreams for far too long. I wipe my hands down the sides of my trousers. Breathe, Ray. Breathe.

No reply.

'That's strange,' says the priest. Looks at his watch. 'He's usually up and about by now.'

He knocks again. 'Dave?'

Nothing.

'He'll forgive me if I intrude,' he offers, and opens the door. I step in before him to find an empty room. If the priests thinks I'm being rude, he says nothing. My pulse slows to normal as I realise my sought-after confrontation is not going to happen. Not today at least. And I can't help acknowledge a feeling of relief.

The room is small. It has a single bed, a pine wardrobe and dresser. The walls are empty apart from a small mirror and a painting of Jesus Christ displaying his heart. A small grass cross, like the ones given out on Palm Sunday, is tucked into the wooden frame of the mirror.

'That's strange.' Father Stephen stands beside me. Now that he's this close I can hear a rasp in his breath. Perhaps all is not well with the local priest, and that's why Martha is so solicitous.

Standing in the centre of the room, I make a slow turn and take everything in. The space feels empty. As if it hasn't been lived in for years. I open the cupboard door. There's nothing inside. The same with the dresser. All of the drawers are bare.

'But…' Father Stephen is clearly at a loss. He looks at me. 'He didn't say a thing.'

'Any idea where he might have gone, Father?'

'He wasn't a man who would share much, son. A bit of a closed book.'

'What do you know about him?'

'Well,' he says slowly and sighs in the manner of a man who continually expects the best in people and can't understand it when they let him down. 'Nothing really. He answered the advert for a handyman. Clearly knew his way about a church. I recognised a kindred soul and gave him the job.'

Kindred soul. The words sour in my mind. Leonard couldn't be further in spirit from this man.

'Did he offer you a CV or any form of references?' I ask.

'No. I took him on trust as I do everyone. I find people tend to match my expectation.'

I look at the grass cross on the mirror. Shiver. The priest misreads my reaction. 'Let's go through to the sitting room, and I'll get Martha to warm us up with some coffee.'

The difference in atmosphere between the two rooms is startling. This room is just like the man sat in front of me. Warm and welcoming. It gives off the sense that many people have been soothed in this space.

'Can't you tell me why you need to speak to him?' he asks.

'Sorry, Father. I can only say that we need his help with an enquiry.'

Just then Martha bustles in with a tray laden with coffee and biscuits. We break off our conversation to allow her to set out the cups and saucers and pour.

'Just milk,' I say.

She hands me a cup and then offers a plate of chocolate topped biscuits. 'You look like a man who likes his biscuits,' she says with a smile. I feel fat-shamed, and my fingers hover over a digestive before I withdraw and say, 'No. Thank you.'

'And Father Stephen won't be bothering with the biscuits either. Sure he'd only be wanting one to keep you company.'

Father Stephen shoots the plate a look of longing. I change my mind and stretch my hand out to spite Martha.

'Actually, I think I'll have one after all. Didn't have a chance to eat breakfast.'

With a beaming smile, the priest picks up a biscuit before Martha can march out of the room with the plate. He takes a large mouthful and, while chewing, winks at me.

'The woman's a treasure,' he says. 'But if the good Lord saw fit to give us delicious food to eat, surely we shouldn't just focus on the bland?'

'My thoughts exactly, Father. We can worry about the heart attack another time.' I pat my belly in solidarity. 'So, back to Dave. We know him as Jim Leonard.' This man is too trusting, and he needs to know not to let Leonard back in his home. 'He has been involved in some … very unsavoury activities. Other than that I can't say. But if he ever comes back, you have to let us know.'

'Good Lord,' the priest says, his hand before his mouth. 'He gave me a false name?'

'Yes, and I'm worried about what other lies he might've told you.'

'He didn't tell us much at all. Only that he was brought up in Bethlehem House in Ayrshire, and from there he went to a seminary…'

'He was in the home. Not in the seminary.'

'He said he was in seminary for a matter of weeks when his parents both died, can't remember how. But that meant he had to go back home to look after his twin brother who was severely handicapped.' He shook his head. 'Another lie, I suppose. Said he devoted his life to his twin brother.'

I think of Leonard's killing spree and the twisted truth in this simple statement. Leonard had woven a tale knowing the mix of fact and fiction would be sufficient to elicit sympathy.

Father Stephen slumped back in his chair, his disappointment tangible. He shook his head slowly. Looked at his watch. 'Shame it's so early. This would be a good time for a whisky.'

'Martha would have a fit,' I say.

'Just what she needs.' Then. 'Why would he lie to me, Ray?'

'It's just what he does, Father. He's probably told so many lies about himself over the years that he no longer knows what the truth looks like.'

'I don't really mind him leaving without a word. It's all transient, this existence.' He waves a hand back and forward. 'I gave willingly, with no expectation.' He brightens. 'And that rose garden last summer was spectacular.'

'Other than the rose garden, what else did Leonard, sorry, Dave do while he was here?'

'Oh, he was really useful. Changed bulbs, painted rooms, hung pictures, carried stuff. For a slight man he had amazing strength. And he did odd-jobs for lots of the elderly parishioners.'

'Did he make any friends?'

'Friends? No, not really.' He pauses and thinks some more. 'Sweet Lord, how could I forget? The Fords. Robert and Ken. They were twin brothers. Identical. He went over there now and again to watch the football.'

Football? My memory of Leonard at Bethlehem House was of a boy completely uninterested in sport. Unless it meant sniping at the other kids with his brother. Why would he spend time with people? He hates other people. And football?

And twins? That makes me sit up. Was Leonard trying to re-create something?

'Could you let me know where Bob and Ken live? Might be worth asking them if they know anything about where Dave might have gone.'

'Sorry. They both died fairly recently. It was awful. Tragic. They were a good age right enough. But fit.'

'What happened?' Leonard had something to do with this. I'm sure of it. My skin is prickling, my hearing on full alert.

He notices the rise in my interest. 'Nothing dodgy, Ray,' he replies. 'Ken had a faulty boiler. Bob was at him to get it fixed just a few days before he died. Sadly, he never got round to it. Died of carbon monoxide poisoning.'

'And Handyman Dave didn't offer to fix it for him?'

'I don't know. Possibly. But he clearly didn't get round to it.'

Or maybe he did. For someone who knows what they're doing, it can't be too difficult to prime an old boiler to pump the wrong fumes into a house.

'Dave, sorry, Jim was a great help to Bob in the days after Ken died. He was round there almost every day. But sadly Bob succumbed to his grief.' He crosses his legs and clasps his hands before him as if bracing himself to use the necessary words. As if he blames himself for what happened. 'He killed himself. In the bath. It was awful.' The last word comes out in a strangled whisper. '*Awful*.'

'You didn't find him, did you?'

'No. Praise the Lord. It was Dave who found him.'

'I bet it was,' I say before I can stop myself.

'Dave was kindness itself during those last few days with Robert.' Father Stephen pales. 'His solicitude towards a grieving man was inspirational. Any doubts I might have had about that man vanished as I watched him help Robert deal with Ken's death. He was a real Samaritan.'

My mind is racing through the possibilities and I don't answer. Identical twins die within days of each other. An accident and a suicide. Leonard had a part to play here, I'm certain. My worries about what he might be doing since the nun's death at Bethlehem House had been ignored. I didn't have the fortitude to think them through. I tucked them away in the same box I placed my concern about Joe McCall.

* * *

Thoughts, theories and suppositions chase through my mind as, wordless, I make my exit from the priest's residence.

'Well?' asks Kenny. 'Thought you were never coming out of there.'

'I can't...' What do I say? I'm a despicable human being.

'Oh aye,' says Kenny looking over my shoulder. And then there's a rap on my window. I turn. It's Martha. Kenny presses a key and the window opens.

'I heard everything in there,' she says. Her mouth is tight. All the lines on her face seem to radiate from it, like it's the centre of her being. 'That man was *wrong*. Just wrong. Father Stephen has a particular view of the world, and it doesn't allow him to see people like that the way they really are. Leonard? You called him Leonard?'

'Yeah.'

'Didn't trust him for a second. Didn't look at me. Looked *through* me as if I wasn't even there. And what he was up to with the Fords? I thought he was maybe trying to worm his way into their wills. No kids...' She sniffs. 'But then he vanished as penniless as he arrived, so that wasn't it. He did help people, but it felt that his motivation was never altruism. A Samaritan? A bad Samaritan for sure. Kindness was never his agenda, but I couldn't work out what he was after. And all that time he spent in front of the computer? It wasn't healthy. Probably doing that masturbation stuff,' she spat.

I can't take in what she's saying. My mind is a storm. I close my eyes against the feeling of self-loathing that rushes in on me like a tidal river bore. That these men died is down to me. I stayed silent, allowed McCall to take the blame.

Permitting Leonard to carry on hunting.

37

Leonard follows the youth out of the bookshop. He takes a right and a right again before walking up Union Street. His pace is leisurely, which suits Leonard. Makes it less likely that he's going to lose him.

Davis reaches the crossing outside a coffee shop. Waits for permission, like a good boy, and then when the traffic has paused before him, he walks across and up the stairs at the entrance to Central Station.

Before he does so, he stops, engages the *Big Issue* seller standing there and buys a copy of the mag. Leonard wants to drag him off and end it there and then. *This boy is too decent for his own good*, he thinks.

Kind deed done for the day, the boy speeds up the stairs like he has been energised by his own thoughtfulness. His speed has increased so much, it takes him through a family clustered at the top. They accept his waved apology with the good humour of the newly arrived tourist. Glasgow has some renown as a friendly city, and these guys want to match that.

'No problem, buddy,' the patriarch of the group hollers at Davis's back.

Their crossing of the concourse is uneventful after that as Davis has slowed down somewhat. Although he does take the occasional slide along the marble floor. Just because he can. And each time he does it, Leonard's contempt for him increases. Fingering the knife in his pocket, it occurs to him that he would take him here under this famous vaulted roof if he could get away with it. *Perhaps it if was just a little bit busier*, he thinks as he avoids an elderly couple supporting each other along to their platform. Their suitcase being pulled behind them like a warning. Ambulant but slow. A crowd can be every bit as effective as the darkest of alleyways. A quick thrust with a knife and he'd be away through the crowd before anyone could react.

The thought gives him such a thrill, his eyes narrow and his senses close to a narrow note of pleasure. With reluctance, he opens his eyes, takes in the hubbub. The shuffle and stamp of feet, the huff of breathing, the high and happy chatter. Sounds that blend and echo at the same time. An orchestra of travel.

It's too much for Leonard, and he stops to take stock. Then he realises he's lost the boy.

He rushes forward, almost tripping over a stocky, bald man and his rolling suitcase. Cursing the man's laziness, he dodges to the left and searches the bobbing heads around him.

There. Just in time. Davis is heading to the far end and the low level trains.

Acknowledging his forethought in buying a ZoneCard, the rest of the journey is much easier. Leonard even takes a seat on the train right behind the boy. Staring at the pale skin on the back of his neck.

He wants to reach out and touch it, it looks so fresh. There's a mole there. A bump of imperfection that adds to the overall. Just above it, the hairline begins. Freshly cropped. Tight to the skull. And from there it layers slightly longer, following the curve and swell of the boy's head.

The boy stands. The train slows to a stop. Thankfully a number of people get off at the same time, and they continue their journey out of the train station, up the ramp, through the ticket barrier and out to the street beyond.

They're in an area of the city that Leonard doesn't know, but that doesn't matter. It will be easy enough to get back to his digs from here.

They walk for only a few more minutes before the boy's pace slows and he enters the pathway leading to a small house.

Home for the Davis family.

Leonard walks past, crosses the road and sees a low wall under an overhanging tree. He sits on it and waits.

And is rewarded.

38

From where he sits on the wall, Leonard has a perfect view of the house. The tree is heavy with leaf, and these create just enough of a shadow. He pulls his feet up on to the wall, making himself smaller, even less visible.

He looks up at the sky. It's getting dark. Better and better.

Minutes after Simon enters the house, the door opens and someone walks out. A broader, more muscular version of Simon. From his gait, Leonard can tell this one isn't happy. His fists and face are clenched in anger.

The door opens again and Simon runs out. Speeds to his brother and they're face to face, mouths moving , neither listening to the other. They're being mindful of whoever is still in the house, judging by how they keep their voices low and both throw glances back up towards the front window.

Interesting.

All is not well in the Davis household. Will make it even easier to divide and conquer.

Then, the muscular one pushes Simon and walks away. Simon calls after him.

'Matt. Matt!'

So that's his name. Simon didn't mention it during any of their conversations.

Matt's pace is fierce. Leonard considers following him, but decides against it when he sees the boy pull some keys from his pocket, aim at a small red car, pull open the door and jump in. Seconds later the car drives off. Fast.

Really not happy.

Leonard settles in to see what happens next. Before long his knees are protesting and he straightens his legs. At that moment a tall figure walks past on the opposite side of the street. Dark jeans. Black top. Hood up. One hand is in his pocket. The other is carrying something. Looks like a letter.

He slows as he approaches the end of the path to the Davis house. Looks left and right. Makes his decision and walk-runs up to the door where he pushes his letter through the letter box. As he walks back down the path to the street, his shoulders are hunched against discovery, and it looks like it is taking everything he has not to break into a run.

Leonard hops off the wall. Crosses the road, and waiting until they are beyond the line of sight of anyone in the house, he approaches the man in the hood.

'Hey. Talk to you for a second.'

'Fuck off, mate.' The man in the hood keeps walking. Leonard reaches out and grabs the man's sleeve. He turns. Snarls. 'Told you to fuck off, mate.'

'So you did,' replies Leonard. Something in his voice makes the man stop. He turns and for the first time Leonard gets a glimpse of his face, and Leonard knows that whatever this guy can throw at him, he can handle with ease. This knowledge transmits itself to the man, and the hostility leaks from his expression to be replaced mostly by fear. He's still defiant though. Trying to save face. But he's a coward, and they both know it.

'What did you put through the Davis's letterbox?' asks Leonard.

'What's it to you, ya prick?' the man replies. Man. Now that they're face to face he can see that he's really still just a boy.

'I'm a friend,' Leonard says and takes a step forward. He knows the rules of this dance better than anyone. This boy might have some inches on him and some width, but it doesn't matter if the smaller man has more fight in him. Leonard has never even bothered to count the number of people he has killed, and he allows this fact to fill his stance. His body is saying, *I could kill you with as much thought as someone else might stand on an ant.*

The boy's voice has a wobble. 'The Davis boy killed that lassie.'

'He did?'

'Aye. And the polis aren't doing nothing.'

Leonard resists the urge to correct his grammar. 'Is that not what Facebook is for? Means rather than just annoying the family, you also get to show the world how pathetic and ineffectual you are.'

'Doing that as well, mate. Lets them know, we know, you know?'

Idiot.

'Which Davis boy and which lassie?'

The boy looks confused. 'Simon. And his girlfriend, Aileen.'

'What's it to you?'

The boy's face tightens in confusion. 'He fucking killed her, mate.'

'Did you fancy her something?'

'Went to a few of the same classes, like. She was a nice lassie.'

'And how do you know Simon did it?'

'Has to be him. She dumped him, and he can't handle it. Goes postal. Kills her.'

Leonard takes a step back. Give the boy space, let him relax and he'll get more out of him. As for Simon being a murderer? No way. Not the boy he's been following all day. Hasn't got it in him. Now, the boy he's just seen running from the house to the car? He's an entirely different story. Strength, aggression and the cold get-the-job-done attitude coming from him was evident. Even from across the street.

'Tell me more,' Leonard says.

'Thought you were a friend?'

'Only of the distant variety.'

'Eh?'

Leonard curbs the urge to lash out. 'I'm an old friend of the family. Just looking out for them.' He guesses that this is not the first time this boy had been at the house. Makes a leap. 'Mrs Davis told me that some little dick was leaving her messages.'

'Aye, well. Feel sorry for her an' that. Can't be easy when your son turns out to be a killer. But I'm thinking of Aileen's family. Her dad has gone crazy. Ran under a bus, man.'

'What's their family name?' This is familiar. He sees McBain's face in his mind, talking to the cameras. A name trips from his tongue at the same time as the youth speaks.

'Banks.'

'How do you not know this? You being a family friend?'

'The word is *why*, not how,' says Leonard. He reaches into his trouser pocket and feels the heavy weight of his flick-knife. He was thinking about letting the boy leave unharmed. But he has seen his face. Might recognise him again.

Before confusion at Leonard's statement can form on the youth's face, Leonard reaches out faster than he can blink. Cold steel punches into warm flesh just under the chin.

39

We're driving away from the priest's house and Kenny looks at me.

'You didn't think he would actually be there, did you? Life's never that easy.'

'Aye. True,' I manage to say and offer a smile as if to say, *look at the idiot who thought it would be that simple.* Find the priest. Drive to his house. Pick up the maniac and drive him to a quiet spot in the hills before driving a stake through his heart.

All very gothic.

And satisfying. And would surely bring this whole chapter of my life to a close. Perhaps then I could find some peace.

Disappointment sours in my mouth, pulls on my shoulders. Did he know we were coming? Nah, no way. How could he possibly have known we were on to him? Where the hell could he be now? We'll never find him. I have a trail of thoughts, all on a similar vein, but I don't give them voice. I'd just sound like a whiner.

I want to get away from my own head. Give my thoughts, my worries, my black hound to someone else. And it was almost all over. A day earlier and we would have had Leonard.

'Don't worry,' says Kenny. 'We'll get him, mate.'

'You didn't answer my question last night.' Time for some deflection.

'Which one was that?'

'If you had ever killed anyone.'

Kenny says nothing. Looks from the road, to me and then back again. Chews on it some. Decides not to even bother with the *What kind of question is that* face.

'Came close,' he says. 'This evil prick was … nah, let's not go there.' He shakes his head. 'Best to let that one go, mate.' He exhales, loud and slow. 'Narrow escape. I've found the threat that I *could* has been enough, so far. Hope to fuck it stays that way.'

'If Leonard had been there, I'm certain the day would have ended with either him or me bleeding out. I've got to bring all of this to an end. Can't take much…' I tail off. Not going there.

'What about Maggie?' he asks.

'What about her?'

'You've got a good woman there, Ray. Don't leave her out.'

'Yeah. Right. The man who can't have a relationship unless there's a fee negotiated from the start is giving advice.'

'Shut it, McBain. Even a blind man can see that Maggie's good for you.'

'Maybe I'm not good for her.'

'She has to be the judge of that.' Kenny shakes his head. 'Arse.'

My phone sounds an alert in my pocket. Saved by the buzz. I pull it out. It's a text from Ale.

'DNA sample in. No match on the system.'

'OK. Thanks for letting me know.'

'Also. Dead body found in a garden across the road from the Davis's house. Stabbed in the throat.'

We both know that when it comes to murder, there's no such thing as coincidence. There has to be a connection. We just have to find it.

'Has the body been ID'd yet?' I send.

'Yeah. Wallet was still in his pocket. With a student's ID card in the name of Ian Cook.'

'Rings a bell.'

'That's cos he was one of the lads we chatted to at the Horseshoe'

My mind provides a mental image. The quieter one. Interesting.

'Murder weapon?' I send.

'Nothing on the scene.'

'Where did he live?' I text. How quickly we adapt. The boy is meat on a cold slab, and we're talking about him in the past tense.

'He was from Dumfries. Rented a flat in the city centre.'

Meaning he was quite a way from his home. I look at the clock on the dashboard and assess how long it will take to get back to the city.

'Be there in 45 mins.'

'What will I tell Peters?'

'That I cancelled the dentist. Bottled it.'

I pocket my phone and look over at Kenny.

'What's up?' he asks.

'Need to get back to the office, big man. So don't spare the horses.'

* * *

Ale is waiting outside the interview room when I arrive. Her eyes are so bright there are almost sparks flying off them.

'We're getting close, boss,' she says. 'I can feel it.'

'Simon's in the room is he?'

She nods.

'Swabbed?'

'First thing we did when he arrived. It's been couriered over to the lab as we speak.'

'Are they giving us any idea of how long it will take to do a comparison?'

Ale shakes her head. 'Got the usual "we'll do our best" answer.'

Which could be anything between an hour and a week. We need this fast. Simon has an alibi for Aileen's murder, so we have nothing to detain him on.

'Does Simon know about Cook?'

'Only if he's the killer. There's an incident tent over the site, so he can't have missed that. It's almost straight across from his house. It was on the news, but with the usual "no name until we notify the family."'

Good. That means we'll get an honest response.

'What about Peters?'

'Held up.' She makes a mock sad face. 'Could be a while.'

'You are a naughty girl, DC Rossi.' I don't know what she's done to get him out of the way, and I don't want to know.

'By the way, Simon was in his house all night last night. With his mum. He couldn't have been the one to do Cook,' Ale says.

'Mmm. Couldn't be too difficult to sneak out without mummy knowing.'

I lean my back against the wall. Thinking this all through. But I can't waste too much time before Peters' fool's errand is over and he's down here wondering what the hell is going on.

'Also, don't know if this is connected, but Helen Davis said she got one of her hate letters last night. Same night as Cook was killed. Could be linked?'

'Yeah, but what the hell does it mean?'

I enter the room with Ale on my heels. Simon is sitting as if he got into that position when we put him in the room and he hasn't dared to move an inch since. His legs and arms are crossed. He's shrinking into himself. He acknowledges me with a nod of his head.

'Good afternoon, Simon,' I say. 'Thank you for stopping by.' He murmurs in reply, and I can't help but be reminded of the difference between him and his twin brother.

'We just want to ask you a few questions.'

'Sure,' he manages to say and coughs as if that might clear the nerves from his throat.

'Could you tell us the last time you saw Ian Cook?'

'Ian Cook?' He sits up straight. The questions has thrown him. He was anticipating more queries about Aileen. 'Haven't seen him since...' He casts his eyes to the ceiling. If I could remember which position the eyes were supposed to be in when recalling something or making it up, I'd be able to work out if he was lying or not. 'I can't remember when I last saw him,' he finishes, and his face flares to full blush.

'For a boy who blushes so easily, you really shouldn't lie to the police,' says Ale.

'Sorry.' He looks from Ale to me. 'I'm not...' He scratches at his neck. He must be feeling the heat generating from there.

'Simon, save us all time. When did you last see Ian Cook?'

'It was the same day that Aileen's dad had a go at me. He came up to me in town and spat in my face. Called me a murderer.' His voice trails off with that last word. Like he can barely get his tongue around the necessary syllables. 'I promise you,' he is pleading with us now, 'I didn't kill Aileen. I loved her.' He starts to cry softly. His head is down. Shoulders moving to the rhythm of his sorrow.

We give him a minute.

'Would you like some water, Simon?' I ask.

He shakes his head. Wipes his face with his sleeve.

'What can you tell us about Ian Cook?'

Simon leans back into his chair. Shrugs. 'Don't really know him all that well. Him and his mate. Jack, I think? Used to stare at me when I was out with Aileen. I think they both fancied her and won-dered what she was doing with a geek like me. And, after, he sent me a couple of messages on Facebook saying pretty much the same thing.'

'Our sources tell us that after you fell out with Aileen, she was seen snogging both of them at the student's union,' Ale says.

'Right,' Simon says, wearing an expression of defeat. 'It's a free world. She was single.' Gets defensive. 'So what? Doesn't make her a bad person.'

'Might make you jealous?'

'Newsflash, I'm human,' he says, and for the first time I see a little bit of fight. Makes me warm to him. A notion I quell instantly. I can't afford to be anything other than objective with this guy. 'They acted like a pair of dicks to me, and Aileen couldn't see that and falls for their chat. So, no I didn't like that. Yes, I was jealous when I heard. Doesn't make *me* a bad person.'

'Do you know anyone who would want to hurt Ian?'

'What?' he asks. I read his expression. He's either a very talented actor, or he's completely unaware of last night's killing. 'What do you mean by hurt him? He's a bit of a dick, but as far as I'm aware he's not into anything suspect.'

'He was murdered last night,' I say.

Simon's mouth falls open.

'Right across the road from your house.'

'What?' he asks, as if the words are reaching his ears through the mouth of a translator speaking a different form of English. 'Across the road? What the hell would he be doing there?' He looks from me to Ale as if either of us might know the answer.

'We hoped you might be able to tell us that,' Ale answers. 'He didn't pop in for a blether? A wee shot on your Xbox?'

'No.' He shakes his head. 'Why would he … I told you, I haven't seen him since that day he spat on me.' His eyes dart around the room as if the answer is caught up in the light that hits the corners.

He makes a connection at the same time I do. 'Mum said that we got one of those letter last night,' he says. 'You don't think, Ian…' He tails off as he realises this gives him, or one of his family, a motive.

'We're getting prints taken,' I say.

'Man, this is fucked up,' he says, and I realise this is the first time I've heard Simon swear. 'Where was Matt last night?' I ask.

'In the house,' Simon answers. 'Went out for a wee while in the evening. Probably to the gym. Came back and didn't leave.'

Time for the silent treatment. I sit back in my chair and cross my arms. Ale reads my cue and does likewise. We both give him the stare. He stares back, looking like a lost little boy.

'You don't think Matt killed him?' Simon asks.

'We just want to know what Ian was doing outside your house last night. If he was the one responsible for the hate mail, it gives you motive. Particularly when added to his previous activity. Do you think Matt killed him?' I ask.

Simon snorts. 'That's ridiculous. I've never known Matt to be aggressive.'

'You're telling me he's never had a fight?' asks Ale.

'Of course he has.' He makes a face. 'Push comes to shove and he can look after himself, but he never goes looking for it.'

'What about you, Simon?' I ask. 'You ever go looking for it?'

He snorts again. 'Matt can look after himself. He also looks after me.' He blushes again. A number of emotions play across the screen of his eyes. The lead one being shame. 'I'm a bit of a fearty. Used to get bullied a lot. Matt always stepped in to stare down the bullies.' He offers a weak smile. 'I'm a lover, not a fighter.' Sounds like an often used line.

'Used to get bullied?' asks Ale. 'Why did it stop?'

'Got some friends? Became anonymous in the crowd? Grew up?' He coughs. 'I think I lost the look of the victim.' For the first time he meets my gaze, as if saying the words out loud had reminded him that self-preservation requires a certain conduct.

I recall my own youth and the almost constant threat of violence that many young males experience. Facing down that violence with a fuck-you grin while trying to ignore the shake in my knees. Knowing that any sign of weakness would be pounced on by any other boys looking to boost their own personal sense of power. The law of our concrete jungle being, look like a victim and you will get victimised. Sounds like Simon eventually learned that lesson for himself.

'The fact is, a boy who spat in your face and who trolled you online has been murdered just across the road from your house. It's not looking good, Simon,' I say.

I hear loud footsteps outside in the corridor leading to this room. Someone is walking with purpose, and I *know* it's not with any favours for me in mind.

Simon crosses his arms. Folds into himself. 'Perhaps I shouldn't say any more until I have a lawyer?'

There's a knock at the door. It opens. DI Peters steps in.

'DI McBain. DC Rossi. Talk to you outside, please?'

Ale gives me a look. We stand up and follow Peters out. He takes a few steps away from the door and turns. His lips are a tight line of irritation. He manages to open them to speak.

'He has an alibi for the night of Aileen's murder. He has an alibi for last night's murder.' His ire increases as each word escapes his mouth. 'I'm the chief investigating officer on this one, Ray, whether you fucking like it or not.' He faces Ale. His expression telling her of his huge disappointment in her. 'DC Rossi. Escort Simon Davis to the public reception area. His mother is there for him.'

'But we're waiting...'

'You might be waiting on Christmas, Ale, but frankly I don't give a shit. Take the boy to his mother. Now.'

40

The moment the knife slid through skin and ligament.

The look in the boy's eyes just before his light dimmed.

The arc and spray of blood.

The gasp and shudder of his own pleasure.

Poetry.

Leonard has set up station in his hotel room. He chose one of those anonymous hotel chains that provide a corporate view of what a dormitory might look like, and it amuses him to think that the length and breadth of the country, men and women, after a day's work away from the comforts of home, accept such a homogenised view of rest and respite.

He imagines legions of these servants of capitalism approaching a receptionist to book into their rooms. Faces the colour of whey, they open their mouth to speak and the only sound to come out is the bleating of sheep.

He looks around himself at his room. Large bed with a dark blue covering. Fat, white pillows. A two-seater sofa offering as much cushion as cardboard and a covering harsh enough to scour skin should anyone be foolish enough to sit while naked. The walls are magnolia, and the wardrobe is fabricated from a factory version of pine.

There's a dresser in front of a large mirror. He takes a seat and stares at his image. Wonders if that is really him. Stares down the wormhole of his own pupils.

Relives the moment of the boy's death again. Feels the rush and heat of pleasure. Draws back from full immersion. He has a job to do.

The killing was a bonus, but he couldn't allow it to become a distraction.

He opens the lid of his laptop. Fires it up, and as he waits for the screen to build he thinks about the various people in his web and how they might help his plans.

The Davis twins and the dead girl. Simon was her boyfriend, so he's going to be the main suspect. Clearly the police have no evidence or he'd be in custody. *If that boy's a killer, I'm a bar of butter,* thinks Leonard. Could the girl have had something going on with the brother?

He has already befriended Simon on Facebook (as his fake persona), so he checks through his friend list. Finds the dead boy's timeline. And with a few well-chosen words, plants a seed. Let's see what the court of public opinion makes of that. Feels a thrill at the possible repercussions.

Next, he goes to the Time4Twin website. Types an apology for Simon's attention and then settles in to wait.

Surprisingly quickly, Simon replies.

'I understand,' his message reads.

'When it came down to it, I just couldn't have that conversation.' Leonard explains.

'No problem.'

'You seem distracted,' Leonard types, allowing a smile to heat his face and knowing what the source of that distraction would be. 'What's up?'

There was a long wait before the screen filled with an answer.

'Just got back from the police station. A guy I know was killed last night. Just across the road from my house. Shit, that was scary, mate. Sorry. I shouldn't be telling you this. That's unprofessional.'

Leonard knew the boy would be conflicted in telling him and yet anxious to be talking to someone unconnected. A conflict that he could manipulate. 'No problem. It's understandable. You must have got a fright. Any reason why the police wanted to speak to you?'

'Well, I did know him. And it happened just outside my house.'

'Do they think you were involved?'

'Don't think so.' Pause. 'Surely not? They were just fishing. Has

211

to be just a coincidence that they had to check out.' Another, longer pause. 'And we got some hate mail that night. If it was the dead guy who sent it, that could throw suspicion on me again.'

'Hope not, mate,' Leonard replies. 'But as far as the police are concerned, when it comes to crime, there's no such thing as coincidence.' Then he stops typing, thinking, *let the boy stew on that a while.*

'Shit. You're right. But they let me go. And my mum told them I was in the house all night.'

'What about your brother?'

'What about him?'

'Was he in the house all night? Could he be involved?'

'Jesus. No. Matt's no murderer.'

'Who knows what we're capable of when we're trying to protect our families? Could he know that this guy was leaving the hate mail?'

'It came in not long after Matt left the house.' Pause. 'Surely not. No. Not going there. Matt will defend himself, but he wouldn't take a knife to someone. No way.'

'OK,' replies Leonard. Another seed sown.

He finishes up the session with an offer to provide a listening ear and a renewed promise to meet up to finally address his issues.

Then he clicks through a number of websites. Takes in the information. Searches the girl's name. Finds the news item about the father's apparent suicide attempt and his subsequent coma. What's going on there? Daddy is consumed by guilt? Why? Did he do it? Does he know who did it and did nothing to stop it?

Another news site and McBain's worn and grey face fills the screen. The sound is on mute, but Leonard fills in McBain's silent mouthings with his own thoughts. Police cliché playing the part of public information service while obfuscating the truth.

McBain's female colleague stands just behind his left shoulder, and Leonard wonders again at this relationship. She was the underling, yet McBain draws something from the relationship. More than friends? Or is it just a strong bond forged in the fire of a trying occupation?

Leonard thinks of his long dead brother. Feels the twist and ache of his loss. It has never diminished despite the passing of the decades.

He remembers that very first killing. All of those children standing round the old man's bed. The old man they thought was responsible for their violation. His feeble attempts at self-defence. The metallic tang in the air as blood was spilled. A cloud of white feathers when the blade missed and hit a pillow.

In his mind's eye, Leonard goes round that bed. Lays to rest each of those white faces. All of them are dead, save him and one other.

McBain.

But there's more suffering to be had before that last one can take his final exhalation.

41

Jack Foreman was in his bedsit. Sitting up in bed. Fully dressed. Mind a swirl of emotions. Unable to pin a name on any of them.

Ian was dead?

They'd only known each other for a couple of years, but what the actual fuck?

Dead?

He crossed his legs, leaned forward, his head in his hands. Felt a tear slide from his eye. 'This can't be happening,' he said out loud, hearing the quiver in his voice. 'Can't be true.' And Jesus, he couldn't remember the last time he cried. At Parkhead, when Celtic beat Barcelona?

What the hell happened, Ian? All you had to do was deliver a piece of paper. Did one of the Davis boys stop you? Did a fight break out? If that was the case it would be Matt, not Simon. Simon couldn't fight his way out of a wet paper bag. Killing women was more his thing, the wee cunt. But Matt looked quite handy.

They were speaking just last night. Before Ian went over to the Davis's house to deliver that latest note. He slumped back into his pillows. Shit. A singular emotion swirled up from the morass. He recognised the sourness of its shape and gave it a name. Guilt.

If it hadn't been for him, Ian wouldn't have even been there.

It all started as Ian's idea. They could see that the police were getting nowhere and decided to do what they could to put pressure on Simon Davis. No way was that wee geek innocent. He'd bet that Davis was having a nightly wankfest at the memory of killing that poor wee lassie.

A mate of a mate of a mate said the polis weren't charging Davis because of a lack of evidence. Sure he was the ex-boyfriend, but he had an alibi for the night of Aileen's death. So they couldn't do him.

Well maybe they can't, Ian said to Jack, *but we fucking could.*

Face-to-face was usually more Jack's style. Up front and in person, like. But Jack was there to be persuaded. His wee sister, Emma, had been date-raped by this sick bastard. Who'd fucked off back to Spain or Italy or wherever the fuck he came from. Leaving him and his ma to hold her hand.

That was a wake-up moment for him. Seeing the impact of that kind of thing on someone he cared about. Sure, he'd taken things a wee bit too far a couple of times. Got the horn so hard he could barely ignore it. But he always pulled back before anybody got hurt. A final no was a no, right?

Wee Emma had been in a right state. Crying all day and all night for weeks. She was getting her act together now right enough. Decided she ain't going to be any sick bastard's victim.

Our Emma's got balls, said his ma.

A fucking huge pair of balls.

And guys need to know that this isn't on.

Jack Foreman is going to be the one to educate them. Starting with Simon Fucking Davis, Jack told Ian and every cunt he could reach on social networking.

They started with poisonous wee messages on Facebook, but it turned out that Davis found them easy to ignore and closed his account on the site. Next idea was to send them some messages. He got the idea from an old TV show, where one of the characters cut some letters out of a newspaper and glued them into a message.

Ian had really impressed him with his attitude on this. Usually he was the quietest guy in the room, as shy as a kid on their first day at school. But he'd really gone for this. Jack was unsure it would be worth all the effort, but Ian delivered the first couple, and then they decided to take turns about.

'Why don't we just stick them in the post and let Mr Postman do the delivery thing?' Jack asked at the start.

'First of all, the envelope would have a postmark. And second, it will really mess with their heads. They'll think it's a neighbour, and they'll end up falling out with them all. It will create an atmosphere around them. Piles on the pressure, mate.'

Jack nodded his assent. Punched Ian on the arm. 'You're a sick fucker,' he grinned. 'And what have you done with my mate, Ian Cook? Let's do this.'

And last night was supposed to be his turn to deliver, but this sweet wee thing called Rachel had sent him a naked text from her shower and an invite to come over. Tits, fanny and everything. Couldn't pass that up, could he?

Ian made a show of complaining. Mumped and moaned, said no fucking way. But it was clear this display was just a matter of form. Didn't want to be seen as a walkover.

Jack whipped out his phone and showed him Rachel's photo.

'Nice,' Ian said, a slow grin forming on his face. 'Fuck me, she's gorgeous.'

'You see what kind of position I'm in?' Jack pleaded.

'Aye. Fair enough,' said Ian before taking another look. A very slow, very appreciative look before Jack pulled the phone back.

'Fuck off, ya prick. Don't you be having a wank over my bird.'

'As if,' said Ian, with an expression that promised as soon as he had the space to himself he'd be rubbing one out. 'But I want a full and frank account of your evening. Got to get my jollies somehow.'

Jack pocketed his phone and rubbed his hands together. 'Not a chance, mate. I'm a total gentleman.'

That was last night. And today, Ian was dead. Murdered just across the road from the Davis's house.

Too much of a coincidence. Innit? The scenario repeats in his mind. One of the Davis boys catches him in the act. Bound to happen eventually, like. It all kicks off. A knife gets pulled, and Ian ends up with his throat cut.

Fuck me. That's brutal.

Jack pulls his phone off the charger. Checks an online news site for any more information. Nothing. The police are keeping this one close to their chest.

From habit, he scrolls through his Facebook page.

Nothing much happening here.

Nope.

Scrolls down some more.

Nobody's doing nothing today.

Finally, a message about Ian. People are going up the site to leave flowers. Maybe he should do that as well? People will be wondering where he was. Best mates with the dead boy and all that.

A sob escapes. A harsh note of pain that is stuck in his throat before escaping on a breath.

Davie boy. What the fuck happened?

He goes back to Facebook. Leaves a quick post.

'**Cannae believe the news. RIP Ian, mate.**'

Within seconds people are piling in to show support. *Fucking rubbernecking bastards*, thinks Jack. '**Sorry for your loss**', one knobhead types. *Fuck off and grow an original thought, ya prick. Don't need your sympathy.* He throws his phone on the bed.

Got to do something. He jumps to his feet. Retrieves his phone. Back to Facebook and scrolling through his contacts. An alert from some guy called Dave Smith snags his attention.

'**Jack mate. Heard from a mate the polis think it was Matt Davis wot done Ian Cook lets get the cunt he was spotted down the town in the student union like he owned the fucking place needs to learn a lesson.**'

First of all, mate, punctuation, he thinks.

Second of all, you are fucking on.

42

Ale is sitting in front of her computer having just sent off an email asking when the DNA results might be in. Who would have thought that austerity cuts would have led to murder suspects being let off?

She drums her fingernails on the desk, wondering if she should phone instead. She phoned yesterday, and phoning again today was just going to piss people off. *Yes, but emails are so much easier to ignore*, she thinks.

'Will you stop that,' says Daryl Drain, a look of indignation on his face.

'What?' asks Ale.

'Drumming your fingers on the desk. It's annoying.'

'Excuse me,' says Ale. Grins. Drums with added zeal.

Daryl raises his eyebrows at her. 'Really mature.'

'This DNA thing is doing my head in,' she offers by way of explanation. She sits back in her chair and crosses her arms. 'What the hell is going on over there?'

Daryl slides his chair over a few inches so he has a better view of her face past her computer screen. 'What else can you be getting on with?'

'The boy, Cook,' she exhales. 'I'm not buying either of the Davis boys for that. Far too...' she searches for a word, 'clinical.'

'What makes you say that?' asks Drain.

'One wound. Appears to be aimed with precision. And who goes for the throat like that for Christ's sake?'

Drain nods in agreement.

Even in her few short years on the force, Ale has seen the outcome of plenty of knife attacks. Sure, they're reducing in numbers thanks to a number of clever initiatives from the suits, but it still happens with alarming regularity.

'With Cook there's no defensive wounds, so my guess is that it was over quickly. Most knife attacks I've seen are aimed at the chest, and when it *is* the neck, if they're attacking from the front, it tends to be a kind of slashing movement. This was a single movement. He was quite literally going for the jugular.'

'Aye. Spot on, Ale,' Drain says. 'This has the feel of an execution. Not a rammy, which it would be if Cook was posting the hate mail and was caught by one of the Davis lads. And besides, none of the neighbours reported hearing any disturbances.'

'It's just not adding up. Who would execute a geeky student?'

'Unless he was more than a geeky student.'

Ale recalls the time she met Cook in The Horseshoe. Sees a body language that suggests, if the Bible is correct, the young man concerned was about to inherit a large chunk of the earth.

'Never say never, but that guy made mice seem positively gregarious.'

'Ooo, gregarious. Who's been reading their word-of-the-day toilet paper again?'

Ale shoots him the finger.

They both sit for a few minutes in silence. Each lost in their own conjecture. Ale chases one thought down after another. Frustrated by the lack of a result in this case and even by the lack of answers.

'Where's McBain?' Ale asks.

'Buggered if I know.'

Back to silence.

Then.

'What else did you get from the scene-of-the-crime guys?' asks Drain.

'Just what we talked about there. No weapon found at the scene, so the perp likely took it away with him.'

'What was Cook carrying?'

Ale looks at her notebook. Reads, 'Wallet, matriculation card, twenty quid in notes. Driver's licence. Mobile phone.' Looks over at Daryl. 'So, it wasn't a robbery gone wrong. Nothing seems to be missing.' Pause. 'I've asked them to...'

There's a knock at the door. A young officer sticks his head in. Short black hair, thick with gel. White shirt, blue tie. Takes one look at Ale and gets his dimples on. *Jesus*, thinks Ale. *Save me from the office Lothario. Thinks flashing the enamel is all he needs to do to get into a girl's pants.* Ale is aware that being one of the few women in the department means there is endless speculation about who is shagging her. Consequently, when the subject comes round she's as quiet as a nun in cloisters. And she gives nothing back when someone tries to flirt with her. She knows it drives them nuts. While there is no way any one of these guys is going to get groiny with her, she's not averse to fucking with their minds.

He walks over to her desk. Sucking in his gut as he draws nearer.

'Can you sign for this, DC Rossi?' he asks. His extends his right hand, which is holding a small bundle. Ale recognises the formal packaging, and she grabs it from him.

'Just in good time,' she says, deliberately avoiding his eye. Looks at Drain. 'It's the phone.'

'Sweet.'

They both look at the young cop.

'You can run along now,' says Ale.

Drain makes a shooing motion with his hands.

'I hope the tech guys have unlocked it,' says Ale as she pulls off the packaging. She's aware that the deliverer is hovering at the door for a moment longer than he needs to, just in case. She gives him nothing. Holds the phone out in front of her. It's a Samsung and yes, it is unlocked. There are a number of apps on the home screen. The usual social networks are there. She enters Facebook.

'Bloody hell,' she says. 'There are literally hundreds of messages on here.' She groans. 'It's going to take ages to get through all these.'

She reads a few. 'Seems like our Ian is suddenly popular. Can you believe he's had twenty friend requests since the news broke?'

'People want to be friends with a corpse?' Daryl checks for understanding. 'I've heard everything now.' He grins. 'You should accept them and see what reaction you get.'

'Now that would be unprofessional and worthy of disciplinary action,' she admonishes him. 'But it would be hilarious.' She scrolls through some more. Thinks out loud. 'Probably best to check what was going on in his timeline last night.' She does so. But there are no entries for the last couple of days.

Daryl reads her expression. 'How about you look at what his mates are saying now? Or what they were saying last night?'

Ale nods in agreement and moves about on the screen. 'His BFF is a guy called Jack…' She scrolls some more. 'And here he is.'

He's changed his profile picture to one that shows him and Ian Cook together. They each have an arm over the other's shoulder, and they're flashing white. Jack's smile says, ladies I'm chocolate and you want to eat me. Ian's says, you really do and I'm happy to take his leftovers.

A message alert comes through. Someone called Billy-Bhoy. And Ale is thinking, there's a nice mix of Glasgow's leading cultures right there. Billy for the "celebrated" William of Orange who is celebrated by a section of the Rangers fans. And Bhoy for the Celtic section of the city.

Billy, even in a Facebook post, is somewhat excitable. 'Got the fucker. Spotted coming out of St Enochs.'

Jack replies. 'No here, Billy. Ya bellend. Omerta!!!'

Ale wonders what the legendary Mafia code of silence has to do with a group of Glaswegian students. She looks down the side of the screen to see which groups Cook was a member of. She expects that if Jack is a member, Ian will be too.

There's only one group. It's called Omerta.

'This detection thing is a piece of piss,' she says to Daryl. 'Especially when the people concerned are as thick as shit.' A press of a finger and she's in.

She can see there are seven members. And hello, here's a familiar name. Karen Gardner. She's the sole female. What on earth is she doing here? Before she can take this thought any further a new post comes through. Lee Kennedy is on Matt Davis's tail. He wants "haunners". A hand from his mates to take Davis on. They're down the back of the St Enoch centre.

'This guy done Ian,' he posts. 'Time for some payback.'

Ale grabs her jacket of the back of her chair. Stands up.

'Right, DD. Things are about to get out of hand. We're on.'

43

When Peters asked, no, *commanded* Ale to allow Simon Davis to go home, it was all I could do to keep my hands away from his throat.

I push my clenched fists into my trouser pockets and hold them there with all the strength I can muster. Ale looks at me as she leaves the room, offering a what-can-you-do shrug.

'How the fuck did you ever get this job, Peters?' I ask. I might even have sprayed some saliva over him.

He's suddenly aware that he's alone in the room with me and backs out.

'Don't worry,' I say, aware that any response from me right now would be excessive. 'Got to see a man about a dog.' I brush past him and leave the room.

* * *

I'm breathing like an untrained marathon runner on the home strait. I somehow make it out the car park without assaulting anyone. But I do collect a lot of strange looks.

My neck heats. My heart beats a supercharged metronome against my ribs. Anxiety has narrowed my line of sight into a thin band of awareness. It's like I'm looking in on myself, and I can't affect what I'm doing.

Where has this come from? One moment I'm speaking to a colleague. The next, something switches, and I'm in full panic attack mode.

My next moment of awareness and I'm knocking on a tall, dark wooden door. It's the church. And the door is locked. Who locks a fucking church door in the middle of the day?

I wait to hear the priest's approaching footfall. Nothing.

I slide down the door until I'm sitting on my arse. Remember the breathing exercises. Focus on the in breath. Follow the exhalation. I imagine I'm inside the cool of the church and under the benevolent smile of the young priest.

Aww, man. How far have you fallen, McBain?

But it works. A little. My pulse has slowed to a jackhammer and my vision is restored. I breathe deep. In for a count of nine and out for nine.

This has to stop, McBain. This is no way to live. I don't get fucking panic attacks.

All evidence to the contrary, you fanny.

Peters just followed protocol and his own internal dickhead rules and didn't really deserve the kicking that I was desperate to give him.

I can't believe that I'm reacting like this. This isn't me. And if I'm being honest, Peters isn't the issue. It's Leonard. Missing him by hours. Can't fucking believe it. Is he psychic or something? Did he know we were coming for him?

A memory of my last visit to hospital just last year. I'd been stabbed in the arse by the deranged Moira Shearer when I acted to save the wee boy she'd kidnapped. Some important veins were cut apparently. The wounds were deep, and coming out of the fog of painkillers a familiar face hove into view. Leonard. And I was the only one who saw him. Or was it a drugged-up imagination?

No, it was him. He was keeping tabs on me then.

Is he still?

He must be. That leopard has indelible spots. And the fact is, he knows where I work. He can watch me on TV news. It wouldn't prove too difficult to watch my movements.

I knock my head against the door. *Calm down, McBain. You're just being paranoid.*

Just in case, I stand and walk back down to the street. Look left and right. Examine all of the people around me. An acne-scarred youth in a grey suit. A blonde beanpole in a red flowery dress and black leggings. A bald guy in faded jeans and dark blue casual jacket hoisting his backpack on to the other shoulder.

See, McBain. Nobody here who wants to kill you.

I hold my hands out in front of me. Hold them steady. Well, steadier.

Back to the breath.

In.

Out.

Can't go back to the office. I pull out my phone and dial a number.

'Converse,' says a familiar voice.

'Kenny, it's Ray.'

'Aye, Ray, I know. These modern phones have a thing where the name and number of the caller show on the screen.' He laughs at his own joke. An alien sound to my ears. People still laugh?

'Smartarse. What you up to? Want to play hookey?'

'Sorry, buddy. Crime never sleeps. People to do, things to see.'

'Round ye.' I hang up.

Ray nae pals. Any other friend I have is in the police. They're kind of busy.

I cough out a barking noise. It's the closest thing I've got to laughter. This is what you're reduced to, Ray. A priest, some polis or one of Glasgow's most notorious.

Or Maggie.

I can't. I'm just going to let her down. I recall what Kenny said. *She has to be the one to say no, don't you say it for her.*

That face. That smile. The way she looks at me. Accepting. Whatever I say and do is alright by her. I don't deserve her. I think of the people in my life. Clever, brave and resourceful, the lot of them. So why did they choose me? I'm letting them all down. They'd be better off without me.

My throat swells. Tightens.

Don't fucking cry, ya big Jessie.

I clench my face against the emotion that threatens to swamp me.

I take a step forward. And another. It's just like the breathing thing, isn't it? One after the other.

The pavement is grey. Scarred with old gum and cigarette ends. I move over it, lost in thought and barely mindful of the noise of the city around me. Then, a phone rings. A girl laughs. Someone crunches his way through a bag of crisps. The rustle and bustle of life is all around me, and I feel removed from it all. Like a patient freshly anaesthetised, on the countdown from ten.

Central Station is on my left. A line of people, all of them wearing jackets in primary colours, waiting for the airport bus. Seems everyone but me has a purpose.

The bronze statue of the fireman. A city's show of gratitude to the firemen who have died in service. I reach out a hand. Fingertips brushing his shoulder, hoping for a transfer of strength. Feel nothing but the indifference of the inanimate. Just like the people who are brushing past me on their rush to put meaning into the meaningless.

Past the Hielanman's Umbrella. The old name always fascinated me. There's no brolly here. It's a bridge taking trains into Central Station from the south and west, over the top of Argyle Street. Tall windows with green painted frames. Under which those seeking escape from the Highland Clearances would shelter from the rain they must have thought had followed them on their long walk from the north.

And on down past the business section of the town and to the River Clyde, and I've walked back almost to the spot I started. The tall buildings here seem to amplify the sounds of the traffic, and it feels like a blessing when I reach the river. The water is high and dark. Oil spilled by the nearby water taxi leaves a trail that's part rainbow, part dust and scum.

I lean on the railings and bend over to get a closer look. Feel the pull of the fall. If I just stretch up on to my toes. Lean forward a little more. It will be like there was no intention involved. A simple case of overextension. I'm not a good swimmer. It would be over in minutes.

Don't they say that death by drowning is a peaceful way to go? Once the initial panic is over and death is accepted.

Then, finally, I would get peace from being haunted and hunted by my own thoughts.

Peace.

I knock my forehead with a fist. I just want the shit in my head to stop.

Checking to my left I see a stand for a lifebuoy. It's empty. A victim of vandals. The lack of replacement probably the fault of austerity. All of which is helpful. Means no passing Samaritan will be able to help save me.

A dark-haired woman runs past me. She's tall, lean, head-to-toe in lycra, and she has the ungainly grace of the practised but awkward. See. Anybody can run. All it takes is the effort and the right, tight clothing.

I feel the bite of the railing's edge on my forearms and push myself back onto my heels. Away from the water's invitation. I lean forward again, rest my forehead on the railing. Feel its chill. What are you doing, McBain? Could you?

A siren in the distance. Part of any city's aural backdrop.

Something off to the left catches my eye. From here I can't exactly tell what's going on. People running. There's nothing strange about that in this city. Seems every other person goes for a jog in their lunch break. But these guys didn't get the joggers memorandum. They're wearing jeans and jackets.

Jesus fuck. You can't even contemplate topping yourself in this city without being interrupted by some idiots. Fuck them. Let them kill each other. Might mean one less scumbag for us to deal with.

44

Harrison is sitting behind his desk, hands clasped on the clear surface. He looks from Peters to me and then back again.

'Somebody want to explain this cluster of fucks?' he says.

As soon as I heard what had happened, I knew that the guys I witnessed running down Clyde Street were the boys involved in the drowning.

My intention was to leave them to it, but I spotted Daryl and Ale pass me in a car and brake sharply at the suspension bridge. I ran along the riverside to see what was happening, but by the time I arrived it was all over.

'Following our intelligence,' Peters says before I can open my mouth to answer, 'we tracked Jack Foreman and some of his friends to Clyde Street where they chased and crowded round Matt Davis on the suspension bridge. Davis tried to fight them off, and by way of evasive action, he stood on the railings. We didn't arrive in time to stop the fight, and Davis kicked out at the other boys, lost his balance and fell in to the water.' He pauses. Actually looks shocked. 'The lifebuoy at the Clyde Street end of the bridge was missing. By the time we sourced another one...'

And I'm thinking, *prick, even when you speak you sound like you're composing a report.*

'By the time Alessandra and Daryl checked the other end of the bridge, retrieved that lifebuoy and threw it to the boy, he had drowned,' I interrupt. Can't take any more of Peters' voice.

'And what was going on with you, Ray? DI Peters told me you had run out of the office a couple of hours earlier, like your coat was on fire.' He stared at me as if he could read my thoughts.

I looked at Peters, a question and an accusation in my eyes. Back to Harrison, thinking, better just be honest. Up to a point.

'I had a panic attack, boss.' And I feel the heat of shame at saying the words out loud to colleagues. 'I had to go out for some air.'

Harrison says nothing. Just looks at me. He's choosing his words with his usual care. Everything that comes out of his mouth is badged with the words self-preservation. And when he does speak, these ones are no different. He's distancing himself from this mess and firmly putting the blame on me and Peters. That Peters is also in the doghouse is a small consolation.

'DI Peters, you are the chief investigating officer on this case. Are you out of your depth?'

'Boss, I...'

'Shut up. That was a rhetorical question.' I steal a look at Peters, and he looks utterly deflated.

'DI McBain? Would any of this mess have happened on your watch if you'd been on your game?' And I wither under his stare. 'If you'd had the balls to admit you were having problems and taken proper care of yourself, we would have managed to get an experienced CIO on this case, and perhaps those two boys would still be alive.' He's referring to Ian Cook and Matt Davis.

I hear the truth in what he says and feel my self-loathing go up a notch. There's a warring thought that it might have helped if he had contributed to an atmosphere where that kind of honesty was even remotely possible.

'Do you really think they're all connected?' asks Peters. 'Cook was...'

'A girl is murdered and two known associates die shortly afterwards. Of course they're connected, you halfwit.' Harrison stands. Shuffles. 'Sadly, I was the one who put you in this position, Peters, and you're all we have at the moment.' He looks at me. 'Ray. I don't want to see you back in this office again until you have been signed off as fit for work.'

'But, boss...' I say.

'But nothing,' he interrupts. 'You used to be one of the best officers under my command, Ray. Now...' he tails off. Then quietly, with a hint of concern, 'Go get help, Ray. That's an order.'

* * *

Ale and Daryl are at their desks. They both look up as soon as I walk in the room.

'Well?' They both ask at the same time.

'I'm officially a basket case,' I say, my grin like a challenge. 'I need to see a shrink and get signed back as fit for work.' I sit at my desk and scan the papers that crowd the surface. It's quite the contrast to the super-organised one I'd just been dressed down in front of.

This is all delay tactics. I don't want to send my thoughts inwards. Then I might have to think about the Davis family and their lost boy. I can already see Helen Davis's face. First a husband. Now a son. How will she ever recover? I open the drawers. There's nothing here that I want to take with me.

'Helen Davis?' I ask, hoping beyond hope that she gets the official word before she learns of Matt's death on social media.

'Harkness is on his way,' says Daryl, his voice deep and sombre. 'Took one of the newbies. They have to go through that sort of thing soon enough.'

I nod. Stand and leave the room.

Ale catches up with me in the car park. She gives me a hug. My arms are down by my side, and I can't quite bring myself to share in the gesture. That would mean I was deserving.

'I saw you, Ray,' she says as she pulls away from me. 'I'm sure it was you. On the way to the bridge. We passed in the car and I caught a glimpse...' She broke off. The wind catches a strand of her hair, blows it to the side like it's a pennant. 'It looked like...' She crosses her arms as if less sure of what she is about to say. 'What were you doing down by the river?'

I see someone else I've let down. Someone else who's view of me has been diminished. Her eyes are full of sympathy, and I feel my gorge rise and I'm down by the river, body tilted towards the fall, considering the water's invitation and that final welcome silence.

I wouldn't have done it. Would I? People say it's the coward's way out. I just learned differently. It would have taken more courage than I will ever possess.

My smile is a brittle thing, and my eyes are stinging.

'I was just taking in some air, Alessandra. Just taking in some air.'

45

Leonard is sitting on a bench under a tree. The cloud cover clears and he turns his face up to the sun. Holds there for a long moment, accepting the heat like a blessing.

He rolls his head, feels the crack in his neck when his head tilts to the back. Could life get any better?

Planting that seed on social media worked a treat. Of course, those boys didn't actually want Matt Davis to die. Their blood was up. They wanted to feel knuckle on flesh. Make sure the boy suffered some pain and then leave him to the police.

But the hunt was on, and when they caught him, no one really knew what to do. It was a real gift that Davis took such evasive action. Leonard couldn't have planned it better.

Every cell is sparking. Blood is dancing through his veins. His brain is so big he notices everything. Locks it all in.

He thinks about Simon Davis. The boy will be in the first stage. He'll need Leonard's help, and the thought is enough to set off heat and joy through his entire body. He places both hands on his head as if to stop the top of his skull from blowing off.

A giggle almost escapes. He catches it. Looks over at the main door of the office building he's in front of. A man and woman are just coming out. He's standing with his arms by his side. She gives him a hug and stands back, suddenly unsure if the gesture was appropriate. His smile, Leonard can see even from here, is costing him. They speak. The man moves away, hands in his pockets, shoulders hunched as if in defence of his own thoughts.

The woman, thinks Leonard, he can catch up with later. And by catch up with, he means *make suffer*. The man is presently suffering enough for two. And Leonard watches the familiar gait and thinks, *It's still not enough.*

Two taxis pull up at the door of the office. One man gets out of the first. Two people get out of the second.

Leonard watches McBain shuffle to his car, and once he's sure he can't be seen, he runs to his own. Fires up the engine and follows.

* * *

Kenny is in his favourite café on Byres Road. His latest attempt at washing his cash through a legitimate business. A double espresso and a newspaper fill the table in front of him. He picks up the cup. Presses it against his lower lip, tilts and allows a small amount of the hot, bitter liquid to fill his mouth. Savours the ring tone of cup on saucer as he sets it back down. Who needs meditation? This is the stuff of life itself.

The door opens, he looks up and offers a smile at the woman who walks in. She nods and sits in front of him.

'Get you something, Alessandra?' he asks. She'd phoned. Prefers to meet to discuss her concerns about Ray.

She sighs. Sits as if being here with him breaches an unspoken rule. She tosses her hair. Meets his eye for the first time. 'Sure. Cappuccino.' And then, like she has just remembered a promise to be pleasant, 'Please.'

Kenny signals to the waiter. Orders. Looks at Ale. Appreciates the view. Long, dark hair, amber eyes and a heart-shaped face. And notes from her uncompromising expression that this lady has smarts.

Thinks, it's a shame she's not for sale.

'Nice day,' he says, less from an attempt to be pleasant, more to mess with her. He reads her discomfort and knows she wants to say her piece and move on. Quickly.

Her cappuccino arrives. She nods her thanks to the waiter.

'*Prego,*' he replies, and mentally Kenny tells him to fuck off, you're from Ruchill, mate, not Rome.

'Life treating you well?' Kenny asks.

Ale tosses her hair like she's brushing him off. 'I'm worried about Ray.'

'Me too,' he admits. 'What's on your mind?'

Ale tells him about Ray's behaviour. Recounts each episode in as much detail as she can remember. Kenny considers telling her about his experiences with Ray and decides not to. Ray needs some kind of privacy and, besides, she has a clear enough picture of the problem.

'And yesterday … I know it's a bit of a leap … and it *was* just a glimpse…' She looks away over Kenny's shoulder and through the window at the passing pedestrian traffic. Shakes her head. 'Och, I'm being silly.'

'Go on,' Kenny encourages. If there's one thing this woman is not, it's silly. He's only had limited dealings with her, but he can see there's nothing fanciful about what goes on between her ears.

'My car was speeding towards an incident. And it was only for a second. But I saw this guy leaning over the railings down by the Clyde. Looked like he was considering a jump.'

'Right.'

She smooths hair away from her eyes, pulls a strand behind her ear. 'It was only when I was past him that I realised it was Ray.'

'You think he was going to jump?' Kenny sits back in his chair. His mind pulling away from what Ale was saying.

'Maybe? I don't know.' She's reluctant to say more. In case saying the words out loud lend them truth.

'He's fucked up,' says Kenny. 'But, suicidal?'

Ale takes a first sip of her cappuccino. Swallows. Crosses her arms. 'Sorry. I'm being daft.' She looks Kenny in the eye, looking for reassurance. 'Ray wouldn't go there, would he?'

'Trust your instincts, DC Rossi. Ray thinks very highly of you. There's a reason for that.' Kenny realises that he is reluctant to face this, but having voiced Ray's view of Ale he begins to accept that what she is saying might have some validity.

'What stopped him, then?' he asks, while thinking, fuck me, Ray is in a worse place than even he realised.

'Dunno.' Ale looks over his shoulder again. 'He was back at work. The boy drowning might have been a wake-up call?'

'Well, that's good,' says Kenny. 'The impulse to do his job could be an important thing in getting him on the straight and narrow.'

'Yeah, but, Harrison has told him to see the doc and keep away from the office.'

'Shit,' says Kenny. And wonders if he should bring up the issue of the missing serial killer.

'Yup,' says Ale. An expression of doubt. She's not sure about saying what she's about to say. 'And has he told you about Leonard?' Her phone rang. She looked at the screen. Apologised to Kenny. 'I need to take this.'

She turned away from him. 'DC Rossi.'

Listened.

'You've got a match. Great.' Her expression lifts. She listens some more. An expression of surprise. Then she cuts the call. As she stands up, she fills Kenny in. 'I know Ray's been benched, but it might help if he knew what was going on.'

'I'll make sure he knows.'

'Ta,' she says and reaches for her cup and takes one last sip.

'Before you go, Ale,' says Kenny. 'How much do you know about Leonard?'

'Ray told me everything.'

'This is some kind of vendetta for Leonard. Everyone else involved in that killing in the home is dead. Apart from Ray.'

'Right.'

'Leonard wants Ray to suffer before he goes after him.'

'Right?'

'He enjoys killing people.'

'Yeah. Where are you going with this, Kenny?'

'If I was Leonard, I'd be targeting people close to Ray. It would really send him off the edge.'

Ale purses her lips. Makes a dismissive sound.

'Just…' He pauses. Now who's taking a leap? 'Just look after yourself, eh?'

46

I'm sitting outside Maggie's house in my car, rehearsing what I'm going to say. Searching for a knot of courage, reminding myself that Maggie is better than me. Deserves better than me.

All I will ever bring her is heartbreak.

I look up at her window. Try to gauge her response to my arrival from any movement I can see from this angle. Which is admittedly a stupid tactic.

What will I say? Hi Maggie. I've been missing you like crazy and oh, by the way, I nearly jumped into the Clyde yesterday and you're dumped. See ya.

Nutshell.

My passenger door opens and Kenny takes a seat.

'Shit. You gave me a fright, big man,' I say.

He answers with his don't-you-just-love-me grin.

'Thinking about sending smoke signals, or are you actually going to go in?' He nods his head in the direction of Maggie's house.

'Smoke signals are SO nineteenth century. I was going with mind reading.' I take the car keys out of the lock. 'How did you find me? *Why* did you find me?'

'In a word. Ale.'

I nod. Figures. Wish that girl would stop worrying about me. I look at him. He's now wearing his serious face.

'If you were thinking of doing something...' he considers his next words, '...fucking stupid, you'd come to me first, right?'

'What are you on about?' I know exactly what he's on about, but honesty isn't my strong suit these days.

He doesn't answer. Just stares at me, love and real concern in his eyes. I can't handle it and look away. There's a tightness in my throat I try to cough out. Why do these people care? I'm fucking useless.

I feel his big paw on my shoulder. 'Anything, Ray. I can handle it.'

'Well handle this,' I bristle. He can take his sympathy and shove it where only his proctologist will find it. 'Fuck off and leave me alone.' I get out the car and slam the door shut. As I walk towards Maggie's door I feel his stare burn into my back. Fuck him and his handling anything crap.

I hear him climb out of the car. 'Ale wanted me to tell you something about the case.'

I turn, all spit and venom. 'Put it in an email to I-don't-give-a-fuck dot com.'

Taking a moment before I knock on Maggie's door, I think, *way to go, McBain. Jesus. I have no patience these days.* I study my shoes. Kenny didn't deserve that. I take a deep breath and look up. Try to find the words for an apology, but he's already turned away.

Brought to you by today's theme tune, folks: Burning Bridges.

I knock. The door opens almost immediately. Maggie steps back to allow me entrance. Her arms are crossed and her eyes full of questions I don't want to answer. Colour blooms in her throat, and she swallows as if there was a piece of dry bread stuck there.

She takes a step towards me.

The words I want to use are caged behind my teeth. My jaw on lockdown.

'Ray,' she says, and it's a soft note of warmth. She pulls me into a hug. I feel her mouth move against my ear. 'Whatever is going on, I don't care. You need this.' From the moment I met her, she always knew more about me than I did myself. It was something other-worldly I refused to acknowledge or investigate.

We stand like that for a long moment. I accept the gift of her human contact for as long as I can. Torn between needing more and feeling I'm not worthy, I pull away. Study the carpet. Cough.

'Can't do this,' I say.

She crosses her arms. 'I felt it yesterday.' She pauses as if considering the wisdom of what she is about to say. 'You reached a crisis.' Her smile is weak but coloured with gratitude. 'For what it's worth, I'm glad you didn't...'

'Didn't what?' I challenge.

'Don't know,' she answers. 'I just got this horrible feeling that you were about to do something...' She searches for the right word. 'Final.'

'Yeah. Well, you're way off base, cos everything is fucking peachy.' And I don't know if I could feel any more loathsome than I do right now. Just don't speak, Ray. Whatever comes out your mouth now will be wrong.

'Sorry, if I've...'

'No, I should be one who's sorry. I can't seem to speak today without getting angry.' Even saying it aloud and I feel the wrong kind of energy flare in my chest. I meet her eyes, trying to send a silent message of apology. 'I should go,' I say and move to the door.

'Please, Ray,' Maggie says. 'You've just arrived.' She reaches out and holds my hand. I pull away from her touch.

I can see the hurt in her face and a moment of acceptance. The corners of her mouth twist downward as she struggles for control.

'Got to go,' I say, pull open the door and leave. *Before I really make you hate me*, I leave unsaid.

* * *

Kenny is leaning against my car. Arms crossed.

'I thought you'd fucked off,' I say.

'You dumped her, didn't you?' he asks, reading my expression.

'Go away, Kenny. I'm not in the mood.'

'That girl is the best thing that ever happened to you, you fucking idiot.'

'Yeah, and I'm taking relationship advice from you?'

'It's not advice. It's a statement of fact.'

I want to run at him and pummel his face until it's mush. My fists and my face clamp.

'Go on,' Kenny says. 'I'll take one punch if it makes you feel better. But fair warning, you won't get to two. Cos then I'll kick your arse.'

It would feel good to wipe that superior look off his expression.

But I know that if my fist meets his face, my fist will come off worst.

'Just leave me alone, Kenny,' I say as I reach the car. I press the remote to unlock it and climb in. He gets in the passenger side.

'What?' I ask.

'Just think of me as your friendly neighbourhood suicide watch kinda guy.'

'I wasn't...'

'Do us both a favour, Ray, and cut the crap.' His eyes are steel. Shame rubs at me. 'Take some pills. Get professional help. There's too many people who count on you.'

'Finished your lecture? *Now* would you kindly fuck off?'

'I'm going nowhere, McBain. Not letting you out of my sight for a second. So, chew on that. And while that's exercising your gums, here's the message from Ale.'

I study his expression, see the resolve there and dampen down the trace of relief that worms its way through my veins. I feel reassured by his presence, but I'd rather scrape the skin off my scrotum than admit that.

'OK. What?'

'The DNA results came in on the Aileen Banks' case.'

'Aye?' My interest is sparked despite my best attempt to disassociate myself from life.

'There's a match on the semen with the...' he searches for a name, '...the Davis guy?'

'I fucking knew it. Butter wouldn't melt the little prick.'

'Don't know what any of this means,' Kenny says with a puzzled expression. 'And they found something else. Some skin under the girl's fingernails.'

'Yeah?'

'So she's given someone a good clawing.'

'Someone?' I'm struggling to compute what Kenny's saying. If the semen sample was a match with the Davis DNA...

Kenny interrupts my thought. 'The skin sample didn't match with Davis, and there's no other match on the system.'

47

Leonard can feel the grief coming through his laptop screen. He soaks it up. Feels it light up every cell in his body. In the middle of the night, just a few hours after Matt Davis drowned, his brother was seeking comfort and understanding. From him. Not his mother or any of his friends. Him.

A message alert. And then.

'What the hell was he doing? Why were those guys chasing him? I can't believe my brother is actually…'

The words tailed off.

Then.

'Are you there? Can we talk? I REALLY need to talk to someone who understands.'

'I'm here for you, Simon,' Leonard typed and felt the electric charge of triumph.

'I can't type fast enough,' Simon writes. 'Can we meet up, please?'

'Of course. When?'

There's a delay of a few moments before Simon replies.

'Sorry. My mum needs me. I'll get back to you later, if that's ok?'

Then a message came up to say that Simon was now offline.

* * *

Ale parks the car, pulls on the handbrake and looks over at Daryl Drain.

'Ready for this?' she asks.

'What else should you be doing at eight o'clock in the morning, other than arresting the twin brother of a drowning victim?' He adds as an aside, 'In front of his grieving mother.'

'When I come back, I'm coming back as a nail technician,' Ale says, 'cos to hell with this shit.' She can already see Helen Davis's face twist with grief when she delivers the news that her son is in fact a murder suspect after all. Just a couple of days after her other son dies. She'd asked Peters for a day's grace before she arrested Simon Davis. Hoping for a couple. But Peters was under pressure from the suits, and they wanted this case put to bed long before now. Any delay when there was an identifiable chain of events was just not feasible. He finished with a withering look and the command: do your job.

'Ale, you didn't make the world. Nor do you make people do the things they do,' says Daryl.

'The world is populated by bloody idiots, if you ask me.'

'Right,' says Daryl. 'No time like the present. Let's go.'

Ale's legs feel like they've been coated in fast-drying concrete as she walks up to the front door. Daryl knocks.

Helen Davis answers even before the sound stops reverberating. She must have noticed them waiting and deduced why.

'You're not taking my son,' she says.

'Can we come in, please, Mrs Davis?' Ale asks. 'We can't really discuss this on the doorstep.'

She turns to the side and allows them entry. Closes the door behind them. Crosses her arms. 'There's something you should know, before you speak to Simon.' Her face is lined and grey. Her eyes are heavy and their light is dim. She looks about ten years older than the last time Ale saw her, just a few days ago. 'Aileen Banks was having a thing with both my boys. Playing one off against the other.' She pauses. Steels herself against what she is about to say. 'Matt was with her on the night she died. Not Simon.'

'Just what are you saying, Mrs Davis?' Ale asks.

'Simon did a DNA test? The results are in, yes?' She sticks her chin up, challenging us for the information.

'We can't divulge that information at this stage,' Ale says, suddenly doubting whether or not this was the case.

'Well, let me save you the trouble of arresting my son.' She gulps back some tears. 'Identical twins have identical DNA. True? Yes?

241

The result you have matches with Simon. But it wasn't him who left the...' her expression sours, '...sample. It was Matt. Because, if you were listening earlier, Aileen had both my boys twisted round her finger. And that night, she was with Matt.'

'Mum,' says a voice from the top of the stairs. 'What are you doing?' Feet drum down the stairs and Simon is beside her mother. He looks as if his eyes have slipped half way down his face. He's wired, anxious and utterly fatigued. He tugs at her sleeve. 'Mum,' he admonishes her.

'On the day after ... the day after my son dies,' she draws herself up to her full five feet. 'The police have arrived to arrest my son. I'm finally ... finally telling them the truth. Can't hurt Matt now, eh?' Her smile is twisted with determination to protect her one surviving family member, and Ale wonders if the truth has also been twisted to help.

'Tell them, son. Tell them,' Helen speaks quieter now.

'Tell them what, Mum?' Simon takes a step back as if he wants to run back upstairs to the safety of his room.

'That Aileen was playing you off one against the other.'

'Mum, please,' says Simon. Ale's reading of this is that the boy is clearly conflicted. But is it with this version of events, or does he want to protect the good name of the girl he was in love with?

Helen is in his face now. 'Was Aileen seeing Matt before she died?'

Simon is a study in pain and silence. He looks like a man about to be placed in front of a firing squad.

'Simon,' Helen says.

A whisper. 'Yes.'

'Did you see Aileen on the night she died?'

His voice remains low. 'No.'

Helen is almost at breaking point but manages to ask, 'And did Matt see Aileen on the night she died?'

Simon's silent response stretches on for more seconds than is comfortable. Helen doesn't press him this time. She simply places a hand on his forearm. Simon almost slumps at the touch.

Then.

'Yes. Matt told me later…' Simon looks from Daryl to Ale. 'But you have to believe me. Aileen was alive when he left her.' He stares his certainty into her eyes. 'You have to believe me. Matt didn't kill Aileen.'

48

Ale and Daryl are on the way back to tell Peters the news. Both processing the information as presented by Helen and Simon Davis.

'What do you think?' Daryl asks.

Ale takes her eyes off the road for a moment. 'If the two of them are singing the same tune, there's little we can do, unless we have some kind of evidence to the contrary.'

'Aye, but do you think they're lying?'

She sees Simon Davis in her mind. The way his eyes flick from his mother to the floor and back. She read a reluctance to answer, and her gut is telling her this was coming from a need to protect Aileen.

'I think Helen would do and say anything at this point to protect her boy. Simon? I'm not thinking "liar" when I see him speak.'

Back in the office, and Peters is duly apprised of the recent information. He gives a single word response.

'Shit.'

'We'll need to get them both in for statements. Get it on record.'

'Yeah,' he says. The thought heavy on his mind. 'Let's give them a break for a day or two first.' He looks over the office towards John Harkness's desk. 'Foreman was clearly the ringleader of this wee barney on the bridge. He needs to be charged with manslaughter. Harkie, see to it, there's a good lad.' Then he walks out of the room like his work is done for the year.

Ale is at her desk. She checks her emails. Nothing needs to be done. She checks her phone. Same story there. She pulls open her top drawer and sees Ian Cook's phone. Thinks, this needs to be returned to evidence.

On a whim, she pulls it from her drawer and switches it on. She checks Facebook. Another couple of friend requests. Ghouls and trolls. The internet does bring out an interesting side of people, she thinks.

She thumbs the icon on the phone to see Cook's photographs. Some selfies of him and Jack, their smiles large and completely unmindful of anything other than the moment. And perhaps getting pissed and then laid. Poor fucker, she thinks. Nobody deserves to have their throat cut and to be just left like that, like trash.

Next she finds one of Aileen Banks.

And another.

And another.

Seven in total.

Thinks, whoa. Haud the bus.

In all of them, she's been taken unawares. No duck-face pouts. No side-on, chest out, stomach in, poses. She's at a table. She's walking down the street. She's talking to someone off camera. In all of them, she doesn't know she's in focus. Ale shivers. She counts the photos in the thread. Yup, seven. What the hell is going on here?

She examines her thoughts in more detail. Sees where the link might be. But something's missing. She picks up Cook's phone again. Scrolls through more images until one appears like a gift.

Interesting. Very interesting.

'You coming?'

'Where now?' asks Drain and looks in the direction of Peters' office. Asking, *should we check with him first*?

Ale makes a face, saying, to hell with him. She sends the photographs on Ian's phone to her work email. Registers that they have arrived and presses print. She stands up.

Says, 'Right.'

'What?' asks Drain.

'We're off to see that daft wee bint Karen Gardner.'

* * *

Leonard's laptop alerts him to a message. He feels a charge in his gut. Hopes it is Simon Davis.

'Can we talk?' It is Simon.

'Sure', he answers. And a moment of elation threatens to blow the top off his skull.

'Not here. Can't type fast enough. AND I need to get out of this house. I can't look at my mum for another second.' There's a pause for about thirty seconds. 'I can't handle her upset and mine.'

'Same place we arranged last time?'

This time the pause is longer.

'Please. Yes. Promise me you'll be there this time?'

There's a world of vulnerability in this last question, and Leonard feels himself respond, but not in his usual way.

'Of course I will. Last time was about me and I'm not good when it's about me.' Leonard pauses in his typing and tries to name the emotion he is experiencing. Could he be feeling something for this boy? They arrange a time to meet and sign off.

He gives the feeling a name. Affection. Drags it into a corner of his mind and imagines huge metal studded boots stamping on it with heart-thrilling abandon.

He thinks, that's a first.

And the last.

49

I can feel Kenny's eyes on me. He's not left my side for hours and it's beginning to get on my last nerve.

'You can relax. The moment's passed.'

'So you admit you were going to top yourself?' he asks, eyebrows almost at his hairline.

'It's like there's this voice. My voice. But I can't control it. Can't shut it up, you know?' I say and search his eyes for understanding. He nods, but he clearly has no clue what I'm on about. 'But it starts with a feeling. My hands sweat, my heart feels like it's being squeezed, my breath … I find it difficult to breathe. And the lights go out. I can barely see.'

'Right,' says Kenny. No judgement, but little understanding. He's always had a healthy conceit of himself. Control over his mind. It's like trying to explain nuance to someone whose worldview is made up entirely of black and white.

'And I can't control it. Don't know when it's going to hit next. Don't know how to stop it when it happens.' I shake my head. 'I'm not losing my mind. I'm not.'

'Didn't say you were, mate,' he says, and I can feel his frustration. He has two weapons: his tongue and his fists. He's equally dexterous with both. If the first doesn't do the job, he can bring in Hurt and Pain. Those are the nicknames he jokingly gave each set of knuckles. And he's in a position now where neither will do the job. Maybe he'll discover that his ears are the necessary tools this time around. 'Another coffee?'

Oh good Christ, he's got his fingernails working through the bottom of that barrel.

'If I have another coffee, I'll burst.'

His phone sounds an alert.

'It'll keep,' he says.

Then another. And another.

He waves it away, his hand pushing through the air. 'It's just work shit.'

Another alert sounds.

'For fuck's sake, Kenny. I'm not going to go rifling through the knife drawer while you look at your phone. Just answer it, eh?'

He makes a dismissive noise. 'I didn't want you to think I wasn't listening…' he tails off as he picks up the phone. Reads the alerts on the screen.

'It's Ale. Four texts.'

Then the phone rings. 'Surprise, surprise.' He smiles. 'It's Ale.'

He answers. 'Were you wearing out your thumbs?'

He listens to her answer, says, 'Wait a minute, Alessandra. I'm putting the phone on speaker.' And her voice comes through.

'I hope you are on your own. I wouldn't want DI Ray McBain to be hearing any of this.' Meaning, I want Ray to hear all of this.

'I'm totally on my lonesome. Thinking of you, as it happens. And those beautiful brown eyes of yours.' He chuckles.

'They're amber, by the way. And another by the way? In your dreams, big guy.'

'Just you keep on fighting it, honey,' Kenny says.

'If you two would stop trying to wind each other up,' I interrupt.

'Sorry,' says Ale. Coughs. 'You can't help the company you keep.'

Kenny chews on his retort. 'See my increasing maturity, Ray?' he asks. 'I'm totally letting this moment slip past.'

'Congrats,' I say. 'Now kindly shut the fuck up and allow Ale to speak.'

'Thanks,' says Ale. 'And yes, I was getting sore thumbs typing out all those texts. Thought I would do it the old fashioned way and actually use out loud words and shit.'

'So, speak.'

'You got the message about the DNA match? But they found another sample. In her fingernails.'

Interesting.

Then I have a moment of appreciation for Ale, and emotion robs me of speech. We both know she shouldn't be doing this. And we both know I can't act on any of this information. She's letting me in on this to make me feel involved. There's a silent acknowledgement that work is the one thing that is keeping me going, it's the one thing that is being denied to me. This time, I'm out. Once and for all. Or the suits will fire my fat arse.

And I acknowledge, the fight has gone out of me.

I get my voice back. 'Sorry could you say all that again, please?'

'Ma Davis and her son, Simon, are saying that the semen on Aileen came from Matt.'

'Convenient. Do you believe them?'

'Actually I do. And,' I can hear a note of excitement in Ale's voice, 'Ian Cook has some interesting photos on his phone. Feels like he was stalking Aileen Banks.'

'Really?' And I imagine his corpse, throat cut, under a tree, behind a wall just across the road from the Davis house. We're missing something.

'We're on our way to bring in Karen Gardner. There's something in that head that will give us the key to all of this. I'm sure of it.' She hangs up with a cheery 'See ya.' And I quash the faint twist of envy forming in the line of my jaw. I can trust Ale to get the job done.

I'm out.

'What's going on in that fat, ugly head of yours, McBain?' Kenny asks.

'Don't take this the wrong way, Kenny. But you need to fuck off.' I put my hand up to silence his ensuing note of protest.

'I'm officially letting you know I'm off the suicide watch list,' I say and offer him a smile by way of apology. Probably comes across like a grimace. I make a decision as I articulate it. 'I'm going to see the doc. Get proper counselling and…' it chokes me to admit I need them, '…maybe some happy pills.'

He stands up. Smooths down imaginary creases on the front of his trousers, not successfully hiding his relief.

'You know I'm only at the end of the phone. And if you need me. Any time, day or...'

'Yeah, yeah. And I love you too, big man.' Can't remember if I've ever said that to Kenny before. Sober or drunk. Fuck, I am losing it. I put my hand on his shoulder. I'm not saying it again, but I'll allow the feeling to transfer through my touch. I squeeze. 'Take me home, Jeeves. I've got legally available drugs to arrange.'

50

Simon is across a small table from Leonard. They're back in the café of the big bookshop on Argyle Street. Leonard has a black coffee. Simon has a glass full of Irn-Bru and ice that he's swirling around with a straw. Apart from an almost silent, 'Hi,' they've barely spoken to each other.

Leonard isn't worried. The boy is here. He'll speak when he's good and ready. Silence has never been a thing of threat to him. Some people act like it burns their ears, and they rush to fill it with any old nonsense. Whatever comes out of his mouth, Leonard thinks, matters. Is leading somewhere.

He looks over the boy's shoulder, out of the window, at the grey building across the street and beyond that, a blue spotted sky. A large gull cuts through the air. Even from here, Leonard can see the glare of focus in its small, dark eyes. On the scavenge. A smile flickers on and off Leonard's face. He can relate.

'Can you remember how you felt when your twin died?' Simon asks.

'Like it was yesterday,' Leonard answers, leaning back in his chair.

'It hurts,' Simon leans forward, tears brimming in his eyes. 'How do you get it to stop?'

'It never goes away,' he says with an expression he hopes conveys solidarity. 'You just learn to accept there's permanent pain there. Just within reach. And you get on with the rest of your life.'

'I can't imagine life without...' he says, and his head falls forward. He places his elbows on the table and hides his face behind his hands. His shoulders move in time with his grief. 'Why me? What did I do to deserve ... First my girlfriend and now my...' His sobs take him off to a place that Leonard knows he will never reach.

He's aware now that people are staring. Perhaps it's time to take this somewhere else. With care, he reaches forward. Touches the boy's arm.

'Not here, Simon. Best not give these people a show,' he says, and to his shock finds that his concern is genuine.

* * *

By the time they get Karen Gardner back to the station, Jack Foreman has also been brought in. Peters meets her outside the interview rooms. He gives her a nod.

'Foreman has been charged already. He's in Room One. We'll put Gardner in Two.'

'OK,' Ale says, wondering where this is going. No need to tell her the bleeding obvious.

'I want you to lead on this,' he says, and Ale takes a step back. Reading her surprise, he continues, 'You seem to have more of a handle on this case than anyone else.' To which Ale silently adds, apart from Ray.

'OK. Cool.' She straightens her jacket, checks the top button on her shirt. Wants to look the ultimate professional. Scare the shit out of Karen Gardner. She hadn't said a word to the girl all the way here in the car. Allowing the silence to intimidate her.

'Let's allow Miss Gardner to stew a wee while longer. We'll speak to Foreman first.'

She runs back to her office, picks up the photographs from her desk, puts them in a brown folder. Runs back.

Peters gives her a strange look.

'Props,' she answers and waves the folder at him. Peters opens the door. They walk in together and each take a seat in front of the young man. Ale gives him the once over. He's wearing a plain, black t-shirt that looks like it might have been taken out of the to-be-washed basket and stretched out to try and get rid of the worst creases before being pulled on.

Foreman is slumped in his chair. Arms crossed, chin tucked into his chest and his eyes on a fixed point on the table between them. Peters clicks on the recorder and speaks to record who is present in the room.

'Hi Jack,' says Ale. 'How are you doing?' A little friendly voice might be just the thing to get him to open up. She places the folder on the table between them.

'Oh, you know, dandy,' Jack answers. Ale can read the small, frightened boy behind the attempt at bluster.

'You understand the charges?'

He nods.

Peters says, 'For the tape, Jack Foreman has nodded his assent to the question.'

Ale recalls the moment she arrived on the bridge and broke through the cluster of angry young men. Matt Davis was standing on the railing, holding on to the supports with his right hand. He swung out with his foot, trying to catch Jack on the side of the head. Jack moved out of reach. Ale was face on to him and could see at that moment he had come to his senses. The chase had got his blood up. And then at the moment that his prey was cornered and in a vulnerable position, his mood changed. Perhaps he recognised the danger Davis was in, for he then held a hand out.

What he said was lost in the shouts that were going on all around them, but to Ale it had the feel of being conciliatory.

'I saw your face just before Matt Davis fell into the river.'

'Aye. So?'

'You realised that things had got out of hand, and you were trying to tell him that he was safe. You weren't going to do anything.'

'Doesn't matter though, does it? He's still deid,' he says, and his eyes move from Ale to the wall to the right. He swallows, and Ale sees guilt and acceptance. Someone's son is dead, and he was the ringleader in the chase to his death. What he doesn't know yet is how he's going to live with that fact. His chin falls onto his chest again.

'Sure, there's no way round the manslaughter charge, but the judge might go a little bit more lenient on sentencing if I testify that at the last moment, you changed. You tried to talk Davis down.'

'Yeah. Well,' he says. His eyes fill with tears. 'I was so fucking angry. I wanted someone to know, you know. But I didn't want anyone to die.' He puts his head on the table and gives in to his tears.

'Can we get you a glass of water, Jack?'

'Nah,' he sits up. Sniffs and wipes his face with his hands. 'I'm just … I can't believe this has happened.'

'The defence will argue that the murder of your best friend, Ian Cook, drove you over the edge. That you're normally not a violent guy.'

'Yeah, well.'

'You have no prior convictions. Not even a parking ticket.'

He nods. Remembers that Peters had to fill in for his last silent gesture, says, 'Aye.'

'And if you are seen to help us with our enquiries, all of this will be in your favour when it comes to sentencing.'

He's listening intently now.

'Right.'

'So tell me, what was Ian Cook doing outside the Davises' house on the night he was murdered?'

'He was delivering a letter.'

'A letter. As in, Dear Mrs Davis, you have a lovely home?'

He attempts a smile. Fails. 'A letter as in, Dear Mrs Davis, your son is a murdering bastard.'

'Is that not what Twitter and Facebook are for?'

'Ian wanted to do it up close and personal.'

'So it was Ian's idea? The hate mail?'

He nods. Looks over at Peters and before he can speak, he says, 'Yes, the hate mail was Ian's idea.'

'Why?'

'He was convinced that Simon Davis had killed Aileen, and he didn't want him to get away with it.'

'Did he have any evidence?'

Jack looks surprised for a moment. 'Evidence? No. He just knew.'

'So, this was like, a superpower thing for him?'

Jack snorts. 'Simon was the boyfriend. It's usually the boyfriend, eh? He hated that Aileen was seeing other guys, so he went postal and in a moment of … I don't know, rage, he kills her.'

'And you have no evidence of this, other than Ian's assertion?'

'Makes sense to me.'

'Right. You were an ex-boyfriend of Aileen's. Why weren't you on Ian's suspect list?'

'Cos we were together on the night Aileen died.'

'All night? You never left each other's sight?'

He looks vacant for a moment, and it's as if he's about to snort again and answer in the affirmative. 'Well, we had to go to the loo and stuff.' He thinks some more, obviously considering that his admission might make him a suspect. 'But, like, it would have been just a few minutes. Not long enough to kill anyone.'

Ale is about to ask, how would you know how long it might take to kill someone, and decides that might not be wise.

'…and Ian has the odd smoke when he has a beer, so he would have left me to go outside for a cig. Other than that. We were together all evening.'

'What happened with you and Aileen?'

'Wasn't much of a thing. Really.' His expression is apologetic as if he's sorry he's about to be disrespectful to the dead. 'There wasn't much of a spark. For either of us. We had a laugh about it after. She said it was like kissing damp wallpaper. I said I got a bigger charge from sooking on a drainpipe.'

'Nice,' Ale says.

'She was cool. Didn't take herself too serious. Liked a laugh.'

'How many dates did you have?'

'About half a dozen.'

'And when did you realise the earth wasn't going to be moving any time soon?'

'On the first date.'

'So why carry on seeing her?'

'Ian and Karen. She totally fancied him and kept pushing Aileen to double date,' he says and makes a face. 'I didn't mind, Aileen was good company, like, and a looker, and she understood if I got a better offer and legged it.'

'And what was in it for Ian?'

'Karen. She was all over him. Made it clear she was his for the taking.'

'And did he *take* her?'

A shrug. 'Far as I know.'

'How did Ian get on with Aileen?' Ale asks, thinking of the group photograph.

'Fine.' His face forms a non-committal expression.

'Just fine?' Ale asks.

He looks quizzical. 'What do you mean?'

'It was Ian's idea to mess with the Davises, yes?'

'Yes.'

'Seems like a pretty extreme action to take for someone your mate had a failed date with and who got on with, just, fine.'

Jack shrugs. 'Never really thought about it before.'

Ale looks pointedly at the folder on the table.

'What's that?' Jack takes the nibble.

'Open it and see.'

With a look at Ale's face, trying to gauge the importance of whatever is inside, Jack lifts up an edge. Pulls back the paper. The first photograph catches his attention.

'She was a beautiful girl,' says Ale.

'Yeah,' replies Jack as he looks at the next one. And the next. Ale puts a hand on his before he gets a chance to look at the very last image.

'What strikes you about these pictures?' Ale asks.

'That the photographer doesn't have the best camera in the world.'

'And?'

He studies the first two again. He looks up at her with a spark of realisation. 'Aileen had no idea these were being taken, did she?'

Clever boy, thinks Ale. Didn't take him long to catch up.

'What's this about?' he asks, his expression wary.

'Carry on,' says Ale, aiming her vision at the pictures.

'It's like she's been papped.'

'Sorry, you'll have to explain that,' interrupts Peters.

Jack looks at him like he's the stupidest person in the city. 'Paparazzi. They stalk celebs, take photos of them in everyday situations and sell them to newspapers and magazines.'

'Interesting choice of words there, Jack,' says Ale. 'Stalk.'

Jack's eyes widen. 'Aileen was being stalked?'

'I couldn't say,' replies Ale.

'Who by? That's your guy then,' he raises his voice. Animation showing for the first time in the interview. 'You've got the guy. Brilliant.' Pause. 'Where did you find these photos?'

Ale picks a photo from the bottom of the pile. Places it in front of Jack.

It's a happy, smiley photo of four young people, untouched and untouchable. Jack and his BFF, Ian Cook, are front and centre. Jack has his arm over the shoulder of Aileen Banks.

She's smiling. But it's clearly fake. She'd rather have someone else's arm in that position. At the other end of the small group sits Karen Gardner. She's holding Ian's hand in hers and is all tits and teeth.

Cook's smile is weak. His face turning away from Karen, focused on the girl at the other end of the foursome. His eyes have an unmistakable look of longing.

Jack looks at it and then looks up at Ale. 'I don't understand.'

'Look at your pal, Ian. Who is he focused on?'

Jack looks at Ale, his face a study in confusion.

'Look at the photo, Jack,' she says gently.

'He looks like he'd rather be sitting beside Aileen than Karen,' Jack says, as if the words cause him pain. He looks from Ale to Peters and then back at the photograph. His mind struggling to take this all in.

'We found all of these images on Ian Cook's mobile,' Ale says.

Jack starts. Jumps back. His hand goes automatically to his mouth, as if holding back the words that might spill from it.

'Oh my God,' he says. 'Ian.'

51

The brass plaque has an almost blinding shine, reads "Chalmers, Crowe and Gibson", and I never thought I'd see it again. It's pinned to a block of sandstone at the doorway to an imposing Georgian terrace. I'm in Carlton Place, and if I look behind me I can see the arched grand entrance to the suspension footbridge from which poor Matt Davis recently took a header. Only the Victorians could have been so extravagant as to adorn a footbridge in such a manner.

With an apology over my shoulder, aimed at his ghost, I press the buzzer.

From a small speaker a voice says, "Chalmers, Crowe and Gibson."

'I have an appointment with Elaine Gibson,' I say. 'McBain. My name's McBain.'

The door clicks. I push and I'm in.

I nod at the receptionist and take a seat in the low, red cushioned chairs, and just as my arse is relaxing into the padding, one of the doors opens. Elaine Gibson walks towards me, hand out.

I take it and shake.

'DI McBain,' she says. 'Nice to see the sun shining after such a miserable summer.'

'Yes,' I agree, struggle to say anything else and wonder, again, at a beautiful woman's ability to turn my brain to mush. Settle for, 'You've done your hair.'

After the "Stigmata killings" – or deaths caused by Jim Leonard, as only I know him – I spent a few weeks receiving therapy here. It was difficult and revealing, but only partially exorcised the ghosts of my childhood. And I was happy to deflect many of the therapist's questions on to the subject of the deranged child abductor I was – unofficially – chasing at the time.

She smiles and, with a flick of her index finger, clears her fringe from her eyes. My brain helpfully provides an image of her stepping out of her shower, naked, wet and gleaming. I blush.

'Shall we?' She points towards her room, and I walk past her through the door and take a seat. As she joins me I take a look around the room. The same plants. The same bookcases. And it feels like the intervening months happened to someone else.

'Thank you for seeing me at such short notice,' I say.

She sits and crosses her legs with the grace and polish of a dancer. 'Luckily we had a cancellation.' Her smile is quiet, non-committal. Meant to confer nothing but a professional interest, and I find myself wanting to see it in full bloom.

Jesus. Enough, McBain.

I bring her up to speed with what has been happening since we last met. She takes notes in her pad. Stops her scribbling every few moments to listen, head cocked to the side. Every now and then she makes a small noise to highlight that she is actively listening. We must have gone to similar training courses. But with her the interest feels genuine.

'So, life has not been without its challenges,' she sums up, once I stop speaking.

'That's one way of putting it.'

'How would you put it?' she asks.

I want to say, *fucked up*. Settle for a smile and, 'Life has had its challenges, right enough.'

'And you say your boss thinks you have PTSD? What do you think?'

'I think he's an arse.'

She raises an eyebrow.

'But...' I continue, 'he may have a point.'

'And the panic attacks? Looking down into the river. Would you have jumped if those boys hadn't thrown you out of that thought pattern?'

I sit back in my chair, arms crossed. Don't think I have the honesty to answer this.

She waits.

'Dunno.'

'Mmmm,' she says and writes something down. 'The important thing, DI McBain, is that you didn't.' Her eyes narrow as she considers her next few words. 'It can often take more courage to go on living.'

I purse my lips. Blow. 'Forgive me, but that's bullshit.' This comes out with a tad more aggression than I intend. 'Sorry.' I swallow it down. Feel my fingers curl into my palm. Nails digging. 'I didn't have the guts to jump. That's the truth.'

'Yes?' She's not agreeing with me. She's asking for clarification.

'I've been to the edge, Miss Gibson. Forgive the hyperbole, but I've peered into the abyss. It doesn't peer back, it pulls you fucking in. Anyway, how can you possibly understand this? Have you ever suffered from any of this shit?'

'My situation is not up for discussion, Ray. But I will say, you don't have to have had a heart attack to become a heart surgeon.' Nicely answered, but we both know my attack on her was a poor attempt at deflection.

'And what,' she continues, too experienced to let my words affect her, 'happened when you got pulled in?'

'Noise.'

'Noise?'

'Chatter. Noise. All of the senseless crap we tell ourselves. Every damaging thought I've ever entertained until it was all I could do to keep breathing.'

'What does the abyss represent to you?'

I don't think about it too much. Just let the words come. 'Me. My deepest thoughts. The unvarnished, the guileless, unprotected, wilful, most selfish, most cruel...' I break off. Look down and see that my hands are shaking.

'Don't you think that it's natural to question your existence? To wonder at your worth in the scheme of things?'

'Yes, but not when the black dog is panting in the corner. Waiting to tear your throat out. Then it's dangerous. The answer more likely to send you into even more of a spiral.'

'Is that what took you down to the waterside?'

I nod.

'What was going through your head?'

'I wanted the chatter, the breathlessness, the sweats, the nightmares ... I wanted it all to stop. I wanted to give my friends a break. It occurred to me that I would be doing them all a kindness if I jumped. Sure, they'd grieve for a while. Then life would be easier. Simpler.' I look away into the distance. Seeing nothing.

I cringe from my words.

'And?'

'And now ... saying it out loud? I can't believe the conceit. That I could be of that importance to anyone.' Pause. And I'm granted an insight. 'I'm worthless.' The last two syllables escape from my mouth in a whisper. I feel a tear moisten my cheek. I wipe it away with my right hand. Elaine waits until I control myself. Waits until I can lift my eyes up to meet hers.

She uncrosses her legs, puts her pad on to the table between us and leans forward. She speaks with an intensity that takes me unawares. 'The good thing is that you've recognised there's a problem, and you want to get help. We can work with that.'

A smile trembles across my lips. I can't help but feel it's too late.

52

Leonard leads Simon Davis past the stares of curious booklovers, out the large, glass doors, and into the bustle and buzz of Argyle Street.

'Want to just walk?' he asks, needing to raise the volume of his speech after the calm of the bookshop.

Simon nods. 'Yeah. Don't want to make a fool of myself again.'

'I have a car. We could go and sit in that. Nobody will see you if you cry.'

'Nah. Let's just walk.' He looks into Leonard's eyes as if searching for something. He puts a hand out. Touches his forearm. 'And, thanks. I barely know you and you've...' he struggles with the right thing to say. Repeats, 'Thanks. You're a real mate.'

Leonard looks away. Discomfited. Can't remember the last time someone touched him in such a way. Honest and grateful. He can feel the heat of it as he judges the traffic, waiting for a double-decker bus to pass before crossing the road. He's only ever been touched in an effort to harm.

A memory so sharp, he stumbles over the kerb. He sees a small, pale face. A weak smile, and a hand touching his arm. The last time he saw his twin brother alive.

Here, in the present, a hand reaches out to stop him from falling. He finds his feet, whirls round to attack and sees that it is Simon. He steps back from the look in the young man's eyes, a flicker of alarm appearing on his face.

'Sorry.' Leonard holds a hand up. 'I'm not myself today.'

'If you want...'

'We're fine. You're fine. Let's keep walking.'

Leonard turns left, walks to the bank at the end of the block and takes a right. A young, smartly dressed man steps in front of them.

Grey suit, purple tie. Slicked-back hair tops a handsome face. Tries to sell them what he calls the bargain of the week.

'You guys got a girlfriend? A mother? They're going to love this,' he chimes, holding out a glossy piece of card. His fake sincerity gleams and Leonard sticks his hand in his pocket, feels the flick-knife resting there and imagines whipping it out and scoring it across the guy's throat.

He leans into his space.

Says, 'Fuck off.'

Two steps further and Simon coughs a laugh. 'Brilliant. I've always wanted to do that.'

'Feel sorry for him, actually,' Leonard lies. 'Can't be easy standing there all day, mustering the energy to sell to every single person that passes.'

They walk past the new glass entrance to the St Enoch subway station, over gleaming concrete and on to the space beyond.

'Where are we going?' asks Simon as his pace slows. He stops.

'What's wrong?' asks Leonard.

Simon is staring straight ahead. Leonard knows what's going through his head.

'That's the river just ahead.' There's a shiver in his voice. 'And that's the actual bridge that...'

'God, I'm sorry,' says Leonard, thinking this is working out nicely. 'I had no idea.' He examines Simon's face. Assesses his possible thought process. Has he misjudged the boy?

'We can go back that way? Up to George Square? Grab a seat there?'

'Nah. Too full of tourists,' Simon answers. He stays locked in position. Eyes aimed at the bridge in the distance.

'You know, it might actually help,' says Leonard. 'Might help lay him to rest?'

Simon says nothing. Simply looks straight ahead. Then, he reaches a decision and without a word starts walking again.

They come to a pedestrian crossing. Simon presses the button and they wait in silence for the traffic to come to a halt.

It stops. They cross and walk up to and under the grand sandstone arch entry. When Leonard has judged they've reached the middle of the bridge, he stops. Simon walks on another pace and turns to face the water. He looks down. Shudders. His face glistening with tears.

'Matt,' he says. 'Matt, what were you thinking?'

Leonard says nothing. Feels the energy of the young man's grief. Savours. Acknowledges his part in orchestrating the whole affair. He takes a step closer, symbolising his willingness to accept some of Simon's burden. Feels his knees weaken. Holds a hand out to steady himself, and again Simon provides the support, reaching out and grabbing him by the wrist.

What is it about this boy, thinks Leonard? His thoughts are interrupted by the drum of feet and a familiar voice.

'Simon? Simon Davis?

Then Leonard feels a pull at his arm that nearly pulls him off his feet.

'Leonard, what the hell are you doing here?' asks Detective Inspector Ray McBain.

53

I leave my meeting with Elaine Gibson feeling utterly drained. Whoever said that confession was good for the soul was full of shit. I just want to take a shower and go back to pretending that everything is just fine.

I walk past the entrance to the footbridge. Think about taking a walk over to the other side, to revisit the scene of my near suicide attempt. Shrink from it in case the water's invitation still stands.

Oh, c'mon tae fuck, I tell myself. *Need to face your demons, Ray.* I look back at the door to Gibson's office. Then over to my left and the safety of my parked car.

Fuck it. Take a walk, Ray.

I pass under the arch and on to the bridge. A man passes by on my left. He's tall, lean as a post and whistling. He pulls his cigarette from his mouth, squints a smile through the smoke. 'Fucking brilliant,' he says.

Right, I think. *Get me whatever this guy's on.* My own face twists into a smile in response. Bloody hell, it's catching.

A couple of steps on and another guys passes. He's wearing a dark suit, white shirt, dark tie. He's bald, with thick spectacles and carrying a briefcase. I pass on the greeting from the previous guy.

He glares in response.

'Can't win them all,' I say out loud, now suspicious of my lift in mood.

A couple of men standing in the middle of the bridge catches my eye. The younger one seems familiar, even from this distance. I take a few more steps forward. Jesus, it's Simon Davis. What the hell is he doing here?

I look at his mate. There's a similarity in height and build. A relative? There is a similarity about the eyes. Then recognition sparks, and I'm off running.

When I reach them I push the older man away.

'Leonard, what the hell are you doing here?' My mind is coming up with all kinds of links. A chain of thought that I dismiss in seconds. Each of them as confusing as the last. The scars on my wrists burn. Adrenalin sparks in my scalp.

'McBain,' says Leonard. 'The proverbial bad penny.'

'Simon, get away from that man,' I say and step up to Leonard. 'He's a murderer.'

Simon looks from me to him and then back again. His mouth falls open. He manages to speak. 'What?'

'Get away from him. He's murdered...'

Something gleams in Leonard's hand. He lunges towards Simon, pulls him into a hug and whispers something in his ear. The boy falls to the ground and Leonard spins and runs off.

He's here within my grasp. Fuck. I'm torn between checking on Simon and chasing off after Leonard.

Simon groans in pain. I look down at him and the blood that's spilling from a wound in his side to flower on his grey t-shirt. I make a decision. Kneel down. Press on the wound with one hand and pull my phone from my pocket with the other.

'You'll be fine,' I try to reassure him. My mind is like a row of spinning plates. Any one of which holds the truth. I dial a number and hold the phone to my ear. 'We'll have an ambulance here for you in a minute.'

The boy begins to sob.

'Are you in pain, Simon?' I ask.

He nods. 'A little.' He tries to shift into a more comfortable position. Grimaces at the pain. 'Who is that man, really?'

'Jim Leonard. He's wanted by the police for a series of murders,' I answer. Or he would be if I had told them the truth.

'What the hell does he want with me?' he asks, his face pale.

'Who knows how that sick fucker's mind works.'

'Do you think he was going to kill me?'

I think over the moment of violence just passed. 'Normally,

people don't survive an encounter with that man. He deliberately stabbed you somewhere non-fatal. It was an attack meant to distract me and allow him to get away.'

'Why?'

I sense that Simon's question is more fundamental.

'What did he say to you? Just then. It was like a hug. Then he whispered in your ear. What did he say?'

Simon shifts his position. Grits his teeth against the pain. His legs are visibly shaking. As I wait for him to speak, I feel a spit of rain on the back of my neck. Then another.

'He said, "Sorry, John".'

54

Ale and Peters wait for a uniformed officer to take Jack Foreman back to his cell. Once he's been led out of the room, Peters turns to Ale.

'Well done, DC Rossi. What's next?'

'Karen. We need her version of events.' Thinks. 'But she needs to stew just a wee while longer.' She looks at Peters. 'I need to go back to my office for something first. Wait here for a second will you?'

As she's half-walking, half-running back to her desk it occurs to her that she just treated Peters as if he were the lower ranked officer. Mentally shrugs. If the shoe fits. He's not half the cop Ray McBain is, and everyone knows it. Even Peters himself.

At her desk she fires off an email to the DNA team, with the heading, *please, please, please.* The content: compare DNA and fingerprints from Ian Cook with the material taken from Aileen Banks. Then she adds, check the fingerprints on the hate mail left at the Davis house.

When she gets an immediate reply, she speaks out loud to the room. 'Well, roger me with a bonsai tree.'

'I'm too much of a gentleman,' says Daryl.

Should have this back to you by the end of the day, it reads.

'What's this?' she says to Daryl. 'Hashtag: efficiency?'

'You are so down with technology, DC Rossi,' he replies.

She stands up. Says, 'Fucking yes.' Rubs her hands. 'Little girl, you are mine.' And walks with a measured pace back to the interview rooms. Picks up the pile of photographs from the table and places them back in the folder, which she tucks under her arm.

* * *

Once the formalities have been observed, Ale studies the girl sitting across the table. She's pale beneath the fake tan, her eyes are puffy from lack of sleep, but her hair is sitting perfectly, as if it had just been arranged by a master hairdresser. Ale makes a mental note to get her hair straighteners replaced. Then swallows a laugh. As if.

She makes a mental comparison with the girl in the photograph. Teeth are hidden behind the thin line of her lips, and her breasts are buttoned out of view under a brown work blouse. Ale looks into her eyes. Sees a girl who has acknowledged that life is not a shiny bauble. It's no longer a series of pissed-up nights out followed by a snog and a grope with the boy of her choice. Judging by the cast of her face, she's haunted by the death of her friends.

Karen opens her mouth to speak. Ale gets there first.

'Thank you for your patience, Miss Gardner. And thank you for agreeing to help with our enquiries.' She's all starch and business. Places the folder on the table.

'Yeah,' Karen replies, not sure where to go next. Settles for, 'Should I be asking for a lawyer?'

'This isn't a TV show, Karen. And as I said, you're just helping with our enquiries. If we decide to charge you with obstruction…'

'Obstruction?'

'Attempting to pervert the course of justice, Karen. When you knowingly make a false statement to the police and it holds up an enquiry.'

'Right,' says Karen and places her hands on the table in front of her, one on top of the other to try and disguise the tremble.

'It's only fair to let you know that the sentence for such a crime can be anything from four to eighteen months. Longer for more serious crimes, like murder.'

'Right,' says Karen, and the tremble from her hands reaches her voice. Ale feels a moment of sympathy but stifles it. Once she knows the truth, that will be time for the supportive Ale.

'Now that we have established the severity of the situation, could you tell us the nature of your relationship with Ian Cook, please?'

'We had sex a couple of times,' she says. Her head falls forward.

'Was he your boyfriend?'

'Kinda. It wasn't a regular thing, like. Just whenever.'

'Whenever he felt like it?' Ale asks.

An expression of humility on Karen's face. 'Aye.' She sniffs. 'He only saw me when we had a foursome with Jack and Aileen.' She looks up. 'I mean a *date* foursome, not a *foursome* foursome.' She grimaces, and for the first time in this meeting Ale sees a hint of personality. 'Yuk.'

'Did you want it to be a regular thing?'

Karen nods. Says, 'Aye.'

'Were you in love with him, Karen?' Ale allows an element of softness into her voice.

'Kinda. Yes.' She nods.

'And you would have preferred it to be a more regular thing?'

'Yeah, but I was happy enough just to see him now and again. Life's for partying, right? Don't want to get tied down with the one guy at my age,' she says, and the lie twists the shape of her mouth.

'How would you typify Ian's relationship with Aileen Banks?'

'Mates. They were just mates.' Her mouth twists again.

'Was Ian Cook in love with Aileen Banks?'

Karen looks up at Ale as if to say, *please don't make me answer this*. She crosses her arms, then gives into the silence. 'Ian had a thing for Aileen.'

'Did you ever wonder if seeing you was the best way for Ian to be in Aileen's company?'

Karen shoots Ale a glare. An unspoken, "*Bitch*".

'Answer the question, please, Karen,' says Peters.

Karen blows out of her mouth. Cocks her head to the side, aiming for defiance and failing. 'Yeah. So?'

'Did Ian kill Aileen Banks?'

'No, absolutely not.' Karen sits forward with the first show of real energy since they all gathered in the room. 'Whoever told you that is a fucking liar.' Her voice is a shout. 'It was butter-wouldn't-melt-in-his-bloody-mouth Simon Davis who killed her.' She pauses, her face a stew of conflicting emotions. 'Actually, if Simon killed Aileen, I'd be amazed.' She speaks softer. 'He really is as nice as he appears. He's a sweet, sweet guy. Truth be told, he was too nice for Aileen.' She puts a hand up to her mouth as she realises what she's just said. 'Oh my God, I'm a horrible person.' She falls back in her chair. 'Must've been some random, cos I know it wasn't Ian. He was gentle, you know. Nice. Wouldnae harm a fly.'

'Nice? As in he'll only shag you after he's been in Aileen's company? That version of nice? Sounds like he was a bit of a prick, Karen.'

'Yeah. Well.'

'Did he discuss the hate mail he was posting in the Davises' letterbox?' Ale asks.

Karen looks genuinely surprised. 'No. He did that?'

'Does that surprise you?'

'Well, yeah. It's a bit cloak and dagger, innit? Most folk just settle for a wee session of trolling online.'

'Do these surprise you?' Ale judges that this is the right time to unveil the photographs of Aileen. 'We found these on Ian's phone.'

'What?' She studies the first couple. 'Wait a minute.' She looks at Ale. 'Really?' For the first time Ale sees a bit of fight in the girl and perhaps a reduction in her loyalty for Cook. 'Holy shit, he was proper stalking her.' She crosses her arms. 'That's scary.' Doubt flits across her eyes. 'I didn't think Ian was capable of...'

'Did Ian kill Aileen?'

'No,' she says. Her voice quieter, less sure. Then again, louder, 'No.'

'In your first statement to the police for that night, you were less than helpful, Karen. Perhaps you can tell us what really happened.'

She closes her eyes. Exhales. 'Doesn't matter if I tell you now. Matt's dead, eh?'

'What do you mean?' asks Ale. 'What does Matt Davis have to do with it?'

Karen's face colours and her eyes dim with the knowledge that she has to present the worst version of herself to strangers. 'Back when I still fancied him, like, I sent Matt a photo. One of those Snapchat things that show up for a second before vanishing forever.'

Thinking, *oh Karen,* Ale asks, 'What kind of photo?'

'And remember that time you saw me and him chatting in the bar?'

'Yes?'

'He met me to show me that he had saved a screenshot of the photo, and if I talked to anyone about the night that Aileen died, he would post it everywhere online and even send it in to my work.' She pleads with Ale for understanding. 'I couldn't afford to lose my job.'

'What was on the photo, Karen?' asks Ale.

'And besides, I didn't really think that Simon did it, so what's the harm, eh?'

'The harm is that you delay a murder investigation, Karen. What was in the photo?'

'I was totally naked. Using my rabbit thingy,' she exhales. 'Everyone has a wank now and again, eh? But to have that on Facebook would have been *totally* humiliating. I would never have lived it down. And my *mother*. Jeez.'

Ale fights the urge to act the disapproving adult. How naïve are these kids?

'You do realise that it would have broken their decency rules and they would have deleted it almost immediately?'

'Aye. Almost. In the meantime, all his friends see it. My friends see it. Everyone takes a screenshot and I'm the slut of the year.' She shudders. 'Social network hell. No thanks.'

Right, Ale thinks, *time to get this interview back on course.* 'The night Aileen died?'

'Right. We were in The Drum. In the corner. Me, Aileen, Ian and Jack. Hanging out. Just having a few drinks, you know? We weren't drunk or anything at that point. Matt Davis comes in with a couple of pals, and suddenly Aileen changes. Before that her and Jack were just acting like mates, having a laugh, you know? But now she's all over Jack, showing off the puppies.' She pushes out her own chest to demonstrate. 'Totally flirting. Trying to make Matt jealous.'

'Matt, not Simon?' asks Ale.

'As far as she was concerned, her and Simon were over. But she had the hots for Matt. She's young and single, why not, she says. But I was like, he's the brother, you don't go there, babes.'

'And? Back to that night.'

'Well, that was the first time I saw that Ian might have a thing for Aileen.'

'Why, what happened?'

'Matt walked past us on the way to the loo. Winked at Aileen, called Ian and Jack a pair of wankers. And Aileen got up to follow him. Ian stood up as if to stop her, and I'm thinking, what the hell, you know? I think...' Her eyes focus on the near distance as if she's recalling these events in full for the first time. 'I think Ian was holding her arm. She tried to twist away. Jack was like, what the fuck, Ian? And Aileen clawed at the back of Ian's hand to get him off her. When he sat back down he had a big scratch and everything.' She pulls a strand of hair off her face. 'Jack was a bit pissed off with Ian, but seemed happy for Aileen to follow Matt down the stairs to the loos.'

'Then what?'

'They were gone for, what, ten minutes? And then Aileen came back with a *huge* smile. Whispered in my ear that she'd...' She pauses while she deals with the guilt of what she is about to say. 'Sorry, Aileen,' she says to the air above her head. 'That she'd given him a blowjob down in the loo.'

Well, thinks Ale, *a possible explanation for both sets of DNA in that wee scenario.*

'Then what?'

'Ian had gone totally silent. In the pure huff with everybody. So I was bored and watching Matt and his crew. I'm sure he told them what he and Aileen had been doing, cos they kept looking over at her. Then Simon comes in and I'm thinking, *awkward*. Simon barely had a chance to get a sip of his pint before he was in Matt's face. I'm guessing one of Matt's pals spilled the beans. They didn't fight or nothing, but Simon came over, said to Aileen, "Well, you must make your parents proud," and left.' Karen stops speaking. 'Any chance I could get a wee glass of water? And a smoke?'

'No cigarettes allowed, Karen,' Ale says. 'A glass of water is fine. We can get you a cup of tea if you prefer?'

'Water's fine, thanks.'

Peters does the needful and the interview reconvenes.

'Then Simon left. Face like thunder. And Aileen stood up to follow him. Ian got up, to reason with her I guess, and got another scratch for his trouble. So then I got in her grill. I was pissed off that Ian cared more about her, you know? Told her she should leave my boyfriend alone and...' Karen's face is clenched in guilt and grief. She whispers, 'I called her a skank and she ran out of the pub after Simon.' She bites on her lower lip for a second. 'I never saw her again.'

55

Leonard is running through the city, snarling at anyone who gets in his way, daring cars to collide with him, speed fuelled by his rage. He's never felt anger like this before. He feels he could fuel a car with it. Zero to sixty in ten seconds.

McBain. The name is a roar in his mind. The focus of all the hate and spite he has ever felt is bound up in that name.

Simon Davis was his. There. Big-eyed. Gullible. Curled up in the palm of his hand. He would have fed off the boy's grief for months.

Then, as the feeding waned, he would die.

Could he kill him? Davis reached through his carefully constructed emotional barriers like no one else ever had.

The realisation strikes him with such force that he comes to a dead stop.

Of course. That was it.

In the eyes. And in a certain light, the cast of his face, the play of his expressions. They even had the same hair colour. As if his twin hadn't died but had transferred into the soul of this child.

He had died, what, twenty-odd years ago. Simon Davis was in his early twenties.

Christ teaches us that anything is possible, he thinks and sends a silent prayer of thanks skywards.

* * *

He can see his hotel in the distance. He picks up speed again. There's something he needs to do.

Back in his hotel room, fury simmering like the flame in a kiln, he takes a shower. Impatient to begin the pleasantries, he rubs a towel over his back, between his leg and over his head. Then he sits naked in front of the mirror.

He opens the drawer of the dresser, pulls out a white mask and a scalpel. Runs a finger slowly down the mask's profile. From the forehead, between the eyebrows and down the nose to the lips and chin. Feeling the lightest of touches as if the pressure had been on his own face, not the mask.

Not since he'd killed the nun has he felt the need to carry through with this ceremony, but the hunger to spill McBain's blood deserves such a celebration.

He places the mask over his face. Holds it in place with pressure from thumb to forefinger under the bottom lip. He picks up the scalpel, and as his veins sing, he places the point of the blade on the soft skin of the lower lid of his right eye. A tiny amount of pressure is enough for the blade to pierce skin, and crimson fluid pearls onto steel and from there slides onto the mask.

And he exalts in the moment as a solitary tear of blood slides down the cheek of the mask. Like a promise of more.

56

I'm sitting with Simon in the hospital, waiting for his mother to arrive. I'd phoned her from the ambulance. Told her not to worry, her boy was safe, but he did need some medical assistance.

Her panicked breathing down the line in response suggested to me that my advice was wasted.

The medical staff shooed me aside while they gave Simon the full check-up and closed the wound. Luckily, the doctor told me, there had been no major trauma. No vital organs had been hit and Simon would make a full recovery.

Just as Leonard intended, I'm sure.

My phone sounds an alert. It is a text from Helen Davis.

'Caught up in traffic. How's Simon?'

'In no danger at all', I answer. Notwithstanding the unfathomable appetites of a serial killer. 'He's had six stitches and is sipping a nice cup of tea.' The cup of tea was a lie, but I was sure it would help reduce any panic and ensure she would arrive at the hospital not having caused any injuries of her own.

I pull back the curtain and walk over to Simon's bed.

'Oh. This is like déjà vu all over again.' I smile.

His answering smile is genuine, but tinged with pain. 'Yeah, that time Aileen's dad gave me a doing.'

'You guys have certainly been put through it,' I say and grip his forearm. 'You just need to be there for your mother. She's had to endure two great losses in her life. Having you by her side will be a great comfort.'

'That's just it,' he says, face brightening, eyes large. 'What if…' He shakes his head. Knuckles a tear from his cheek. 'Never mind. Tell me what I need to know about that guy, Leonard?'

I wonder for a moment where he is about to go, but park the thought and answer his question. I have to impress upon him the danger he was in.

'He's a very dangerous man who has murdered a lot of people, and you were quite possibly his next target,' I reply, while thinking I'd probably bumped him down to number two on the list. A surge of anticipation in my gut lets me know that his attempt would be welcome. We needed to sort this out once and for all. 'How did you guys meet?'

'I work as a counsellor on a website that helps bereaved twins. He was one of my clients. He seemed so genuine. Only another twin could understand what that kind of loss might mean.' He stops speaking as he thinks this through. 'How could he have fooled me so completely?'

'That's because he was speaking the truth,' I reply. 'His twin brother died when he was just a kid. It has – understatement of the year – screwed him up badly.'

'But why me? Why home in on me? And *how* did he home in on me?'

I think about my visit to the church in Perth. The priest's story about the twins there who had died within days of each other. Both seemingly accidental. With Leonard around, *nothing* was accidental. I think of him at the orphanage. He was never the cleverest of boys, but he had street smarts and a survival instinct that was uncanny.

The job as parish handyman would be his first stroke of luck after he fled from the bodies in Bethlehem House. Fitting in to that kind of environment would have been simple for a man with his cloistered background. I remember the postcard he sent to McCall. *Gone hunting*, was all he wrote. So, his second piece of luck was finding a target. The twin brothers. And that had sparked off a new purpose.

'It's me,' I say to Simon. 'I'm the reason he found you.' And I realise the truth of it as the words sound out of my mouth. 'Our paths have crossed before. I'm the only one of his previous targets who survived…'

'Holy shit,' Simon interrupts.

'I like to think of myself as his nemesis,' I say airily, aiming for a moment of levity. Fail spectacularly. 'The press seem to like me.' I hold my hands out to the side. 'Fat, grizzled detective guy. And the suits had me fronting the press briefings for Aileen's murder. The man's a ghoul, so he would have fixed on that. And when he found out that you, the early suspect, was a twin, that would have set his pulse soaring.' I pause. Shake my head. None of this would stack up in a court of law, but the range of the man's thinking was there, undeniably.

'You have an online presence? An interweb shadow footprint thing?' I ask.

Simon grins. 'Of course. Who doesn't?'

'Jesus. You kids have no idea how dangerous this stuff could be in the wrong hands. Does any of your online stuff mention about you being a counsellor on this website?'

His eyebrows crowd together as he thinks this through. 'Possibly,' he replies. 'Probably,' he goes on to assert. 'Bloody hell, that's quite a leap.'

'Yeah, so, he tracks you down…' I make another connection. 'Oh fuck. He'd have been watching your house. He will have seen Ian Cook deliver his poison pen letters…'

'Do you think he killed Ian?'

'I'm pretty damn sure of it,' I reply, thinking it through. 'And,' I carry the thought on, 'I'm pretty sure he would have had a hand in the hunt through the city for Matt, before he drowned.'

'No.' Simon has his hand over his mouth.

'It all worked out beautifully. Probably better than he could have ever imagined. He made his previous twin killings look like an accident and then a suicide…' I'm getting ahead of myself here. There's no evidence to back up this theory, but I feel it as truth. 'The priest said he was a great comfort to the second brother in Perth. So, he would have enjoyed the proximity. The grief…'

'No,' says Simon. 'He would have got off on the man's grief?'

'Anything's possible with this guy,' I say.

Simon shivers.

'Did you know there was an online hunt for Matt? People posting his whereabouts like a Facebook lynch-mob?'

'No!' says Simon, his face long. 'No,' he repeats. Hides his face in his hands as he cries and contemplates his brother's death.

'I'm sure they didn't want to kill him. They just wanted to vent. People rarely take their online shit into the real world. Like all bullies, they're cowards. But somehow, this one got out of hand, and I'm pretty certain Leonard would have had a hand in that. How I can prove that one, I've no idea.'

Simon falls back onto his pillow. 'I can't take all of this in. it's too much. It's … fucking obscene.'

'There's just one thing I need to know,' I ask. I see Simon and Leonard on the bridge. Their posture. The apparent link they had already forged. The physical similarity. The way Leonard had pulled him into a hug before wielding the knife.

This had become something other than a hunt for Leonard.

Simon looks at me with a question in his eyes. 'Who's John?'

'Sorry?'

'Leonard. He said, "Sorry, John", on the bridge. Didn't occur to me as strange at the time. I was kinda busy trying not to bleed,' he jokes. Then sobers. 'Who's John?'

My phone sounds another alert. Helen Davis.

'Still in bloody traffic. I HATE this bloody city.'

'Don't worry. Everything's fine here.' I thumb and press send.

'That's his brother. He died when we were just kids.'

'We?'

I grimace. 'We have a shared history.'

'God, that's creepy.'

'When were you born?' I ask, not quite sure why I need to know.

'1992.'

I do the figures. 'That's the year John died.'

57

I pull back the cubicle curtains. The sound of the metal rings singing against the pole sounds high-pitched in the room.

'Detective McBain, there's something I need to tell you,' Simon says to my back.

'In a minute, Simon. I just need to…' I walk away past the nurses' station and out into the large hallway at the lifts.

I thumb to a name and number on my phone.

'Elucidate,' says Kenny.

'Arse,' I reply.

'Alright, Mr McBain. Anything I can help you with?'

'Listen up. There's not much of a charge on this phone.' I tell him about my meeting on the bridge and my subsequent conversation with Simon. 'So, I think Leonard's got me in his sights.'

'Well, we knew that,' says Kenny.

'You're supposed to say, that's rubbish, Ray. It's all in your imagination, Ray,' I feel the surge of fear in my thighs. I don't fight it. Could save my life.

'I don't do bullshit, Ray. If you want that, phone one of your bosses down at Police HQ.'

'Maggie,' I say. 'He'll go after Maggie or…' I follow the thought. He's been stalking me, I'm sure of it, for weeks. He'll target anyone and everyone he thinks I have a relationship with. 'Ale,' I say. I'm discounting Kenny. He's more than capable of looking after himself. 'Maggie and Ale are the two obvious targets.'

'What about the lad, Simon Davis?' Kenny asks. 'Do you think he'll go after him?'

'Anything's possible,' I say. 'I'll get on to the team. Get an officer posted to his ward.' I grit my teeth. 'And if he thinks he's going to get Maggie, he'll need to go through me first.'

Kenny reads where I'm going. 'And I'll see to Ale.' We both know she'll refuse official help. Kenny sitting outside her house in his car will be a more effective option in any event.

Relieved that's been taken care of, I hang up and go back to Simon's bedside.

'Right,' I say, surprised at the affection I feel for the young man. Was I ever that wholesome and naïve? 'I'm all yours. And all ears.'

He breathes out. Long and deep, as if he'd been holding it in since I left his side.

'You know you said about the connection Leonard thinks I have with him?' He looks like he's about to start crying again. 'Maybe it's not the brother thing. Maybe it's a killer thing? Maybe I'm...' His face is bright as if it's about to burst.

'Simon, son, you're not making much sense.'

'I lied to you. When we first spoke. I did see Aileen the night she died.'

'And?'

'Will you arrest me?' he asks. 'Can you wait until after my mum's been?'

'Simon, can you start talking sense, son? And besides, I'm not on active duty. I'm off on the sick...' and the thought occurs to me that I might just resign anyway. Me and this job just aren't working out anymore. 'So tell me what you need to tell me, but in words I can understand, eh?'

'We were all in The Drum. I arrived later than everyone else. One of the guys said that Aileen had given Matt a BJ down in the toilets. I went over to where Aileen was sitting and said something nasty. Then I left.'

He bites his lip and closes his eyes against the memory.

'She was walking when I last saw her. Honest. And talking. Well, shouting actually. Told me I was a cunt.'

'What happened before that point?'

'She came after me when I left the pub. Found me up one of those lanes. I heard her coming a mile away on those stupid high heels.'

I get a mental image of her legs under the incident tent. And those stupid red high heels.

'I was having a piss. She caught me and tore into me while I still had my dick in my hand. Told me I was a loser. A wimp. Not a patch on my brother. I told her she was drunk and if she wanted to shout at me to wait until the morning when she would at least know what she was saying. She just looked at me. Then began taunting me again. Simon the bloody counsellor, she said. Always knows the right fucking thing to say. I zipped up and faced her. She pushed me. I pushed her back, and she lost her balance. Fell on to one of those huge metal bin things. The corner of one caught her right in the temple.' He pauses in the telling, eyes seeking mine, telling me there was no way this was the blow that caused her death.

'I tried to help her back on to her feet, but she pushed me off. Pulled herself back up. Then she started on me again. But even worse this time. She was furious. I've never seen her so furious. So…' He stops again, his bottom lip trembling, the effort to speak all but impossible. 'I walked away. She told me to fuck off. She never wanted to see me again. So I did. I walked away.'

He stares at me, face frozen in a mask. Begging for absolution.

I can't give it.

'That's what killed her, Simon.'

'Noooo,' he cries. 'Please. No.' I feel the spray of his saliva on my cheek. 'But she was walking. Talking,' he says with desperation.

I recall the forensics report. 'She took a blow to the middle meningeal artery. Via the temple. It causes a build-up of blood in the cranium. An epidural hematoma, I think it's called, or something like that.' I take refuge behind the Latin, like any good doctor might.

'Oh my god,' he whispers.

'People who have this are often lucid for a period. Which is why she was still able to curse at you. Then they grow confused, and if they don't get immediate surgical help…' There's no need to finish the sentence. He can fill in the blank.

And he does, judging by the howl of protest and the look of horror etched onto his face.

58

When I walk into Maggie's house, she takes one look at my face, takes my hand and pulls me into her bedroom.

There, she slowly takes off all my clothes.

'Wait … but…' I try to speak. She silences me with a kiss, and there's a surge of pleasure from that beautiful, light pressure that carries all the way down to my groin. She pulls away. Her look coy.

'What were you saying?' she asks.

I close my eyes and push out my lips, and trying to speak in that ridiculous position I say, 'Who was speaking? Not me.' It can wait until morning. Then we're out of here.

She laughs and trails the lightest of touches from my neck to each nipple to my belly button, and from there she curls a finger under the head of my dick and starts to stroke. I don't think I've ever felt anything quite so exquisite.

I groan. And groan again.

'If you don't stop that, this is going to be all over in seconds.'

She giggles and steps away.

'No,' I say and make a face. 'Don't stop.'

'My turn,' she says and pouts. I take the hint and take her clothes off. I blow on each of her nipples, and copying her movements on me, run a finger down her body and feel the welcome wetness between her thighs.

'What,' I grin, 'you no want foreplay?'

She chuckles. Grips my shaft. Says, 'I think you know where you need to put this, Mr McBain?'

'Indeed I do,' I say and push her back onto the bed.

The first time we make love, it is indeed over in seconds. I try to apologise, but it is difficult to sound sincere when every cell in my body is sparking with pleasure.

'Oh look,' I say and point at my still erect penis. 'Mini me hasn't had enough yet.'

'Mini me,' Maggie chides. 'You're an idiot, McBain. But stop admiring it and please your woman.'

A small voice nags from the corner of my mind. I need to tell her about Leonard, and I need to get her to leave town until he's safely behind bars. Or pushing up thistles.

But the promise of pleasure is too great, and I have to do as my woman asks, no?

* * *

When I wake up, there's a glimmer of the hint of light that signals dawn. I stretch and yawn and recall the pleasure we'd shared the night before. I can't remember our love-making sessions ever having such a charge. Can't remember a night when I'd slept so well.

My cock is hard again. I look over at Maggie, see that she's still sleeping and decide it will keep. I'm on leave. She's off work. We have all morning to repeat last night's performance.

I stretch again, and then with a smile forming on my lips I turn over onto my side, away from Maggie. There, I curl into the foetal position and relax, waiting for sleep to claim me.

But something surges in the reptilian part of my brain. I sit up. Peer into the gloom of the room. There's something not quite right, and I can't put my finger on it.

Then I hear a voice from the far side of the room. At the bedroom door.

A deep, male voice.

'Morning, Raymond.'

59

'Leonard, what the fuck?' I sit up so fast my head spins.

'It seems almost a shame to spoil this little perfect scene of domesticity,' he crows. 'But spoil it I must.'

'Over my dead body,' I growl and lean protectively over Maggie.

'That will be my greatest pleasure, Ray,' he says. My eyes are getting used to the low light and I make him out, standing in the doorway. He's holding a knife. My first thought is that I have to find one of my own. In the kitchen. But I can't leave Maggie on her own.

Then it dawns on me that she hasn't stirred. Surely the noise of two men talking would wake her up.

'Maggie,' I say and push on her shoulder. 'Maggie,' I repeat. 'You need to get up.'

I hear the sound of a chuckle coming from Leonard.

I pull the cover off Maggie's shoulder, and as I do so, the image of Leonard in the corner fixes in my mind. The knife. It wasn't shining. It was dull as if covered in something thick and wet. I pull at Maggie's shoulder. She falls over onto her back, and I can see a small wound on her neck, just under her chin and a thick, heavy pouring of blood that has stained her breasts and her side of the bed.

'Brings a new meaning to the question, who gets to sleep on the wet patch, dontcha think?' Leonard chuckles.

Something bestial takes over, and unmindful of my nakedness or the stained steel in his hand, I clear the bed and I'm on him in seconds.

The speed and certainty of my movement takes him by surprise. He falls out of the room into the hall with me on top of him. My hand is on his wrist, and I twist so the blade is poised over his heart. He locks his elbows. Resists. I'm astride him. Leaning over. My buttocks on his hips.

Making hate.

I grunt. My full weight pressing down. Pushing. My grip now on the handle. There's nothing I want more in this second than the strength to win this battle. For him to weaken and the knife to find its target. To slip through skin and sinew and slide between ribs before piercing his twisted heart.

But he's strong. Deceptively so for such a lean man.

The effort is bright in his face. Tendons are strung tight like ropes down either side of his neck. His eyes are large, bulging. There's a dictionary of emotion there, and I read them as if flicking through pages.

Hate, anger, pity, fear, joy. He's actually enjoying this.

He snorts, spittle flies from his mouth to my cheek. I want to brush it off like it's Ebola. I can feel it infect me. It all but burns. For a moment I want to lean my face onto my shoulder and wipe it off. But I can't take any pressure off.

'Fucking useless, McBain,' he laughs. 'Can't do it. Can you?'

I squeeze out more effort. Lean into him just a little more. He tightens his jaw as he fights against me.

I can't talk. Won't talk. I just want him to die, and I want to be the one to make it happen.

'What's keeping you, McBain? Kill me already. It's not like you haven't killed anyone before.' There's a mad sparkle in his eyes as he speaks. Saliva froths at the corner of his mouth.

He bucks his hips, trying to throw my weight off, but I've got a good three stone on him and it doesn't have the desired effect.

I lean forward some more, forgetting that I need to keep equal pressure on the shoulder and hip pressed against him. A shift. He bucks again. I tilt to the side. The knife falls, but he is no longer directly under me and the blade dents nothing but carpet.

'Whoa!' he shouts in my ear. Warm air on my cheek. He laughs. 'That was close.' I manage to get purchase with my left knee and right myself. Resume the position. Poised for murder.

'Die you fucker, just die.' I squeeze the words out from between clenched teeth. My talking is enough to weaken my pressure on him, and he pushes up. The blade is further away from its target.

'C'mon, McBain. Fucking do it!' he roars. 'End me.' As he speaks he pushes with his left hand, forcing me a little off balance. I don't know where he gets his strength. It occurs to me that if he was on top he could win this battle. Good reason for me to keep the pressure on.

His hips thrust up again. I tilt to the side. He senses me weaken and smashes a knee up. It connects with my right buttock. There's little pain, but the power is surprising. Pushes me even more to the side.

The two of us still have both hands on the knife, but it is now some way from its target. He takes advantage. Heaves forward. Smashes his forehead against my temple.

My vision blurs, I shake my head to clear it. Think of the injury sustained by Aileen Banks. If that's how I go, fine. But I need to kill this fucker first.

Another bloom of pain. Flashes of light in my sight. I lose my hard-won balance again, topple over. With a sharp movement he knees me in the balls. The pain is massive. I want to be sick. I grit my teeth, fight it.

He lets go of the knife, bounces to his feet and steps away from me.

I stand, grip the knife in my right hand. But I'm bent over, willing away the twisting, surging waves of pain that rush from my balls to my gut.

He's out of breath too, chest heaving, but he's smiling as he inhales large gulps of air. I'm in charge of the weapon, but I can't shake the feeling that he's the one in control. A memory of him leering before me, sliding another blade across my wrists. A memory that has infected my dreams for these last few months. A year? Fear weakens me. I feel my legs wobble. A slick of sweat on my forehead. With my free hand I brush it away. I have to end this soon, before I run out of energy. Before he finishes what he's tried to do before.

He looks like he could carry on for days.

'Look at you,' he laughs. 'All naked and everything. Should I take my clothes off too?'

I don't speak. Stretch forward, slash at him. But I'm tired and slow and regretting that I've let my fitness slip. He dodges my thrust with laughing ease.

'Whoop!' he yells. Skips from one foot to the other like a prize-fighter just entering the ring.

I run my eyes over him, assessing any damage. He has a small cut over his right eye that I can't remember inflicting, and his shirt is ripped in a line from his right nipple down towards his belt. There are a few spots of blood, but there can't be much of a wound if his energy levels are anything to go by.

Assessing my own hurts takes me a couple of seconds. Pain sparks in the right side of my face, and my balls are only aching now. I take a deep breath. Shake my head, like a dog shakes water from its coat. Trying to get rid of the fear. Aiming for clarity.

Until I remember what this man before me has done, and hate brings a brightness all of its own. Murder is in my sight, and I won't be denied.

'Before I slice you, tell me. Why did you have to do it? She was nothing to you, Leonard. Her whole life in front of her.'

He gives an elaborate shrug. Makes a face. 'It was something to do?'

'Fuck you, you arsehole.' I run forward and stab at him. Again he dodges and dances out of range and laughs.

I rage.

'You laughed at my brother all those years ago. Called him the names suggested to you by Mother Superior,' he says. His words reach memory, and I see the tight, cold face of a nun leaning into the small, harried face of a boy being punished for wetting the bed. John Leonard. Who died just days later. 'And you were every bit as culpable as that vicious woman of God.'

'I was a kid for fuck's sake. Just a kid.'

'And she taught you well.' He pauses and looks at me. Looks *through* me. 'I won't know peace, McBain, until you are dead. Until one of us is dead.'

'You first, ya nutjob.'

He dances forward and roars in my face. I am so surprised I take a step back. Stumble. But he is so caught up in his own fury he can't take advantage. He has a glass ornament in his hand, throws it at me. I duck, it hits the wall and splinters into a hundred shards.

He runs into the lounge. I follow. Relieved to be further away from the sight of Maggie's dead body. He moves to the coffee table under the window. Lifts it up and throws it across the room. Next he aims a kick at the TV. Knocks it off its table.

'Hey!' is my absurd response.

He ignores me. Can't hear me, so deep is he in his rage. I run at him before he can destroy any more of Maggie's stuff. Forget I am holding a knife and catch him in a bear-hug. Squeeze for all I am worth.

His face in front of mine. All teeth, spit and snarl. I struggle to keep a grip on him as he fights my hold. In a bizarre dance we move around the room until we fall over the edge of the sofa onto the floor. He lands first. Me on top. I lose my grip, and he is on his feet and out of range.

Fuck.

I get to my feet and realise I no longer have the knife. I scan the room. Leonard does likewise. His eyes brighten when he sees it. I follow his gaze. We both dive. He gets there first. Wraps his fingers round it and holds it high like a prize.

'Again, you lose, McBain. You had me. Coulda killed me. Nae bottle for a big guy.'

I look around the room for something else I can use as a weapon. A fake fur throw and a couple of cushions weren't going to cut it. Or him.

He sits on the arm of the sofa. Exhales. Shoulders sagging as if exhaustion has taken a hold of him. His eyes are dark. His expression a slump of self-loathing. I couldn't follow this guy's mood with radar.

He looks at the knife in his hand like he has no idea how it got there. He moves the wide blade up to the side of his head and slaps his temple with it. Then runs his thumb along the sharp edge.

He looks at me, and I can see the small boy I knew all those years ago. There is little sign of the man he has become. I fight the recognition while reading the pain. Someone needs to put him down like he's a rabid dog.

When he was just a boy, his twin brother had died before his eyes. A victim of ill treatment from people who should have known better. A chest infection was ignored. The boy sat for hours in a cold bath as punishment for wetting the bed. Repeated infections and punishments led to pneumonia. And the adults we had to trust to look after us ignored this young boy's suffering.

The Twins, as we called them, lived at each other's side. In a world where the grown-ups served their own vision of how the world should be, the boys had no one else. And when his brother died, the surviving Leonard's maturation was arrested forever. To this day he still harbours the spite and malice that only an unloved child could have.

He stands up as if a decision has been made. Walks towards me. All fight has gone. Leaking from his eyes like anguished tears.

I don't move, caught in his spell.

He stops in front of me and holds the knife to his throat.

'Give me your hand,' he says.

'Fuck off, Leonard.'

He reaches down, grabs my right wrist, and with a strength that again surprises me, brings it up to the handle. I grip it, despite myself.

'It needs to be you, McBain. Don't you see? The church hates a suicide.'

After all he has gone through, he's still wary of the teachings of the Catholic Church?

'What?' I say, struggling to make sense of the sudden shift and his apparent lack of fight. Wondering how he is going to try and turn this to his advantage.

'You just need to push,' he says, his eyes bright with longing. 'And it will all be over.'

I pause. Can't quite believe that the moment is here.

Leonard's eyes go large. He makes a loud noise. Like an alarm. 'Bzzz! Wrong answer.'

He grabs my wrist with one hand, twists the knife from it with the other. And strikes.

60

Kenny's had a long night on the front seat of his Range Rover. Sure, it's a comfy seat, but all fucking night? McBain owes him, and he better appreciate it.

He looks out of the windscreen at Ale's flat on the second floor. It's a classic Glasgow tenement. Large sandstone blocks. Big windows. The same across the street, and people peering into each other's lives.

Her curtains open. Her face appears at the window. She moves away. Then back. Stares down at him. She mouths a question that Kenny can read from where he is sitting.

What the fuck?

Seconds later, her front door opens. She appears and waves him in. Mouths the next question.

Coffee?

He gets out of the car. Stretches. Craves a lie down on a soft bed. But Ale has said the magic word. Follows her in through the door and up to her flat.

She walks into the kitchen. He follows, admiring the swell of her backside in her tight, black jogging pants.

Ale reaches the worktop. Reaches over to the kettle. Flicks the switch. Turns and says, 'You better not have been staring at my arse.'

'It would've been rude not to.' Kenny grins.

She throws him a finger. 'One lump of cyanide or two?'

'Sounds like a Ray McBain line, that,' Kenny answers.

Ale grins. 'Yeah, I've been working with that eejit for far too long.'

'Just milk, thanks,' Kenny says.

Ale does the necessary, and moments later they're both holding warm ceramic as if it's a lifeline. She takes a sip. 'Right. What the hell are you doing outside my house at this time of the morning?

Is Ray OK?'

'I've been there all night, Ale. Is that you just noticing?'

She makes a face. 'All night? Why the hell would you do something like that?'

Kenny tells her about his conversation with Ray the day before.

'Right.' She takes a sip. 'Thanks, I think. But if that psycho comes anywhere near me, it's him that will be needing assistance.' She smiles. 'I may be a lady, Kenny O'Neill, but I'm no pushover.'

'I didn't say you were. I was just doing something that would help keep Ray's mind at rest.'

'Well,' she makes a small bow, 'it is noted. And appreciated. And now you can piss off.'

'There's gratitude for you.'

'What about Ray?' she asks. 'Have you heard from him yet this morning?'

'Nope,' he replies. 'He was spending the night with Maggie.' He makes air symbols with both hands. '"Protecting her."'

Ale laughs. 'So Maggie gets the good stuff, I get a stiff in a car.'

'A Range Rover, if you don't mind.'

Kenny drains the last of his coffee. 'Anyway. Enough with the banter,' he says and looks at his watch. 'It's gone eight o'clock. We should probably phone. Just to check in, eh?'

'Sure,' agrees Ale.

Kenny pulls his phone from his pocket. Dials Ray's phone. It rings. And rings. No answer. There's a faint note of concern in the back of his mind, but he decides to ignore it for now. Could be nothing.

'When I spoke to him yesterday, he said his phone was almost out of juice. Do you think he'll keep a charger at Maggie's?'

'How the hell should I know? Anyway, chargers for lots of modern phones are interchangeable, aren't they?' Ale asks.

'We're talking about Ray McBain here. What's the likelihood of him having a modern phone?'

'He has mastered the art of texting, to be fair.'

'You got Maggie's number? Try her?' Kenny asks. 'Just to be sure, eh?' The faint note of concern has become a chill in his gut. He pushes the worry away and waits for Ale to call.

The phone rings. And rings. Goes to her answering service.

'That was too quick to go to a message. Try again,' Kenny says.

As Ale dials again. Kenny dials Ray on his phone. Neither respond.

'Right,' says Kenny. 'I'm going over there to check.'

'I'm coming with,' says Ale, reaching for her handbag.

'No. You're not,' says Kenny and runs out of the house, down the stairs two at a time, out into the street where he jumps into his car.

As he pulls on his seatbelt, the passenger door opens and Ale climbs in.

'Think about it, Ale,' says Kenny as he fires up the engine. 'If, and it's a big if, something is going on, you can't be a part of it.'

'But it's Ray,' she pleads.

'Exactly. Now kindly get your cute, well-formed arse out of my car, before I push it out.'

As gracefully as she can manage, Ale exits the car.

Kenny sees her in his rear-view mirror when he stops to judge the traffic at the end of her street. Dark hair, and a pale, worried face.

* * *

Kenny parks in front of Maggie's house. Notes that Ray's car is still there. Looks up at the windows. All the curtains are still drawn. So? They're having a long lie. Nothing weird about that.

The nagging in his gut is a full churn.

He reaches across to the glovebox. Opens it and pulls out a pair of black leather gloves, which he puts on with practised ease.

He gets out of the car. Locks it. What's the worst that can happen? He pushes the door open to find Ray's white arse pumping away between Maggie's thighs. They can all laugh about it later.

Still.

Concern sharpens his vision. Adds a lightness to his tread. He's in full battle mode, and if anyone gets in his way, they should be afraid. Very afraid.

He reaches the door. Twists the handle. It's unlocked. They were probably in such a moment of passion last night, they forgot to lock up. He pushes it open and steps inside.

The first thing that hits him is the smell. The metallic tang of freshly spilled blood.

The next is the sound of weeping. Quiet and in a high tone. Man or woman, he fails to guess as he silently makes his way deeper into the house.

'Ray?' he says, trying to keep his tone low and reassuring.

There's no response.

'Maggie?'

Nothing.

The sound is coming from a room straight ahead. Kenny makes for it, his tread light and sure. If there's anything to worry about there, it won't catch him unawares.

He opens a door.

The room beyond is in chaos. Furniture and soft furnishings cast about as if a cyclone had passed through. There's a figure sitting on the one chair that's upright.

Male.

Naked.

Sobbing.

And he's too skinny to be Ray McBain.

The man's head moves. He opens his eyes. There's a resignation there. Whatever this intruder wants to do to him is fine.

Leonard, thinks Kenny.

'Where are they?' he asks.

Leonard moves his head to the side. Slowly. As if the effort costs too much.

Kenny follows the direction of his nod and walks into the bedroom. And sees a sight that will haunt him for the rest of his life.

Maggie is lying on her side as if sleeping. The lie of this notion betrayed by the red tidal slick of blood, from her throat all the way down her side.

McBain is beside her. On his back. Naked. A blade sticking out of his chest.

He turns, walks back into the room where Leonard has stayed, stock still. To Kenny, it looks like he has lost the power of movement. He's just sitting there. Staring, yet unseeing.

There is no decision to make here, thinks Kenny. Not really. And as the white heat of rage hits all points of his body, he somehow retains a cold, clear focus. He remembers one of the last conversations he'd had with Ray. His question, have you ever killed anyone?

Standing in front of Leonard, Kenny asks, 'Do you know how many bones are in the human body?' And he can't quite believe how calm his voice sounds to his own ears.

'Me neither,' he answers his own question. 'Well, I'm going to break every one of yours. And then, the real fun can begin. You might have known suffering in your life, Leonard. But that was just a warm up to what you are going to go through now.'

Then, with a quiet fury, he sets to work.

Acknowledgements

Writers can have such a rich internal life that at times it is difficult to face the "real" world and your failings. In that regard the people who breathe life in to your work are where the proper riches lie. To all of you my thanks, affection (and the odd hug) are due. The gang at Saraband (especially Sara Hunt) – one of the very best independent publishers around. Douglas Skelton, for the cover image and for keeping me right. Jenny Hamrick for a painstaking edit. To the wonderful crew at Crime & Publishment in Gretna – the crazy gang in THE Book Club – all the troops in the Crime Scene – you guys keep me sane, you rock! And a special (too many to) mention to all the reviewers, bloggers, booksellers and readers – without you there is no book. Thank you for your enthusiasm and your continued passion for reading.